Wembley's Hallowed Ground

A Kenna Hannigan Mystery

Dan Winkle

DISCLAIMER

DEDICATED TO

Sav ... a great artist with an infectious zeal for creativity that inspired me to continue putting my stories into the computer.

SPECIAL THANKS TO

My critics for their brutal honesty and undying support:
Kevin, Lynn, and Skip.

PROLOGUE

"It's not whether you get knocked down,
it's whether you get up."
—Vince Lombardi (1913 – 1970)

LUHANSK, UKRAINE—10 MARCH 2020

For a man past his sixtieth year, Alistair Rensenhaus carried his tall, thin frame with the agility of a man many years his junior. That he would crash-and-burn was inevitable. He drank too much, smoked too much, and worked too damn much. The word *relax* somehow escaped his vocabulary … and lifestyle.

A hard-line, old-fashioned newsman, he had been British News Corporation's bureau chief in Ukraine since the country broke the shackles of a USSR vassal state. With his career winding down, he wanted to avoid the trouble that frequently presented itself, the same he had welcomed when he had a younger man's head of hair. Yet, as with most things, what you often wished for wasn't what you got.

Since the Russian incursion into Ukraine in 2014 and the annexation of Crimea, tensions had been on the rise, notably in the Donbas region. He had received troubling reports from sources on the Russian side of the imaginary line that separated them from the Ukrainians. Reports he could not ignore.

Dim sunlight through shaded and partially blacked-out windows illuminated the small, messy office. Lingering in the air was a mixture of mildew, cigarette smoke, and Horilka. The small metal desk and old wood table that doubled as a credenza were overloaded with haphazardly stuffed folders. Metal chairs rounded out the décor, indicating this was a working office and not just for comfort. A corkboard on the side wall held a map of Luhansk, with documents and photos hanging on it.

A lit cigarette his constant companion, Rensenhaus cared more about content than organization or flare. If one shaved every day or brushed his hair, if his clothes were pressed and neat it was of no consequence to him. He focused on finding and reporting the news, not analyzing it, as did so many of this age. To him, a newsman or woman's job was to report what happened, not how they felt about what happened.

He had called London for help, not knowing if it would come. COVID-19 had shut down the world. The only reporter from the West of any merit was a Yank … a female Yank. Also being old school, but to a much greater degree than Rensenhaus, Sir Clifton Toll, the company's venerable head, had ventured outside his paradigm and recommended her.

Kenna Hannigan's credentials were impressive, even to an old hardliner like Rensenhaus. The clinching factor was her pedigree … her grandmother. He had known Fiadh Dougherty-Lockwood before she added her husband's surname. Her successful criminal investigative work was common knowledge in news circles; many would say legendary. Upon meeting Kenna, it was obvious the fruit had not fallen far from the tree. That investigative sixth sense would be needed for the job he had in mind.

The only problem was that Kenna Hannigan was in Ukraine on a personal mission.

In a Ukrainian-style woman's winter clothes, no makeup, and hair pulled into a slapdash bun, Kenna moved to the corkboard. She knew where this discussion was going and decided to *hit any objections head-on*, as Gran Lockwood taught her.

"Yes, sir, Anson Beck," Kenna said. "He murdered my grandmother. Just before the travel ban, I got a lead he was in Ukraine."

"I was told you had a partner … a Jeremy Heffernan," Rensenhaus said more than asked.

"Like everyone else in the world, locked down by this damn Chinese bug."

Rensenhaus lifted two glasses from the desk drawer and blew into them as if to clean them. He uncorked a bottle of Horilka, poured two fingers into the glasses, and handed her one.

"This stuff kills all forms of bugs," he said and lifted his glass. "Prost."

"Cheers," Kenna said. They toasted; she downed the drink without hesitation or reaction.

"This won't be easy, Kenna."

"Nothing worth accomplishing in life is, Alistair."

"Words from yer gran's lips."

Rensenhaus stared into those emerald eyes, seeing how a younger man could be trapped by them. He knew deep within, though, that Kenna wasn't in Ukraine for a tumble in the hay. She was there to work, plain and simple, and to find a murderer. He admired that and dragged the bottle like a pointer along a street on the map.

"Like a halfway line on a rugby pitch, it separates the Russians from the Ukrainians … some of the time," he said and moved the bottle along a line on opposite sides of that street. "We'll call the area between the two ten-meter lines, no-man's land."

"No problem … I'm not a man," she said.

"No humor where you're going for the next few days."

"Wiggy, that is Jeremy, always says *'if ye don't have humor, ye die,'*" she said, pointing into the Russian area of the map. "Word is Beck's beyond your no-man's land, Alistair. If you want me to locate Russian military installations or troop build-ups while I'm there, consider it done."

"Since your partner … uh, Wiggy … isn't here, I arranged for one."

Rensenhaus motioned to the door. The silhouette of a thin man appeared in the glass, followed by a knock. Without waiting for a reply, Oleksandr Shwetz stepped inside. His looks were stern, a middle-aged man who'd led a hard life. His sinewy physique and scars told a potential adversary that Oleksandr could take care of himself. His carved, all-business expression was that of a Ukrainian ready for anything thrown at him. He stepped forward and extended a hand; Kenna accepted it without hesitation.

Rensenhaus handed him a glass and filled it; they raised them in a toast, "To the story."

"Prost," "Cheers," "Budmo," Rensenhaus, Kenna, and

Oleksandr said at the same time.

*

It was dark, a cold, overcast night made colder by the wind that carried the acrid scent of death and destruction. Both wearing camo clothing, Kenna followed Oleksandr as he inched along the shadows of a muddy, snow-covered, war-torn street. She lifted her phone, turned off the camera light, and videoed their approach to a damaged shack. An unintelligible whisper from the darkness; Oleksandr paused and crouched low. Men in the distance shouted orders in Russian, followed by sporadic gunfire and screams of pain. A flare popped overhead, brightening the next block. Kenna turned the phone for a selfie; she flinched at a close explosion and automatic gunfire.

In a guarded whisper, she spoke to the phone, "We have intel that this shack …" she spun the phone to the shack, "is where a high-level Russian military meeting is about to take place."

Oleksandr turned, "Ssshh … quiet."

Their attention was drawn to the front of the shack. Two Russian UAZ-469 "Jeeps" roared down the street and skidded to a stop. Kenna trained the phone on two men and two women, well-dressed in civilian clothes, who jumped out and moved rapidly into the shack. Armed drivers remained at the vehicles and watched the street. As if on cue, a third UAZ and an armored Russian Tigr approached from the opposite direction and stopped.

Well dressed and beaming with arrogance, a tall blonde woman with a Russian model's chiseled looks stepped from the UAZ. A beauty in her 50s but looking 30, she had a cold, calculating mind and eyes that transmitted it. There was no doubt she was in command.

"Svetlana Pavlovsky, FSB," Oleksandr whispered. "Get her on video."

"Who's the other?"

"Her lover, Lyuba … beautiful and deadly."

In her early 30s, Lyuba was pretty and unafraid, an equally tall and muscular woman with hair the color of death. Her cat's bedroom eyes breached the darkness with a deceiving smile. Beneath the beauty lurked a killer who executed Svetlana's will in whatever manner required. Armed soldiers escorted them to the shack and took station at the door. Looking back at the street, Lyuba obediently followed her lover and boss into the shack. A young lieutenant stopped at the door and turned to the street.

Stepping from the Tigr and looking uncomfortable with the surroundings, Anatoli Novikov was a disheveled man in his 50s. He leaned back inside and said something out of earshot. Five heavily armed soldiers jumped from the Tigr. Novikov's anxious order to the officer beside him was clear without hearing it: *Die before you allow anyone inside this Tigr.*

Novikov turned and hurried for the shack. The lieutenant opened the door and followed him inside, the last to enter.

Oleksandr crouched low and moved at a quick pace for the shack. Still videoing, Kenna followed. He eased aside a portion of the destroyed rear wall; they slipped inside.

In near-total darkness, they paused in a damaged kitchen straight out of a horror movie. Though parts of it were undamaged, the majority was strewn across the counters and floor; the ceiling partially collapsed inside. In the adjacent room, the voices of the women and men murmured an indiscernible conversation. Oleksandr and Kenna inched through debris to a battered door. At a gap in the wall, Kenna videoed the other room.

Illuminated by battery-powered lanterns, Svetlana took charge at a weather-beaten table. There were no introductions; only Svetlana knew the identities of all present. The four well-dressed men and women moved forward from the shadows. To the opposite side, Novikov stood out from the others, a ragged oddity, twitching nervously.

He doesn't like being in this building ... or these people ... or both, Kenna thought.

"You all have your assignments," Svetlana said. "If you have reservations, now is the time to speak."

Her glare scanned every face at the table; all knew if they spoke, they would not see the sunrise. The hard looks of each gave her the answer she demanded. Novikov stepped forward and handed Svetlana a thick folder titled in gold. From it, she lifted five envelopes and handed them to the lieutenant. He circled the table and handed one to each of the four men and women. In the shadows behind the others, he handed the final envelope to a third man.

Kenna watched the phone and cursed beneath her breath ... not enough light to read the folder or even catch their faces clearly. She turned the phone. With a jacket hood up, the third man, tall and slender, face hidden, stepped forward from the shadows. For an instant, the lantern illuminated his face, then darkened to a silhouette. Kenna zoomed on him ...

"Beck," she whispered, cursing, catching the image too late.

Not one hundred percent certain, she stiffened and tried

another angle. None was available. She placed a hand on the pistol in her shoulder holster. Oleksandr stayed her hand, *quiet, stay calm*. She snapped away, phone steady on the meeting, trying for a facial image.

"It's him, dammit," Kenna insisted, though still not certain.

In the other room, Svetlana lifted her attention to the kitchen door. No one else had heard; she pulled Lyuba aside, motioning that direction with only her eyes.

"See if anyone's in there. If it's two-legged rats, you know what to do."

In the kitchen, Oleksandr took Kenna's arm and pulled her for the rear opening. Without looking to the other room, Kenna continued to video behind. Oleksandr pulled her outside. At the opening, Kenna's coat snagged on the wall. Just as it ripped free, she made brief eye contact when Lyuba entered the kitchen.

In the rear alley, an unsuspecting soldier walked the perimeter. Oleksandr lunged from the shadows, tackled him, and, with a pistol, knocked the soldier unconscious. Soldiers in the front heard the commotion; loud Russian voices and running footsteps approached. *Time to move*. The five soldiers at the Tigr readied weapons for a fight.

"Intruders!" Lyuba yelled from the kitchen.

With urgency, Oleksandr ordered Kenna, "I'll lead 'em away."

"Halt!" a soldier yelled from the side of the shack.

Kenna sprinted for the darkness and videoed behind without looking. Lyuba stepped out and lifted a pistol; the young lieutenant followed. Kenna ducked behind a pile of rubble. A spotlight illuminated her but an instant. Gunfire from behind; bullets peppered the buildings and ground behind her as she ran into the first alleyway.

Oleksandr fired from the opposite direction, drawing the Russians towards him. Within seconds, he disappeared into the darkness of the ruins. From the front of the shack, two UAZs with Russian soldiers sped in opposite directions to encircle them.

Kenna ran into a narrow alley as a UAZ passed and swept its spotlight along the street behind. At the next intersection, she reached an aged four-story apartment building. Soldiers' voices echoed through the buildings, closing on her. Sweeping spotlights darted through the streets. She looked up to an aged metal fire escape, climbed onto a rubbish tip, and grabbed the metal ladder.

"Like climbing a tree," she mumbled to herself, climbing

the rungs to the stair landing.

Just as a UAZ entered the street below, Kenna reached the top landing. Pausing to hide in the shadows, she waited until the UAZ passed. She climbed over the roof parapet and ran the full block to the western end. With caution, she looked over the edge.

Spotlight scanning the area, a UAZ growled along the street. Checking behind shrubbery, in every alcove, and behind the detritus of war, soldiers with torches hurried through the streets and alleys.

Kenna looked over the parapet. In the distance, UAZ headlights illuminated the street in front of the shack. Kenna flicked on the phone video and zoomed on the distant shack. A flare popped overhead and illuminated Svetlana at the front of the shack. Soldiers walked from the Tigr with … a flare popped directly over Kenna.

Panicked, Kenna dropped into the corner, leaned against the parapet wall, and shut off the phone. Anxious, suddenly very cold, and weary, Kenna flinched when a second flare popped above her, illuminating the rooftop. She pushed back into the shadows but couldn't avoid the light.

No good ever came from sitting on your laurels expecting something good to happen,' Gran Lockwood instructed in her mind, *'Only failure will result from others*

Spitting out fear, Kenna glanced over the parapet wall. The street was empty. She ran to the roof access door and opened it. Inside, she ran down the stairs to the ground floor and eased open the exit door.

Soldiers searched in the rear; spotlights illuminated the streets and buildings. Overhead, flares weakened and died. A UAZ passed a block over. Sounds and searchlights waned. She gathered a big breath, opened the door, and ran. At the street a UAZ backed into view on the street over, directly across from her.

"There!" a soldier yelled to the driver, then to Kenna, "Halt!"

A spotlight illuminated her; the soldier swung an SR-2 Veresk submachine gun off his shoulder. The UAZ sped for her; the soldier raised the Veresk to fire.

"Hal—"

An RPG round steaked across the night. It hit the UAZ, blowing it nearly in half, and throwing dead Russian soldiers in different directions. The concussion catapulted Kenna to the side. She slammed into the building; air exploded from her lungs. The destroyed UAZ spun in a violent dying dance, rolling to within a meter of Kenna. Fire erupted from within.

Was this death? She wondered.

An overwhelming sense of mortality, one she had never experienced, slapped her across the face. A child's dream evolved into the authenticity of life. She saw the world around her more clearly. It was here, alone and bleeding, that she fully realized the ability … and, yes, perhaps even destiny … of humans to destroy each other. As a child, wars had been games with sticks as swords. Now, as a woman, the animalistic urge driving mankind to kill was infinitely clearer, infinitely closer, and infinitely more painful.

Semi-conscious, the raging fire snapped her to the present. Fighting for breath, she lifted blood from her head. *Was that her talking or someone else?* She wondered, trying to clear her head.

Ukrainian soldiers sprinted across the street, exchanging gunfire with the Russians. A soldier with a medical armband knelt beside her. He held her chin and waved a bright penlight across her eyes.

"Are you alright?" he asked, as if in a deep well.

He pressed a temporary wound patch on her head. Gathering her senses but hearing only a screeching buzz, Kenna nodded. He helped her stand and pointed past the UAZ to the west.

"Then, go … go!"

Kenna staggered, gathering her balance and breath. Ukrainian soldiers flooded into the area. Behind, gunfire and explosions filled the night. Another flare popped overhead; she staggered/ran in pursuit of her shadow, which led her through the buildings into darkness.

VICTORIA STATION—LONDON—18 FEBRUARY 2022

Yuri Zelenko was thick and muscular, a Ukrainian who had been on the receiving end of too much evil in life. Though 30, he had savored the life of danger as an investigative reporter and had spent most of his adult life reporting on Russian activities. He wore the face of a man many years his senior, deepened even more by the uncertainty that consumed him.

Nerves on edge, eyes observing every person, movement, and nuance of the terminal, he hesitated before stepping from the train. *Had word of his travels gotten out?* burned in his brain. The trip from Ukraine had been trying, every instant anticipating the bullet or blade that would send him into eternal darkness.

But the dread of that darkness greeted him that night. He ignored passengers trying to push past him and board the last train to Dover. A whistle: he stepped off. The train jolted away from the platform. The air was heavy, matching the night. Light fog drifted through the immense open-air terminal building. Passengers rushed along the walkway; he joined in the exodus.

Loudspeakers barked arrivals and departures; his thoughts drowned them out. A flood of people poured through the hallway with opposite destinations in mind: tracks and exit. Ducking away from the crowd, he rounded the corner only to be faced by a greater pulsating crowd.

His eyes never stopped moving. If they did, he would be dead. *London,* he thought, *what a dreadful place to die ... stay alert.*

He leaned on the wall, watching the hallway. He pulled a photo from his pocket and focused on the fuzzy grey-haired man in the background, far back. He brought it closer to his eyes, squinting, unable to make out the man … or woman. He swallowed the dryness in his throat. *Stop,* he insisted silently and jammed the picture into a pocket.

In a shop window, a reflection, if ever so brief. *Don't turn, don't look, just move,* he commanded himself.

He quickened his pace through the crowd. In another window, like a mirror, a tall and thin man in a dark hoody quickened his step to keep pace. Yuri studied the man's walk; he'd never seen it, he was certain. *Who are you? How did you know I would be here?*

Gathering resolve, an escape plan fixed in his brain, Yuri

hurried around a corner. With a sleight of hand and without stopping, he lifted an addressed courier envelope from his overcoat and slid it into a "PREPAID COURIER SERVICE" collection box. He cursed, wanting to have hand-delivered that parcel.

Total attention now on survival, he glanced to the corner behind. The man in the hoody did not look up directly. Yuri felt inside his overcoat for a pistol that wasn't there. *Fucking security!* A sinking feeling consumed him; fear strangled courage.

The station's layout flashed across his memory; sweat burned his eyes. With the crowd moving for the exterior door … ten meters, he tensed … five, muscles tightened … two, his heart raced. He stepped out into the blaring traffic noise at the passenger arrival area of Terminus Place. He ran, fighting through the crowd, ignoring angry, yelling people.

He weaved through cars and busses. Horns and squealing brakes greeted him. He vaulted the fence in the center of the street and didn't look back. He didn't have to; the man was there. He didn't stop at the crossing street; neither did the man chasing. *Don't stop, run, run!* he yelled in his mind.

Yuri ran against the traffic to a construction area at the side of the road. He looked back; the man was gone. *No, he's there, somewhere!* His heart raced. He leaped onto a rubbish tip and jumped over the temporary metal construction safety fence.

He landed awkwardly with a yelp and reached for an ankle. He stood and limp/ran across the building construction area, avoiding debris and equipment. At the end of the street, he paused, flexing his ankle. He stepped out across the heavy traffic, narrowly missing a lorry. He glanced back as he entered another construction area. When he turned back, the hooded man was there, five meters in front. Yuri froze. The hooded man fired a suppressed PB 9mm semiautomatic pistol. The bullet ricocheted from a metal beam; Yuri spun.

"No need to run, Yuri," the man said with a forced accent.

The second shot hit Yuri in the leg. He faltered and collapsed against scaffolding but held on and forced himself to a boarded walkway. The assailant fired again, hitting Yuri in the shoulder. He collapsed atop a pile of demolition rubble. When he rolled over, the hooded man stood over him, a streetlight silhouetting his face hidden by the hood.

"Where is it, Yuri?" the hooded man insisted and stepped forward. "Where's the video?"

"Video?" Yuri hesitated, then broke into pain-stricken laughter. "That's what you want? I thought you were after the Halibeck fol…"

Yuri froze, his lips locked tight. The would-be killer leaned forward and aimed the pistol at Yuri's face. With a grin from the darkness of the hood, the assailant ground a boot into Yuri's wounded leg. He cried out, unable to hold back.

"The video and folder … disappeared in the fire with Rensenhaus," Yuri said. *Go to hell!*

"You and I both know that's not true," The killer's hand tightened on Yuri's throat, the pistol pressed against his forehead. "I thought you understood."

"And I thought," Yuri struggled while being choked, "you were … smarter than this."

"You should have listened in Luhansk," The assailant said without rancor. "You have become unreliable."

Yuri's eyes defied the fear that filled him … not for the moment … but for the unknown of what awaited him … *I am going to die.*

While choking, "See … you … in hell …"

"Say, what's happening here?" a security guard yelled from the street and blew a whistle.

The killer crushed Yuri's throat. He fired a bullet into Yuri's forehead just above the left eye. Yuri's head snapped back against the wood security wall. His dead body slid down, streaking the graffiti with blood and gore. The security guard frantically blew his whistle. When the killer turned the gun, the security guard ran towards the terminal.

The killer rifled Yuri's pockets, lifted the photo, and shoved it into his hoody. Frustrated when he found nothing else, he tossed Yuri's passport to the side. He removed the suppressor from the pistol and walked without concern from the construction area.

II

LONDON—19 FEBRUARY 2022

Keena slept fitfully on a queen size poster bed, wrestling with the pillow and the down comforter that confined her. Blinking eyes followed the nightmare that filled her mind. Gunfire! Panic! More gunfire! Screaming children! *"No,"* she screamed in her mind. Fighting the ropes that confined her, she screamed at the fire. She struggled to move away but couldn't. Her eyes snapped awake with the mind.

"No," she whispered and closed her eyes, breathing hard.

As the morning sun broke through the overcast and struck her face, she swatted at it like a fly. The more she fought, the tighter the comforter confined her. Her phone alarm clattered like automatic gunfire; her struggle reached fever-pitch.

"No … stop!" she bawled.

She shot upright as if searching for cover, eyes flashing from side-to-side, not at first realizing where she was. Cold sweat covered her face and torso. In a flash of memory, she was in the street fighting again. She slowly gathered her bearings, *no, not Luhansk … the alarm … hotel room …* and fell back onto the pillow.

A gas fire burned in the fireplace and reflected off the full wall windows that overlooked the waking city. She stared at the reflection but didn't see the organized fire of the fireplace. She saw the destruction and conflagration of battle. She turned away and stared at the dull morning sunlight that filled the hotel suite. It wasn't fancy, but it was warm, basic, and clean, save her clothes littered about the floor.

With a frustrating effort, she untied the comforter and hurried into the bathroom. While relieving herself, she rubbed sleep from her eyes and squinted at sunlit clouds out a tall window.

"Fucking Luhansk nightmares."

She flushed and stripped, then flipped on the shower. She turned on a wall radio:

"Time to wake up, London," the disc jockey whined over the radio speaker.

"Rather be sleeping," she hissed.

"And to help, we'll start the weekend off with a hit by The Weeknd, 'Blinding Lights.' "

Kenna stepped into the shower and sang the song:

"Yeah, I've been tryna call. I've been on my own for long enough."

Fifteen minutes later, *Easy on Me* by Adele played on the radio. Kenna walked from the bathroom wrapped in a towel, sponging her hair. Suddenly cold, she hurried to the bed and yanked off the comforter. Wrapped like a cocoon and wearing Wiggy's good-mood flip-flops with the puppy dog ears, she walked into the suite's living room. At a small glass table by the fireplace, she flipped open a laptop.

For some reason, she thought of a Gran Lockwood teaching: *'Fear's a tangible object in oneself when faced with death. Control it to avoid its wrath.'*

Thanks, Gran, for that cheerful morning wakeup, she thought.

Kenna had experienced such fear more than once. The worst had not been in Luhansk, as most believed, but in Virginia. It had been dark as pitch when she watched the last breath leave her grandmother's chest … the most frightened she had ever been.

At that instant, she saw not the cliché of life before her eyes but the enraged anger of her new reality. There were no flashbacks to childhood happiness. Those had been cast into a void of blackness, a past that no longer existed. She remembered how, in less than an instant, her entire body had turned to mush, the saliva in her throat had thickened to mud, and a shrill explosion erupted in her ears with the crack of

Anson Beck's gun.

She hadn't been prepared for her grandmother's death. Like all humans, she expected the woman she loved to be around forever. And the man she sought more than all others … the murderer … was always just out of grasp.

Anson Beck, if you're in London, I'll find you, filled her mind.

She lifted her cell phone and punched a number. "Wiggy, I need coffee, please."

As if on cue, the room door opened. Jeremy "Wiggy" Heffernan entered, disconnecting a call on his cell while carrying a tray of coffee. Joining the rest of the world during the pandemic, Wiggy had put on about twenty pounds. He blamed it on lack of work. When the same volume of food and drink entered the intake unit during solitary times as it did in active times, what other result could there be? At least, that was his theory.

"Ya could'a just knocked on me door," he said, setting the tray on the table. "The Kenyan ya prefer, nice and strong."

"Just like my men," she chuckled, savoring the first drink.

"Ain't seen many of 'em since pretty boy in D.C.," he

smiled.

She frowned, "Had the damn dream again … correction, the Luhansk nightmare."

"The title of yer memoirs," he chuckled, then seriously, "Ye gotta get Ukraine outta yer brain, kid."

"It's Beck that fuels 'em," she said. "Still can't figure out why he was with the Russians."

"We'll know soon enough," Wiggy concluded. "Now, stop messin' about me computer before ya delete me work."

Kenna walked into the bedroom and dressed. Stepping out while Wiggy was on the computer, she pulled on riding leathers and lifted a colorful motorcycle helmet and backpack. Not pleased, Wiggy typed in several items, then sent them as a message; Kenna's phone dinged.

"That's the leads we have so far on where Beck might be stayin'," Wiggy said. "For now, just go by and see if anyone's been there."

"Yeah, yeah, I know," she said. "No funny stuff, especially…"

"If ya see him, call me too swift. Don't do anythin'," he demanded.

"I hear ya, pops," she said with a smile and finished the coffee with a bawl of satisfaction. "If it's one of his dead-ends, I'm having brunch with Addie. I'll call later to see if you've made any progress."

"Ya know I don't like ya ridin' that contraption," Wiggy said, as would her father.

"It's a motorcycle, the fastest way around this city."

"I'll not mend yer broken bones if'n—"

"Advice noted, pops."

"And stop callin' me that!"

Kenna smiled and opened the door to leave.

*

Swinging on the backpack, Kenna walked from the rear of the hotel. It was chilly by her measure, not cold. But the low clouds meant it might rain … *welcome to London.* She unchained a Honda CMX 1100 Rebel motorcycle, swung on, and started it. She pulled on the helmet and gloves, eased the Honda to the street, then looked left.

"Wrong!" she admonished herself. "Right first, then left."

As a car passed, she accelerated into the left lane to follow, singing a Rolling Stones song:

"I don't get noo … satisfaction …"

III

With the collapse of the Soviet Empire in the 90s, many of Russia's nouveau riche migrated to London. The wealthiest congregated in Belgravia and purchased lavish terrace houses along Eaton Square. Hence, the area's nickname, *"Red Square."* The owner of the corner home, #50 Eaton Square, was Ukrainian and rich enough not to be outdone by his Russian counterparts. He purchased two and combined them into a single residence, making it the largest and most expensive in the area.

Standing on the balcony outside a living room fit for a tzar, Kostyantyn Vasyl Kovalev cut a handsome, arrogant, and well-conditioned swathe in his late 50s, even in a gold-trimmed bathrobe. Though the sun was hidden by overcast, it didn't lessen his mood. He welcomed the day as he did all days, *being an air-breather.*

Though not cold, he rubbed his hands together and blew out cigar smoke. The park across the street was void of activity. That would change as the square awoke with the new day. Kovalev brushed the ash from the Cuban cigar into a crystal ashtray. Those deep, all-encompassing eyes revealed that he quite enjoyed London.

Like many along Eaton Square, Kovalev took advantage of the Soviet Empire's collapse. Many outsiders branded him rapacious, if not a thief, but he ignored them. He thought of himself as an opportunist. When the Berlin Wall fell, he pilfered money from the crumbling KGB and, still in his twenties, became a millionaire literally overnight. Over the next few years, he multiplied that wealth a thousand-fold in the Crimean oilfields, exporting oil and natural gas to Western Europe.

His greatest challenge had come in 2014, though. When Russia annexed Crimea, he scrambled and paid off the right politicians to maintain his holdings. Today, most believed he was in London to ensure nothing upset that steady stream of business and money. In reality, Kovalev was here to feed his one true passion … American Football.

Kovalev's bodyguard, Illya, was born about the time his boss walked from KGB headquarters in Kyiv with travel trunks full of U.S. Dollars, gold, and Crimean oilfield leases. Of the same mold as his boss, Illya was never without a sidearm but preferred the business side of the job. He listened when Kovalev spoke and followed his mentor's every move.

Ukrainian with a pleasant demeanor, a young house staffer pushed a gold-trimmed cart with silver service through the arched open entryway. Illya inspected it and waved her through. With a bright smile, she stopped the cart at a glass breakfast table. Under Illya's watchful eye, she assembled the meal and China table setting to perfection.

"Ah, breakfast, I'm famished," Kovalev said. "Thank you, Anna."

"Enjoy, sir," she said and pushed the cart from the room.

Kovalev turned to Illya, "I want the number of that newsman at British News Corporation. It's time I gave that interview."

Illya walked to him and extended a cell phone, "On the screen, sir."

"While I'm talking to the Brit, see if you can locate Oleksandr Shwetz." He lifted a piece of bacon and took a bite, pleased while chewing, "British bacon, the best. He's somewhere in London."

Illya was taken aback and warned, "The last time you saw him, he promised to put a bullet in your heart, if you recall, sir."

"Oleksandr was never one to … how do the Americans say … beat around the bush," Kovalev said. "But whatever happens, I need his involvement."

"If you don't mind me asking, for what purpose?"

Kovalev did mind but would appease Illya to train him, "To keep Svetlana and Medved in check while I conclude my business. I want no trouble until that's done."

"Then, I suggest contacting the fishing boat captain instead, sir," Illya offered. "He will gladly pass on the information and leave your name out of it."

*

BRITISH NEWS CORPORATION—LONDON

In suit and tie under an overcoat, Douglas Thurnbull strode arrogantly through the pristine but blandly decorated foyer. It was a large and dark rectangular room with far too few windows. Floors of boring pale tile matched the receptionists' and visitors' expressions when he walked past. The only color was the company logo in tile on the wall behind the front desk, a globe encircled by large round analogue clocks displaying the time of twelve major world cities.

He ignored the lifts, never used them, and took the stairs two at a time. He was in good condition … could still run a football pitch … for his 50-plus years, and was determined to remain that way as long as Mother Nature allowed. As would any military man, he double-quicked down an equally bright but blandly decorated hallway and marched through a glass door with a stencil: "ON-LINE REPORTERS."

A dozen reporters tapped on computers, talked over cell phones, and read printed articles. Some lounged, having worked through an all-nighter. Those who saw him paid tribute to their boss as he walked past. Thurnbull swelled with a hint of pride, knowing how much he had improved things since his arrival.

Corina Barker was in her late 30s, a plain brunette who made herself plainer by wearing black-rim glasses, heavy makeup, and shapeless clothing. Her desk was full of work but organized. She stood when Thurnbull approached.

"How was the gym, sir?"

"Same as every day, Corina," Thurnbull said.

It was obvious to everyone that Corina didn't like her boss and thought him an arrogant twat. Thurnbull knew but didn't care. Corina did good work, the only thing that concerned him. She followed him through the door that announced him: "Douglas Thurnbull — Editor On-Line News." She took his overcoat and hung it on a coat tree.

"Would you care for anything, sir?"

He looked at her like, *when do I take anything in the morning?* Corina looked at him. *If I didn't ask, you'd belittle me.*

"Any headlines this morning?" he asked.

"No rumblings yet, sir."

"Day's young, Corina," he said. "Lotta time for news."

"Sir," she said, turned, and walked out.

Thurnbull draped his suit jacket over the back of the office chair. He lifted a simple aged pipe from a clean ashtray, wanting a smoke. He stared at the company logo on the wall, then allowed a glance at the display case that held a Distinguished Service Order with a gold bar for exemplary leadership in combat that read, "Iraq 2003." Beside it stood a photo of him in the field with his men, all in uniform, the signature pipe clinched between his teeth.

The son of abusive, alcoholic parents, he left home at 13, stuck with his studies, and joined the Royal Marines at 17. Military life suited Thurnbull, though he initially struggled with authority figures. He righted those shortcomings, passed officer training, and was made lieutenant. After a wound during peace-keeping operations in Iraq, his superiors forced him from the service. He hated the decision … and the men who made it, feelings he had never divulged.

It surprised most who knew him when he joined a covert SIS operation in Ukraine in 2014. With the cover of a newsman, the objective was to gather intelligence on Russian operations. He excelled at it, having gone behind the Russian lines to report on their activity. It hadn't been Sir

Clifton Toll's first exposure to Thurnbull, but it was the one that caught the Executive Director's eye.

The phone on Corina's desk rang; she snapped it up, "Mr. Thurnbull's office."

On the balcony of his home, Kovalev finished the cigar, "This is Kostyantyn Kovalev. Is he available?"

"Yes, sir. I'll place you on hold for a moment," she said without emotion.

Corina stood with a pad and pencil, straightened her dress, and tapped on the glass pane door. Without waiting, she eased the door open. Thurnbull looked up with a raised eyebrow: *Who is it?*

Corina stepped inside, "The Ukrainian oil man, Kostyantyn Kovalev, sir."

"Very well. Stay and make notes. Never know what these oligarchs have in mind."

Thurnbull cleared his throat and punched the desk speaker phone, "Mr. Kovalev, good of you to ring. I was—"

"I've decided to do that interview we discussed some time back," Kovalev interrupted.

"Excellent," Thurnbull said pleasantly, the Ukrainian's ill manners aside. "I have a team in Kyiv—"

"Not necessary, I'm in London," Kovalev interrupted

again.

"So, the rumor's true about this venture into American football," Thurnbull said as much as asked. "That makes it easier for everyone."

"I want the woman that was in Luhansk to do the interview," Kovalev demanded. "She was straight-forward with me then; I expect she will remain so."

"I have no idea if she's in London. She's a Yank, you may recall," Thurnbull offered.

"Exactly why I want her. She knows football, the American brand," Kovalev said with emphasis. "I think you will find she's in London and amenable to doing the interview."

"We have many fine reporters who know sports—"

"As I recall from our time together in Ukraine, listening was one of your shortcomings, Thurnbull. It's not a request," Kovalev demanded. "Her or no interview. I will be at Wembley this afternoon ... make it three."

The line went dead. Thurnbull's anger was swift and obvious, though he brushed it aside as a minor annoyance. Corina saw through him, as she always did. *Very good at hiding emotion,* she thought. *What else is in there stowed away?* She wondered with a devious smile.

"Rather boorish of him, sir," she said, wanting to say more.

"He's Ukrainian, can expect no less," he said. "Find that bloody Yank and the Boston hooligan she runs with."

"Tommy Henson's become friends with her, I believe. I'll ask him to make contact."

Corina walked out the door. As it closed, Thurnbull's expression soured. *What the bloody hell are you really doing in London, Kovalev?* He lifted the phone and punched an exchange.

"Mrs. Pemberton, is he available?"

IV

At a roundabout, Kenna accelerated the Honda past a slower car, then roared onto a multi-laned busy street. Maneuvering rapidly through traffic, she was an aggressive, instinctive rider who changed directions without hesitation, without fear, and passed slower cars like in a competition. Alistair Rensenhaus taught her the *art of riding* in Ukraine. She had taken naturally to it and enjoyed the rush.

Her phone rang. She accelerated around a taxi and tapped the Bluetooth, "This is Kenna."

In the busy reporter's room of British News Corporation, Tommy Henson was fighting the hangover from celebrating his 30th birthday. Tommy spent his formative years as a ground-pounder in the Army, where he was an accomplished marksman. A knee injury in Afghanistan sent him to the Army Royal Corps of Signals, where he excelled at information gathering and processing. He joined BNC after the Army as a content editor and was now its senior video analyst. He wanted more out of life, but after surviving COVID, Tommy was happy to have a job.

A plain-looking man, Tommy knew his future wasn't in front of a camera; his goal was to someday occupy

Thurnbull's chair. He sat in an orderly cubical, stared at a bio of Kostyantyn Kovalev on the computer screen, and adjusted a phone headset.

"Tommy here. How goes it, killer?" he asked, ignoring the pounding headache.

Annoyed, Kenna stopped catty-corner from a building that matched the address on Wiggy's text message, "I woke up this morning, Tommy toilet. That's the best part of the day."

"I get it. You don't like the nickname," he replied with a chuckle. "Too bad, it's stuck in my head."

"Having brunch with Addie, you coming?"

"You got her to take time off? She won't do that for me," Tommy said, half-serious.

Across the street from Kenna, a young woman with a toddler in-hand and pushing an infant in a stroller stepped down the stoop of the apartment building. A working man … not Anson Beck, she noted with disappointment … followed them out and locked the door.

"Actually, this is a work call," Tommy continued. "Thurnbull himself received a specific request for you to do an interview."

"Me?" she asked and deleted the first address on her

phone. "He's never liked my *Yankee independence.*"

"Three this afternoon at Wembley, with Kostyantyn Kovalev."

"Wow, didn't think I'd hear that name again," she said, pocketed the phone, and accelerated past the couple and children. "Why'd he ask for me?"

"Pretty obvious … Luhansk," he said. "If you're interested, I'll send over the details."

"Certainly … an opportunity to clear up loose ends between us," she said, concentrating on traffic. "Some not pleasant."

"I don't need to remind you but will anyway … don't mention this to Adelaide. She might kill both of us."

"You know I can't keep secrets from her, T-squared," she chuckled.

"T-squared?"

"Tommy toilet," she laughed. "Anyway, Gran taught me *full disclosure is always best.* Send the info to Wiggy. I'll call him before seeing the evil witch."

*

After observing two more residences with no sign of Anson Beck, Kenna swung the Honda between stopped cars and onto the sidewalk in front of a corner pub with a swinging sign over a blue door: "BLUE BOAR." On the window, another sign: "FULL ENGLISH BREAKFAST—ALL DAY". She chained the Honda to a lamp post, unfastened the helmet, and tapped the Bluetooth.

"Call Wiggy's cell," she said. It rang only once.

"Missed me already, eh Fiery," Wiggy said in the hotel suite, working on his laptop.

"Cross those addresses off your list. Dead ends all," she said.

Wiggy's fingers flashed across the computer keyboard, "Getting some new intel from the MI5 lads; we'll go over it with 'em later."

"Have to fit it in with some paying work for BNC," Kenna said.

"Somethin' arranged by yer old man?" Wiggy asked.

"Don't think so, a special request from …"

"Gettin' Tom Terrific's email now … Kovalev, eh?" Wiggy doesn't like that at all. "Don't ya remember how the last one ended?"

"Different time, different place, Wiggy."

Kenna wanted answers, as much as closure to a bad situation. She knew that getting either from Kovalev would be more than a challenge. Though he helped her in Luhansk, he was also at the base of the problem, or so it seemed. Everywhere she and Alistair Rensenhaus turned, Kovalev was there to block their efforts. He had said it was to protect them; it seemed more of a control mechanism.

"But I hear ya … yesterday's friend, today's enemy."

"I'll text the details while yer enjoyin' brunch," he said, then added in a serious tone. "Gotta watch our backsides around him."

"You just like lookin' at mine," she said with a chuckle and disconnected the call.

The pub was a well-known hangout for lovers of sports, football to darts. From humble beginnings a few centuries ago as an Inn for horse carriage travelers, it had occupied several buildings on the same corner for more years than the U.S. had been a country. The present structure was a replacement for the one wiped out during the Blitz in World War II.

Quaint with a rough edge, dark, long, and narrow, the pub had a bar along the side wall and a dozen tables. Patrons turned as Kenna entered but ignored her. Her sense of its history evoked thoughts of those travelers from centuries past imbibing an ale … and perhaps enjoying other nefarious things that accompanied ghostly surroundings.

At a table by the front window, she embraced Adelaide, a pretty but reserved woman roughly Kenna's age. Adelaide played down her looks, partially for her work in the Foreign Secretary's office and partially because she didn't like men hitting on her. Much like Kenna, to Adelaide, work took precedence over romance. Kenna sat across and admired the charm bracelet on Adelaide's wrist … *oops.*

"Forgot … not in Boston."

Kenna moved to the bar. From the other end, the toothy middle-aged bartender lifted an eyebrow. By his expression, he hated mornings … or maybe it was just Yanks.

"Coffee, if you have any."

He gave her a glare he probably gave all foreigners, especially those who ordered coffee, but she smiled and accepted the cup. At the table, she sipped the coffee and frowned, then added lots of milk and sugar.

"Today's road tar," she shivered. "Should-a gotten tea."

"Bitters are more their specialty, Kenna," Adelaide said, patting her hand. "I ordered food. You look like you need some."

"No thanks, mother hen. Stomach's in a knot. That damn dream again."

"That makes two of us, love," Adelaide said,

immediately sad. "Can't stop thinkin' about me dad."

"Luhansk … the nightmare that never ends," Kenna touched the bracelet. "The one he sent you."

"Yes, his last gift," Adelaide said and sipped the tea. "Why do you do it, Kenna? The dangerous stuff."

Kenna shrugged, "Don't know. Started out life interested in it, probably like your father. Then, it just became second nature, a part of me, as strange as that may sound."

"Wouldn't know," Adelaide said. "I was the child that came around late, the mistake."

"He never thought of you like that."

"Still, he wasn't around much, always in Ukraine."

"That second nature thing … addicted to the work," Kenna offered, wanting to diffuse the conversation. "It consumes you."

"Like you riding that motorcycle pell-mell through Piccadilly."

"A rush of adrenaline might get you out of the doldrums."

"Papa taught me to be a thinker, Kenna," Adelaide added. "He always said he'd take care of the heavy lifting."

"Which he did. Look, I'm still working to get the proof of what happened," Kenna said. "But there's still no news on my video unless you've heard something."

"The foreign secretary's received nothing. Everyone's tellin' me to drop it."

"I'm getting the same dribble at BNC," Kenna agreed. "Douglas No-Bull avoids the conversation every time I bring it up."

Adelaide slid the cup of tea to the center of the table, "All this … it just ruins my brunch."

"Sorry, it wasn't intentional," Kenna said and paused. "Look, the good that came from it was our friendship."

"Papa would have been pleased with that. He liked you very much, and I can't say that about many people he worked with," she snickered and added, "Certainly not Mr. No-Bull."

Both chuckled in a guarded sense, but neither knew why.

"Thank you … and in that vein," Kenna swallowed hard. *Time to pour salt on the wound,* Gran would have said. "I'm interviewing Kovalev."

Shock hit Adelaide, followed by instant anger, "You're going to sit across from the man responsible for my father's death?"

"We don't know that for certain and won't until—"

"Bollocks. Who else was it, then? Dammit, you were

there!" Adelaide slammed her hand on the table; everyone in the pub turned.

"BNC wants his story, and he requested I do it," Kenna insisted, taking Adelaide's hand, only to have it jerked away.

"Tell me when and where," Adelaide demanded, "and I'll run a shiv into his heart."

"Relax, Addie. I'll broach the subject at the right time. You'll know what I know."

"You could have said no," Adelaide said, disappointed.

"And miss an opportunity to learn the truth?" Kenna asked. "Not in my genes. In grandmother's words, *'No self-respecting granddaughter of mine would say no to a fight.'*"

The bartender slid a plate of bread, cheese, and meat across the bar, "Order up, Adelaide."

At the table, Adelaide lifted the knife and stared at it with intent. *What would it feel like to shove this into a man?* she wondered, then spread butter thick on the bread.

"Should try it without butter someday," Kenna said to lighten the mood. "Might surprise you."

"No self-respecting Englishwoman would ever have bread without butter, Kenna."

"Unless it's fried in bacon fat."

Kenna chuckled. Adelaide glared at the knife and took a

big bite. Kenna forced down a piece of cheese. *Saved by the bell*, her cell phone dinged; she looked at the text message, pleased.

"Wiggy, you're brilliant."

"Jeremy," Adelaide said, "another heavy lifter."

"Heavy lifters like Wiggy and your father can also be brilliant thinkers and doers, Addie," Kenna showed Adelaide her phone. "He's arranged lunch, which means beers, with his mate from MI5. Good thing I didn't eat."

"Take me when you interview Kovalev," Adelaide insisted. "I want to hear the words from his mouth."

"No, Addie. I'll tell you what we discussed."

Kenna grabbed a piece of cheese, kissed Adelaide's cheek, and spun for the door. Outside the window, Kenna started the Honda and accelerated away. Adelaide lifted her cell phone.

"Tommy, I just spoke with Kenna. Where and when is she meeting the Ukrainian?"

V

The executive office suite of British News Corporation was not frugal, but it was, as well, not lavish. What Sir Clifton Toll demanded of his staff, he practiced. His private office was a working office, though decorated with plaques and letters from Prime Ministers since Margaret Thatcher, his personal favorite, several American and French Presidents, other heads of state and dignitaries, many civic awards, and trophies.

The conservative white notepad in the upper left-hand corner of the highly polished but small desk remained within easy reach and bore no name, no initials. The legendary slanted "CT" slash, which had remained the same since youth, placed at the bottom told a person of a note's origin and its significance.

From the old school of note-taking, Toll disliked recorders, though he reluctantly accepted them as more accurate. People were uncomfortable speaking into a recorder or phone, which stole the personal touch from an interview. Giving to progress, though, he had capitulated on that rule, an infrequent event at the BNC.

Each morning, a crystal bowl was fully stocked with

freshly sharpened pencils and placed within easy reach of the telephone receiver. His distaste for a disorganized person was equally matched by his contempt for the ball-point pen. The businessman's abilities today seemed to be measured by what he carried in the pocket of his Tyrwhitt, not by the work or, more importantly, the profits he generated.

All that was needed to calculate and facilitate a merger or record meeting notes was a pencil; a handshake was all he needed to solidify a deal. He loathed how the ball-point pen brought the necessity for solicitors, which brought the necessity for signatures on everything, fostering distrust between men and the agreements into which they entered.

Incoming mail was placed in the tray according to importance and date received, as was the outgoing in hardwood separators stacked front and center. Both elements were equally important in deciding who or what was answered first. That responsibility had fallen on the thin shoulders of Mrs. Thelma Pemberton twenty years ago and remained hers today.

In the outer office, Mrs. P., as Toll called her, was a wisp of a woman, well-dressed and attentive to duty at her simple desk. As was customary, her work area was immaculate and organized to perfection. She had joined Sir Clifton's staff after raising three children. Toll often said that hiring her had been his best staff decision. When Toll ordered, Mrs. P. often repeated it to the unfortunate recipient of the executive director's wrath when they walked out.

As Thurnbull entered, she punched the aged intercom … sometimes, simple things were better than high-tech. As a ritual, Thurnbull paused at attention alongside the desk.

"Mr. Thurnbull, Sir Clifton," she said and released the intercom button.

"Send him in, Mrs. P.," came the raised voice from behind the closed door, which was also customary.

Turnbull walked past Mrs. Pemberton while she held the door open. As the door closed, Toll pressed lengthy, thinning white hair against his narrow head and eased a Woodford pocket watch from his vest. He popped the face open to check the time. Passed down through the generations by his great-great-grandfather, the timepiece had been a gift from his mother. The Woodford was a ritual everyone encountered upon meeting the *"old man."* The tradition remained intact as he snapped the face of the watch closed.

Today, time, or loss of it, mattered as much as had the days of the Falklands campaign or Iraq, Toll thought.

Toll held the glare of a man intent on success but knew the tasks he must undertake to avoid failure. Doubt was short-lived in his mind; failure was a thought he never entertained. He accepted only success and expected his staff to be of the same ilk.

Thurnbull sat across from him, stiff-backed like a military man, "I received a call from Kostyantyn Kovalev, the Ukrainian. He's agreed to an interview on—"

"Your first assignment with us was in Ukraine, right?" Toll interrupted, though he knew the answer to the question. Caught off-guard with the information, he needed time to think.

Thurnbull found this opening curious, given his master's penchant for brevity. He shifted uncomfortably. His insides balled; his hands tightened on the arms of the chair. He wasn't good with being probed and questioned. He preferred to state the facts and end the conversation. He had no desire to debate Sir Clifton and, indeed, would never dream of it.

"Yes, sir. When I assisted Rensenhaus before returning to London."

"Odd … London," Toll said, though he knew why.

"He's finalizing the lease of Wembley for the American football club he's buying," Thurnbull said, then wondered aloud, "Do you have a problem with him, sir?"

"Don't know the man," Toll lied. "Why are you

bothering me with this?"

"He's asked for the Yank, Ms. Hannigan, to interview him."

"The Yank, yes, I remember her. An outsider, Thurnbull?" Toll questioned. "We have sports broadcasters for that."

"He was rather insistent, sir," Thurnbull offered. *Why had Kovalev specifically asked for Hannigan?* He asked himself again.

"Dammit, man, how do you get tied into these Gordian Knots?" Toll insisted. *What's the real reason you're in London, Kovalev?* He wondered. "Well, did you have problems with him in Ukraine?"

"Sir, and some none too pleasant," Thurnbull said. "He can be obstinate."

Toll chuckled, "Human nature to protect one's territory."

Curious wording, Thurnbull noted, "Quite, sir."

"You're not in Intelligence Service now, Thurnbull; you're at BNC," Toll demanded. "Can you remain objective about it, or do I need to find someone else?"

"Of course, sir. I'm more worried about how he treats Ms. Hannigan," Thurnbull said, though uncomfortable. "They had issues in Ukraine. Some quite intense, according to Rensenhaus."

"Are you sure it's not because the bloody Ukrainian demanded it be her … and not you?" Toll snapped, though he knew that wasn't the situation. "You don't see it, do you? Damn, man, why do I pay you?"

"Sir? See what, sir?" Thurnbull stammered.

You've made my point, Toll thought, "He's obviously requested her for something that happened during her time in Luhansk. And that's the news, not some fluff piece about a stadium lease."

"So, are you saying she's the right person for the job, sir?" Thurnbull asked.

"Rensenhaus is dead, which leaves you and Hannigan with knowledge of Kovalev and the Ukraine. Take this Kovalev situation and run with it."

Still in the chair, Thurnbull snapped to attention, "What exactly do you want done, sir?"

"Thurnbull, I brought you in for your ability to run operations."

"Which I have always appreciated, sir," Thurnbull said, drawing Toll's glare at the gratitude. "But my duty there was to seek and verify the enemy's location and strength."

"Now, you're understanding," Toll said, but Thurnbull

clearly didn't. "Put your best man on the content and keep it quiet. I want no leaks out of this office. Understand?"

"Yes, sir, quite," Thurnbull said.

Knowing he had been dismissed, Thurnbull stood and left the office. His mind raced; his insides soured. Dazed more than when he arrived, he walked to the outer office and paused at Mrs. Pemberton's desk.

"Is the old man well, Mrs. Pemberton?"

"Perfectly well, Mr. Thurnbull. Why?"

Thurnbull shrugged, "No real reason seemed out of sorts."

Toll opened the door between inner and outer offices, unamused, "Time versus motion, Thurnbull. Nothing's accomplished loitering and gossiping."

"Was just going to ask Mrs. Pemberton to gather the troops, sir."

"Isn't that why we hired you a P.A., man?"

"Time versus motion, Mr. Thurnbull," Mrs. Pemberton reminded him.

"Yes, sir, immediately, sir," Thurnbull said, turning out. As the door closed …

"I want to know what he's doing at all times, Mrs. P.," Toll ordered. "Put his P.A. on it, she's a sneaky little shit."

"Of course, sir," the obedient subordinate replied, pleased with the skulduggery, and lifted her desk phone.

"And, Mrs. P., I was expecting to hear from Yuri Zelenko. Make contact, if you will."

Toll walked back into his office and stared out the window over the city. *So, you want Ms. Hannigan, Kovalev,* he thought. *Which means you've come to collect. Yes, that must be it.*

He lifted his cell phone and punched a contact. The phone rang several times. A woman's soft voice laced with a heavy Eastern European accent answered:

"Good morning."

"Have you arrived?"

"Haven't had time to change my travel clothes."

"Don't bother. Meet in one-hour, same location." He paused for a moment. "Be on time!"

*

Thurnbull's mind whirled with questions as he walked into the "On-Line Reporters" room. Something was off about that meeting with Sir Clifton. The old man knew something about Kovalev being in London that he wasn't saying.

Not the fluff piece, he recalled. He brushed it aside and

approached Corina. She hung up the desk phone and stood with an infrequent smile.

"Corina, you and Henson in my office, if you will," Turnbull said without stopping.

"Sir," Corina said and lifted her phone. "Tommy …"

Thurnbull stepped into the office, closed the door, and draped his suit jacket over the back of his chair. He once again looked at the Distinguished Service Order, remembering the incident well. He turned when the door opened; Tommy and Corina entered.

"We have a discrete assignment from the almighty himself," he said, pointing his pipe in an attempt at humor; it didn't work. "This assignment stays between the three of us."

He waited for silent acknowledgments, then continued:

"Has the Hannigan woman agreed to interview Kovalev?"

"The woman you met in Ukraine a couple of years back, sir?" Corina asked.

Annoyed, Thurnbull responded, "I returned to London before she arrived, Corina," then, to Tommy, "Well?"

"Anxious for the opportunity, sir," Tommy snapped.

No doubt, Thurnbull thought and ordered, "Then, it's a

two-prong assignment. Monitor Kovalev and Ms. Hannigan's every move, Henson. In fact, I'd rather you directed her moves."

"You don't know Kenna … uh, Ms. Hannigan, sir. She's not one to be directed, prefers to follow her own path."

"One could conclude that's why she's an independent journalist, sir," Corina offered.

Thurnbull continued with authority and a hint of annoyance, "As for this independence … Well, that's not how we do things here, but I see your point. That's your charge, Henson. Get her on the same path. You follow?"

"What about her colleague, Wiggy?"

"Wiggy?" Thurnbull chirped, unamused. "What kinda bloody name is that?"

"Her assistant, analyst, and cameraman, all wrapped into one, sir," Tommy said, then added. "He's quite the computer guru."

"Don't care if he's a bloody tzar. Make sure they're up to our standards when they interview this Kovalev chap … no mistakes. Which means, I want you on-site." He made direct eye contact with Tommy, *follow*? Tommy nodded. Thurnbull turned to Corina, "I want a report every night."

"For one interview, sir?" Corina half-objected.

"This is big news, and we're getting the exclusive. So, we'll treat it like that."

"Sorry, sir," Corina said, only half meaning it. "Just didn't realize American football was big news over here."

"It will be if the bloody Yanks have their way," Thurnbull said with rancour.

"Yanks?" Tommy quipped to goad Thurnbull a little. "Kovalev's Ukrainian."

"Where do we start, sir?" Corina asked, preventing Thurnbull's rejoinder.

With a glare at Tommy, Thurnbull continued, "Our previous bureau chief in Ukraine, Alistair Rensenhaus, had an assistant, Yuri Zelenko, that worked out of Luhansk. Make contact and see what information he can give us on Kovalev's venture into American sport."

Thurnbull's desk phone rang. Corina lifted it, "Mr. Thurnbull's office." She listened for a long moment. "Yes, sir. It's confirmed. Ms. Hannigan will be there."

VI

Wearing a billionaire's three-piece tailored Savile Row suit, Kovalev stood at the balcony balustrade with a cigar. He smiled, watching children play in the park while supervised by nannies. He wondered how his children and their children were and made a mental note to phone when business was concluded.

A black Chevrolet Suburban stopped on the street below, taking his attention away from his family. A man Kovalev knew and expected stepped from the rear and looked up; they made casual eye contact.

David Camden's silver hair shined in the grey overcast morning. In his late 60s, he was tall and lean and carried himself with confidence. One look told people in their line of work he was the CIA. His innovative and analytical thinking coming out of Yale in the 80s caught the Director's eye.

Camden was, however, an anomaly compared to his Langley colleagues. Regardless of climate, he preferred a white linen suit and Sagan Classic Nubuck Crocodile shoes to the company's drab standards. Permanently brown, he stood out in any London crowd. Brits confused his color with a tan, but Camden was the byproduct of his mother's Cuban ancestry. Even a casual observer could not avoid his father's contribution … the cold calculation in the brilliant silver eyes that matched his hair.

A Butler in suit and tie met him at the house door and showed him inside. With his career winding down, Camden believed he had one more hurrah left in him, a final mission that would leave a lasting mark on his legacy. The Agency's new hierarchy … he referred to them as *the political children* … had no knowledge of and were incapable of true espionage. Succinctly, they couldn't hold the *proverbial jockstrap* of Cold War spies that went behind the Berlin Wall and into the bowels of the *Evil Empire*. No, today's intelligence network was just that, a network of bytes in a database floating through cyberspace.

Like the old dinosaur the younger generation considered him, Camden held onto his means and methods that had not varied over three decades. There was never doubt of his confidence and his belief in the mission. It was well known throughout the Agency that Camden never acted unless the plan was perfect … which meant it had to be his. The days of their work being romanticized were gone. He hoped to recreate it one more time as if turning back the clock. In truth, he would miss it when it had run its course.

The butler ushered him to the living room, where Illya met him at the open arched entrance. Though they knew each other, neither offered a hand.

"Good to see you again, Illya," Camden said, neither meaning it nor remembering the last time he saw the man.

"You as well, Mr. Camden," Illya responded out of courtesy, though that was as many words as they had ever spoken.

Camden stepped onto the Persian carpet that defined the room's opulence. However, what Camden saw was the contrary. In his eye, the grey sunlight through the open balcony doors added to a stuffy, drab, and depressing room that reeked of England's past glory.

Chrome, leather, and flash were more to Camden's liking.

From the balcony, Kovalev watched his business associate with a keen understanding. Prior to the end of the Cold War, they had been young rivals, if not enemies. When the Berlin Wall came down, and Svetlana joined the FSB, she acted as an intermediary to pull them together. Kovalev needed funding for an oil pipeline to the West. As head of Halibeck International, a fledgling CIA cover that would grow to become the largest construction conglomerate in the world, Camden wanted the contract to build it. It was but one of many steps in his overall plan and worked to both men's benefit.

Svetlana had wanted their relationship to be a cat-to-rat marriage, with both ready to pounce at any moment. Sensing an opportunity, she planted a seed of dissent to drive a wedge between them and to bring herself favor with FSB's hierarchy. It nearly worked, but Camden and Kovalev discovered her treachery, called a truce and decided to work together. In pointing out Kovalev's betrayal to her FSB boss, she received glowing reports and promotion.

Svetlana's interference nearly cost Kovalev everything in 2014, something he would never forget … or forgive.

"You know I don't like mornings, Kostyantyn, so what's so important it can't wait for a civilized hour?" Camden asked.

"Svetlana is in London," Kovalev said with a leading tone.

Taken by surprise, Camden hesitated for a moment, "That's a conversation better had over cocktails."

As if on cue, Illya handed both men a clear drink, vodka. He offered Camden a Cuban cigar and lit it. Standing at the balcony door, looking out at the city, neither fully trusted the other. Perhaps by some measure, that's how their partnership had worked, even thrived.

"Svetlana … I wondered what that razor-sharp shashka was up to," Camden said with appreciation. Mind whirling, he took a drink and inhaled from the cigar. "Why London, and why now?"

To stop me, Kovalev thought, sipping the drink, eyes never leaving Camden, "I have my suspicions. If she phones to meet, I'll have an opportunity."

"And if she doesn't?" Camden asked.

Kovalev smiled, "Svetlana's ego won't allow her to go unnoticed by the men she failed to defeat."

"Once again, the snake slithers from the weeds," Camden growled. "It's time we did something about that."

"I agree," Kovalev said, waving the cigar. "And London is the perfect place."

"After we know why she's here," Camden said. "She wouldn't risk being captured just to come for us."

"But she might if she thought she could bag all three of us."

Camden nearly choked on his drink with surprise, "Oleksandr is in London?"

"SIS brought him and the others out two years ago after Rensenhaus was killed," Kovalev said. "Our temptress has something big in play."

They lifted their glasses and toasted, their minds devising a plan on how to eliminate their mutual enemy. Illya refilled their glasses.

"There's another piece of business I wish to discuss," Kovalev offered.

"You're buying an NFL franchise," Camden said. "I am a sports fan, Kostyantyn."

"Not that," Kovalev said and gazed into Camden's eyes. "I want to buy Halibeck International."

Camden's immediate reaction was a broad frown that eased into a hesitant chuckle. "Absurd … Halibeck is the backbone of our operations worldwide, you know that. You buying it would be akin to buying the CIA itself."

"You know why I want it," Kovalev said. "We could call it an exchange … for the Rensenhaus folder."

Camden's thoughts froze, "Chernobyl. It's taken you three decades … this is about fucking Chernobyl."

"And may be why Svetlana is here," Kovalev offered. "It was, after all, your plan."

"But Halibeck? No way."

"I just recently became aware of the truth," Kovalev said and gave Camden a glance that said, *I know what you know.*

"I won't be denied this purchase, David, and neither will Ukraine."

"The political children … the president and Intelligence Committee … would never consider it. They—"

"Haven't heard my terms," Kovalev interrupted, then continued when the CIA mastermind cracked. "And you, my friend … for your retirement—"

"I can't be bought, Kostyantyn, you know that."

"I don't want to buy you, David. I want Halibeck," Kovalev hesitated for a long moment to finish his drink. "If denied … well, there is information on CIA activities in Ukraine and Russia that could be very damaging if brought to light."

Camden stiffened, anger rising. *You have the folder, you bastard,* Camden thought, "It's not smart to threaten the Central Intelligence Agency, Kostyantyn."

"It's no threat, David," Kovalev said as Illya filled his glass. "America's press would say that the public has … well, let's just say, I would be blind to your public's right to know."

"There are more permanent ways to achieve silence, Kostyantyn," Camden warned.

Anger darkened Camden's steely eyes that remained

fixed on Kovalev. He set the drink on the table and walked

out.

65

VII

Like an old man out for a lazy midmorning stroll through Hyde Park, Sir Clifton Toll was bundled against a cool breeze in a Savile Row tailored trench coat … one of his two extravagances, fine clothing. But for Toll, this was far from a lazy stroll. It was business, part of his duty to the Crown. The Queen's Knight was well-preserved for his 60-plus years and showed no signs of slowing. The cane was used more as a status symbol than a necessity. Those who knew the elder statesman knew he didn't consider himself old and never did anything without purpose. He had a newsman's eye for detail, a billionaire's confidence, and a spy's presence.

He walked the vacant footpath past several barren trees. *That time of year*, he thought briefly and saw the parallel with life. He wiped down a bench across from the Statue of Achilles and sat. The Woodford pocket watch from his vest told him the time. Not yet annoyed, his narrow eyes revealed signs of it mounting.

Footsteps turned him away from the brief but warm sun. The annoyance dissipated, but his expression soured. He snapped the Woodford closed. Wearing a dark hoody and workout lycra, Lyuba walked the footpath towards him. Though her exotic beauty was breathtaking, Toll saw her value elsewhere.

When she joined Svetlana's inner circle, Lyuba had no way of knowing the impact that decision would have on her life. The day she met Alistair Rensenhaus, she realized she had entered a realm where she had no business being. That meeting was accompanied by a sinking feeling that there was no getting out; Toll confirmed that with only his eyes.

But for Lyuba, there was always a solution, as there had been to get her family out of poverty. She joined Toll near the bench but did not sit.

"Kostyantyn Kovalev is in London," he said. "He has the folder, and I want it."

"Have him arrested; you have that power."

Oh, to be your age again, he thought. *I would put a bullet in your brain and drag you to a farm to feed the pigs.*

"I didn't interrupt my morning for a negotiation," he demanded.

Lyuba didn't weaken and refused to beg or plead. However, she knew her beauty had no effect on Toll. Her dilemma remained … she was stuck between two masters, maneuvering for survival. What followed was a demand:

"I want out."

"And sacrifice the lifestyle and the rewards, Lyuba?" he asked and stood.

"Which carry a price-tag beyond reason," she said, looking down on the older man who was half a head shorter.

"Squeamish about soiling those pretty hands?" he wondered aloud and tapped her leg with the cane. "Why the sudden change of heart?"

"Svetlana grows suspicious," she said, then changed the subject. "The promises you made in Ukraine … do you intend to honor them?"

"Ukraine … where you failed," Toll said, tiring of the tit-for-tat. "Your childish dribble is unbecoming. Other arrangements can be made, ones not favorable to you."

"You promised that within two years, I'd be free," she insisted. "That was—"

"I know when it was, Lyuba!" he snapped, then paused to scan the area. "Honor your commitment, or I will return you to Luhansk, gift-wrapped for execution."

"Damn you," she hissed. *I will have my own life, with or without your help*, she thought.

Toll's anger mounted like the increasing pressure in a steam boiler. She would pay if her insubordination jeopardized this mission. He grabbed her by the sweater and pressed her against a post that protected the statue. His strength surprised her, but she glared at him without fear. Both knew she could kill him in a heartbeat, and both knew she never would.

"Get what I want or face the consequences!" Toll demanded.

"Kovalev won't just turn it over to me," Lyuba countered.

"Use whatever means of persuasion is in your little bag of tricks, Lyuba," Toll suggested. "Kovalev has an interview at Wembley, three this afternoon, a perfect time."

Though equally angry, a sinking feeling told her there was no escaping this corner Toll had painted her into. "He will kill me if he finds out!"

"Then, I suggest you beat him to the punch, if necessary," Toll demanded without hesitation. "You have two days. Don't contact me again until you have the folder."

Their eyes locked. Her glare said *I will kill you.* Walking towards the street, he felt Lyuba's eyes narrowing on the back of his head like a pistol sight. Not bothered, he knew some things were more important than life … hers or his.

VIII

A sign over the back bar of the busy pub read: "WELCOME TO THE DARK HORSE." The boisterous mid-day weekend crowd wore tailored *casual clothes* and lingered with pints, wine, and cocktails. Plates of food were picked at, not eaten. Wiggy stood alongside a lone MI5 suit, toasting pints. In riding leathers, wearing the backpack, and carrying the helmet, Kenna entered with an investigative stare that covered the crowd. Strange environs had long been second nature to her, especially quaint pubs.

At the bar, Wiggy waved her over, "Here she is."

Turning and anxious, Barnaby Scriven was a stately balding man on the cusp of retirement but wearing a well-fitting suit without a tie, his casual look. An infectious grin at Kenna curled up into a grand smile. *My God*, he thought, *what I wouldn't give to be thirty again.*

"A double," he said, taking her shoulders, as would a long-lost relative. "You look exactly like Fiadh Dougherty. Barnaby Scriven at your service, young Fiadh. It is alright if I call you that, is it not?"

"I'm not worthy of being mentioned in the same sentence with Gran, but thank you," Kenna said and accepted his fatherly embrace.

"Humility was one of her greatest traits. She'd be pleased it's trickled down."

Wiggy handed Kenna a pint. They toasted and, as would two investigators, she and Barnaby, sized each other up. Kenna approved; she'd heard Gran's story of the handsome English investigator who captured her heart at a young age … something about subtle British charm.

"And you for having noticed," she said. *Gran told me everything* she did not say.

"Barnaby's helping us on this side of the Atlantic to find Anson Beck."

"Anything in honor of your grandmother," Barnaby insisted. "She helped us more than once and never wanted anything for it."

"She would say *'it's about the game, their side versus ours,'* and…"

"*'May the better side win,'*" she said at the same time as Barnaby and Wiggy.

As if to a dream, Barnaby lifted his pint to the sky, "To Fiadh, may she be holding our seats at the right hand of the Maker."

"Aye," Wiggy agreed. "But I must warn ya, my man, that

like the Grand Ole Dame, when the work face is on, the younger version doesn'a take ta small talk either."

Barnaby took her arm, "Anson Beck, what a worthy adversary you've chosen to hunt."

"Any information on him?" she asked.

"One of my original questions to Jeremy was, how does he fund his life as a jet setter?" he suggested.

"Why gran was hunting for him," Kenna said. "He's an accomplished jewel thief."

"Which was the basis of our search," Wiggy said. "We plotted his exploits."

"And traced his arrival in Ukraine back to Warsaw, Poland," Barnaby said.

"We had suspicions of that a couple years ago, but COVID blocked Wiggy looking into it," she hesitated. "We lost track when Beck went into Luhansk."

"Aye, the Russian sector, which you know all too well, lass," Wiggy said.

"We confirmed that Anson Beck is not his name," Barnaby said. "At least not the name given to him at birth … Antoni Brzezicki."

"Checking criminal associates, family, the usual," Wiggy said. "Could be he's tied in with the Polish mob and meth production, possibly even heroin coming out of Afghanistan."

"That's a new angle for him, but certainly more profitable," she said, then asked, "Is his base in Warsaw, then?"

"Not sure, lass," Wiggy said. "But we're tightenin' the noose."

Kenna's phone rang. She looked at the face, walked to the side, and answered, "Yes, Tommy. What's up?"

In the On-Line Reporter's room of BNC, Tommy sat in his cubical. On the computer screen was an image of "Yuri Zelenko."

"The Kovalev interview is now at two," Tommy said, ignoring the computer. "But there's something else."

"Get to it, Tommy. I'm in a meeting," she said.

"You worked with Yuri Zelenko in Ukraine, right?"

"Yes, why?"

"How well did he know Kovalev?"

"No idea … again, why?"

"Thurnbull wants background from him on Kovalev."

"Seems like a waste of time since we're interviewing him," Kenna said.

"Kinda what I thought, but he's the boss."

"I'm going to get Kovalev to meet after the interview," she said. "I'll ask him then. Is there anything else?"

"I'll be doing the live feed from Wembley's media room," he said, stared at Yuri's image, and saved it to the desktop. "See you there."

Kenna disconnected the call and walked for Wiggy and Barnaby as they toasted another pint. By their expressions and conversation, friendship between them was natural and as obvious as was their sense of duty.

"The interview with Kovalev's been moved up an hour, Wiggy," she said, downing her pint.

"Then, we best be about it," Wiggy said and turned to Barnaby. "You've made an acquaintance with the Ukrainian, eh Barnaby?"

"Yes, a piece of work, that one," Barnaby offered. "Eastern Europeans can be a nasty lot, and he's no exception."

"The other NFL owners approved him, and they're very picky," Kenna countered.

"They like his money if what I heard he paid is half true," Barnaby stated.

"How well do you know him?" Kenna asked.

"Had some dealings with him years back in my

Intelligence Service days," Barnaby said, thinking. "Don't care to relive 'em."

"SIS," she said, impressed and curious. "Why did you leave?"

"Missed dreary ole London," he said. "As to Kovalev … I'll just put it this way, he didn't become a multi-billionaire being a nice guy."

"He and I butted heads in Luhansk. I hope to iron out the issues after the interview," she said, knowing it wasn't going to be that simple. "And Beck?"

"Jeremy and I will continue to coordinate efforts," Barnaby said. "If the wanker's in London, we'll source him out."

"And if he isn't?"

"Then, we'll hunt him 'til we corner him, even if it's in bloody Hong Kong," Barnaby promised. "Been meaning to return, found and lost the love of my life there in the 90s."

"During the turnover of the colony to the Chinese, if I recall the story correctly," she said to his surprise. "I'll be forever in your debt if you help us capture that animal."

"Anything for your grandmother, Fiadh. No other reason required."

With a silent thank you and a hug, Kenna walked for the

door. Wiggy shook Barnaby's hand and hurried out after her. On the sidewalk, he watched as she unchained the Honda.

"The BNC equipment's at the hotel," Wiggy said.

"Hop on," she said, swung on, and started it.

"Me … on that?" Wiggy chuckled. "Not in yer lifetime, kid. I like the metal of a car 'round me. Have a van in a lot around the corner."

As Kenna strapped the helmet, she looked to the pub's front window. Barnaby lifted a fresh pint to her; she nodded in return, then smiled, having seen what attracted Gran to him.

"I don't like the sounds of this Kovalev interview, lass. No good'll come from it."

"We still have a little time, Wiggy. I need some background," She revved the engine. "I can't softball him; he knows I wouldn't do that."

"But you don't want to piss him off either," Wiggy suggested. "Barnaby's right. He was ruthless in the early days of his oil venture."

"That's why they're called roughnecks. Tough men willing to fight for what they want. That's the background I need."

"Already done in the hotel, kid," he said, to her surprise.

“And an idea how to parallel it with professional football.”

“Race you there,” she said and accelerated away.

IX

A variety of vessels moored at South Dock of Canary Warf, the water dark and ominous in the grey day. Light waves of a slow-moving speedboat slapped against the concrete embankment. A tug howled in the distance, breaking the silence.

Ashore and certainly out of place in the upscale shopping and dining area, Evhen Chayka was a gruff, middle-aged black Ukrainian fishing boat captain. His badge of honor was an aged, soiled uniform and sweat-stained cap. He puffed the last of a cigarette and dropped it to the stone walkway beside other blackened, squashed butts. He took his eyes from his objective long enough to smash out the latest addition. Ignoring the cool, still surroundings, he looked up.

Moored twenty meters from him, the flamboyant eighty-meter luxury yacht *"Worldly Light"* flew the tricolor Russian flag. On the aft deck, Svetlana wore dark skin-tight workout lycra and trainers, covered by a dark tailored overcoat with a hood. A self-made woman, she smoked a cigarette in a holder. Like her male counterparts, Svetlana had made rank in the FSB through hard work and an intelligent, if devious, mind, not by using what she had between her thighs. She had refused encounters of the flesh when offered; defied those demanded by superiors and peers. She had left more than one man bleeding, wishing he had not made an unwelcome advance.

Walking the gangway to board the yacht was Alexi Medved, a 30-year-old Russian FSB agent. A man as lethal with his hands as with a weapon, he was a trained assassin with a handsome boyish face that contradicted his nature. Hatred of London was written on that face like a Shakespearean sonnet. When he and Svetlana made eye contact, a second sonnet revealed that she hated him, and he hated her. However, on this mission, duty demanded they set their animosity aside. But it was always there, just beneath the surface like an active volcano.

She offered coffee, which he waved off. "Are you sure, Alexi? Imported from Tanzania, it's excellent."

With a contemptuous glare, he said, "I have no interest in small talk, Svetlana."

She responded with a sarcastic grin, "One of your great failings, Alexi. You never enjoy life."

Ignoring him for the moment, she sipped coffee and watched the speedboat rumble slowly from the harbor like a tiger pacing in a cage. All business, Medved ignored the boat. He demanded attention to duty above all else. Sensing his impatience, she turned … *time for business* … and placed a photo on the table.

"Kostyantyn Kovalev, Crimean oil. What of him?" Medved asked.

"Do what you do best, Alexi … today. I want to know why he's in London," she said. It was not a request and said with enough emphasis to remind him who commanded this operation.

"To finalize the purchase of an American football team," he said without interest.

"American football," she chuckled, continuing the small talk just to annoy her petulant subordinate. "The game escapes me. During a match, the foot contacts the ball so seldom."

"Americans are an oxymoron by nature, Svetlana," he offered. "Kovalev's negotiating a lease with Wembley."

"That may be the advertised reason," she said, paused, and pressed out the cigarette. "Remember, Kovalev is a master deceiver; his every move is by design toward the end game."

"What we do is no game, Svetlana."

She patted his cheek just to anger him, which it achieved. He jerked her hand down, not to hurt her but to make the point: *don't touch me.*

"How wrong you are, Alexi," she said and lit another cigarette. "I want to know if he's here to derail our assignment, intentionally or otherwise. Once we know that, we will know how to proceed."

"I already know the answer to that," he jabbed. "We should deal with him my way."

"Patience, my impatient friend," she ordered. *Yes, this must be dealt with,* she thought. "Do what has to be done."

Svetlana sensed there was something stewing inside Medved. He wanted to say more, much more. Surprising her, and without closure, he walked to the gangway. She allowed an annoyed frown to sour her expression and thought, *oh, how I love angering that rogue.*

Approaching from the side, Sergey was deadly serious in a suit, a young armed Russian guard, trained military, and void of humor. "Word from the embassy, director. Your diplomatic pouch from Ukraine has arrived."

"Very well, Sergey," she said as Medved accelerated away in a Jaguar F-Type. "Have Filipp bring her here."

She punched a number on her cell phone and waited for an answer:

"Kostyantyn, I heard you were in London. A word

outside your apartment, if you don't mind," she said and listened. "Outside the Mandarin Oriental then, in one hour."

In the shadows of the upscale shops, Evhen's eyes followed Medved as he drove away. He inhaled from a cigarette, walked the opposite direction, and lifted a cell phone …

*

WHITECHAPEL, LONDON

In boxer shorts, Oleksandr slept on a sloppy bed, snoring. Dull sunlight through the window accentuated his rough looks and the scars from just below his left ear and along the bottom of his jaw. Empty beer bottles sat on the table beside a yellow pad covered in notes. In the open window, a black cat stared at him from the sill.

A cell phone rang loudly. He struggled and yelled. Still half-asleep, his eyes opened. The cat scampered out the window. Panic snapped him upright; he slammed his head on the wall. Fear and rage consumed him; the cell phone rang loudly.

The hall outside Oleksandr's room was void of fixtures and dark, lit only by dull sun through a single window over the stairway. In the room, the cell phone rang loudly. Mrs. Kohut was a forty-something angry manager of Ukrainian descent and had done this more than once. She dropped a cigarette on the wood floor and ground it out with a slipper. In the room, the cell phone rang loudly. Mrs. Kohut knocked.

"Bear, answer the fuckin' thing!" she yelled.

"Yeah, yeah," Oleksandr mumbled from the room.

In the hall, Mrs. Kohut turned away … the cell phone rang loudly. Now, she's really angry. In the apartment, Oleksandr grabbed his head, then a mostly empty beer. He took a drink … the cell phone rang loudly … with instant revulsion and anger, he spit out a cigarette butt and slammed the bottle on the table. Mrs. Kohut pounded on the door … the cell phone rang loudly.

"Christ! Hang up! Fuck 'em!" Oleksandr yelled.

"It's your phone!" Mrs. Kohut yelled from behind the closed door. She pounded on it. "Bear! Answer it!"

Oleksandr rolled to the side … the cell phone rang loudly. "Alright … alright!"

The door lock clicked; the door burst open. Mrs. Kohut moved rapidly and lifted the cell phone from a pair of trousers as it rang loudly. Oleksandr walked for the toilet. Mrs. Kohut connected the call:

"Stay on the line; he's drainin' the dragon." She dropped the phone on the table and walked for the door. "Ya need ta keep proper hours!"

"These are my proper hours!" he barked, coughed up a lung, and spit.

Oleksandr relieved himself, flushed, and splashed water over his face. For a moment, he stared at his reflection in the cracked mirror, not liking what he saw. Walking to the table, he grabbed a full beer, opened it, and took a swig. He lifted the cell phone as Mrs. Kohut slammed the door.

"Yeah?" Oleksandr belched into the phone.

On the cell phone at South Harbor, Evhen walked along the yacht and tipped his cap to Svetlana. She ignored him and turned inside the salon. The guards on deck, however, watched his every move.

"Just watching yer girlfriend and her boy toy from the FSB."

With immediate recognition, Oleksandr perked up. "Impossible, I killed that son-of-a-bitch in Luhansk."

"Like you, O.S., many lives," Evhen said. "Both in the flesh on the company yacht in South Harbor… and she's givin' the orders."

Oleksandr's attention was now keen. "Did you get an opportunity to ask why they are here?"

"Perhaps to meet the man they hate more than you,"

Evhen said and paused for effect. "He's in London, as well."

"Kovalev," Oleksandr surmised, hatred filling his eyes.

"It was his man that contacted me to watch for 'em."

"What you suspect they're up to?" Oleksandr asked.

"Won't be no good, whatever it is. And, no doubt, about what they were doin' in the old country."

"So, they've all come together," Oleksandr thought aloud.

"With the Russians believin' yer dead," Evhen suggested. "Which presents an opportunity."

"Indeed, but why would Kovalev contact me?" Oleksandr said with stiffened anger. From under the pillow, he lifted a Glock 17 pistol and placed it on the table. "I could inform SIS or CIA and let them do the job for us."

"Kovalev's no fool," Evhen said. "Whatever he's doin', it's for a good reason."

"And known only to him, Evhen."

"He knows you want the pleasure of watching the other two bleed out, my old friend."

"Do you know where she's laying her head?" Oleksandr asked.

"Hasn't moved from the yacht," Evhen said. "If she does, I'll make it so we can follow without her knowing."

"Kovalev?"

"Has an apartment in Red Square," Evhen said. "Rumor is that he will be at Wembley this afternoon to finalize the lease for his American football team."

"I look forward to getting reacquainted."

Oleksandr disconnected the call. Now filled with mixed emotions … anger, sorrow, hatred, and joy, he was no longer tired and hungover but wide awake. Subconsciously, he ran fingers along facial scars, then placed them on two gunshot wound scars on his upper chest. The black cat moved to the windowsill; Oleksandr rubbed its fur.

"Ah, my good luck charm," he said to the cat. "Kovalev, Svetlana, and Medved … one big, happy family. I've been waiting a long time."

The names lingered on Oleksandr's tongue like acid; he took a drink of beer and opened a pistol cleaning kit.

X

Kenna sped the Honda along Olympic Way and merged onto the pedestrian ramp leading up to the stadium. She stopped at the six-meter-tall bronze statue of Bobby Moore, a tribute to the only captain to lead the British team to a World Cup title. A large electronic sign wrapped repeatedly around the stadium: "WEMBLEY CONNECTED BY EE". Jameson, by the name on his uniform, an unarmed British Guard at the main entrance, walked in her direction. She swung off and lifted her press credentials.

"I have an appointment to interview Kostyantyn Kovalev, Mr. Jameson," she said.

"They are expecting you, Ms. Hannigan," Jameson said. "Just received word that Mr. Kovalev is running late and asked that you join the lads on the pitch."

"Lads?"

"American footballers."

"Didn't realize I was interviewing the entire team."

"A half side by my measure, Ms. Hannigan," Jameson said and opened the door.

"That'll give me time to get to know the lads," she said

with an annoyed smile.

"I like your work, what I've seen of it."

"Not much of it these past two years."

"Yeah, bloody COVID kicked us all in the bollocks."

"Some of us, anyway," she said with a chuckle.

A strange sense consumed Kenna when she stepped into the largest stadium in England. Here, on any given match day, ninety thousand lunatics would drink enough beer for the entire city, blow horns and whistles, and scream until their lungs burned. Win or lose, though, the event would not be complete without a fight or ten; after all, it was English football.

When she walked from the tunnel onto the pitch, a sense of belonging overcame her. If papa had gotten his wish … her being born a boy … she might have stepped onto this pitch in uniform to the roar of the crowd. In lieu of the soccer net, American football goalposts had been erected at the goal line with two tall chairs centered. Near the goal posts, a group of American professional football players lounged on the grass, most concentrating on their cell phones.

"I'm gonna like playin' here," a tall, lean wide receiver said, "if all the women are like this fine English lass."

"Sorry to disappoint, Texas born and bred," Kenna

countered. "Irish Gran, though."

The one twirling the football on his palm, the quarterback, motioned to her riding leathers. "You some kind'a motorcycle daredevil?"

"It's been said," she replied. "A reporter here to interview the new owner."

"The Russian?" a lineman asked.

"He's Ukrainian, actually."

"Ain't no difference," the cornerback said.

The smartass, Kenna thought. "Don't say that to his face when it's time to sign your pay check."

As if to catch her off-guard, the quarterback tossed her the ball, impressed she caught it. She removed her boots and relished her feet on the grass. She tossed the ball to the cornerback; he snatched it with one hand.

"I come from a football family," she said. "My father played for the Longhorns."

"Where'd you play?" the smartass cornerback said with a chuckle.

Catching the cornerback off-guard, Kenna knocked the ball from his hands and caught it in mid-air. She ran around the players with the cornerback in pursuit. The other players laughed, egging him on:

"No wonder you ain't got no interceptions.", "Can't catch a girl in leather tights?", "Yer slower than me, and I got a hundred pounds on ya."

Just before the cornerback reached her, she lateraled the ball to the quarterback. The cornerback gave her a forearm shiver in the side, knocking her from her feet. She landed heavily and rolled in the grass. While lying there, a smile filled her face. When she rolled over, a frown replaced it. He offered a hand apologetically; she accepted it with a huff and stood.

When he turned to the others, Kenna buckled his knee and ran down the pitch. The quarterback passed the ball and hit her in perfect stride. In the open, she celebrated and spiked the ball. The players shouted their approval and gathered around, giving her high-fives.

"Offensive pass interference," the cornerback whined with a laugh.

Carrying two large duffel bags, Wiggy walked onto the pitch. "Come to play football or do an interview, Fiery?"

"Just teachin' the guys how the game's played," she replied and pointed at Wiggy. "Here's a real man; plays rugby."

A lineman joined Wiggy and shook his hand. "Tried it

once in college but couldn't get the hang of it. Nonstop, no breaks. Guys my size need air ever once in a while."

"Gettin' a little long in the tooth, but still game for a good scrum now and then."

Wiggy assembled temporary lighting in front of the chairs. From the side of the pitch, a maintenance man unrolled a power cord towards them. Wiggy assembled the camera on a tripod in front of the chairs at the goalposts. The players applauded and whistled as Kenna peeled off the riding leathers.

"Come on, guys, act like you've seen a woman taking off her clothes."

Much to the players' chagrin, beneath the leathers, she wore a pants suit and blouse. She pulled flats from the backpack and slid into them. When done, an amazing transformation had taken place, from motorcycle riding and football playing tomboy to professional reporter. Wiggy fixed the handsfree microphone to her blouse and pulled a strand of grass from her hair. He found her in the camera frame, focused, and punched his Bluetooth:

"Call Tommy," Wiggy said and waited for an answer.

Wembley's Media Room overlooked the pitch. Tommy sat at the control panel, and the large screen in front of him came to life. As the image of Kenna and the players came into focus, he answered.

"Got it, Jer. Hear you loud and clear," Tommy acknowledged.

"How's the video, T-squared?" Wiggy asked.

"Not you, too … T-squared," Tommy objected. "Don't call me Tommy toilet!"

"Toilet? No, Tom Terrific," Wiggy said, confused. "How's 'bout the video?"

"Looks good," Tommy offered. "Close on Kenna; let's make sure she's not like a ghost."

"No Casper the friendly some days," Wiggy said in jest, then waved his hands at Kenna. "Fiery, Tommy wants a test. You players gather 'round."

"Gladly." "That's my spot." "I'm next to her," the players said, jostling for position.

Kenna fussed with her hair as the players assembled sloppily around her. From behind the camera, Wiggy gave her a thumbs-up, then twirled his hand. Kenna began, as if from a script:

"What better venue than the hallowed grounds of Wembley to interview a man vying to enter the sacred society of team ownership in the American National Football

League."

"Okay, that's good," Wiggy said. "Powder yer face for the real thing."

"She don't need no powder," the cornerback countered.

"Believe me, on the screen, I do," she said.

"Sorry 'bout roughin' ya up," he offered.

"No biggie. Been hit harder, believe me," she said honestly. She clapped, drawing the players' attention. "While waiting for Mr. Kovalev, I'd like to get some words from you guys … one at a time, please."

The cornerback jumped into the chair first. "Fire away, sister. Rashon Hill at your service."

XI

Cool and cloudy, a breeze brushed across Canary Wharf. Shoppers and diners were bundled against the chill and filled the area with conversation and laughter. Various types of music from pubs mixed for a variety of listening pleasures … or confusion.

A black Aurus Senat Russian limousine stopped on the street near the end of the gangway onto the deck of the Russian yacht *"Worldly Light"*. Filipp stepped from the driver's side and opened the rear door. He was past middle age but didn't show it, gruff and scarred with hollow eyes. Those eyes, however, never stopped moving. He was not just a driver; he was also Svetlana's bodyguard, as good with a pistol as he was behind the wheel.

Filipp reached inside the car, revealing the handle of a Russian PB 9mm pistol in a shoulder holster. With effort, he lifted out a heavy suitcase-sized "Diplomatic Pouch." Following it out the door, Lyuba wore a fashionable dark overcoat with a hood over dark lycra. Though having no rest after a long, tiring journey, Lyuba's expression and looks were fresh and crisp. She walked up the gangway towards Svetlana on the rear deck. Filipp followed, pulling the heavy suitcase on wheels. Sergey joined Svetlana as she embraced Lyuba.

"Remarkable how the young manage perfection after a long journey."

"Not what it feels like behind my eyes, Svetlana," Lyuba responded.

Svetlana motioned to the suitcase. "Sergey, bring the case to my stateroom."

Sergey carried the suitcase and followed Svetlana below. Filipp left the yacht and stood at attention alongside the limousine. Lyuba walked the deck, admiring the luxury. Though her eyes did not show it, she was consumed by the bold display of wealth. This was why she had agreed to this operation. She would not be satisfied until she had this.

Her childhood in Ekaterinburg flashed through her mind. Her father worked tirelessly to feed the family. Every night, he returned exhausted, soiled, and sometimes beaten. He was a sickly man and couldn't cope with the rigors of forced labor. Every night, mama cried herself to sleep. There was never enough food … until Lyuba took it upon herself to change things.

That first venture into crime in her mid-teens nearly cost her everything, including her life. Avoiding gunfire, she had escaped after stealing food, vodka, and medicine from a small shop. When home, she was confused when papa whipped her with a belt for such stupidity. All that aside, they ate and drank as they hadn't in years. Her father forgave her that transgression and those that followed, accepting that she had done it for the family.

Around her 18th birthday, her life changed forever. It was when she first saw Svetlana, dressed like a queen, hair perfect, nails painted. But what struck Lyuba the most was a woman giving orders to men that dwarfed her physically. That's when her game to join Svetlana's inner circle began.

Her plan had been simple: steal from Svetlana, plant the evidence on one of her associates, and inform the lady that she had been swindled. When she told the story, though, no one had believed her. Without emotion, Svetlana watched as Medved beat Lyuba. On the second day, they were joined by another man … Kostyantyn Kovalev.

'I swear to you, she has the jewels, madam,' Lyuba had cried, bleeding, badly beaten. *'She's a seamstress, no? Check the linings of her clothing.'*

Lyuba looked at the index finger that would not straighten, remembering that time. Yes, she would have her revenge. She took a seat in the main salon with a clear view of Canary Wharf's shopping area. A young female Russian server poured a glass of wine.

"The Chardonnay madam said you preferred," the server said.

"Yes, thank you," Lyuba said.

Svetlana joined her at the table but did not sit. She kissed Lyuba hard, with authority; Lyuba accepted it eagerly. These last few days had been the longest they had been separated in several years. Animal lust overcame them, but Svetlana broke away and caught her breath with frustrated satisfaction.

"I have a meeting with Kostyantyn Kovalev. Relax and enjoy the wine, my love."

"Kovalev's in London?" Lyuba asked, pretending surprise. It was, after all, why they were all in London.

Lyuba's curiosity beamed, wanting to ask if she should follow him. But she wouldn't; she never asked. If she was to be told, Svetlana would tell her. Over these past few years, she had gotten close to Svetlana, closer than she ever thought possible. She had become not just Svetlana's lover but also her most trusted courier. But Lyuba was, if nothing else, a realist. She knew that any relationship with Svetlana was like walking a razor's edge.

How was she going to get close to Kovalev? She seduced

him once before, but all that resulted was sex, not the long-term relationship Svetlana wanted her to secure. Svetlana's anger was overwhelming, beating Lyuba so badly that scars remained today. It was the closest Svetlana had come to killing her. Lyuba had considered running at that time but decided to stay for the long play.

Lyuba massaged Svetlana's thigh just the way she liked it. As much as she enjoyed the attention, Svetlana stayed Lyuba's hand. Time for that would come later.

"What is it, Svetlana?" Lyuba asked.

"I can read your mind, Lyuba," Svetlana said. "Kovalev. I believe he has information from Luhansk, information I require."

"If you want me to watch him—"

"No, there is too much between you from the past," Svetlana said.

"That I slept with him has no bearing on how I do my duty, Svetlana," Lyuba insisted. "As I recall, you slept with him, as well."

Svetlana calmly grabbed Lyuba's face and, with her other hand, a breast. As she had with Toll, Lyuba, the obedient warrior, did not resist. Svetlana saw something in Lyuba's eyes she had never seen. *Could it be fear?* She wondered, savoring it.

"You owe me your life, my beautiful lioness," Svetlana snarled. "Don't force me to collect on that debt."

"You know I will do whatever you require, Svetlana," Lyuba offered.

Svetlana's anger dissipated in an instant. "Yes, then, I do have a task for you. You know the newsman, Sir Clifton Toll?"

Stunned, Lyuba tried to hide it … she lied, "Of him, yes."

"There is a part of my past that must go away, specifically kept from him."

"Luhansk, I take it," she surmised … *knowing*.

"Yes, information stolen from our mission by his bureau chief, Alistair Rensenhaus," Svetlana said. "It details my FSB involvement with Ukrainian separatists. Find it and bring it to me."

"How will I know what to look for?"

"You remember the meeting in Luhansk, the Novikov folder?"

Lyuba nodded. "Of course."

"It is similar to that," she said and kissed Lyuba's cheek. "Tomorrow, we celebrate your delivery … and I will have a surprise."

As Filipp drove Svetlana away in the limousine, Lyuba motioned to Sergey. He joined her while she finished the wine.

"There is somewhere I have to be and will be gone a few hours," she said. "Please have one of the men hail a taxi."

*

Filipp eased the Aurus Senat limousine to the side of the street in front of the exclusive Mandarin Oriental Hyde Park Hotel. The area teemed with wealthy businessmen and women. Svetlana knew Kovalev relished being around his Western allies. She, on the other hand, loathed the arrogance and flamboyance, not once comparing it to her own. For her, the hotel's only redeeming quality was its close proximity to the embassy. Filipp stood out, inspected the street, and opened the rear door.

"Stay close," Svetlana said, stepping out.

"Of course," Filipp said, stepped into the car, and drove away.

Svetlana lifted a cigarette from her handbag and placed it into the holder. Children walked with their nannies across the street towards the Hyde Park playground. She smiled with her eyes, though deep within, she felt only the annoyance of family, pleased to have avoided it.

She sensed him before he appeared. Walking from the hotel like an omnipotent ruler, Kovalev lifted a cigar; Illya snapped a lighter to the end of it.

Oh, to put a bullet in the heart that keeps that bastard alive, she thought.

"A private discussion, Kostyantyn," she requested. Kovalev nodded to Illya.

"I'll bring the car, sir," Illya said and walked down the street, lighting a cigarette.

"It's been a long time, Svetlana. Such a coincidence," he said, laced with sarcasm. "Had you phoned earlier, I would have ordered coffee … a Tanzanian blend, as I recall."

"We never meet by coincidence, Kostyantyn."

He waved his hands at the city. "Yet, here we are, together once again in the *den of iniquity,* I believe you call it."

Kovalev enjoyed barbing Svetlana. It was like toying with a child, bringing her to the point of anger, only to knock the hot air from her sail. He continued with the sarcasm:

"I understand you are staying on the company yacht. How wonderful they named it after you."

Svetlana hated Kovalev's word games in an attempt at control. Today, those feelings took on greater meaning by the importance of her mission. Failure was not an option. Kovalev would not be allowed to get in the way of her success … no man would.

"If you are here to interfere with my business, it will not end well for you," she warned.

He frowned: *you would threaten me?* "When will you learn … I don't respond to idle threats?"

"It wasn't meant as idle, Kostyantyn. I will do what I must to succeed," she said, her demanding eyes boring into him.

"Spoken as the seraph you are, my dear."

"Stay out of my way … and, more importantly, out of my business."

"It pleases me your ego has not waned, Svetlana. Alas, I forgot about you long ago." Kovalev relit his cigar and exhaled toward her, knowing she loathed it. "You know why I'm here, and I don't give a damn why you're here."

Illya stopped the Rolls Royce at the curb beside them; Kovalev waved at it. "I'd be happy to take you where you desire."

"It's my intention to survive the night, Kostyantyn," Svetlana objected.

Kovalev allowed a wry smile to crease his cheeks.

Another exhale, this time away from her. He flicked the cigar ash dreadfully close to her tailored overcoat.

"Had I wanted you dead, Svetlana, I would have sunk the yacht in the middle of the Black Sea." He paused, inhaling. "I know every step you take before you take it. You have a job to do; I have a job to do. Stay out of my way and there will be no problems."

"From a man who has never kept his word."

"To a woman paranoid of a leaf falling from a tree."

"Once my business is concluded, I will leave London, never to return." She leveled those devious eyes. "Get in my way, and you will never leave, Kostyantyn."

XII

The owner's suite at Wembley was chock-a-block with sports memorabilia. Men and women's Football, Rugby, American Football, and special events mementos lined the walls, stood on tables, and filled display cases. Team flags hung from the ceiling, encircling the suite. Kovalev walked to the glass door that overlooked the pitch and slid it open. With pride of knowing this was the venue from where he would watch his football team, he toasted the pitch with a shot of Horilka. Watching Kenna and Wiggy, he accepted another shot from Illya.

"A great day, Illya," he said without turning.

"Yes, sir. Will lift the spirits of all Ukrainians."

Tommy knocked and entered the suite, his eyes all-encompassing, like a child at a toy store. "We're ready when you are, Mr. Kovalev."

"We'll be right down," Kovalev said.

On the pitch, Wiggy spun the camera to the owner's suite, capturing Kovalev and Illya in the door. The Ukrainian lifted his glass, drank, and turned back into the room. Tommy looked out and gave Wiggy a thumbs-up. He turned to the outer room and lifted his phone.

"We're ready, sir. Was just in the owner's suite with Mr. Kovalev. He and the bodyguard are going down now."

On the field, Wiggy got Kenna's attention. "He's on the way down, Fiery."

"I want a word with him before we start recording, but get me greeting him."

"I have done this before, kid," he said with a hint of sarcasm.

A few minutes later, Kovalev led Illya down the stadium steps and onto the pitch. With pride and radiating arrogance, there was no doubt who was the man of the hour. Kenna walked over to greet him. Both hesitated, then embraced and kissed each other's cheeks.

"Kenna Derick-avna, my apologies for being late," he said in a business greeting. "It has been a long time."

"Some would say, too long. Others would say, not long enough," Kenna said in hopes of breaking the ice that had frozen their relationship in Luhansk.

"How is your father? I enjoyed our brief time together in Kyiv."

She now realized why she had trouble with Kovalev in Ukraine. He was exactly like her father, authoritative and demanding. She brushed it aside.

"Well … thank you for asking. He promises to be here for the first game," she said, already tired of the small talk. "Before starting with the interview, thank you for asking for me."

"After Luhansk, it was perfectly logical, so I phoned Thurnbull to arrange it."

"Most importantly, though, thank you for helping me get out of Ukraine two years ago."

"Your gratitude is not deserved, Kenna. I was doing what any man … father … would do," Kovalev responded. "Besides, you were in no condition to combat the Russian Army."

"Is anyone?" she wondered aloud.

"Or to find the man you sought, which is what brought you to London," he offered. "Has the information from Luhansk been helpful?"

"Only time will tell," she said, and added, "It's very much appreciated."

The lead on Anson Beck that brought Wiggy and her to London was a detailed account of Beck's movements in Ukraine, specifically his contact with the Russians. She wasn't sure why Kovalev had supplied it, though that would be her first question later. That Wiggy and Barnaby had discovered he was Polish filled some of the black holes about him. There were many more.

"I owe you an explanation for events in Luhansk," Kovalev said with feeling, surprising Kenna. "Which is why I asked for you. To begin, though, I wanted to offer my condolences on your colleague, Rensenhaus. The times I worked with him, I found him to be the consummate professional."

'Worked with him' caught Kenna off-guard; she was instantly uncomfortable. *Was Adelaide right? Had Kovalev's actions led to her father's death?*

Her mind drifted to Luhansk two years before, the automatic gunfire, explosions all around, and the BNC office in flames. Her heart sank, remembering Nadia, a frightened child clutching onto her for life. Kenna's tears nearly fell again, reliving that horrible moment when the charred, unrecognizable remains of Alistair Rensenhaus were pulled from the smoldering debris. At that moment, it hadn't mattered what happened to the video of the clandestine Russian meeting.

Now, two years later, it did. Only Yuri Zelenko … and possibly Kostyantyn Kovalev could tell her that. *Question number two,* she thought, mentally editing her interview strategy.

"He was a good man," she said. "I look forward to discussing those times ... and Anson Beck, off camera."

He took her arm, as would her father. "I have a short meeting after the interview, no more than an hour. Come to the Owner's Suite; the Horilka will be chilled."

"Now," he continued with *man-of-the-hour* vibrato and walked her towards the players, "let's meet these modern-day gladiators that play this American game."

Kenna joined Wiggy while he filmed the greetings, new owner to players. The quarterback presented Kovalev an autographed football and team flag. The only thing missing was Horilka, black caviar, and Cuban cigars.

At the edge of the pitch, unnoticed by Kenna and Kovalev, Illya spoke into his phone. While talking, he looked up at the owner's suite. He disconnected the call, then hurried off the pitch and up the stadium steps.

"Let's begin with a group shot," Kenna yelled and clapped. Like a choreographer, she moved them into a line, with Kovalev in the center. "A simple T-formation but in reverse. Defense plays offense today."

The players were impressed with her knowledge and took her orders as if their head coach. She placed each player in the formation, looking to Wiggy for approval.

"Join us, Kenna," Kovalev insisted. "You brought us all together."

Kenna wondered what he meant by that and joined them. Surrounded by men twice her size, she felt physically inadequate. Wiggy panned the camera slowly across them, then looked up, listening to Tommy on the Bluetooth.

"How about some men on a knee in the front," Tommy relayed from the booth.

When Wiggy repeated the request, the quarterback yelled an audible. As if during a game, the players shifted. Rashon Hill went in motion across the team, handed Kenna an autographed football, and said:

"Your first professional touchdown … but it was still offensive pass interference."

"Thank you, Rashon," she said. "It's only a penalty if you get caught, right?"

He laughed and patted her shoulder. She clutched the ball and stood behind Rashon and several other *smaller* men on a knee in front. Wiggy listened to the Bluetooth and then gave them a thumbs-up.

"That's good," he said. "Now, Kenna and Mr. Kovalev walking to the chairs."

"Are we getting married, or is this an interview?"

Kovalev asked to the amusement of the players.

"He's a picky choreographer, Kostyantyn," Kenna chuckled.

On the chairs, Kenna fussed with her hair a final time. The players lingered on the grass behind the camera. Wiggy fastened Kovalov's cordless microphone, got everything in the camera lens, and motioned:

"Three, two, one, action."

Holding the football, Kenna began the interview without script:

"Kenna Hannigan for BNC, reporting from Wembley's hallowed ground to interview Kostyantyn Kovalev, the first Eastern European to become a team owner in America's National Football League," she said. "Thank you, Kostyantyn, for agreeing to meet."

"The pleasure is mine, Kenna," he responded and smiled with his eyes. "Thank you for having me."

"How excited you must be about the prospects of your team in this great arena."

"I'm humbled that the other NFL owners have accepted me and that Wembley's owners support the team. I look forward to the challenge of having the first team in Europe." Waving a hand across the players, he continued:

"With this fine group of athletes, as you said, on these hallowed grounds, I have no doubt a Super Bowl is on the horizon."

"Perhaps here," Kenna added with a broad grin.

*

A half-hour later, Kovalev walked from the pitch with the players. Kenna sat on the chair with a beer. Wiggy disassembled the equipment and loaded everything into the duffel bags. When finished, he took a big drink of beer and punched his Bluetooth.

"Call Tommy." He took another drink while Tommy answered. "Do you want any follow-up shots while I'm here, Tommy boy?"

"Everything looks good, Jer," Tommy said. "Just about through adding Kenna's intros. We'll air as-is. You guys are good at this."

"Been doin' it a long time, my man. Beer's on you later." Wiggy disconnected the call and turned to Kenna. "Got a text from Barnaby. Has something he wants to discuss."

"I'll call when I'm through with Kovalev. Do me a favor," she said and tossed him the football. "Put that someplace safe."

He tossed it into the air and caught it. "Last time I was

here was in '15 to watch the Rugby World Cup."

"I remember. Gran helped investigate the safety deposit heist from London's Hatton Garden," she said. "Ingenious caper, as I recall."

"Aye, until their capture. The World Cup was several months later. The Grand Ole Dame said I earned some time off, so I stayed behind," he said.

"You're leaving something out, Wiggy," she hinted at his modesty. "The story I got was your leg was broken in an altercation during the investigation."

"Gave me the opportunity to meet some pretty nurses," he said.

"Ah, yes, the nickname," Kenna said with a grin.

Wiggy grumbled and placed the football into the duffel bag. "If I'm not at the suite, you know where to find me."

He gathered the duffel bags and started to walk away but stopped and flicked his eyes to the owner's suite. "Remember what I said … watch yer backside."

As Wiggy walked to the tunnel out of the stadium, Kenna looked up to the dark owner's suite. She looked at her phone for the time and took a drink of beer. Her eyes circled the stadium, enjoying the sudden and complete silence.

She came away from the interview with a different

opinion of Kovalev. He had been kind and courteous and freely answered her questions. The man on Wembley's pitch was a much calmer man than she met in Luhansk. Maybe what she had told Wiggy … *different time, different place …* had really changed things. She was anxious to see if the same would hold true when they met later. The questions that swirled around her brain were nothing like those she asked about Wembley and American football.

They were about the deaths of a good man … and a ten-year-old girl.

XIII

In the waning hours of day, the well-appointed pub was brightly lit and situated with a view of Wembley Stadium. As one would expect, it was decorated with sports fanatics in mind. Oleksandr was at ease with himself, in a reflective mood, as he entered and walked for the bar. Conversations softened, if ever so slightly, and he felt more than saw the investigative stares lifting from pints to scrutinize him. He sat on a stool and leaned on the thick wooden top.

In London, by necessity, he missed much about his homeland. Perhaps highest on the list was the local bar he frequented. It was larger and more open than most in London. Most important, though, at home, he could depend on having chilled Horilka. The British believed everything should be served at room temperature.

Staring into the full-back mirror, he fiddled with a lighter, wanting a smoke. Another reason he missed home; his bar allowed smoking. Without stepping in Oleksandr's direction, a short and thick, flat-nosed bartender lifted a fighter's punchy eyebrow in a silent question.

"London Pride," Oleksandr said. "And Horilka, if you have it."

"Russian or Polish, mate."

"Polish it is," Oleksandr said.

The bartender poured a pint and a shot. He didn't look at Oleksandr until he slid the drinks across the bar. Oleksandr pushed money forward, lifted the shot, and drank it.

"Big weekend, mate?" the bartender asked.

Oleksandr slid the shot glass for a refill. "I'm alive; they all are."

The television behind the bar flashed: "BNC Sports Report". Eyes fixed on the stadium, Oleksandr rolled the pint in his hands. On the television, a Female News anchor mouthed words silently. The bartender turned up the volume.

"Big doin's at the stadium today," the bartender offered.

"Hadn't heard," Oleksandr said, annoyed by the small talk. *He knew perfectly well.*

A camera view from the end of Wembley's pitch panned to the owner's suite, down to the pitch and a group of players, and then to Kenna and Kovalev on chairs in front of the goal posts. Oleksandr nodded with a reverent smile:

"The woman born of fire … Kenna," he mumbled, surprised. "Turn this up if you would, lad."

The bartender turned up the volume. Kenna leaned to Kovalev with a reporter's smile:

"What was it that drove you to want this, an American football team, I mean?"

"I know that guy," the bartender interrupted.

And I, her, Oleksandr did not say. "Kostyantyn Kovalev, a Ukrainian here to lease the stadium for his American football team."

"You know him?" the bartender asked.

"Follow the sport when I have the time," Oleksandr lied.

Oleksandr's mind whirled. The camera turned to Kenna with her infectious smile and addictive eyes. Numb with thoughts of their adventures in Luhansk, Oleksandr did not hear the interview. Headlights through the drizzle snapped his attention from the television. *Relax*, he scolded himself, *it's not the Russians*. A Vauxhall Combo panel van drove from the stadium and sped down the street.

"I had no idea. He's become a regular," the bartender said. "Usually sits at the bar."

"Good P.R., if you want my opinion." Oleksandr downed his beer, dropped a tip on the bar, and stood. "Looks like he's busy and won't be coming in tonight."

In front of the pub, eyes on the stadium, Oleksandr allowed light rain to dampen his face. He pulled a flask from his pocket and took a drink. He lifted the pistol from his back belt and shoved it into his overcoat pocket. He took another drink and walked across the street to a rusty, beat-up vintage Vauxhall Brava pickup.

"You have chosen a very bad time to be in London, my American beauty," Oleksandr said to himself as much as to the stadium. He lifted a hood over his head. "Kovalev and Svetlana couldn't leave well enough alone ... and soon, they will come for me."

XIV

Light rain passed over Wembley. On the pitch, Kenna looked up, *welcome to London*. She finished the beer, threw on her backpack, and hurried for the sideline. She ran up the steps and paused under the cover of the stadium seating overhead. She brushed rain from her clothes, pulled out her cell phone, and tapped Bluetooth:

"Call Wiggy's cell." She continued up the steps.

"Aye, have ye met with him already, Fiery?" Wiggy answered.

"On my way now; was wondering what Barnaby had to say."

"Not there yet … London traffic."

"Didn't slow you in D.C.," Kenna said with a chuckle. "I'll call after I speak with him."

Standing at the top of the steps in the darkening stadium, all that went wrong in Luhansk flashed before her eyes. There were good moments, but they were overshadowed by the battles and death. An unarmed stadium guard moved in her direction. She lifted her credentials.

"Oh, apologies, mum, didn't know you were still here,"

the guard said.

"I have a meeting with Mr. Kovalev in the owner's suite."

"On me rounds, come along," he said. "So, how is he to work with?"

"We have a saying in the States," she said. "He's a tough nut to crack."

"Me ole man always said, *do yer job best ye can and fuck the naysayers*," he said. "Apologies for me language, mum."

"My grandmother said much in the same," she replied with a smile. "With that attitude, you'll do just fine with him."

He led Kenna up a series of stairs to a long, dark hallway lit by an occasional night light. Even in darkness, the shrine to sport did not escape her. The walls held photos and posters of sporting events at Wembley since the first stadium opened in 1923, including the Olympic games in 1948.

"Is it always this dark?" she asked.

"Saving energy, mum," the guard offered. "The suite will be brighter."

She recalled seeing the suite dark. Her response was a silent but questioning, *not from the pitch*. The guard led her to the door; he knocked, then knocked again.

"Mr. Kovalev, sir, the reporter is here," the guard said. With concern, he grabbed the door handle and eased the door open. "Mr. Kovalev?"

Kenna entered the dark outer room behind the guard. "Kostyantyn, it's Kenna. Kostyantyn?"

It's dark and eerily quiet until … a scuffle in the suite startled both Kenna and the guard. He gripped his shoulder microphone. She moved forward; he reached out to hold her back.

"Sir, something's not right in the owner's suite," he said into the mic.

In the suite, the scuffle became a full-fledged fight. Screaming, grunting, shattered glass, crashing furniture. Kenna broke away from the guard and hurried for the door. With greater urgency into his mic, the guard followed and said:

"Sir, send more men; there's a fight in the suite."

Kenna reached the door before the guard and jerked it open … a suppressed gunshot followed by a brief grunt. The guard grabbed her. The dark shadow of a body collapsed and hit the floor, gurgled breathing of a man drowning in his own blood.

The silhouette in a hoody hurried for the service door.

The guard and Kenna hurried after … bad decision. The silhouette turned the pistol. The guard jerked Kenna to the side. The silhouette fired and hit the guard in the chest, spraying Kenna with blood. They fell. The silhouette ran for the service door.

On the floor, Kenna checked the guard … labored breathing … and hurried to Kovalev. She knelt beside him; blood pumped from the heart shot. She felt for a pulse; he struggled to pull her close:

"Package … safe … Mandarin Hotel—"

Kovalev's body relaxed; he stopped breathing. Voices of running guards outside the suite. She tapped the Bluetooth, jumped up at a run for the service door, and flipped on her phone's video.

"Call Wiggy's cell!" She threw the service door open and hurried out. "Wiggy, Kovalev's been—"

A bomb exploded in Kenna's head. Her legs folded; she fell. Her eyes blurred; her head slapped the concrete walkway. A blurry silhouette in a hoody bent over her. Muffled yelling from the suite. As vision faded, Kenna held firm the phone until the silhouette ran away … and light faded to blackness.

"Fiery?" Wiggy yelled over her phone. "Fiery, talk to me!"

XV

With *Dear God* panic on her face, Mrs. Pemberton hurried along the hall towards Toll's private office. Staff members watched with some amazement if not amusement; none had ever seen Mrs. Pemberton in such a hurry. She threw open the door.

During the day, the offices had clear views of the Thames and Parliament. On clear nights, lighting along the buildings reflected from the river, providing the semblance of double lighting. This night, Mrs. Pemberton ignored it. She sat behind the desk, panic on her face, perhaps a little more aged than she was a few minutes ago. She lifted the phone and punched in a number with a pencil.

*

Edgar Boone was Toll's 30-something tall and lanky chauffeur. A former rally driver in a car sponsored by BNC, Edgar retired from the sport when a crash in the Belgium Ypres Rally nearly took his life. Loyal to employees who gave all to BNC, Toll had offered Edgar a less strenuous profession in some regards, driving him with an occasional need to act as bodyguard. Edgar appreciated the opportunity and performed both duties to his utmost ability.

Behind the wheel of Toll's vintage Rolls Royce Phantom VI, Edgar was now more reserved in his approach to driving. He slowed in front of the "British News Corporation" building, a stone edifice that matched its surroundings. In the rear seat, Toll's inquisitive eyes watched pedestrians on the dark street.

For some reason, he thought of the work it took to transform the family tattler in Kent nearly forty years ago. He was fought every step of the way by his weak, lazy, and loathsome older brother. While the younger was willing and eager to fight for what he wanted, the elder wasn't up to the task. Pushing the incompetent nincompoop aside … as he so often liked to relate in his later years … Clifton orchestrated major acquisitions that defied logic.

Clifton took advantage of certain situations for rapid expansion. Many within the investment and banking communities questioned how a little-known man and under-financed company could compound so much wealth so rapidly. Aggressive transactions, most secretive, had increased the holding company's net worth a hundred-thousand-fold since the day he cast his brother into a life of drunken uselessness … where Clifton was positive his sibling was happiest.

The means by which this was made possible was, to this

day, a matter for a few eyes only, mainly those occupying Number 10. It had all begun with the Falklands War and the secrets he discovered while in Argentina. Information that led to the sinking of the Argentine warship ARA General Belgrano.

He was brought to the present when his cell phone rang. "Mrs. P., I'm coming in now."

Mrs. Pemberton came to the point, as Toll had instructed on her first day, "Kostyantyn Kovalev's been killed, and the Yank, Ms. Hannigan's been injured but not badly."

"Were any of our lads with her?"

"No. She had just finished the interview, which went on-line just before the incident occurred," Mrs. Pemberton said with a bit of sadness.

"Kovalev dead, you say," Toll said in reflection. *This changes the game,* he thought. Of Kenna, he stated, "She's a resilient lass, eh, Mrs. P.?"

"She is at that, sir, just like in Ukraine a couple years back." Uncharacteristic of her, she asked, "Do you feel these things are related, sir?"

"Won't know until we get into it, Mrs. P.," Toll said, though knowing full well they were. "Tell Thurnbull to get on top of the situation immediately and to clear his calendar.

We have work to do, Mrs. P.!"

"Sir!"

Staring out the window with calculated concern, Toll disconnected the call. He thought of the early years when he took control of the family tabloid. He had known what he wanted the business to become and was willing to sacrifice everything to achieve it. That conviction split him from his family and created animosity that was never repaired.

This situation would require the same conviction and the same motivation. Not just from him, but every member of the staff. What he wouldn't give to be a younger man and to tackle this situation head-on. *I envy you, Ms. Hannigan*, he thought. *We will discover if you really are made from your grandmother's mold.*

"It's begun, Edgar. The bastards killed Kovalev."

"Sir."

"Number 10, I'll ring on the way."

Edgar smiled; his rally driver instinct took over, and he accelerated aggressively into traffic.

XVI

Wembley Stadium was brightly lit, from the pitch to the suites. Police were everywhere, it seemed. The room outside the owner's suite was as busy as the London tube at rush hour. Wearing crime scene protective suits, technicians of the Major Investigation Team carried equipment into the suite; others carted evidence out. Two officers stood at the door; one checked the identification of those who entered, then recorded their names, ranks, and the time when they arrived and left.

In the outer room and more than a bit annoyed, Kenna sat on a barstool behind the stadium-style seating that overlooked the pitch. A female medic taped a gauze pad to the rear of her scalp. The medic was a hard woman who had, no doubt, seen worse than Kenna's bump on the head. As Kenna gazed into the suite, the medic forced her to look forward and checked her vision with a penlight.

"Vision's fine," Kenna said while the medic removed a blood pressure cuff.

"Miracle, no signs of concussion," the medic said without fanfare.

"Splitting headache, though," Kenna quipped.

The medic was not amused. "You could'a ended up like the two in there."

Passing them, two paramedics wheeled out the guard on a gurney. Covered in blood, he was connected to an IV and a ventilator. A female paramedic followed with a handheld monitor, speaking into her Bluetooth:

"Thirty-year-old unconscious male, single gunshot wound to the chest appears to have shattered the sternum. Labored breathing, very low BP ..." They hurried from the outer room.

"He gonna make it?" Kenna asked.

"We'll know soon enough," the medic said and finished the head wound dressing. "You appear to be the fortunate one."

"I'd say the killer was," Kenna countered.

"Still, you're blessed he ignored you," the medic said.

"Thought you gave medical, not spiritual assistance," Kenna said. "But yeah, that's the first question I'd ask ... without the gender designation."

Walking from the suite in a crime scene protective suit, Detective Chief Inspector Reginald Attwood was in his 40s but looked young for the job. Unaffected by the rigors of the work, he was tall and fit, with a pleasant demeanor and professionalism that belied any age concerns. Behind dark, inquisitive eyes, underlying it all was a no-bull-shit attitude. His job? Prevent cockups and succinctly get results … quickly.

He received the *okay to interrogate* nod from the medic. Following him was a short, round technician in a protective suit with a sample kit and a large evidence bag. She wore neither a smile nor a frown, a rare breed who had mastered the art of having no expression.

"All right then, Ms. Hannigan, why were you spared?" Attwood asked in a deep voice. "And are you saying the assailant was female?"

"Would like to ask whoever wielded the pistol, or whatever it was," she responded.

Packing her medical bag, the medic handed Kenna some pills. "For the pain. From your wound, I'd agree … the butt of the pistol that killed the Russian."

Kenna thought of correcting her, but the pounding in her head convinced her otherwise. "Then, to your other question, chief inspector, I have no idea why I was spared."

Attwood pointed to Kenna's hands. The technician opened the kit and lifted out nail-scraping tools, cotton swabs, and capped plastic tubes.

"The scraping, the gunshot residue test, and a DNA sample are all voluntary, Ms. Hannigan," the technician said, her monotone voice matching her stone face.

"Kovalev had significant scratches on his face and arms," Attwood said.

"From the fight we heard," Kenna said. "Do what you have to do. I'm familiar with the procedure, as well as its importance."

The technician took the samples from under Kenna's fingernails and continued as if Kenna hadn't spoken. "Whoever did it would have the victim's skin under their nails."

"Might find a little dirt from the pitch, but that'll be it," she offered.

"Ruling you out as a suspect, Ms. Hannigan," the technician said, handing her a protective suit. "We'll need your clothes and shoes, mum. Also, at this point, voluntary."

The technician accompanied Kenna into the toilet room, where she changed. Returning to the outer room in the protective suit, she tried to recall what had happened, but it had been so fast, it was …

"Mostly a blur, DCI Attwood. I don't recall much of anything."

"With that knock on the head, it might take time to start remembering," Attwood offered. "You had your phone in your hand when you were found."

"I was calling for help … I think."

"Our switchboard received no emergency calls from your phone," he said. With Kenna's blank expression, Attwood moved on. "Unfortunate that you had to witness this. Are you sure you're alright?"

"Yes, I've been around this sort of thing before."

"I recall your reports from Ukraine." He motioned to the suite. "With our victim, Kovalev, being Ukrainian, a coincidence or?"

"No such thing, DCI," she offered.

"Just let me see the lass!" Wiggy's voice boomed outside the room.

"And if I find what links everything, you'll be the second to know."

"Second?"

Wiggy entered the outer suite with two policemen attempting to hold him back. Attwood waved the policemen away. Wiggy made his way to Kenna and examined her injury. Kenna eased his hand away. *I'm alright.*

"The first, I take it," Attwood said more than asked.

"Yes, and who I was calling," Kenna said.

"Any idea who would want Kovalev dead?" Attwood asked them both.

"You mean anyone jealous of his wealth or hated the idea of an Eastern European owning an NFL franchise and playing in Wembley, or the Russian and Ukrainian politicians he snubbed to achieve what he did?" Wiggy rattled off.

"I see ... a daunting task ahead for all involved," Attwood concluded.

Kenna added, "I knew him, but not well. Our paths crossed in Ukraine, but that was about it."

"I understand you do a little sleuthing on the side, Ms. Hannigan," Attwood said. "I ask that you leave it to us from here on out."

"Mr. Heffernan and I have enough on our plate, DCI Attwood," Kenna offered. "We are searching for the man who killed my grandmother."

"Could he be involved in this?"

"The lads at MI5 think there's a possibility," Wiggy said. Attwood turned a *don't get them involved* look and a silent question. "Supervising Agent Barnaby Scriven and I are mates."

"Don't know him, but if he's a supervising agent, you're in good hands." He handed both a card. "If you remember anything, please ring me." Then to Wiggy, "Even if it's for the Security Service."

"Would it be possible to take a look at the scene?" Kenna asked, motioning to the owner's suite.

"Allow us to do our job, Ms. Hannigan," Attwood insisted in a polite way. "You need to get some rest."

"Wasn't trying to do your job, just thought it might spark a memory of what happened."

"The lass has a keen eye, sir," Wiggy said.

"You could be right," Attwood agreed, then to Wiggy, "Suit up, and let's take a look."

In crime scene suits, Kenna and Wiggy followed Attwood into the owner's suite. The forensic team had the entire room identified with Crime Scene tape, plastic numbered evidence "tents", chalk outlines, and projectile trajectory string. Cameras flashed every few seconds, digitally recording every square inch of the space. Shell casings, drops of blood, blotches of mud and water, broken Horilka bottles and glasses, chalk dust from the pitch, and anything else material to the murder were bagged or bottled, labelled, and recorded. Two evidence technicians with trollies organized everything and recorded it on tablets.

Two uniformed Coroner Service officers lifted the body bag that held Kostyantyn Kovalev and placed him on a gurney.

Wiggy motioned to a camera at the ceiling. "Should have the entire thing on CCTV."

"Unfortunately, shut off at that time," Attwood said.

"The guard escorted me to the door," Kenna said and indicated. "While outside, we heard a fight, and the guard called it in."

"That's confirmed by his supervisor," Attwood said. "What I don't understand, Ms. Hannigan, is why the assailant didn't shoot you, as well."

"I can't speak for what was in the killer's mind, inspector." She took in the room and recalled looking up at the window from the pitch. "Where's his bodyguard? Illya was Kovalev's constant shadow. Yet, when we entered, I don't recall seeing him…"

"Unless…" the three of them said at the same time.

XVII

Edgar dimmed the Rolls Royce's headlights, turned towards a security gate on Downing Street, and stopped before a line of armed guards wearing flak vests. Toll rubbed a sagging chin with an age-spotted hand. An improper, though necessary, grunt cleared his wrinkled, loose-skinned throat. The guards checked the car, recognized Toll, and waved them through. As the gates opened, Toll's weathered lips puckered as if swallowing lime.

Toll hated getting old but believed his mental state remained as sharp as it was in his thirties. With a hint of satisfaction, he recalled what it had taken to get to this point … driving with impunity into the Prime Minister's sanctuary.

He set those thoughts aside as Edgar stopped the Rolls Royce in front of the most famous door in the world. Toll stepped out and passed an armed British Guard that opened the door. Neither acknowledged the other. There was no need; they saw each other frequently.

Escorted by a middle-aged secretary, Toll walked into the posh conference room. At the head of the long conference table sat Sir Keegan Benton-Smythe, the Chief of SIS, more commonly known as MI6. The same age as Toll, he was not known to waste time on trivial matters such as greetings. These two titans had been friends since Cambridge, had the same value system, and forged a working relationship that hummed like a Woodford watch.

Benton-Smythe initiated the conversation. "The Russian woman?"

"My source verified she's in the city," Toll said. Noticing Benton-Smythe's raised eyebrow, he continued, "I have a close ally in her camp, Keegan."

"Did she orchestrate this Kovalev hit?"

"Orchestrate it? Possibly, but the messy work would be the FSB agent, Alexi Medved if the bugger's in the city. They're thick as thieves."

"Sickens me how these people enter London with impunity," Benton-Smythe objected.

"Members of the diplomatic corps, the buggers," Toll said, as disgusted as his colleague. "Not all that different from what we do in Moscow, though."

"Doesn't mean I have to accept it," Benton-Smythe said. "Should we bring 'em in?"

Toll was direct. "Let's learn their end game before revealing ours."

Benton-Smythe went to a sideboard and poured two whiskeys. He stared at a painting of Winston Churchill, then handed the drink to Toll; they toasted.

"What's she looking for … to risk coming to London, that is?"

"At the moment, I could only speculate, which I don't do." Toll took a long sip, thinking. "It has to do with this."

Toll lifted a folder from his satchel and handed it to Benton-Smythe. Printed on the cover: "LUHANSK, UKRAINE". Benton-Smythe skimmed the documents, not liking the contents.

"Rensenhaus was one our best men, Clifton, very thorough," Benton-Smythe said.

"If he says she was involved in what he reports, we can bank on it," Toll agreed.

"Sponsored by Moscow?"

"She doesn't have it in her to go rogue," Toll said, then continued, "There is another folder that details everything. Rensenhaus was in possession of it a couple years ago, then it disappeared … until Kovalev made contact that he possessed it."

"I gather there was a quid pro quo on the table?"

"From us, to expedite the Wembley deal, which was

easily enough done," Toll said and paused. "The second part was something from the Americans."

"Then, I suggest we have a chat with them."

"I've reached out to David Camden, CIA Section Chief. Waiting for a confirmation," Toll said. "Right now, we need to find that folder. I have two people with first-hand knowledge of what happened in Luhansk, possibly with Kovalev."

"If one was Yuri Zelenko, you'll need a replacement," Benton-Smythe said. "Received a secure message today that he was found murdered outside Victoria Station."

"What a tangled web they weave," Toll said and swallowed a hearty amount of whiskey. *Welcome to the game, Ms. Hannigan,* he thought. "I'm grooming someone on my staff to take over for Rensenhaus, but he's not ready. Which means we have no senior people in Ukraine."

"Exactly what the Russians want," Benton-Smythe said, then thought aloud, "And leaves us totally in the dark."

"Not totally, but presents us with a more challenging scenario. Not impossible, just more challenging."

"This video Rensenhaus references, any word on it?" Benton-Smythe asked.

"Ms. Hannigan's work," Toll said. "Zelenko cabled two

days ago that he was sending a pouch through but didn't mention what was in it."

Benton-Smythe shoved the report to Toll. "The officer at the scene reported he had no possessions, not even a travel bag."

"Multiple gunshots, nine-millimeter, foreign, and strangled, rather messy," Toll pondered. "Zelenko must have decided the evidence was important enough to personally deliver. And whatever it was got him killed."

"Are you speculating, Clifton?" Benton-Smythe asked.

"The man is dead, Keegan," Toll said flatly. "An educated conclusion."

"This could indicate that things are about to get messy."

"Rensenhaus, Zelenko, and now Kovalev," Toll said and paused. "Appears things already have, Keegan."

"Does at that," the government man agreed. "And if it escalates?"

"We do what must be done, as always," the civilian said with finality.

"Very well, I'll see to it and brief the PM," Benton-Smythe said. Toll stood. "One final thing, Clifton. We don't want any headlines about this affair."

"Not possible, ole boy, that cat's already out of the bag,"

Toll said as a reality check. "The Russians started this game, not us. If we handle it right, though, they'll end it themselves."

"Yes … their specialty … roulette."

Without acknowledging his colleague, Toll walked out.

XVIII

Kenna leaned on Wiggy for balance as they walked from the owner's suite onto the concrete outer walkway around the stadium. She was unsteady as if she had entered a surreal vortex without normal shapes, no connecting images, or lines. A bizarre shadow continuum where everything floated in space randomly, without logic or reason.

Is this what it's like to take LSD? She wondered.

They paused at the temporary lighting that illuminated where she had been knocked unconscious. She blinked hard against the bright lights. When she opened her eyes, the moment flashed across her memory; she steadied against Wiggy. She felt the impact against her skull again but not the impact with the concrete. Where she had fallen, two forensic technicians in crime scene protective suits swabbed blood that stained the concrete. Another technician to the side photographed a partial footprint in blood.

"Who found you?" Wiggy asked.

"Are you alright, mum?" the lead forensic analyst interrupted.

"One of the guards," she said to Wiggy, then to the lead analyst, "Yes, on the mend, thank you. I believe you'll find that was mine."

The lead analyst swabbed blood and used a Blood Type Testing kit to analyze the sample. He believed her but had a job to do. *No detail left unturned* was his motto.

"So far, we have three blood types out here," he said and raised the sample.

"Three?" Kenna asked. "I'm O-negative."

"Now, we just have to discover who owns the other two," the lead analyst said.

"Sir," a younger female technician said, "shell casing, nine-millimeter."

"That makes two shooters," the lead analyst said. "The gun inside was a forty caliber, probably a Glock."

"This one looks foreign," the female technician added.

Kenna's memory flashed to when she ran for the exit door: *a gunshot outside, this one not suppressed.* Her head spun thinking of it and leaned on Wiggy for support.

The lead analyst pointed to blood drops leading away. "If you're walking out, mind 'em. I've yet to get to 'em."

Kenna paused, thoughts battling in her brain, eating at her. *Give it time; it will come,* she told herself.

"We'd be happy to place evidence tents as we leave," she offered.

"No bother, we'll get to it. Looks like you could use some rest."

Kenna took Wiggy's arm and walked towards the exit. "Why is everyone trying to get me into bed?"

"Perhaps because ya can't stand of your own accord, kid," Wiggy responded.

Her memory flashed again: the *fuzzy image of a man was doubled over and hurried for this exit, limping, holding ribs.* She quickened her pace, following the drops of blood.

"What is it, lass?" Wiggy insisted, keeping hold on her arm.

"He was hurt," she said, doubling over as had the killer. "His ribs and right leg."

"Kovalev must'a landed a few before he was shot," Wiggy said.

"Not so sure, Wiggy," she said, thinking. *Was the injured man the killer?* She wondered. "I remember the shots, just not how many."

"Unusual you bein' uncertain," he said. "We need to get you to the hotel."

A bit unsteady as the corridor spun, she stood upright and gripped Wiggy tight. In the darkness of the down ramp, she lifted out her phone and flipped on the light. Slowly, they followed the blood trail down to the service entrance of the parking garage. Moving towards the Vauxhall van …

"Wasn'a exactly true, you not knowing Kovalev well," Wiggy said.

"DCI Attwood was right about one thing: this is linked to Ukraine." The pain intensified in her head; she ignored it as best she could. "Which means we have suspects—"

"From here to Luhansk."

"Got yourself a job, Wiggy … narrow the list," she said.

"So, I take it we're ignorin' the DCI's instructions?"

"We can't ignore the fact that Beck could be involved," Kenna said. "Even so, it's not just about him, but he's there in the background … like always. Someone helped him, beginning in Warsaw, but it leaves us with the same list."

"The Grand Ole Dame called it *'cuttin' down the trees to see the bloody light 'a day,'* " he recalled.

Kenna took Wiggy's arm to stop him. Using the phone light, she highlighted the garage floor. The blood trail had stopped.

"Must'a been parked here, lass," he offered. "Could be anywhere by now."

She examined the area closely, panning the light in a wide half-circle. A few feet away, blood smeared the pavement in an arch … a struggle. She walked the perimeter. It stopped again, another area with evidence of a struggle … and more blood.

"So, the killer leaves, and whoever helped me followed him. They struggled down here, and the killer left." She searched the area with the light. "So, where's the body?"

"Not enough blood for a killin' … but here," he said, pointing.

From that point, marks indicated a body dragged to the garage door. Outside the door, an overhead light illuminated the area. The drag marks ended with more blood. Kenna squatted and panned the light; something sparkled. She moved for it.

"Your pocketknife," she said with an extended hand.

Wiggy snapped open a switchblade and handed it to her. She dug into a seam in the pavement and popped out a brilliant charm bracelet that had been run over by a tire. She lifted it into the light. Her heart sank. With sad eyes, she looked at Wiggy.

"This could explain why the killer spared me," she said.

*

As they drove from the stadium, Wiggy blended the van with heavy night traffic. From light rain, the streets were bright and glistened like the bracelet. Kenna lifted her phone and punched in a number. The phone rang and went to voicemail.

"Addie, call me when you get this. I found something of yours," she insisted, then disconnected.

"Yer supposed ta be restin'," Wiggy insisted.

"The Honda's in the back, isn't it," she said. "A nice warm bath is what Dr Kenna ordered … but first."

"You really think that's Adelaide's?" Wiggy asked.

"She was wearing it at brunch," Kenna said, thinking. She dialed again, but it went straight to voicemail. "Dammit, pick up the phone, Addie!"

She slammed her finger on the phone to disconnect the call. With deep emotion, she said, "This morning, she told me she'd like to stick a shiv into Kovalev's heart."

"Ye don't think it could'a been her, do ya?" he asked, not believing it.

Kenna drifted into thought and stared at the phone for a long moment. Lorry headlights flashed into her eyes at a roundabout. *The suppressed gunshot filled her mind; Kovalev fell.* In fear, she looked up at the headlights. *The second suppressed gunshot; the guard fell.* The lorry's horn filled her ears. *The assailant in an all-black hoody ran from the suite.* Wiggy steered out of the roundabout. In the rearview mirror, a car hit the lorry; Kenna turned to look.

Kenna snapped around and stared at the phone. A memory flash: *an unsuppressed gunshot outside the suite. She moved away from Kovalev and flipped on the phone video.* She swiped a finger across the main screen and opened the "Camera" icon, then "VIDEO".

"What is it, lass?" Wiggy asked with concern. "You okay, Fiery?"

"I forgot … I …"

At the bottom of the screen, she punched the video. *The interior of the owner's suite bounced on-screen as she ran for the service door. Just outside, a suppressed gunshot* at the same instant she said, *'Wiggy, Kovalev's been—'*

The impact with her head. She collapsed, the phone still in her hand and recording. The assailant knelt over her. Silhouetted by a ceiling light behind the hooded image, an indiscernible face in shadow came faintly into view …

"Illya?" Kenna wondered aloud.

"So, it was Illya that did that to ya?"

"It's not a good image … I don't know," she said

honestly.

On the screen, *the hooded man turned, then ducked away off-screen. The sound of impact, a deep grunt, a heavy metal object dropped.* Kenna punched speed dial and waited for an answer.

*

The Metro bus roared along the street, its windows dark and streaked with rain. Nervously watching the Kovalev interview, Tommy sat alone at the rear, away from three other passengers at the front. He was pleased with the effort but always looked for ways to improve their work. This time, though, his eyes concentrated on the background, watching the shadows.

The follow-up piece will be a career-maker ... or breaker, he thought.

His phone vibrated; he wiped sweat from his brow and answered, "It's late. What's up, killer? If you're lookin' for a drinking companion, you're too late."

Kenna ignored the question. "Where are you?"

"On the way home, left as soon as the interview aired."

"Have you heard the news?" Kenna asked; Tommy was silent. "Kovalev was killed."

"Killed?" Tommy said. "Who ... why?"

"That's what we're going to find out," Kenna said. "Where's Addie? I've been trying to reach her, but she's not answering."

"Haven't heard from her," he said. "That's why I went to the Boar, hoping she couldn't resist a glass of vino. But I'd meet again if ya want."

"Can't. Got a bump on my head and need to rest tonight."

"Bump? What happened?" Tommy shouted. "Not like you to refuse a drink."

"We'll discuss it later," she insisted. "I need to talk to Thurnbull about a follow-up piece. It's obviously taken on new meaning."

"When I left the stadium, he said he was going to meet with Sir Clifton …" Tommy thought for a moment. "I'll work on some ideas for the follow-up, as well. Look, rest tonight and come in tomorrow. It'll give us time to think on it."

"My pounding head says that's the good play," she said. "I have a video of the man that attacked me. Do you have facial recognition capabilities?"

"Antiquated version," Tommy said, stiffening, closing his laptop. "But send it along, I'll take a look. Was it the killer?"

"Don't know. We'll take a stab at it first," she said. "And don't tell Thurnbull, please."

"He'll cut off me bollocks if he learns I withheld something from him."

"Damn, Tommy, you gotta grow a pair before he could cut 'em off," Kenna said and disconnected the call.

Tommy pulled the "next stop" cord and stood. The bus slowed and pulled to the side of the street.

XIX

Sir Clifton sipped a whiskey neat, then eased back in the posh yet firmly cushioned red velvet parlor chair of his private study. He preferred the stiff, straight back to a sofa and had never understood the infatuation with recliners. A large fire warmed him; the whiskey soothed him. This was the aged master's inner sanctum, where confusion met logic, where impossibility met probability.

The three-story residence that housed the eccentric billionaire was centered within "The City", a convenient post to conduct business and be attuned to the heartbeat of London's legal, financial, and business communities. Few people possessed the wealth necessary to own such an exclusive address: One had to be not only of means but also of influence.

Long days that often stretched into nights found the "old man" toiling at the simple, neatly organized, highly polished slab of granite … the desk. A mind of impeccable recall and an infinite grasp of detail constantly worked to yield the greatest result, be it in business or intelligence.

Sir Clifton was not, however, a man entirely devoted to the collection of capitalistic victories and the almighty pound sterling. After the Falklands, he proposed an integrated approach to intelligence gathering between his news agency and MI6. Keegan Benton-Smyth had been his biggest supporter. Indeed, they had created the plan together.

They sold the concept that the intelligence gathered by BNC for the Crown would be provided directly to the Prime Minister without the bureaucratic meddling of Whitehall, Parliament, or the Five Wise Men (The permanent undersecretaries of the Cabinet Office, the Foreign Office, the Home Office, the Ministry of Defense, and the Treasury).

For nearly forty years, Toll had supplied this information, clandestine and otherwise, to the Prime Minister. Yet, the time to turn over the reins was rapidly approaching. With this Ukraine business behind him, his plan was to do just that.

His aged, deliberate hands unfolded and pressed a single sheet of paper across a writing board on his lap. He cleared his throat and took a drink. Pensive eyes studied the maze-like pencil outline of narrow rectangles, three at the top. Two straight lines from each led down to a row of six blocks, one-third down the page. From that row, two more lines fell from each box above to a row of twelve directly below. From that series, lines angled down and met at a final single box. Each was designated by number.

So, she's entered the game, he thought. *Seems Rensenhaus wasn't such a fool after all.* He marked an "X" through the fourth block from the left in the row of twelve. Above this line, all boxes were "X"d, representing events that had taken place … absolutes.

The fortunes of war, his kind of war, he chuckled at the thought … *a war of intellect.*

He looked up at three brisk knocks at the study door. He folded the paper and stuffed it into the pocket of an aged heavy wool sweater that had warmed him for forty winters. It was the only surviving memento from his mother … *bless her departed bitching soul.*

"Yes, Graves?"

The surly, dependable butler entered. *A perfect match for Mrs. P.,* Toll thought once again as the round-faced, tall man stepped effortlessly into the room.

"The American and Sir Keegan, Sir Clifton," Graves said.

Benton-Smythe led Camden into the holy shrine of Britain's leading newsman. They had met here several times, always over business, always over matters of national security for both their countries. This night would prove to be no different.

Overall, Camden didn't like working with the British. However, he could never question their abilities as spies. He admired them most for how they intertwined the private sector into intelligence gathering. The CIA had failed miserably in an attempt to copy their approach, with the exception of Halibeck International.

It was here, in the master's chambers … so Toll thought of it … that Camden wondered how much the "old man" knew of the events leading up to the Russian invasion of Ukraine in 2014. How much did Toll know about his involvement? Of the company's involvement?

Camden smiled to himself, knowing it really didn't matter what Toll knew or how he reacted. He wore the protective cloak of the CIA; there was nothing more powerful. A sharp glance revealed Toll's distrust; Camden enjoyed it.

"David," Toll began, standing but not offering a hand or a drink. "Thank you for coming."

"Would you care for a drink, sir?" Graves asked on cue.

"Whatever Toll's having."

Graves bruised the whiskey, contrary to the preparation of a drink for Sir Clifton, handed it to the American, then backed away without emotion. He raised the corner of his lips for only his master to see, then closed the door.

Benton-Smythe took a chair across from Toll. The "old man" looked across to the American with a wrinkled grimace. His ears warmed; his battle lines deepened.

"I was under the impression this was to be an informal meeting, Toll…" Camden began, refusing to acknowledge the formal British title, "… not one that involved the Secret Intelligence Service."

"We both report directly to the P.M., David," Toll said.

Camden replied dubiously, "But that's not why you asked me here."

"Our man Zelenko was found dead outside Victoria," Benton-Smythe said.

That took Camden by surprise. "I hadn't heard. But that means—"

"We have no senior people in Ukraine," Toll interrupted.

"Any idea who's responsible?" Camden asked.

"Several," Toll countered. "But let's not get ahead of ourselves. First, we want to know if this is part of your game?"

"My game? You think I—"

From his desk, Toll lifted Rensenhaus's folder titled "LUHANSK, UKRAINE" and slid it across the desk.

Camden's facial expression did not change, though his mind raced with curiosity. He ignored the file; he knew what was inside.

"I want to discuss Halibeck's operations in Ukraine," Toll said succinctly. Camden sipped whiskey without responding. "Specifically, I want the entire file for your plan coming out of Yale. The one Rensenhaus references in his report."

"Afraid that's not possible," Camden said, then hesitated, stomach tightening. "Classified."

"Ballocks," Benton-Smythe clamored. "You stand on the precipice of the cliff where we British have already stood. But you Americans, within your finite capacity to think, never comprehended joining us there."

"Flowery prose as always, Keegan," Camden said and tried to ignore the burning in his stomach. "But what the hell does that mean?"

"As the Romans also discovered ... empires don't last forever." Benton-Smythe took a drink of whiskey. "I suggest we, as you Yanks say, cut to the chase ... Chernobyl."

"In due time, Keegan," Toll interjected to Benton-Smythe's surprise. He turned to Camden. "These murders tell me that your plan isn't classified. It's not even in your possession. We need to know how this information fell into Russian hands …” Toll cut Camden off before he could object. “We know they have it. But more importantly, we want to know what they intend to do with it.”

Camden stood and walked to the sideboard to refresh his drink. The room suddenly became very confining. The last hurrah seemed on the verge of becoming a crash landing. *Never,* he thought.

“At this point, I agree and think it’s about time we both laid our cards on the table,” he said and sat with the drink. “Where do you want to start, gentlemen?”

*

The door closed behind the American. Benton-Smythe sipped whiskey and stared at Toll. His eyes circled the study, and he wondered who would fill Toll’s position after he stepped aside.

“Opinion?” Benton-Smythe asked.

“Frightened children,” the old master said. “As they say, they shit in their mess kit.”

“Then, you believe they actually implemented the plan?”

“No doubt,” Toll said, gathering his thoughts.

“It’s been thirty years,” Benton-Smythe reflected. “Our next move?”

"You're at the right hand of the P.M., Keegan. You tell me."

Benton-Smythe dabbed at his chin with a linen napkin. He enjoyed working with Toll, a man who came to the point. All their adult lives, they had enjoyed a working relationship few others could duplicate. He would miss their exchanges when they decided to call it a day.

"Brief the P.M., of course."

"To tell him what, exactly? He will want to arrest and deport them all."

"Which is what should be done," Benton-Smythe said.

"Not before we know their intentions, Keegan," Toll demanded. "We must discover their intentions before we take suitable action."

Benton-Smythe wrinkled his brow for a moment. "I see your point. We have nothing of substance to report."

"Precisely. But there is someone who may be able to provide us useful information." *Ms. Hannigan,* he did not say.

Toll looked out the window that overlooked the courtyard between wings. Graves escorted Camden to the side door out. Camden looked up at him. Caesar smiled from the window as the American lifted his umbrella in a perfunctory salute. Toll lifted his glass in return and believed he heard the gladiator's valediction:

'Ave Imperãtor, Morituri Te Saluttant.'

XX

Kenna didn't bother to look at the time; her body said it was late. She sat on a lounge chair, beer in-hand, staring out at the city lights. She finished her sketch of the crime scene and slid it onto the coffee table. Wiggy sat on a barstool doing the same.

"I'm so tired, I can't think straight," she said.

"That knock on the head might have somethin' to do with it."

He finished the sketch, walked to the chair next to her, and dropped it on the table. Given all the fancy technology utilized by MIT investigators, Kenna and Wiggy used their intellect and experience. But they weren't entirely old school … technology was a great tool. They didn't use it for anything other than that … a tool.

Though appearing like a simple execution, Kovalev's killing was more complex, much more. On that, they both agreed. Their notes were similar, confirming what both saw and felt. No forced entry, so the killer either had access or was allowed to enter. Kenna included, *'Perhaps a member of the stadium security?'*, then had lined through it. Both noted the precise location of the bullet's impact in Kovalev's chest, with a note that the guard had been wounded in nearly the exact spot. That shot during a struggle would either be pure luck or be made by an expert. But when it came to two shots, neither believed in luck. *Firearms Expert!* Both had noted.

"Kovalev knew the killer," Kenna said, followed by a drink of beer.

"Curious, though, why the bodyguard wasn't in the room," Wiggy said. "Perhaps a private conversation that turned bad."

She handed Wiggy her phone. He downloaded the short video into his laptop and watched it play through.

"Barnaby will have access to equipment that can pull this image up better than anything we have," Wiggy said.

"Put your Boston charm on him and convince him it's for Gran," she said. "They were very much in love at one time."

"Aye, saw it in his eyes when ya walked in," he said.

"Look into Kovalev's movements, phone calls, all that good stuff since he arrived."

Kenna finished the beer and walked for the bedroom. Wiggy opened his laptop and began his background work. A light knock at the door; he opened it. A bellboy extended an envelope addressed to "Ms. Kenna Hannigan".

*

20 FEBRUARY 2022

New wound patch on her head, Kenna walked from the bedroom to welcome the morning sun. Pleased her senses had cleared, she joined Wiggy at the table where he sat in front of the laptop. Wiggy slid a cup of coffee her direction.

"You get any sleep?" she asked.

"That's my question," he countered. "I'm not the one got knocked on the head."

"Actually, I feel good."

"Don't lie to me, lass," he said deviously.

"Can't ignore it, but can't dwell on it either," she said.

The dull pain remained, but it hurt for a completely different reason now. In a way, it was a feel-good pain. It meant she was alive, regardless how close she had come to joining Kovalev and Alistair Rensenhaus.

She moved to the wall of windows that overlooked the city street, her mind whirling with what happened the day before. It was meant to be simple: Go to the stadium, do the interview, set aside the differences with Kovalev, then continue the hunt for Anson Beck.

"Wiggy, would you check on the guard this morning?"

she asked. "He saved my life, and I need to thank him."

"Sorry, lass, after you went to bed, I saw on the news he hadn't made it," Wiggy said.

"We need to get word to his family."

"I'll take care of it." He motioned to the unopened envelope on the table. "And that came for ya."

Kenna sliced open the envelope with Wiggy's knife. She pulled out the police report and read. Her eyes brightened, then narrowed in anger. She fought off emotion, refusing it. The video … *how was she going to find the video now?*

"Yuri Zelenko was killed entering the U.K.," she said sadly, handing Wiggy the report.

"The one worked with Rensenhaus in Ukraine, right? What's he to you?" Wiggy wondered aloud.

She sat heavily. "With Kovalev dead, he was the last hope for finding my video."

"There's no such thing as last hope unless you've seen it destroyed," Wiggy said firmly. "We still have this case, lass, and it could lead us to it."

"A thousand miles away," she said, then asked herself aloud, "Why did he come to London?"

"The answer might solve the puzzle," Wiggy said.

She sipped the coffee and heard Gran Lockwood

admonishing her for lazin' around and feeling sorry for herself. *'Now,'* she would have said, *'get off yer arse and get to work!'*

"It might at that, Wiggy," she said, standing. "I'll add it to my list."

"When you get back, we can review the suspects from Ukraine," he said without looking up. "And I'm lookin' into Wembley's CCTV."

"DCI Attwood said it was turned off."

"Coppers don't always look beyond what's in front of 'em, kid. This side of the pond or ours," he said. "Now, we begin fillin' the Grand Ole Dame's blank spaces."

"I'm going to the Russian Embassy for a comment on the killing," she said, pulling on the riding leathers.

"You sure you're up to it, lass?"

"That's why God gave us aspirin, Wiggy," she said. "I'm just going to talk, not invade the place. After that, I'll nose around where they found Yuri."

"Take it easy, and don't do anythin' crazy on that contraption," he insisted.

"This started in Luhansk, Wiggy; we'll end it here." She walked to the door and paused. "You gonna help me unload the Honda?"

"Did that while ye were sleepin'," he responded. "Somethin' tells me what we're facin' has been in play long before yer time in Luhansk, lass. Watch yer backside."

*

At the rear of the hotel, Kenna sat on the Honda while it idled. She fastened the backpack, looked up at the overcast sky, and lowered the helmet visor. *'Starving animals eat their own,'* she heard Gran Lockwood say from years past, believing she finally understood the meaning. She accelerated the Honda onto the busy street, weaving through traffic. Her phone rang; she tapped Bluetooth.

"This is Kenna," she said, leaning through a roundabout.

With a phone to his ear, Rashon Hill walked along the street across from Wembley Stadium. "Kenna, this is Rashon … Rashon Hill."

A moment to remember … *the smartass* … "Yes, my favorite cornerback. What's up?"

"Look, I know I ain't supposed to be at the stadium, but I saw somethin' last night." He paused, making sure no one was listening. "The owner's bodyguard was chasin' a guy. Took some video on my phone. Anyway, thought we should talk about it."

"Indeed, we should," she agreed. "I can meet you in a

couple hours."

"Good enough. Buzz me, I'll meet you outside the suite," he said. "See ya then."

She disconnected the call and tapped Bluetooth. She slowed with the traffic and maneuvered through a roundabout, avoiding an aggressive Jaguar.

"Call No Bull cell," she said. It rang and went to voicemail:

"Thurnbull, leave a message," the recording said.

Kenna disconnected the call and turned onto the jammed A5 heading for Kensington Gardens. With deep concern, she tapped Bluetooth again.

*

Climbing the steps of the British News Corporation building, Tommy was disheveled. In Alistair Rensenhaus's world, that wouldn't matter. But he was about to enter Douglas … not Doug … Thurnbull's world, where slovenly attire was akin to a mortal sin. His phone rang; he paused at the top step and answered:

"Good morning, Kenna."

Kenna weaved through stopped vehicles. "Does that mean you heard from Addie?"

Tommy's eyes flicked across the busy street and

sidewalks. "Nothing."

"Keep trying, she'll show up," she said. "Let Thurnbull know I'll be in later."

"Everyone raved about the Wembley piece," Tommy changed the subject. "Because of what happened after the interview, Thurnbull wants you to come in first thing to discuss the follow-up."

"Toward that end, I'm on my way to the Russian Embassy to get a statement on Kovalev's death and —"

"Why the Russians?" Tommy interrupted. "He was Ukrainian."

"He mentioned working with them to facilitate the deal."

"The stadium deal?" Tommy asked, surprised.

"One of many questions I have," Kenna said, leaned the Honda through a roundabout, and accelerated ahead of two lorries. "After that, I'm going back out to Wembley."

She needed to see the scene again, this time with a clear head. Something wasn't adding up, and she was determined to get to the bottom of it. Perhaps it was the information that Rashon Hill had … the killer's escape. And then, there was Adelaide … she shut off the thought.

"Thurnbull said you were to come straight in," he suggested. "In his words, he wants to *script how we can parlay your interview into what happened afterward.'*"

'Script how we can parlay' caught Kenna off-guard. It seemed an incredibly cavalier way to talk about a double murder, a triple including …

"Did you hear Yuri Zelenko was killed at Victoria Station?" she asked.

Panic filled Tommy's eyes; he hadn't expected that. "Now I know why I can't reach him."

"I didn't know you were trying," Kenna said.

"On Thurnbull's orders," he said. "I think you should do what Thurnbull said and come straight in. Forget the Russian comments; this is getting crazy."

"Already is, Tommy," she corrected him.

In Luhansk, Rensenhaus had told her that Thurnbull was a hard-nosed newsman but also a man who followed a strict protocol, one developed over Thurnbull's pay grade, Sir Clifton Toll. *Just like Papa,* she thought, *the master of his realm.*

"If the Russians respond the way I think they will, I won't be long. Besides, I'm almost there."

"You mentioned Wembley," Tommy said. "Why you going out there again?"

"One of the American football players called. He

remembered seeing something last night and wants to talk about it."

"Saw something? What?"

"We didn't go into it … I'm here, gotta go." Kenna disconnected the call and accelerated past the planters in the middle of Notting Hill Gate.

"Kenna?" Tommy snapped, cursed, and hurried for the door. "Bloody Yank."

*

'Yuri Zelenko was killed at Victoria Station,' rang through Tommy's mind. He walked across the On-Line Reporters room to Corina's desk. She screwed a cap onto a bottle of nail polish.

"He's not in from the gym yet, Tommy," she said and blew across her nails.

You wouldn't be doing that if he was, Tommy thought. "I'll try his cell. Want to get started on the follow-up story about Kovalev."

"If there's anything I can do, let me know," Corina offered, blowing across her nails.

"No time for a manicure," Tommy said and turned. He paused when Corina took his arm with her unpainted hand.

"Don't give up hope on Adelaide."

"I haven't. One of these days, she'll pop up." He glared at
her hand until she released him and walked away.

"Wanker," Corina said to herself.

XXI

Where Notting Hill Gate transitioned into Bayswater Road, the street was clogged with stopped traffic. Horns filled the air, a scene from the third world as if noise would move the masses of metal occupying the pavement. Surprise filled Kenna as she eased the Honda between and around vehicles.

Surrounded by a three-meter-high stone wall, the Embassy of the Russian Federation sat across from Kensington Gardens in the heart of London. A crowd of several hundred filled the front street. Kenna maneuvered around a pack of demonstrators that held placards covered with crude writing and chanted the slogans:

"Kovalev murderers!", "Death to Imperialist Russia!", "Return the Crimea!", "Free Donbas forever!", and "Get out of Ukraine!"

She had not anticipated such a response to Kovalev's killing. His murder, though, was the obvious catalyst fueling the outpouring of anti-Russian sentiment, the proverbial *straw that broke the camel's back*. The protest was a continuum of Ukrainian-Russian relations and the multitude of intricate parts, all telling Kenna where to direct her energies.

'Never allow emotion to run your investigation,' Gran had instructed.

Though she was deeply moved by Kovalev's killing, perhaps mostly because she had seen his last breath, she could not allow those feelings to dictate how she approached the case. Just as she could not allow this gathering of emotionally charged people to influence her thought process, now was the time for conscious, rational thought and concentration on the facts, not emotionally charged rhetoric, however logical or correct.

She chained the Honda to a streetlight and fixed her phone to a selfie stick. Without hesitation, she turned on the video, raised the phone, and spoke loudly over the din of the mob:

"Test, test." Satisfied, she turned for the mob with a huge breath of apprehension.

A foot sergeant took her arm, "Safer ta stay outta that lot, lass."

"Can't play the game from the sidelines, sergeant," she said, revealing her press credentials.

"Yer crazy fer such a wee thing," the sergeant said.

"I'll take that as a compliment," Kenna said with a

hesitant grin.

The sergeant released her. She draped a press credentials lanyard over her head and stepped into the crowd. Thoughts of Ukraine filled her mind: the sights, the sounds, the smells. As she forced her way into the crowd, a realization struck her. The base of Gran's crime pyramid was what happened in Luhansk. Every event that happened since filled it, regardless how trivial.

The pulse of the crowd … *this isn't trivial*, she thought … a wave of humanity dragged her towards the large building where the tri-colored Russian flag waved in the breeze. Russian guards armed with nightsticks stood at equal intervals along the security wall and at the entrance gate. What began as shoving intensified slowly, and then … a Russian guard knocked down a protestor.

Pandemonium broke out and spread like wildfire. Fists flailed, signs became clubs, and bottles crashed against the security fence and wall. Though outnumbered, the Russian guards fought the crowd back. The struggle became out of control rapidly; guards and protestors fell from blows. Trying to break it up, a policeman's horse neighed and reared, throwing him. A mounted policewoman moved her horse through the mob, controlled the other horse, and helped her fellow officer aboard.

Screams of angry men and women dwarfed the sudden shrill of pulsating sirens. The heavy scent of sweat, blood, and fear sickened Kenna as it had in Luhansk. She spun the phone for a selfie of her and the mob.

"This is Kenna Hannigan for BNC at the Russian Embassy," she yelled at the phone. "An angry mob protests the killing of Ukrainian businessman Kostyantyn Kovalev yesterday, which this reporter sadly witnessed."

Ukrainians chanted and screamed. The mob forced Kenna towards the gated entry. Whistles pierced the air over the roar of the mob. Dozens of police with riot shields and nightsticks unloaded from vans down the street. More mounted police arrived with them. All advanced in an organized Roman-like phalanx, shields locked a great human chain.

"Caught in a wave of Ukrainian protestors battling with Russian guards, I can barely move!" Kenna reported. "More police arriving … at the far end of the street … ahhh!"

In the middle of the mob, Kenna spun the camera 360 degrees. She ducked signs swung at the Russian guards. One hit the side of her head; she drew back blood and fought a burst of dizziness. The day before flashed before her eyes, followed in an instant by the street fighting in Luhansk. She fought the images and gathered herself. The riot police phalanx slammed into the far end of the mob.

"What began as a peaceful demonstration turned violent when a Russian guard clubbed a protestor. Signs are no match for Russian nightsticks. Is this a microcosm of Ukraine itself?" she yelled. "The arrival of the police has worsened things for the protestors, now forced to battle in two directions … the police … and the Russians!"

Fighting continued, collapsing quickly into numerous one-on-one brawls. Ukrainian screams intensified; the mob shifted towards the police. More Ukrainian civilians arrived and joined the fray. More sirens as a line of paddy wagons stopped at the outskirts of the melee. Behind the wagons, an armored police vehicle with a water cannon turned onto the street. More sirens converged on what had become a riot.

"Russian Embassy delegates and employees watch at the windows," she yelled, turning the phone to capture them. "Perhaps wondering if the fighting will breach the security perimeter."

She captured armed security guards running across the embassy grounds towards the security fence, "Armed Russian reinforcements are arriving at the fence." *Dear God,* she thought, *a bloodbath in the making.* "They've called in the military!"

The protestors were undeterred. Screams of angry men

and women drowned out the sirens. A car horn and a flash of black through the mob spun Kenna's attention. Continuing to honk, the car eased slowly through the riot. She fought against the mob in that direction, as did the Police.

"The ambassador's arriving," she yelled. "I'll try to get close enough for a comment."

Hit by a great force, Kenna was thrust through the fight. Unable to contain the mob, the riot police phalanx broke. Unorganized and screaming at the passengers, protestors assaulted the black Aurus Senat limousine with clubs, fists, and signs. Bottles broke against the windscreen.

"Protestors are attacking the diplomatic limousine," she said, jostled and hit several times. She yelled at the protestors, "Let me through here!"

Startled, she was thrown through the mob and slammed against the passenger door. For a brief time, she stared directly at Svetlana in the rear. Kenna aimed the phone to video Svetlana just as she lifted a file and covered her face. Without recognition, Kenna yelled:

"Do you have a comment on Kostyantyn Kovalev's killing? Any comment?"

A Russian guard jerked Kenna away and reached for the

phone. She fought against him, screaming. The mob beat the guard and dragged him away. With the video still running, she yelled into the phone:

"It's not the ambassador! And I don't recognize the woman!"

The Aurus Senat inched through the mob towards the gate. Guards pushed the steel barred gate open against the mob. As the limousine drove through, Medved met the car. Another Russian, Pyotr, a scarred and angry-looking young man, joined him and opened the door. Svetlana stepped out, yelled orders at Medved, and pointed directly at Kenna.

The water cannon converged on the mob and blasted the rioters. Kenna spun and screamed to herself, *Get out of here!* But she couldn't. Medved and Pyotr left the compound and fought through the mob directly for her.

"I'm gonna get wet!" she yelled into the phone, not seeing their approach.

Kenna pocketed the cell phone and fought against the spray and the mob. Fighting his way through the mob, Medved slammed a fist against her face. She fell just as the water cannon blasted Medved, forcing him back. Kenna covered her face as Medved leaned over her.

"Who are—" she demanded.

His fist silenced her, and he demanded, "Give me your phone!"

Medved backhanded her, knocking her to the street. Blood ran from her mouth, dizzy; she kicked him to no avail. He kicked her side and jerked her up by the blouse, ripping it. She slammed the selfie stick against his face; he knocked it away and drew back a fist. Several large Ukrainian men jerked him back.

"Police!" Pyotr yelled and pulled Medved away just as the water cannon blasted them again. "Deal with her later!"

Pyotr and Medved blended into the mob and fought for the entrance gate. As if propelled by some explosive, Kenna was thrown back five layers of protestors. Several bodies fell beside her and forced her down, grinding her face against the pavement. Her vision fogged; she forced herself up to an elbow and swiped bloody water from her face.

Rioters blasted by the water cannon stepped across, over, and atop her. Many fell beside and over her. Screams of anger, hers and others, became cries of pain. She beat away two men atop her and forced herself up. Jerked back by a large hand, she was turned to the sergeant. Protectively, he pulled her away from the center of mass hysteria. Outside the police line …

"Think we'll call this full-time for you, lass," he said,

motioning to the blood. "EMS vans will be arriving."

Acrylic baton at the ready, the sergeant turned back into the melee. Kenna reconnected the phone to the selfie stick and flipped on the video. She extended it to where she was in the foreground with the riot as background.

"As you can see, a little bloodied but not broken. Reporting the facts for BNC, this is Kenna Hannigan signing out … for now."

She removed the phone from the stick and climbed onto the Honda's seat. Television Vans arrived down the street. With a smug expression that she beat them to the punch, she videoed the on-going riot and the embassy grounds inside the security walls. Through the mist of the water cannon past the police line and security fence, she zoomed on Medved. He glared directly at her.

"Who are you, my violent Russian friend?" she wondered aloud. "A good job for Wiggy."

She shoved everything into her backpack, started the Honda, and winced while pulling on the helmet. She focused on the street, unsure of her balance. With hesitance, she accelerated slowly and cautiously away from the mob.

Out of earshot of the riot, she pulled to the side of the street. She lifted a bottle of water from her backpack and took a drink. Gathering her thoughts and breath, she looked at her shaking hands, then tapped Bluetooth.

"DCI Attwood," he answered.

"This is Kenna Hannigan," she said. "Are you at Wembley?"

"Still in the office," he said.

"Meet me at the owner's suite," she suggested. "One of the American football players saw something yesterday and wants to discuss it."

Kenna disconnected the call, gathered herself, and put on her game face. She accelerated into traffic, singing along with the Led Zeppelin song, 'The Battle of Evermore':

"The pain of war cannot exceed the woe of aftermath. The drums will shake the castle wall; the ring wraiths ride in black ..."

XXII

Determination and urgency filled Svetlana as she marched along the hallway. Still wet from the riot, Medved and Pyotr followed, rubber sole shoes squeaking on the floor. In keeping with the grand exterior of the Russian Embassy, the interior was polished and bright. Tapestries and paintings by Russian masters, from Aivazovsky's sweeping seascapes to Levitan's landscapes, lined the walls. Basic furniture sat in strategic locations in the long hallway where tables held classic Russian art objects of many eras. On a table outside the conference room, a dichotomy in a locked glass display case … a glistening Fabergé egg.

They paused at a door: "Безопасность посольства" (Embassy Security). She swiped a security badge against a lock; it clicked, and they entered.

A single room was the heartbeat of security for the embassy, consulate, and ambassador's residence. Twenty large computer screens were fixed to the wall. Sitting in straight-backed chairs at symmetrical lines of tables, five young computer geeks managed specific areas of surveillance. The uniformed manager sat on an elevated platform at the rear of the room.

Occupying that chair was the eldest in the room, Feodor. A captain in his mid-30s, thin and short, he jumped to attention. There was no escaping the fact that Feodor seldom saw the sun outside; he was pale, nearly albino. The other computer geeks of similar pallor stood immediately, paying homage to the FSB director.

"Deputy Director, I am prepared," Feodor said, motioning to a chair, though he knew Svetlana would not take it. "Please take a seat."

Svetlana ignored him and looked at the screens. "If you were prepared, the tape of the protest would be on a screen, Feodor."

Immediately uncomfortable, as were the other computer geeks, he sat and flashed his fingers against the keyboard. Four screens before him flashed to life with differing angles of the on-going protest cum riot.

"She doesn't want what's happening now, Feodor," Medved demanded. "Start where the woman comes from the crowd and approaches the director's car."

Medved stepped to the screens; Svetlana joined him. Over the past few years, this was the closest the two had been without anger and screaming. Without sound, the events of the riot unfolded. Approaching from the side, the black Aurus Senat limousine inched through the mob towards the gate. Protestors converged on it, hitting it with signs, clubs, and fists.

"The woman, I recognized her," Svetlana said evenly, concentrating on the screen.

"The question is, did she recognize you?" Medved asked.

"It didn't appear so, but this operation is too important to take the risk." Svetlana pointed to the screen. "There, the woman with the selfie stick. Show me her face, Feodor."

Feodor paused the footage, segregated the area, and moved it frame-by-frame for the best view. He zoomed close to a full-face but fuzzy view of Kenna Hannigan.

"That's the best I can get, Director Pavlovsky," Feodor offered.

"Hold that … Yes, I remember now. Luhansk …" she paused, thinking. "Must be two years ago. She became a minor nuisance."

Medved frowned. "Minor? Enlighten me."

"She worked with a Ukrainian that supported British News Corporation—"

"I don't watch news; I make it," Medved interrupted. "What about him?"

Svetlana touched Medved's arm, surprising him. "Oh, but Alexi, you knew him well." She turned to Feodor. "Bring up the file on Oleksandr Shwetz."

"Shwetz? He was killed in Luhansk," Medved insisted.

With several strokes on the keyboard, a screen flashed facial images and the U.K. passport of "Oleksandr Shwetz". Taken aback, Medved attempted to show no emotion, but his eyes betrayed him. The more he glared at the image, anger, and hatred balled his hands into white-knuckled fists.

"We all thought so, but I learned he is very much alive … here in London," Svetlana confirmed.

"So, he is the real reason you are here," Medved said with a knowing glare.

"No, he's the reason I asked for you. Unfinished business for both of us." She studied Oleksandr's image. "Business that must be completed to avoid complications with my mission."

"He lives under his real name," Medved said with admiration. "He has balls."

"A man that never ran from a fight," she agreed. "Always willing to charge."

"With one exception," Medved corrected her.

She tightened her grip on his arm, *don't go there.* Medved knew why Shwetz was in London, why they were all in London. Yes, the mission, but that required settling old scores. *You won't escape this time, Oleksandr,* Medved thought.

"And now, this Kovalev interview and a journalist sticking her pretty little nose where it shouldn't be," Svetlana said.

Medved turned to Feodor. "Print everything."

"Her presence is troubling. Was she with Kovalev simply for the interview?" Svetlana wondered aloud. "I don't like coincidences, Alexi. Find her. She and I must talk."

"And the others?" Medved asked.

"You know the importance of our mission," Svetlana said. "No loose ends, Alexi."

When Svetlana walked out, Medved stared at the screen. He ignored the image of Oleksandr and glared directly at Kenna.

"Feodor, while we're out, cross-check what we have on Kovalev against ..." he opened a leather flip wallet and looked at Kenna's press credentials. "An American journalist named Kenna Hannigan. Where she lives, known associates, the works."

"I'll put my best man on it," Feodor said.

"Did I say put your best man on it?" Medved snapped.

Feodor's scolded dog look gave Medved the answer he wanted. "After the director arrived inside the compound, a motorcycle rode away. Put it on the screen."

Feodor zoomed on the Honda as Kenna rode away. Medved pulled Pyotr to the screen, and both studied Kenna and the Honda, from the riding leathers and helmet to the make and model and registration number.

"Find that woman and follow her. I'll find Shwetz."

"But the director said to—"

"She has her mission; we have ours," Medved interrupted. "Keep track of the journalist's every move, Pyotr: where she goes, what she's doing, who she meets."

Medved handed Pyotr Kenna's press credentials. Medved turned to Feodor.

"Now, Feodor, that man you mentioned … who's your best," Medved said, "bring him over; let's talk cell phone tracking."

XXIII

Under a bright, infrequent sun, Kenna stopped the Honda at the Statue of Bobby Moore and swung off. She hesitated, stretched a sudden twitch in her hip, and looked up when the stadium entrance opened. With a look of concern at Kenna's injuries, Jameson, the guard, held open the door. Inside, another guard stood to the side.

"You alright, mum?" Jameson asked.

"A question with many answers, I assure you," she said.

"The superintendent's waitin' for ya," he said, motioning her inside.

"He is?" she asked, taken aback. "I received a call from one of the American football players—"

"At the owner's suite, mum," Jameson said. "I'll escort you."

"I know the way."

"Sorry, mum. Orders from the superintendent."

The other guard opened the door, and Jameson followed Kenna inside. From his sad expression, she knew something was off. Her heart sank. The burning in her stomach became an inferno, like the aftermath of eating Maxi's Thai food outside D.C. times ten.

Kenna and Jameson walked along the brightly lit hallway. Security guards stood at regular intervals and increased the closer they came to the owner's suite. They slowed when they entered the double doors of the outer room. As she entered, Jameson remained at the door.

Zachary Carter, superintendent of stadium security, might have been in his 50s, but one would never know by attitude and physique. Stern faced, his muscular body filled the suit with the Wembley emblem on the chest. A retired Royal Marine, though always a Marine, he stood as rigid as the Bobby Moore statue a meter from the dead and bloody body of Rashon Hill.

"Nobody's been near the body, ma'am," Carter interrupted her thoughts.

"With one obvious exception, superintendent," she countered.

"Yes, ma'am," he agreed without emotion. "I meant since, ma'am. I made sure of it."

"Not intended to point out a flaw, Mr. Carter, just me thinking aloud."

"Understood, ma'am. I do much in the same."

Kenna shook his hand. "DCI Attwood is on the way."

Turning to Rashon's body, Kenna's heart sank. Such a young, talented player and person snuffed out … for what? It was becoming a familiar question in this case. Keeping her distance, she squatted close enough to Rashon to smell the death she had not on Senator Harvey William Chamberlain at Congressional. A thousand-dollar track suit, personalized running shoes, diamond studded signature sunglasses on a gold fob, a five-thousand-dollar Rolex. If she found his wallet, it would hold money and every gold, platinum, and black credit card imaginable. This wasn't a robbery; none of them were … then … for what?

"How did you know about this?" Carter asked.

"I didn't," she said. "His name's Rashon Hill. He phoned me earlier to say he'd seen something yesterday. I agreed to meet him with DCI Attwood. Did you see his cell phone?"

"No, ma'am," Carter offered. "But haven't looked either. Thought I'd leave that to the police."

"These guys live on their cells," she said. "If it's not here, the killer has it."

And knows he called me, she thought.

Carter's radio squawked. "Go ahead."

"The police arrived," came the guard's voice over the speaker.

"I'll go down to escort 'em," Carter said to Kenna.

Carter spun from the room. Without getting close, Kenna reviewed the all-to-familiar scene. In a flash of memory, she saw Harvey William Chamberlain dead in the sand trap near the 18th green of Congressional. Just like with that scene, there was also something missing here … Rashon's cell phone.

It didn't escape Kenna that had she come directly to the stadium when Rashon called; this scene might be very different. Perhaps she could have helped prevent this … or, in all likelihood, she would be lying beside him.

Erasing the thought, she lifted her phone and punched his number. A phone buzzed … to the side. She looked under the stadium seating. In a direct line from Rashon's dead outstretched hand was a flashing, buzzing phone. She disconnected the call. With a cloth napkin from a serving tray, she lifted the phone and placed it on the table. The face was smeared with his blood.

'I saw the owner's bodyguard chasin' a guy. Took some video on my phone.'

Kenna pulled up the "CAMERA" icon, then tapped on the most recent video. It began with Rashon doing a selfie while running through Wembley.

"Hey ever-one, wanted to show ya where I'll be playin' next season—"

Loud voices from the hallway. Kenna shut down the video, hit "send as message", entered her number, and sent it. As the phone swooshed, she shut it down and placed it back on the floor.

DCI Attwood and DS Jenkins entered the suite. Jenkins' stern looks and trim, muscular body left little doubt that it was *hands-off* with her. She had only one interest: the job. With a grimace, Kenna greeted them.

"Looks like you've had better days, Ms. Hannigan," Attwood offered with genuine concern.

"Went to the Russian Embassy looking for a comment," Kenna said, "and was greeted by the welcoming committee."

"You certainly don't lead a sheltered life."

"You were there for the riot?" Jenkins asked more than said.

"Ms. Hannigan seems to always be in the wrong place at the right time, DS Jenkins," Attwood said. "Now, about this American footballer?"

"Just what I told you," Kenna began. "He called to say he remembered something."

Carter stood to the side while Attwood and Jenkins

surveyed the scene. "Appreciate you keeping the scene under control until we got here, superintendent. We'll get forensics on the way."

Attwood nodded to Jenkins. She turned away, lifting her phone. Kenna followed Attwood to a discrete distance from the body.

"Looks like the same shooter," Kenna said. "Single shot to the heart."

"Nobody heard a thing, sir," Carter said. "Must'a been suppressed."

"Consistent," Attwood agreed. "We're dealing with a professional."

"Is the CCTV up and running now?" Kenna asked Carter.

Carter silently questioned her; Attwood nodded. "It's on, but I haven't been through it."

"Have 'em wait, and I'll go through it with you," Attwood said.

"Maybe that'll tell us where he'd been while here," Kenna offered. "Any chance I could sit in on the review, DCI Attwood? This assassin did give me the lump on the head."

"The first of many, it appears, Ms. Hannigan," he said without humor.

"There's something you should check. At the time of Kovalev's killing, was the stadium's CCTV on outside?" Kenna asked.

Attwood turned to Carter, who hesitated. "I'll have to check." Then, to Kenna, "Why do you ask?"

"I was looking for a friend that may have been in the vicinity," she said but held back the details. "She wanted to come to the interview."

"I take it you didn't find her," Attwood deduced.

"No, and I'm very concerned," she said. "Another nagging issue: We discussed the bodyguard's absence briefly, but did anyone actually see him leave the stadium?"

"Meaning, he could still be inside," Jenkins returned and stated the obvious.

*

The sun was on its downward fall when Kenna stepped from the stadium with DCI Attwood. Jenkins remained in the security room and was reviewing the footage to see if Illya could be located.

Attwood lit a cigarette and leaned on the police interceptor. There was no need to discuss further what they had seen. It told them of the work that had to be done. This was no ordinary killer.

"There's another thing," Kenna said.

"There always is in murder cases," Attwood said, concentration broken.

"There was a man killed outside Victoria Station, Yuri Zelenko," she said.

"How do you know that?" he asked. "That's been sealed by MI5."

"I knew him; Kovalev knew him. Their killings are linked," Kenna said. "As is Rashon's. I believe ballistics will confirm it."

"Positive speculation, I take it," Attwood said.

"The link is Luhansk, Ukraine," she said. "Specifically, my time there."

"Then, how does Rashon Hill fit into that?"

"A player on Kovalev's team," she suggested. "He must have seen the killer."

"Maybe you should come in so we can discuss it more formally."

"I'd rather not, but will if you think it's necessary," she said.

"We'll see how things progress, but don't leave London."

"Not my style to run from trouble, DCI Attwood."

He chuckled. "That's obvious, Ms. Hannigan."

"This assassin let me live once; don't think he will a second time," she said. "How about this? Come by the hotel, and we can do a round table with my associate."

"I'll ring you when I'm free," he said, ground out the cigarette, and walked for the door.

*

Kenna rode away on the Honda, her mind recalling the CCTV video. Rashon Hill hadn't done anything out of the ordinary while in the stadium. There had been no evidence of an intruder entering the stadium or walking through it to reach the owner's suite. He was smart, this killer, and had known the black holes where cameras didn't record.

The only glimpse of the killer had been when he entered the outer room, the hoody concealing his face. Rashon had stood, smiling, assuming it was her, no doubt. When he turned, he was greeted by the barrel of a .40 Caliber Glock 22.

The single bullet to the heart had ended the career … and life … of a fine young player and man. As much as she prayed the assassin was Beck, she knew it wasn't. Just like at Congressional Country Club, this killer was far too organized, but mostly, far too calm. Beck would have blown up the stadium to kill one person.

A trained assassin … that's what they were after … and she knew of one that had the motive, training, and possibly even orders to pull this off.

XXIV

There hadn't been time for a shower. Covered in the blood, mud, and grime of a struggle reminded Kenna of returning to see Alistair Rensenhaus at BNC offices in Luhansk. He had been joyous as much as concerned, not just of her video but of her condition. When Oleksandr arrived an hour later, the bottle of Horilka was opened for an all-night celebration.

Line of dried blood down her forehead, Kenna walked through the revolving door into the foyer of "British News Corporation". Its bland nature matched her mood. She ignored it, the receptionist's blank stare, the clocks on the wall and continued to the bank of lifts.

Reaching for the "up" button with a shaking hand, Kenna startled when a male executive took her shoulder. He backed off apologetically.

"My apologies, Ms. Hannigan. Are you alright?" he asked, keeping his distance.

Silence was her answer; distant eyes said, *I'm not sure.*

"We have a nurse on staff," he offered.

The lift door opened; she ignored him and stepped inside. Surrounded by silently admonishing BNC employees,

Kenna drummed her fingers on the helmet. *Assassin,* she thought, and stared blankly at her reflection in the stainless-steel door, trying to ignore them as the snail-paced floor indicator dinged.

Single bullet to the heart. She pressed the dangling end of tape against her head to cover the origins of the dried blood. Hands still shaking, she felt the vice-like grip of her Russian assailant's hand on her lapel.

The woman in the limousine covered her face just like arrested criminals, she thought. It was telling; she had something to hide. Kenna's trembling stopped for a moment; the Russian attacker's eyes came into her mind's eye, his hands. She reached for her ripped blouse …

In a flash of memory, *Medved stood by the Aurus Senat limousine on the Embassy grounds and held her press credentials in the air.*

Her eyes remained beyond the lift doors; thoughts transfixed on the sights and sounds of the riot: the sign slammed against her forehead, the cackle of horses' hooves, the roar of the water cannon, fists against faces, nightsticks against bodies, shattered bottles, shrill police whistles. But most of all, the screaming, demanding, angry voices. The lift door opened to a burst of light; she startled.

"Ms. Hannigan," the executive said and pressed the

door-open button just as it slid across to close. "This is your floor, I believe."

She snapped to the present. "Yes … yes, it is."

Helmet tucked under an arm, she stepped out and paused. She lifted her phone and sent Rashon's video to Wiggy. The call went to voicemail.

"Wiggy, see if Barnaby can share the file on Yuri Zelenko's killing outside Victoria Station. I just sent you a video from Rashon Hill. Take a look at it; we'll discuss it later." She paused. "This killer's good, Wiggy, very good. Don't let your guard down for a second."

The Russian at the embassy flashed before her once again. She had filmed something he didn't want shown. It had to be the woman … but why? Kenna stood in the hallway, numb, wondering, *could that be the real reason no one has found her Luhansk video? Perhaps it wasn't meant to be found … or shown? But what's the parallel to Rashon Hill?* She walked through the swinging glass door of the "On-Line Reporters" room.

"Good heavens, love," a female reporter bawled. "Where have you been?"

"I wanna party with you, girl," another laughed.

Kenna didn't hear the comments and found no humor in

her appearance. Her eyes went to Corina at her desk outside Thurnbull's office. On the phone, Corina saw her and pointed to Kenna's right. Thurnbull had the answers to her questions, of that, she was sure. She turned down a short hallway.

Kenna lowered her hand from the bloody cut and recalled what Gran Lockwood had drilled into her all those years: *'A great investigator, not detective, feels, hears, and smells the true essence of the case.'* She had to see the killer's next move before it was made: *'Know how they will act before they ever think about it'.*

She walked to "Media Room #1" at the end of the hallway and reached for the handle. As she touched it, she paused when Thurnbull's voice resounded from inside the room:

"I can't be two places at one time, Henson, and can't do your work for you. Your work's been sloppy. You're not preparing properly or thinking things through. Concentrate!"

"Yes, yes sir, it won't happen again," Tommy apologized. "Just that Adelaide—"

"Being a professional is working through adversity, Henson," Thurnbull said. "Think about it if you want to take the next step up."

Kenna knocked. Thurnbull pulled open the door, resplendent with his grumpy demeanor and dinosaur newsman's glare. His expression eased as he examined her like mulling over an injured racehorse. In the darkness behind him, a pulsating light against a whiteboard wall was like a strobe that silhouetted him.

"All this time, I thought you wanted to be a sports reporter, Hannigan."

"Situations dictate the real story," she countered. "Or so my father says."

"Yes, quite."

"Why you slinking around the halls, anyway?" he growled, then gathered himself after the lecture as she entered. "I wanted you in here first thing."

"As you often remind me, Mr. Thurnbull, I don't work for you," Kenna challenged. "I followed my intuition and was right."

The dimly lit room had a rectangular table, six chairs, and a simple sofa. Laptop and desktop before him, Tommy turned his concentration to the Wembley video that ran in slow motion on the whiteboard wall.

"Old news, Tommy," Kenna said and sat at the table, totally exhausted.

Tommy finally looked at Kenna; shock hit him. "Damn, killer, knew there was a riot, just didn't know you were in it. You should see the nurse."

"What I took at the riot as part of the Kovalev follow-up piece," she said and slid her cell phone across the table. "There's something else that needs to be worked in. One of the football players was killed."

"When?"

"Henson said you were going to Wembley," Thurnbull interrupted. "Must be the reason for all the traffic on the police scanners."

"He was dead before I arrived … just before DCI Attwood," she began, subconsciously placing a finger on her heart. "No doubt, the same killer."

While the riot video downloaded, Tommy watched her intently. "You alright? You seem out of sorts?"

"The question of the day," she said and changed the subject. "Who sent an assassin after Kovalev?"

"Don't you mean, who is the assassin?" Thurnbull asked, redirecting her.

"I'm thinking of the man, not the act," she countered. "In Luhansk, he was considered one of the good guys."

"A rare breed in that part of the world," Tommy offered.

"In my time there, I can honestly say I never met a local that was a *good guy*."

"That was Afghanistan, Tommy," Kenna objected.

"Different mountain range is all, killer," he said.

"I agree with Henson on this, Hannigan," Thurnbull said. "And I was there."

"That's narrow-minded for men with your knowledge of the world."

"It narrows when it reaches that side of the globe, Hannigan," Thurnbull insisted. "Acquired that in the Army, never left me. Now, enough chit-chat … the follow-up story."

Tommy flipped the keys on his computer; the riot video began on the screen. Kenna looked up as her image said:

'This is Kenna Hannigan for BNC at the Russian Embassy.'

Kenna stood alongside the whiteboard, pointed, and narrated while the video ran. Thurnbull and Tommy watched in silence until she was thrown against the limousine.

"Here," she said. "A woman in the ambassador's limo … I should know her … from Luhansk."

"Don't waste my air on Luhansk," Thurnbull insisted and lifted a thick eyebrow. "History, Ms. Hannigan, is in the hands of those who can produce it. Until you show me the video from Luhansk, it doesn't exist."

"I just wanted to see if I captured her face, sir." On the screen, Svetlana held up the folder to conceal her face. "There, she's holding something, a folder. Let's look at that again, Tommy."

"You're getting bogged down in the minutia, Hannigan," Thurnbull stiffened in surprise, then instructed, "Move on, Henson. This riot's a piece of the follow-up, not what this bloody Russian reads! Everything must tie with Kovalev's killing in the follow-up."

"And Rashon Hill, sir, the football player," she said.

"What the bloody hell's he have to do with the riot?" Thurnbull asked.

"Nothing that I know of, sir," she said. "But—"

"Stop derailing the follow-up, Hannigan."

Tommy froze the screen on the image of Svetlana holding the folder. "Do you recognize her, sir?"

Thurnbull grimaced at Svetlana's image. "Another Russian model."

"I'd like to look at that folder," she said.

"Do it on your own time, Hannigan," Thurnbull demanded. "I told you to move on, Henson! Get back on point with this follow-up story: Kovalev's murder and the riot. You need to link them. We'll get to the American football player … and the bloody Russian model later."

Tommy started the video again. The limousine pulled into the compound; Kenna was swallowed by the riot. The water cannon blasted the mob, concealing Kenna and Medved. She pointed at the image.

"This is when the Russian took my press credentials and ripped my blouse."

"Well, if he didn't before, he knows who you are now," Thurnbull snapped, more than a bit put-out by all the interruptions.

"This might amuse you, sir, but the only thing on his mind was killing me."

"Melodramatic, even for you, Hannigan."

"You didn't see his eyes," Kenna insisted.

"Russians bow their backs when people attack their embassy gates," Thurnbull offered. "You have a video of the riot, good. Get to the follow—"

"But—" Kenna interrupted.

"We'll get to Luhansk later, as well, Ms. Hannigan."

Tommy cleared his throat. "Sir, about the Russian. We could reach out to MI5. They might—"

"First good idea you've had, Henson," Thurnbull interrupted. "You have inroads with one of their people, eh Hannigan?"

Barnaby Scrivens flashed across Kenna's memory. "My sources are private, Mr. Thurnbull. You, of all people, understand the importance of that."

"Yes, of course," Thurnbull said. "Don't want to upset the apple cart. Do what you must to get to the bottom of it."

'People look at things wrong when they say they want to get to the bottom of something. That's the bloody crime, the beginning,' Gran often said. *'Getting to the top is the result, leanbh.'*

Kenna thought of Gran's teachings, as well as the thought of revealing a source. Were they that desperate for the story, and Thurnbull, just another annoying journalist? She wasn't Thurnbull's employee and would do what it took to get to the top of what was happening. Afterall, to her, this wasn't just a story. It was about finding a murderer.

"Get those injuries patched up," Thurnbull ordered. "You're no good to me on the sick list."

Thurnbull walked out. Tommy shut down the video and slid Kenna her phone. She took his hand and waited until he looked into her eyes.

"What was that discussion with Thurnbull before I entered?"

Tommy's face wrinkled with hesitation. "Him reminding me who's boss."

"If I can help, let me know," she offered.

"I'm worried about Adelaide," he said. "I'm going to make some more phone calls."

Tommy walked out. Kenna sat alone, her mind jumping to every event, and ended with … *Adelaide, damn you, what did you have to do with this?* Tommy had a right to know of her suspicions about Adelaide, but she shook it off. There were too many things in play to be worried about one item.

'Concentrate on what will solve the case, leanbh. Leave the inconsequential to others,' Gran hissed into her ear from the past.

She pulled up the riot video on her phone and froze it on Medved's image, then found the image of Svetlana holding the folder. She took them as screen images, put them into a message, and sent it to Wiggy. Her phone swooshed; she pushed Bluetooth.

"Call Wiggy's cell," she said and waited for the ring.

"Where ya been all day, kid?" he asked.

"I'll fill you in later at the hotel," she said. "I text you two images. The first is a Russian that attacked me today—"

"Attacked? Are ye alright?"

"Not to worry," she lied. "The second is a woman from Luhansk. She's holding a folder. Find out everything you can about a company named Halibeck International."

They disconnected. Kenna shoved the phone into her riding leathers. Throwing on the backpack and taking the helmet, she walked from the room, for the first time wondering if an assassin's bullet would hit her in the heart when she stepped out.

XXV

Svetlana sat alone at a high table in the exquisite Mandarin Oriental Hyde Park Hotel bar. International voices and laughter filled the room. "BNC News Special" flashed on the television behind the bar. She didn't think much about it until the camera focused on Wembley Stadium. A subtitle tracked across the screen, "Second Murder in Wembley Stadium—Details Developing." Svetlana's brow furrowed as a male anchor spoke from a studio desk:

"An American football player was found this afternoon—"

"Permanent solution to any problem," she said and lifted her wine glass to the sky. "To you, Kostyantyn, may you rot in whatever corner of hell you have landed."

In a sudden excellent mood, she eyed a tall waiter in a tuxedo as the sex object she would like him to be. A smile punctuated her fantasy as he stood at the bar and turned. Her eyes did not leave him as he walked for the table and added wine to her glass.

Her eyes held his in a lengthy embrace. She placed money into his palm and whispered in his ear … he smiled, liking that idea. She handed him a card.

"It will be my pleasure, madam," he said.

"For that amount of money, the pleasure better be mine." She brushed a hand across his bum when he walked past.

"Ms. Pavlosky, is it not?" the deep British accent came from the side.

She turned into the inquisitive eyes of Douglas Thurnbull. Recognition close to shock filled her; she turned back to the television and the news broadcast. He presented a card; she ignored it. At the door to the restaurant, Filipp stepped forward; she waved him off with her eyes.

"Douglas Thurnbull, British News—"

"I know who you are," she said. "How did you find me?"

"London is a large city with many eyes, Ms. Pavlosky," he offered. "That follow us everywhere."

"What do you want?"

Without asking, he sat beside her. "I find it interesting that you are out in public after the riot in front of the embassy this morning."

"It is the nature of people to complain about something," she offered.

"One of our reporters came to the embassy to get a comment from you on Kostyantyn Kovalev's killing," he said and waved off the waiter.

"Why would she want a comment from me? I barely knew the man."

"She's paid to investigate, Ms. Pavlosky," he said. "She is quite tenacious … and good."

Her facial expression registered a hint of surprise but more curiosity. She had seen the reporter as a nuisance more than anything. She would wait to see what Medved found on her.

"So, tell me, how do you find London compared to Moscow?" he asked.

"Warmer this time of year," she said. "Now, if you don't mind."

"Just one more question, if I may?" he asked. Her glare said *you may not*. He ignored it and continued:

"She photographed you in the embassy limousine. In that photo, you were holding a folder titled, 'Halibeck International'. "

He allowed that to sink in. Svetlana's expression soured; anger gripped her wine glass with white knuckles. Brows furrowed deep; small lines of concern creased that perfectly painted and Botox'd forehead.

"I would be very curious to see what's in that folder," he said.

Svetlana waved the waiter to the table. She handed him money and walked out. Thurnbull and Filipp made unfriendly eye contact. With a hint of satisfaction, Thurnbull walked out behind.

XXVI

When Kenna entered the hotel suite, afternoon light was slowly deepening to grey. She expected the full Wiggy juggernaut of questions and fatherly advice on what she should and should not have done. She was in no mood for it, which was clear by the hardened scowl. He looked up from the laptop and shook his head.

"Coffee in the pot, beer in the frig," he offered.

"Shower first," Kenna said.

"Was gonna suggest that. I'll put a new patch on those war wounds when yer done."

"London is rapidly becoming a must-not-visit-again city, just like Washington, D.C."

"Watched the riot at the embassy," he said. "Ya need ta work on yer cinematography skills, kid."

"Not funny, Wiggy. I hurt where I didn't think there was anything to hurt."

"They must'a cut that you'd been in a scrap."

"Really? Was the best stuff … *a little bloodied but not broken* … blah, blah, blah," she said. "What you got for me?"

"Barnaby brought facial recognition software, downloading it now," he said. "Didn'a need it for the woman in the Rolls, though. He recognized her immediately, Svetlana…"

"Pavlovsky," they both said.

"FSB director in occupied Ukraine," he said.

"Oleksandr recognized her at the clandestine meeting in Luhansk," Kenna said from the bedroom. "She leaves Ukraine for London … why?"

"The answer to that and why Yuri Zelenko was here might put a lot of the puzzle together, lass," he concluded.

Kenna pulled off the riding leathers and the ripped blouse. Wiggy followed her into the bedroom. They'd seen each other naked before and didn't give it a second thought. She disrobed and entered the bathroom while he sat on the bed.

"Her presence perked up Barnaby's interest, that's for certain," he said in a raised voice.

"He knows her?" she asked from the shower.

"Of her," he said. "But I get the feelin' he'd like to get acquainted … in the interest of the Crown, mind ya."

"He and I are of like mind on that, with the exception of doing it for the Crown," she shouted, lathering.

"With his help, I found a way into Wembley's security system. Yesterday's history is runnin' now. When ya get out, we'll go over it."

"What about that folder Svetlana had?" she asked, stepping out with a towel. "Halibeck International and Rashon's video?"

"My one machine can only do so much, Fiery. I'm workin' on it," he said and stood.

"Then, get another if you need it."

"What I need is a second set of eyes and hands," he said.

"Can't help ya there," she said.

"When yer ready, come out to the table. Oh, and Barnaby says he'll get us what he can on Zelenko's killing, but it'll be tough."

Within ten minutes, Kenna sat at the table beside Wiggy. Wrapping her hands around a cup of coffee, she relished its warmth as it eased the pain from her hands. New bandages covered her facial and scalp injuries.

"While you were out, DCI Attwood phoned," he said. "Wants to chat, in his words."

"That'll be about Rashon Hill. Same killer, one bullet." She pointed to her heart.

"Bloody hell, and ya think the Russian had somethin' to

do with it?"

"If I knew who he was, I could answer that," she said.

"Barnaby didn't recognize him," he said. "Let's put everything ya want me to do in order."

"My bet is he's FSB or ex-military," she said. "We both thought that about Kovalev's killer."

Wiggy pointed to Medved's image on the screen. "If this lad's Russian, your man from Luhansk might know him."

Kenna swallowed hard, hating that idea. "Oleksandr? No! No way!"

"Ya told me ya didn't know if he was involved in the ambush."

"That innocent little girl vanished before my eyes!" she said with great emotion. "He did nothing!"

"All you want's a name to this face, kid. Your words, Oleksandr knows every Russian in Ukraine," he said and handed Kenna a sheet of paper. "His last known address and phone number."

"You already ran it?"

"In Barnaby's files," he said. "If you want to know who this Russian is, go see him."

Kenna stared at Medved's image, hating that Wiggy was right. But Oleksandr? She was almost afraid what might happen when they saw each other again. She remembered Nadia but, more importantly, how Oleksandr had done nothing to help her.

Kenna stopped twirling the paper and stared at Oleksandr's face, just like she had two years before. She lifted the cell phone and punched in the number. The phone rang and went to voicemail:

"You know what to do," Oleksandr's gruff voice recording said, followed by a ding.

Kenna frowned, recognizing the voice. "Oles, I miss our fireside chats. Call me."

Wiggy leaned on his elbows and stared at her with his patented, *I'm not dropping it until you talk to me*, glare. "It's time you told me what happened in Luhansk."

Kenna's mind fixed on Luhansk two years before … and that horrible day …

***

LUHANSK, UKRAINE—17 MARCH 2020

Flames spread rapidly through the BNC offices, engulfing it in seconds. Kenna ran out, clothes smoldering, dropped and rolled in the moist, muddy street. An explosion sprayed the street with burning debris. Gunfire riddled the building. A man inside screamed … Alistair Rensenhaus.

Frozen in shock, Kenna was stunned to silence. She wanted to go in, but the flames kept her back. Holding a dead child while staggering from an adjacent building, a burning woman screamed, fell, and didn't move.

Armed with a Kel-Tec SUB-2000 semiautomatic rifle, Oleksandr didn't see her and ran across the rubble-strewn street towards the fighting. Shaking in total fear, Nadia was 10, filthy in tattered clothes. She ran to Kenna and embraced Kenna's arm. Grenades exploded close.

Russian and Ukrainian fighters converged on the buildings across the street, exchanging gunfire. Nadia broke away, running between the converging warriors after Oleksandr. An explosion partially masked Kenna's words as she yelled, *'No, Nadia!'*

Machinegun fire riddled buildings around Kenna as she stood. Debris showered her; a close explosion catapulted her several meters. She slammed against a building, knocking her semi-conscious.

Dazed, a jagged bloody cut on her head, she looked up from the ground. A separate explosion. When the dust cleared, Nadia was gone. Masked by the fighting, Kenna crawled that direction and yelled, *'Nooo!'*

Through the dust in the shadows, Oleksandr stared blankly and screamed, *'Nadia!'* which was silenced by gunfire …

***

At the hotel window, Kenna lowered her hand from the head wound, looking at her fingers. She took a sip of coffee … then another until the cup was empty.

"Yesterday reminded me a lot of that day."

"If for no other reason, that's why you should talk to Oleksandr," Wiggy offered. "Never met the man, but you should hear him out."

"Can't force him to call me back," she said. "Have a feeling he's doing the same thing we are."

"I don't like offerin' advice, but we might be over our heads on this one, kid." Wiggy took her shoulders. "If Oleksandr's doin' as you say, then we should work together. Like we're doin' with Barnaby."

She knew he was right. There were things Oleksandr might know that were still a void in her mind. It began with Kovalev's involvement in Alistair Rensenhaus's killing. It all led to the doubt about Oleksandr … *whose side was he on?*

Wiggy motioned to the laptop and took her mind away from the thought:

"The balance of the CCTV from yesterday has

218

downloaded, lass. Let's take a look."

"So, it was on?"

"Only views of the pitch and outside the stadium. The inside cameras were off," he said.

She remembered the dark hallway, *saving energy.* "Doesn't make sense with all the bigwigs there for the meeting."

"Speaking of which, while downloading, I reviewed several hours before we arrived. I didn't see any brass arrive," Wiggy said. "From what I can tell, Kovalev either lied or had the meeting somewhere else."

"Could be why he was late, a change of venue," she concluded.

"Aye," Wiggy offered. "Possible Kovalev wasn't the target at all and surprised the would-be killer who expected someone else."

"You spent too much time with Gran, Wiggy," she countered. "But she was right … *simplicity is never the answer; there is never a direct line from bottom to top. ' "*

They turned their attention to the CCTV footage that came to life on the computer. It began with ten small images occupying a part of the screen, four overlooking the pitch and six around the outside of the stadium.

"Go to where I found Addie's bracelet," she said.

He isolated that image and moved to the dock those he deemed unimportant. He increased the size of the service entrance at the parking garage. A two-tone Mini Cooper, appearing black over grey on the screen, sat just outside the entrance.

"That looks like Addie's Mini," Kenna said.

Wiggy pointed to the date stamp and said, "Just before the Kovalev interview."

She twirled a finger; Wiggy fast-forwarded. Two figures left the stadium. He paused, reversed, and ran it at normal speed. Within a few seconds, an uninjured man dragged someone in a dark hoody from the stadium.

"Illya … and that must be Addie," Kenna said.

"That's why he left the pitch before the interview," Wiggy said. "She must'a been causin' a row in the owner's suite."

Illya opened the Mini and shoved Adelaide inside. He said something sharply, slammed the door and hurried back into the stadium. Wiggy froze the frame. He went to another screen, pulled up the interview video, and compared the date stamps.

"She's still in the car after the interview ended, and I left on the other side of the stadium," he confirmed.

Kenna snapped open her phone and looked at the video date stamp when she was knocked unconscious. "Just before the guard and I entered the suite."

Wiggy went back to the stadium CCTV and continued in fast forward. Inside the Mini, Adelaide moved, collected herself, and stood from the car. A Jaguar F-Type sped from the garage. Adelaide ran for the Jaguar, waving hands, screaming silently. The Jaguar slid to a stop and reversed hard. Adelaide hesitated and didn't move. The Jaguar slammed into Adelaide, throwing her against the Mini.

Kenna gasped, "Why didn't she move out of the way?"

"Hopefully, we'll get the chance to ask."

"That's exactly where we found the bracelet," Kenna added.

In a black hoody, the Jaguar driver stepped out. He spun to the side in panic, then jumped inside the Jaguar. Injured and in great pain, Adelaide crawled to the Mini and pulled herself in. The Jaguar sped away. The Mini weaved away in the opposite direction.

On another screen, Wiggy pointed to flashing emergency lights approaching the stadium. "Police, Kovalev's dead."

Wiggy reached to shut it down, but Kenna stayed his

hand. "Wait, let's see if we know what happened to Illya."

Wiggy fast-forwarded the video while they watched the screen. No-one else left the stadium until the police and emergency vehicles arrived.

"Must still be inside the stadium," Wiggy said.

Kenna silently agreed. "I have to tell Tommy about this."

"Go easy on the lad."

"He has to find Adelaide. We don't have the time," she said, lifted her phone, and walked into the bedroom. "I want to know what the hell she was doing there."

When Kenna walked from the bedroom in the soiled riding leather, she tapped the Bluetooth. "Call Tommy's cell."

"Hi, Kenna," Tommy said softly.

"Have you found Adelaide?" she asked.

"No, was about to go to the Boar to see if she shows."

"I'll pick you up out front, and we'll go together. I'm on the way now."

Kenna disconnected the call. She grabbed the helmet and threw the backpack over her shoulders. Wiggy walked her to the door and turned her.

"Like the Grand Ole Dame always said, *'pay attention to the darkness more than the light,'* " he said. "I'll call DCI

Attwood."

Watching the Rashon Hill video had lost its importance for the moment. He was dead, and there was nothing she could do about that. However, there was a chance Adelaide was still alive. She had to do everything in her power to keep her that way.

"Isolate that sequence at the Mini and send it to my cell." Kenna wasn't sure why, but she reached up and caressed Wiggy's cheek. "Find that fucking Jaguar."

XXVII

Fuming with anger, Medved stood nose-to-nose with Sergey on the aft deck of *"Worldly Light"*. Armed, they glared into the other's eyes, both unafraid. Weapons were a heartbeat from being drawn; lives an instant later from being extinguished.

"I take my orders from Svetlana, Alexi," Sergey said.

"Perhaps you should rethink that," Medved countered. "Her orders are from the director; mine are from the president."

"We all live—"

"Or die," Medved interrupted.

"By a chain of command," Sergey continued, ignoring him. "Bring me orders that I report to you, and I will do as you wish."

"I am telling you now … next time you see that Ukrainian, kill him!"

Medved hurried down the gangway from the yacht. The guards joined Sergey on deck, glaring at Medved with anger equal to their boss's. However, like Sergey said, all followed the chain of command, and that began with Svetlana.

"Incompetents," Medved yelled to himself more than them, "unable to capture that Ukrainian vagabond."

Two years ago, he had a very similar opportunity to capture Oleksandr. The resulting gunbattle was long and bloody. Though involving many men, his attention had been on Oleksandr, as the Ukrainian's attention had been on him. He had believed the British press when they reported the Ukrainian was dead. Anger boiled within him for not verifying the kill when he had the opportunity. He would not make that mistake again.

He marched to an Aston Martin Vantage and glared at the low, dark, overcast dusk, hating the damp English cold. *Does the sun ever shine here?* he wondered. He popped open the boot, lifted out a SR-2 Veresk submachine gun, checked the magazine, slapped it back in, and chambered a shell. He set the safety and slid the weapon behind the passenger's seat. Inside the car, he accelerated away and steered onto the street towards the exit of Canary Wharf. He tapped the phone screen.

"Call Feodor," he said and pulled out a cigarette. The phone rang over the speaker.

"Security," Feodor answered from in front of his computer terminal in the embassy.

"Trace Shwetz's phone again," he ordered. "The idiots

at the yacht lost him.”

“Haven’t turned it off, sir. Just need to re-acquire,” Feodor said, following the highlighted object on his screen. “Let’s see where he’s going. In the meantime, I’ll text Shwetz’s known associates.”

“I need this quickly, Feodor,” Medved demanded. “Don’t want him slipping away again.”

Feodor enlarged the screen map with the highlight. “He’s on the move, sir … a few moments for me to get a fix.”

Impatient, Medved stopped at the side of the street, waiting, and lit the cigarette. His phone dinged. He pulled up the attachment on the screen and reviewed it. Anger mounted with every second.

Feodor smiled at the screen. “Got him, sir. He’s on the A-11, driving east into Tower Hamlets.”

Medved pulled up Tower Hamlets on maps and punched “Directions”.

“At first opportunity, make a U-turn,” the metallic female GPS voice said.

Medved reversed at full acceleration with bawling tires. Shifting, he accelerated hard and spun a U-turn in front of on-coming traffic. To blaring horns and screeching brakes, he floored the accelerator. In a half block, he slid around a corner, ignoring pedestrians and a red traffic light.

"You are exceeding the speed limit," the metallic voice reminded him.

He shot the phone screen with a finger pistol and lifted the SR-2 Veresk submachine gun from behind the seat. He shoved it between his leg and the console.

"Definitely on track for the safe house in Tower Hamlets," Feodor said over the speaker.

*

With concentration more on what must be done than the road, Oleksandr slowed the old beat-up Vauxhall Brava pickup in heavy traffic. Stopped at a light, he cupped his hand over the flame to light a cigarette. It was one of those rare moments of pleasure, though he knew how bad it was for him. But then, his life had been forged in doing bad things for good causes … not necessarily good people. He punched a number on his phone.

"Yes, Bear."

"Evhen, where are you?"

Several kilometers in the opposite direction, Evhen drove a well-used Vauxhall Arena delivery van. "On my way. You?"

"Just left the FSB on the yacht. He was mad about

missing you, I think," Okeksandr said. "The tracking device is working perfectly. I followed the countess yesterday to a meeting with Kovalev, didn't look too friendly. Then, to the stadium."

"Maybe she did us a favor with Kovalev," Evhen offered.

"I have an idea where she's going," Oleksandr said. "Appreciate you doing this."

"Wasn't a problem. She left the limousine unattended while having cocktails. I could have stripped it had I wanted," Evhen chuckled. "Want me to meet you?"

"You came to London to leave all this behind, my friend," he said. "If you don't hear from me, tell Mrs. Kohut I'll see her on the other side."

"They aren't good enough to kill you, Bear," Evhen insisted.

"Appreciate your confidence … wish I had the same."

"Then, why do it?" Evhen asked.

"You know the answer," Oleksandr said. "Thank you, brother."

"See you after you've taken care of business," Evhen said reassuringly.

Oleksandr disconnected the call and turned onto a

narrow street between row brick warehouses. Halfway through the next block, he stopped and stood out. He opened the swinging doors of a storage garage, then drove the Brava inside.

XXVIII

In the lengthening shadows of dusk, Kenna stopped the Honda on the sidewalk in front of the BNC building. For a moment, it seemed like she had parked in front of Texas Television Studios in Dallas, and her father was waiting. Her report would be brief; his response curt. Yet, in a strange way, she wanted that to happen again someday. After Congressional, they had made progress toward repairing their relationship; she wanted it to continue.

That she had gone to Ukraine alone in search of Beck hadn't pleased her father and undoubtedly prompted his silence over the past two years. Perhaps it was the fear that poured from her mother's eyes when she left that fueled her father's antagonism. He was protecting the love of his life, which Kenna could never condemn. Someday, she wanted the opportunity to finally set things straight with him. That day would come … when Anson Beck was dead.

Swinging on a backpack, Tommy walked from the building, followed shortly by Thurnbull. Kenna tossed Tommy a helmet. On the top step, Thurnbull lit his pipe, nodded, and saluted them with it. A security guard stepped out beside Thurnbull and watched the street.

"I hope to hell she's there," Tommy said, swinging on behind.

"Surprised Thurnbull let you out," Kenna said.

"Something about getting my head around work."

"A heartless old school master, Tommy," she said, thinking of her father.

From behind Thurnbull, Corina ran from the building with an envelope, waving it at Kenna. "Kenna … Ms. Hannigan!"

Kenna paused until Corina joined them and extended the envelope. "A courier just brought this. Thought it might be important."

"Courier on Sunday?" Kenna asked. "Thanks."

Kenna shoved the envelope into her backpack and accelerated onto the street. Behind, a Vauxhall Corsa sedan pulled from the curb to follow. Thurnbull and Corina watched curiously, but his thoughts were interrupted when his phone rang. His conversation was masked by the traffic noise. He turned inside, motioning Corina with him.

*

Driving with traffic, Kenna couldn't help but think of her father, Kovalev, and Thurnbull. They were all cut from the same cloth: strong-willed, arrogant, and demanding. The only thing that separated them was nationality. She thought of throwing Toll in the mix, but there was something distinctly different about him. Hadn't put her finger on it yet but would.

Tommy leaned over her shoulder and yelled over the wind, engine, and traffic noise, "Have you learned anything about Yuri Zelenko's killing?"

"MI5 has it bottled up," she yelled over a shoulder.

"Was he coming to see you?"

Undoubtedly, she thought, making a sharp turn. "I'll never know … that makes three."

"Three what?" he asked.

"Three of the five men I worked with in Ukraine, Rensenhaus, Kovalev, and Yuri, are dead. And Illya is missing."

"So, Oleksandr Shwetz is the last man standing," he concluded.

That comment surprised Kenna, but Tommy was right. Oleksandr was the last man standing. And, quite possibly, the last man that could help her find the video.

He's the only other person that knows what happened in Luhansk, she thought.

In the passenger seat of the Corsa, Pyotr slapped the driver's arm. Vanya was an intense man in his 30s, a Medved disciple ready for a fight. A few cars behind the Honda, he accelerated the Corsa through the heavy traffic to remain within sight.

"Could easily take that motorcycle out, Pyotr," Vanya said.

"Medved wants us watching for now," Pyotr said.

"A waste of time and energy," Vanya countered.

"The time will come, Vanya. For now, we follow orders."

Through the twists and turns of London's busy streets, the Corsa followed. At the "Blue Boar", Kenna leaned the Honda onto the sidewalk and stopped. She and Tommy swung off, chained the Honda to a streetlight, and walked inside.

When the Corsa reached the front of the pub, Pyotr pointed across the street. Vanya pulled onto the street across, parked, and turned off the engine.

"Rather be in there than out here," Pyotr said.

"Why not go in? You could hear their conversation," Vanya suggested.

"She's seen me." They settled back for a long wait.

*

In the pub, Kenna sat at the dimly lit bar. Tommy motioned he was going to the toilet. A boisterous evening crowd talked and laughed. A group of men played darts at the rear. Ian, the frowning bartender, brought two pints.

"You're gonna start calling us regulars if we keep coming in, me yesterday morning, Tommy in the afternoon."

"Don't remember seeing him, but we were rockin'. It was Saturday," he said with a shrug. "Where's Adelaide?"

"Getting her hair done, knowing her," Kenna chuckled.

"She doesn't need it; looks good the way she keeps it."

That surprised Kenna but also saddened her. He lifted a bottle of whiskey and slapped two shot glasses on the bar. She waved him off.

"Riding the bike tonight, a pint's good for me," Kenna said. "Tommy will want one, probably many."

Ian filled one shot glass; a patron at the other end of the bar yelled for a pint. He turned that direction just as Tommy left the toilet with a down-trodden gaze. He lifted the shot glass; they toasted and drank.

Kenna caressed Tommy's arm, attempting to ease his mood. When his eyes lifted, the expression remained the same. *This isn't going to lift his spirits,* she thought.

"About Addie—"

"I was half-hoping she would be here, drunk on the floor," he interrupted.

Kenna stared into his eyes. His weakness was troubling. She had never seen that in him and didn't expect it. Now was a time to be strong. Perhaps that was at the heart of Thurnbull's lecture in the media room.

"She could be in big trouble, Tommy."

"You're reading my mind again," he said and drank the shot. "She won't return my calls."

"She was at Wembley yesterday. I'm positive of it," she said.

"Wembley? How do you know that?" he asked with forlorn hope.

"It's just possible she can't return your calls."

Kenna watched Tommy's eyes as every bad thought possible filled his mind. Yet, his reaction wasn't what she expected. Perhaps it was his military background, much like Thurnbull, the deadpan expression when confronting pain. She turned on her phone, brought up the CCTV video of Wembley, and pressed play. She spoke while Tommy watched:

"This is CCTV outside Wembley at the time Kovalev was killed." She lifted the bracelet from her pocket and placed it on the bar. "I found this where the Mini was parked…"

On the phone screen, the Jaguar hit the Mini Cooper driver … Tommy gasped.

"The Jag," he said and paused.

"That's Adelaide's Mini, isn't it?"

He nodded; the deadpan military expression remained. "Her father sent this bracelet for Christmas. Do you have any idea where she is?"

"I'm depending on you to find out," she said. "Let's plot the hospitals close to the stadium. If badly hurt, she might have gone there or was taken there."

"What are you going to do?"

"Find the driver of that Jaguar."

Tommy pushed away from the bar to stand; Kenna took his arm. "Don't go off half-cocked, Tommy. Sit, we need a strategy on what to do if things go bad."

XXIX

With the Aston Martin stuck in a line of traffic at a roundabout, Medved's frustration mounted. Streetlights flicked on but were overpowered by flashing police and ambulance lights. He covered the stock of the submachine gun and pulled his jacket tight to conceal the shoulder holster. Police guided traffic slowly around a crashed delivery lorry and a car while paramedics tended to several injured in the middle of the street. Looking at the injured with no reaction, Medved eased the Aston Martin past. He spoke into the speaker phone:

"Talk to me, Feodor!"

In the embassy security room, Feodor sat at his console. He took a large drink of vodka and improved the screen image. He smiled.

"The phone stopped at the safe house, sir. Stationary now and hasn't moved."

"If it does, let me know. I'm close."

Medved turned off the GPS and steered out of the roundabout. As traffic moved, he accelerated with screaming tires and weaved through and around slower cars.

"Get outta my fucking way!" he screamed.

A few blocks later, he turned off the main road into the warehouse district and slowed. Ahead, an aged Vauxhall Arena delivery van pulled away from a warehouse. It turned around and drove for Medved. With total concentration, he lifted the submachine gun to his lap and flipped off the safety. Without slowing, the delivery van passed. Medved stared at the driver, Evhen, not recognizing him. Medved watched in the rearview mirror while the delivery van drove to the end of the street and turned.

"What the fuck?"

"What's that, sir?" Feodor asked, still fixed on the screen.

"Is it moving, Feodor?" Medved asked, anxious.

"No, sir, still stationary."

Medved slowed in front of the warehouses, then stopped short. His eyes took in every building, rooftop, and window along the darkening street. More streetlights flipped on. Leaving the submachine gun, he stepped out with the pistol and hurried to the building's sliding door.

On the pavement was a small box addressed to: "Alexi Medved". He sliced it open with a switchblade. From inside, he lifted out a cell phone. He illuminated the screen, surprised and angered by the text message:

Welcome to London. I'm sure we'll see each other before you leave. As I recall, I owe Svetlana something ... two bullets. Get in the way, and I'll repay through you.

Filled with rage, Medved lifted the phone to throw it. He hesitated, jumped in the Aston Martin, and pounded his fist on the steering wheel.

"Fuck!" he screamed. "Feodor!"

"Sir," came the computer geek's hesitant response.

"I'll call when I'm near the embassy. I want you to do something with a phone," he ordered. "Where's Svetlana?"

"The last she reported, she was going to a flat in Eaton Square."

"Dammit," he yelled. "When will she learn?"

Medved disconnected the call and looked in the rearview mirror. The delivery van was gone. He pulled up the list of Oleksandr's contacts and enlarged the photo ... "Evhen Chayka," he mumbled to himself. *Well done, my Ukrainian friends,* he thought sarcastically, *but don't get comfortable. I'm coming.*

*

The Brava idled in front of the open warehouse doors. A canvas top covered the cargo box, with a sign on the side: "Garden Maintenance". Oleksandr closed the swinging doors and jumped into the cab. He opened a GPS tracker and waited for it to acquire the signal from Svetlana's limousine. With a ding, it provided a location in Belgravia, Eaton Square.

"You are a horrible person, Svetlana," he said to himself. "Time for someone to discipline you in the harshest manner."

Oleksandr accelerated the rattling Brava along the warehouse road. He set a burner cell phone on a Kevlar vest next to two Glock pistols in opposing shoulder holsters on the passenger seat. With a hint of brief satisfaction, he lit a cigarette. His eyes narrowed. Mind fixed on the job ahead, his expression hardened to that of a man going into battle.

XXX

On separate missions with entirely different body language, Kenna walked from the "Blue Boar" with Tommy. She wasn't comfortable with his depression, but she had neither the time nor the inclination to get him out of the doldrums. At the bus stop, she took hold of him, this time firmly. The nice girl routine hadn't worked.

"What the fuck's wrong with you?" she demanded. "Addie's missing, and you're moping around like a scolded child. Get your head outta your ass and find her!"

She shook him hard with frustration, then released him. She unchained the Honda and watched. Nothing had changed. Had he given up hope? Or did he know that Adelaide had been involved in Kovalev's death? Kenna couldn't believe it, but she refused to speculate and couldn't rule it out. Facts spoke the truth. She pulled on the backpack and helmet.

*

Across the street, Vanya sat in the driver's seat of the Corsa, head resting back. Pyotr leaned on a streetlight, smoking a cigarette, partially concealed from Kenna's view. His phone rang.

"Yes, Alexi?" Pyotr answered.

Driving the Aston Martin, Medved yelled into the phone screen, "Break off following the woman. Meet at Kovalev's apartment in Eaton Square … Now!"

"We're on the way."

Pyotr jumped into the Corsa and slapped Vanya's arm. "Eaton Square, let's go."

*

A bus rumbled to a stop in front of Kenna and Tommy; they embraced. He walked aboard. With a cloud of black smoke, the bus rumbled away. Vanya accelerated the Corsa onto the street and turned in the opposite direction of the bus.

Kenna watched the bus while she cinched the helmet strap. Weakness aside, something was off with Tommy. He hadn't seemed himself during the conversation. Yes, Adelaide was missing, but it was as if something else was at the rear of his brain, either guiding him or confusing him. She couldn't tell which. *The Thurnbull lecture?* she wondered.

A Corsa police interceptor stopped at the curb, snapping Kenna from the thought. DCI Attwood stood from the car. DS Jenkins stood from the driver's side to join him.

"You are one tough woman to see, Ms. Hannigan,"

Attwood said.

"I thought we were going to continue this in my hotel room with my associate?" Kenna asked.

"Circumstances have changed about the bodyguard, I'm afraid," Attwood said.

"Illya," Kenna said. "What's—"

"Do you know his surname? We find nothing in the system," Jenkins interrupted. "Immigration has no record of anyone by that given name entering the country."

Kenna replied, "Come to think of it, I never heard his surname. He'd been with Mr. Kovalev as long as I'd known him. Don't even know if Illya is his given name. It's an Old Testament name and could be a derivative of Elijah."

That deflated Jenkins' ego a bit; she lifted her phone and tapped in a text. When she looked up, that brazen attitude returned.

"Forensics matched your blood outside the suite," Attwood said. "There are two others that don't match. Did you see anyone else?"

"Just the shadow in the hoody," Kenna said, "which I believe was the attacker."

"Man or woman?" Jenkins asked, angered by Kenna's earlier interruption.

"I didn't get a good enough look to tell, actually," Kenna said. "What did the blood samples tell you, man or woman?"

Jenkins ignored Kenna with a step forward and said accusingly, "The shooter had to be looking at you when he shot the guard."

Stand your ground when accused. Kenna's anger flared; she held it back but confronted Jenkins face-to-face. Attwood stepped between them and eased Jenkins back.

"Keep it civil, ladies," he said and glared at Jenkins. "What did the lab say about the blood?"

Jenkins swallowed hard, "Both male and female."

"See, that wasn't so difficult," Kenna said to keep the fire lit. "Now, as your lead technician said, we just need to find whose blood it is."

"All right, I'm calling a truce to this right now! Or …" Attwood demanded, then to Kenna. "I'm sending you downtown," then to Jenkins, "And I'm sending you home." He paused. "Got it?"

Kenna and Jenkins reluctantly agreed and backed away from each other.

"Where was I? Yes, my interest right now is the bodyguard," he said. "There was no CCTV footage of him leaving the stadium."

"As I said before, when the guard and I got into the suite, he wasn't there," Kenna said. "Check my credentials, DCI Attwood. We are after the same thing: the truth about what happened."

"I appreciate that, Ms. Hannigan, but we do things a little differently on this side of the pond," Attwood advised. "I want to know what you're doing before you do it. Moving forward, ring me, or there will be consequences."

"I understand," she said. *Spoken like a true bureaucrat,* she thought. "A quid pro quo if you don't mind … keep her away from me … please."

Attwood exhaled the long day from his lungs. "Anything else can you tell us?"

"I am returning to my hotel to review what we have," Kenna said while Attwood walked to the police car. "I'll phone with anything of substance."

Attwood and Jenkins waited as a double-decker bus stopped at curbside in front of them. Kenna's investigative gaze followed the people who alighted and boarded. She trusted none. Not the man in the suit with the smartly dressed woman. Not the teenage girl in holey blue jeans listening to music on her earbuds. Or the mother that carried the infant. Finally, a brown man leaned on a building and rubbed a scruffy, salt 'n pepper beard, all with deep and dark penetrating eyes that trained on her, as if to … pull a concealed weapon.

Kenna shook it off and started the Honda. Her phone rang; she tapped Bluetooth while pulling on riding gloves.

"Finally, Oles, we need to—"

In his office, Thurnbull stamped tobacco into his pipe and, for the first time, put a light to it. He inhaled, relishing the flavor and more … It felt good breaking a rule.

"Thurnbull, I'm afraid," he said between inhales. "Come in, we need to clear the air … and discuss everything."

"You had an opportunity for that," she replied, put out. "Now, I'll do things my way."

"There are some developments, Kenna, and you need to be privy to them."

Kenna? she wondered. *Who's this stranger I'm speaking with?* "Does this have to do with Kovalev, the riot, or Luhansk?"

"And Yuri Zelenko."

The double-decker bus roared, and with clean exhaust, it lumbered away. With a final glare at Kenna, Jenkins accelerated the police interceptor behind it, then passed.

"What was that … I couldn't hear because of a bus."

"It's time we talk about your Luhansk work," Thurnbull

offered.

"Tired of talking, sir," she said. "I have work to do if I'm going to help solve these murders."

Losing it, anger consumed Thurnbull, "If you want to report on sports for BNC, you'll come in!"

Kenna disconnected the call, accelerated into traffic, and screamed, "Don't tell me what to fucking do!"

*

In his office, Thurnbull stared at his cell phone, "Hannigan, are you there?"

His face turned ghost-like with anger. When he looked up, Corina stood in the open door. There was a long moment of silence, both evaluating the other, both waiting for a reaction. He calmed instantly. *Not in front of the troops,* he scolded himself.

"Contact Henson and have him track her phone, Corina," he said.

"He's looking for his girlfriend, sir. She's missing."

Don't tell me no! he screamed inside. Corina eased back to the door and stiffened.

"Dammit, everything over the story!" he said to himself. "It's supposed to be the other way around!"

Biting back hesitant fear, knowing there was nothing she

could do, Corina turned out. In shock, Thurnbull knew he'd lost control of this story. At the sideboard, he poured a whiskey and drank it in one gulp.

XXXI

Kenna brought the Honda to a stop at a traffic light. To her right, Victoria Station was well-lit, teeming with vehicles of all makes and models that off-loaded and picked-up travelers. The London landmark had seen millions of men and women shuffled off to war, had survived bombings during declared and undeclared wars, and had greeted millions of foreign visitors. Yet, hollowness ate at her stomach while watching the unknown faces, just as it had when she left the Blue Boar.

It was impossible for something to happen here without someone seeing it. Conversely, she had known many people who stared directly at something and never saw what happened. She had been trained to see and recall everything …

***

OUTSIDE BOSTON—13 YEARS AGO

Snow blanketed the field and forested area of Gran Lockwood's estate. Trees were barren, the only green on the evergreens. Wrapped for the cold and walking arm-in-arm with Gran Lockwood, Kenna had just celebrated her 18th birthday. It was the day Kenna revealed her calling in life;

she wanted to follow in her grandmother's footsteps.

Gran Lockwood stopped Kenna and cupped hands over her eyes. *'Your first lesson. Tell me what you see, leanbh.'*

'Blackness,' Kenna responded honestly.

Smiling with approval, Gran Lockwood continued, *'Describe what's around us ... use your other senses.'*

'The breeze is cold against my face, rustling the trees,' she said and lifted her foot. *'The ground is frozen; it crunches. Most of all, the silence ... no cars, no people, no animals.'*

'Anything else?'

'A hint of your perfume carried by the breeze.'

***

Goosebumps rose on Kenna's arms; her body shivered as it had that day. This was no longer just a story, no longer about a video. It was a struggle for survival. A policewoman approached and blew a whistle, waving. Kenna eased the Honda along Terminus Place past the station entrance. She weaved through car barriers, stopped off to the side, and lifted out the Yuri Zelenko police report:

Victim arrived on the Dover-Victoria Southeast train at 20:21. Indications are that victim left the station alone without personal belongings. As seen by a Security Guard for the construction works underway on Wilton Road ...

Kenna spun just as the policewoman approached. She accelerated along Terminus Place, then turned towards the office construction on the corner with Wilton. The site was surrounded by a tall metal security wall. She eased the Honda onto the sidewalk and stopped at car barriers under a streetlight. She lifted the police report:

... Indications are that the victim vaulted the temporary security fencing, suffering an ankle injury in the process. At the temporary boardwalk, the perpetrator fired several times, hitting the victim in the leg and chest. Cause of death was strangulation. Postmortem, a coupe de grâce was administered over the victim's left eye, trajectory indicating the shooter was righthanded. The weapon was .40 caliber and suppressed.

Kenna lowered the report and walked along the temporary security fence. In the distance, "Westminster Quarters" chimed from The Elizabeth Tower. She stood on a vehicle barrier and looked over the wall.

From all indications, the killing was random, a simple robbery that got out of control.

Kenna looked back at the report, then over the wall again, surprised. The location where Yuri Zelenko had been killed was clean, left without a trace of blood or any signs of a struggle. There was no crime scene tape, no markings where the body fell.

"Say, there, lass, what's yer business?" the security guard asked, illuminating her with a torch while approaching from the side.

Kenna jumped down. She reached for her press credentials that weren't there. She moved to the elderly man, ex-police, by his demeanor. She offered a hand.

"I'm Kenna Hannigan, BNC news," she said.

"Ah, the Yank that's been on the tele," he said, accepted her hand, and softened his attitude. "Seen ya doin' the report on the Russian buyin' the American football club. Sad that."

It no longer seemed worth the effort to correct people about Kovalev's nationality. "Were you on duty the night the man was killed here?"

"Aye, walked up right when the bloke went through the lad's pockets."

"So, was he a thief?" *That's what the report says.*

"Didn'a act like it, but he had a gun, and I wasn'a gonna wait to ask."

"Did you get a good look at the shooter?"

The security guard backed off a little. "Sorry, lass, I was told not to talk to anyone about this."

"I'm just trying to figure out if this killing was related to the one in Wembley."

"They's a long ways apart, lass."

"Both men were the same nationality, in London at the same time, and both killed. Too many similarities to be coincidental."

"Guess it won't hurt nothin'," he said. "Besides, I didn'a see anythin'."

"But you saw the killer."

"Not his face, just what he was wearing … a dark hooded jacket."

"A jacket with a zipper, not a jersey?" she asked.

"It was dark, but yeah, that's what it seemed."

Kenna opened her phone and pulled up the video from Wembley with the assailant leaning over her. She paused it and showed it to him.

"Something like this?"

"A hoody's a hoody," he said and nodded. "Yeah, like that, draw strings and all."

*

Riding away on the Honda, Kenna's mind echoed with the report. Two shots, strangulation, and a coup de grâce, not pretty and certainly not quick. The killer took his time, which seemed personal, and allowed time for interrogation.

She didn't know Yuri well, but Alistair Rensenhaus trusted him, which was good enough for her. Kenna believed the report was a fabrication, a politically doctored one at that. A random killing would not have involved a man running from his pursuer. A robbery victim would not run away from the safety of Victoria's crowd and security. *He wouldn't,* rang through her mind. There were no defensive wounds … only the bullets.

She looked at the report again. The first shot to the leg … *kept him from running.* The second, to the chest … *disabled him.* Strangulation during a brief interrogation … *silenced him.* Without an answer, or with one, a crushed larynx … *killed him.* The coupe de grâce in anger … *or to make a point.*

'That's been sealed by MI5,' DCI Attwood had said when she brought up Yuri's killing.

Whose side are you on, Barnaby? she asked herself.

XXXII

Svetlana and Lyuba walked hand-in-hand into an apartment bedroom fit for a Tzar, Kostyantyn Kovalev. Organized like a study in geometry, everything was positioned symmetrically. Linens and pillows on the king-plus bed bore the initials KVK. She walked along the dresser, easing her fingers along the masculine jewelry box, the cigar humidor, and a case for watches. There was no dust, not a smudge on the dresser mirror. Perfectionism equal to her own was one of the redeeming qualities that attracted Svetlana to him.

She rubbed the bedspread, then lifted her hand and smelled it. "Ah, Kostyantyn, such a grand lover but so misguided."

Lyuba extended an envelope. "As documented by Sir Clifton Toll."

Angered, Svetlana jerked it from her. "You read it?"

"I had to make sure it was genuine before I stole it," Lyuba said.

"How did you get it?" Svetlana asked. Something was off with Lyuba; she wanted to know what.

In a memory flash, *Lyuba stood under a dark overpass.*

Edgar stopped the Rolls Royce alongside her, handed her the envelope, and sped away.

"Even old men enjoy pleasures of the flesh," Lyuba said as if in a dream state. "And set in their ways, have habits that are easily followed."

Curiosity filled Svetlana. "If you've been to his residence, then you could access other information?"

"Of course," Lyuba said. "Have you forgotten how we met? Doing this was what brought us together."

"No, my dear," Svetlana corrected. "It is what saved your life."

Lyuba had not forgotten. After Medved finished his interrogation, Svetlana gave Lyuba an opportunity. Steal damning information on her superior officer. When Lyuba presented it, Svetlana used it against him. For all Lyuba knew, the man was still spending winters in Siberia.

Lyuba redirected the conversation. "Why are we here?"

"There's something in the safe I want," Svetlana said. "When his bodyguard arrives, we will have what the Ukrainian stole in Luhansk."

"Illya, you know him," Lyuba said more than asked.

"I arranged for him to be Kostyantyn's bodyguard through an associate in Luhansk. He has been loyal since we occupied Crimea."

"Where are the police and staff?" Lyuba wondered aloud.

"Such an inquisitive mind, my love," Svetlana said, embracing Lyuba. She motioned to the room's grandeur. "This grand chamber to a traitor's ego is now ours."

Lyuba controlled the excitement that filled her. She took Svetlana in her arms and kissed her passionately. Usually, the aggressor, Svetlana, was surprised and enjoyed the approach. Rapidly, she pulled Lyuba's clothes down as Lyuba disrobed her.

They fell onto the King-plus bed naked, kissing passionately. Svetlana lay back while Lyuba went down on her; she moaned with pleasure. The room door clicked. Looking up with pleasure in her eyes, Svetlana smiled:

"Ah, the surprise I promised."

The tall, handsome young waiter from the Mandarin Oriental Hotel entered the room. He paused for a moment, then smiled warmly and moved to the bed. Both women stood, kissed him, and removed his clothes.

On the nightstand, Svetlana's cell phone lit but did not ring on silent ... an incoming call, *"Medved"*. She was too occupied to notice.

*

Medved roared the Aston Martin through traffic, braking to slide around a corner. He punched the dash and passed slower traffic at an intersection. Over the car's phone speaker, it rang and rang, then went to voicemail.

"Leave a message," was Svetlana's recording, followed by a ding.

Frantically, Medved yelled into the microphone, "Svetlana, get out of the apartment! Shwetz may be on the way! I'll arrive as soon as traffic allows!"

Medved disconnected the call. Infuriating him, traffic came to a virtual standstill.

*

Approaching from the opposite direction, Oleksandr enjoyed the wind on his face. He thought of the warm summers of Odessa, driving through the countryside and flying kites with Nadia on the beach. How he longed for those days and wished he could reverse time. He would have left everything to have them with him now. They had been his entire life, all that mattered, but that was what he realized now. At the time, he had been too obsessed with work to realize it and too blind to see it.

With Kovalev dead, it left Svetlana and Medved, the two

258

that betrayed him. He would have preferred to kill both in the presence of the other, but they were surrounded by protection. One at a time suited him just fine … beginning with the woman who orchestrated it all.

XXXIII

The overcast night was black as pitch and soured Kenna's mood. She leaned the Honda onto a lazy, narrow street between dimly lit rows of brick tenements. She wondered if the lives of the people who occupied the buildings matched the monotony of construction. One after the other, all the exact same design. The thoughts did nothing to brighten her mood. Two laughing middle-aged couples crossed the street ahead of her.

Stick to solving crimes, not analyzing people, she thought. But analyzing people was exactly what she did. Crimes didn't commit themselves; people did. The bland, mechanical male voice in her ear broke the thought:

"In one hundred meters, your destination is on the right."

"Welcome to Whitechapel," she said to herself. "You out tonight, Mr. Ripper?"

She flipped off the Honda's headlamp, slowed, and eased to a stop at the curb. On the corner stood a four-story brick apartment building much in need of repair. Room lights dotted the façade like a dragon's eyes, glaring at her, daring her to enter. When she turned off the engine, the neighborhood was silent. A distant car engine broke it, a cat screeched in an alley, and a couple argued in an apartment.

"Always said you wanted the good life, Oles," she mumbled and swung off.

A light breeze whispered to unnerve her. A black cat scampered from the alley and ran towards the building. She imagined Edgar Allan Poe following it, penning his story, *"The Black Cat"*. She brushed off the curse of bad luck and walked for the building. So as not to tempt fate, though, she avoided the cracks in the street.

At the building entrance, she hesitated for a deep breath. Hairs on the nape of her neck bristled; goosebumps formed on her arms. She didn't recall ever hesitating … but she also didn't remember two days like these outside Luhansk. She opened the door.

Silence caressed the darkness in the bland foyer. She stepped inside to creaky floorboards. A dull streetlight through a window at the end of the hall laid a long, thin line of light to an aged staircase. *Yes, Poe is definitely here*, she thought. *Or is it the Ripper?*

A cool breeze brushed aside a ragged curtain and rattled a broken blind that held on by a single strand of fiber. Stairs creaked lightly as she climbed to the first floor, the second to her. A dull yellow ceiling light added to the disquiet in the air. At the top of the stairs, she tapped on the door and hesitated when it eased slightly open.

As if fingernails dragged across a chalkboard, the door hinge squawked when she pushed it fully open. The single room was all but empty, the toilet dark and silent. The only sound was the click of a bell alarm clock.

"Oles," she whispered, entering.

A sound outside the open window, like that of a rattling rubbish-bin. She jumped when the black cat lunged into the window, entered, and sat on the table, staring at her. She swallowed hard, *how many years bad luck?* She stepped forward, kicking an empty beer bottle across the floor. A breeze forced open the door with a creak, but her attention was forward.

"Oles," she mumbled.

Silent as a whisper, a shadow slipped in behind her. Mrs. Kohut's sinewy hand gripped Kenna's arm, startling her. Kenna sucked in a breath and lifted her chin high as a razor-sharp stiletto snapped against her throat. *The Ripper!* Eased against a wall, she remained silent.

"Why you here?" Mrs. Kohut asked with a thick Ukrainian accent.

"To help a friend," Kenna offered.

Mrs. Kohut held the knife firm. "Friend not come like

thief."

"I thought he might be in danger."

Kenna turned slowly to face her. Unafraid, Mrs. Kohut stared into her eyes. What Kenna saw surprised her … curiosity.

Mrs. Kohut eased her grip on the knife. "He go … Not know where. Think in plenty trouble."

"So, he said nothing?" Kenna asked, sensing the woman was not being truthful.

"Take what he come with, old backpack," Mrs. Kohut said. "Where you know from?"

"Luhansk, we worked together." *I know that backpack well,* Kenna thought.

"He say he put past behind; you should too, perhaps," Mrs. Kohut suggested in a kind way. "He hide to stay away from trouble … from you, I think."

"He isn't in trouble; he just needs his friends," Kenna said. "If he returns, tell him the woman born of fire wants to talk."

Mrs. Kohut's leery glare softened. Standing at the window, she watched Kenna walk from the building. They made eye contact when Kenna swung on the Honda and pulled on the helmet.

Kenna's gut wrenched, knowing there was only one man who could give her the answers she wanted. She stared at the apartment window and pulled on the riding gloves.

In the apartment, Mrs. Kohut lifted a cell phone and punched a speed dial number. "You had visitor."

*

Behind the wheel of the Brava, Bluetooth in his ear, Oleksandr steered around a parked vehicle, then turned at a street sign "Cliveden Place" on the corner of an upscale terrace house. He ignored a couple walking the opposite direction, puffed the last of a cigarette, and threw it out. Before exhaling, he pulled another from the pack.

"The Russian with the snake's eyes?" Oleksandr asked, exhaling.

"No, woman … from Luhansk, skinny with head of fire … American, I not remember."

"Interesting, she would be looking for me," Oleksandr said, looking at his phone. *So, that's who's been calling*, he thought. "The apartment building has been compromised. You know what to do."

"I pack now," Mrs. Kohut said and disconnected the call.

The street of Eaton Square made a loop around the two parks, traversing in front of the lavish terrace houses on both sides of the parks. Private mews for parking ran along the rear of the houses, with access on the side streets. The A3217 passed through the center of two parks that stretched the length of "Red Square".

Oleksandr eased the Brava off Eaton Square onto the lush, green, grassy area across the street from #50, Kovalev's home. He stopped in the dark shade of trees away from streetlights and ground out the cigarette in the overflowing ashtray. He turned off his cell phone and looked up at the building.

Svetlana leaned on the balcony door while the Waiter had sex with her from behind, both kissing Lyuba. Oleksandr smiled and turned off the GPS tracker.

"Kovalev was right, Svetlana," he mumbled to himself. "You never could separate business and pleasure."

Oleksandr stepped out. He pulled on the Kevlar jacket, then the two-shoulder holsters. At the rear of the Brava, he eyed the street and park all directions, then lifted out an IWI-Mini Uzi machinegun. He chambered a round, then pulled on a full-face stocking cap. He stepped into the street … *time to kill … or be killed.*

XXXIV

In the living room, with the glow of sexual satisfaction, Svetlana and the waiter relaxed in robes on the sofa. At the full bar, Lyuba poured shots of Beluga Gold Line vodka and opened a bottle of wine. Though pleased, Svetlana was anxious for Illya to arrive. It wasn't good practice to stay in the enemy's lair for long.

In the partially lit mews between the terrace houses, Oleksandr hurried through the shadows. Hugging the building, he climbed the steps to the rear door. With an inhale of hesitation, he lifted the pistols and screwed on suppressors. Hesitation with the pistols revealed the length of time since he used one; had hoped he never would again. A great inhale … *now is the time*.

He picked the door lock with little trouble and eased the door open. He stepped into the modern kitchen, eased the door closed, and paused. Laughter and light conversation from the front room drew his attention. He moved to the service door and paused briefly.

Life is cruel, never kind, he reminded himself. He eased the door open and moved out to the long, dark hallway.

In the open living room, Lyuba poured glasses of wine.

A distraction to the side caught her eyes: Svetlana's phone flashed *"Medved"*. She took it and the wine to Svetlana; she punched it to answer.

"Medved, we just—"

*

The Aston Martin roared past parked cars along Eaton Square. Medved pulled the Veresk submachine gun onto his lap and spun his head in recognition when he passed the Brava.

"Get out! Shwet's in the house!"

*

In the living room, Svetlana jerked a P-96 pistol from under a pillow and made panicked eye contact with Lyuba. Lyuba squatted behind the bar and lifted a paring knife. Instant fear filled the waiter; Svetlana pulled him down and slapped a hand over his mouth.

Svetlana yelled to the other room, "Intruder! Get in here now!"

Oleksandr lunged across the arched opening, fired, and rolled to the side. Svetlana fired too quickly and blew holes in a parlor chair and chunks from the marble columns. Oleksandr came up to a squat, firing over a chair. Svetlana pulled the waiter in front of her as a shield. Oleksandr took aim but hesitated.

At the far end of the room, a guard slammed the door open, gun leveled. Before he could acquire a target, Oleksandr fired and hit him in the chest. Using the bodyguard as a shield, Filipp ran in and fired continuously at Oleksandr's position until he reached Svetlana. Firing with a second pistol, Filipp pulled her across the room while Svetlana fired.

The waiter crawled behind the bar with Lyuba. Frantic beating on the front door, glass broke.

Oleksandr fired, winging Svetlana on the shoulder; she screamed. Filipp fired and hit Oleksandr in the flak vest, throwing him back to the floor. Fighting for air, he rolled up and aimed just as Filipp pulled Svetlana from the room.

Oleksandr jumped up as the front door broke open. Medved entered, firing the machine gun. Returning fire, Oleksandr maneuvered through the heavy furniture towards the bedroom.

In the bedroom, Filipp hurried Svetlana to the closet. She beat him off, rushed to the bed, and grabbed her large handbag. He threw clothes from the closet and opened a hidden door on the rear wall. When Svetlana joined him, he helped her down the dark steps.

Close to the bedroom entrance, Oleksandr fired the Uzi. A bullet grazed his shoulder above the Kevlar vest. He screamed and blindly returned fire. Medved threw himself behind the bar beside Lyuba.

"Stay here," he ordered, then pointed at the waiter, who shook with fear on the floor. "And take care of him."

Oleksandr ran, firing the Uzi at the bar. Wood, glass and alcohol bathed Medved, Lyuba, and the waiter. When the firing stopped, Medved jumped up and lifted his phone:

"Pyotr … Shwetz is coming out! Kill him!"

In the bedroom, Oleksandr reloaded the Uzi and jumped into the steep stairway down just as the door at the bottom swung shut. He took the steps down two at a time and threw open the door. Medved entered the stairway above and fired.

In the dark confines of the private parking garage, Oleksandr moved to the side. Bullets riddled the door. The Aurus Senat limousine roared from the end of the garage and crashed through the door.

Oleksandr ran in pursuit and reached the street to a light rain. The Aurus Senat roared away, zigzagging. He fired the Uzi. Bullets peppered the bullet-proof car with little effect. A car engine whined from behind; he spun while on the move for the tree cover of the park.

Medved ran into the street, firing. In the Eaton Square Coliseum, the two 21st-century gladiators fired at each other. Pyotr slid the Corsa to a stop twenty meters from the Aston Martin. The animals were unleashed in the Coliseum as Pyotr, Vanya, and the other Russian jumped out, firing. Distant sirens bit into the darkness. Outgunned, Oleksandr returned fire with the Uzi as he ran into the trees and bushes. Bullets riddled the other Russian; he dropped dead.

Staying in the shadows, Oleksandr reloaded the Uzi. He ran through the trees in a long arc towards the Brava. Determination filled his eyes, defying the heaviness in his legs and labored breathing.

Medved led the Russians into the trees, motioning them to spread out. Sirens approached rapidly, now from two directions. A shadow darted through the trees; they all fired.

Oleksandr ran and fired the Uzi. A bullet hit him in the side; he faltered and slammed against a tree. He spun and emptied the Uzi's clip towards the trees. He ran as best he could in full retreat.

Reaching the Brava, Oleksandr jumped in and started it. He shoved another clip into the Uzi. Medved appeared from the trees and fired. Oleksandr ducked as bullets blew holes through the windscreen and metal, missing Oleksandr by a hair. Medved's submachine gun emptied; he jerked out his pistol.

Accelerating past, Oleksandr fired the Uzi, spraying the area just as the others left the trees. A bullet hit Medved in the side; he went down. Another grazed Vanya's arm; he dropped his pistol. Pyotr fired as the Brava roared away.

Sirens echoed through the neighborhood. Pyotr and Vanya lifted Medved from the ground.

"Let's get out of here!" Pyotr yelled.

Medved tossed keys to Vanya. "Bring the Aston Martin."

The Corsa and Aston Martin sped away from the Brava, the sirens, and the flashing lights. Wearing only a bloody robe, the waiter ran into the night on the side street.

*

The sounds of battle gave way to approaching sirens. With a deep limp, bloody bandages around his midsection and leg, Illya hurried across the dark garage. Pistol drawn, he climbed the rear stairs, ran out of the bedroom, and into Kovalev's study. To his surprise, the safe was already open. He sensed more than heard movement from the night shadows.

"Seems we were both too late, Illya," the hooded man said and stepped from the shadow into a shaft of light from the street.

Recognition flashed across Illya's face; he lifted the pistol. The assassin shot him in the heart; life escaped Illya's eyes rapidly as he collapsed. Without urgency, the hooded assassin left the room. He hurried down the stairs, out the rear of the building, and into the mews.

A distant movement … he lifted the pistol and turned. Lyuba ran around a distant corner and shoved an envelope into her robe. The assassin jumped into a Jaguar F-Type and roared that direction, leaving behind the sirens and technicolor flashing of emergency lights on Eaton Square.

XXXV

Fighting for breath in great pain, Oleksandr passed the police interceptors that sped past in the opposite direction along the park. The Brava slowed and weaved; he jerked the wheel to avoid a parked car. At the end of Eaton Square, he eased off the Kevlar and tossed it aside.

"Lotta fuckin' good you did," he growled at the vest.

Checking his wounds while he turned onto A3217, Oleksandr pulled back blood. The street came in and out of focus. Headlights and streetlights blurred and brightened; a car honked, clear one moment, from the end of a tunnel a moment later. He swerved back to his lane, fighting to stay awake. He stopped, ripped away part of his shirt, and stuffed it against the side wound. He took a swig from a flask, lifted the phone, and hit a speed dial number.

"Leave a message; I'll call back," Kenna's recording said, followed by a beep.

"Athena, wherever you are, you aren't safe," Oleksandr forced out. "Come to my flat. We need to tackle this together."

Oleksandr bit back pain, disconnected the call, and accelerated into traffic.

Going too fast, Pytor slid the Corsa sedan along Grosvenor Gardens and turned onto a one-way street the wrong way. Headlights and horns of a lorry met him. He swerved, sideswiped a parked car, and bounded headlong towards the park. The Corsa crashed through the fence surrounding the park. Pytor did not slow and sped through the grassy commons past the Jonathan Kenworthy sculpture.

The Corsa crashed through the fence on the opposite side of the park. Screaming pedestrians bolted in all directions as the Corsa bottomed out on the sidewalk in a shower of sparks, fishtailed, and power-slid onto the street.

In control, Pytor accelerated the Corsa into traffic on the street.

"Had your fun now?" Medved yelled, bleeding in the rear seat. "Get me to the embassy!"

*

Driving the Aurus Senat limousine, Filipp sliced through heavy traffic like a surgeon. He never used the horn; there was no need. London's traffic either allowed you to breathe or suffocated you. The Aurus Senat was powerful enough to accelerate around trouble and nimble enough to avoid it. But sometimes, like tonight, the only thing … patience.

"Why are you slowing?" Svetlana screamed.

"Traffic, ma'am," he offered. "I'll find a way around it."

With the flashing lights and sirens behind them, Filipp steered the limousine through a busy roundabout. Covered by a jacket, blood on her face, Svetlana's head was on his lap.

"Are you alright, director? Are—"

"Yes! Get me to the embassy!" Svetlana screamed, angry at herself more than Filipp.

"For now, stay down. It's not far."

Filipp turned onto Kensington Gore along the southern edge of Kensington Gardens. Several more police cars passed, lights flashing, sirens blaring. None saw the evidence of bullet pockmarks on the rear metal and impact spiderwebs in the rear window.

XXXVI

Kenna eased the Honda through the maze of London's streets, occasionally wiping rain and overspray from the helmet visor. There was no moon, which seemed appropriate. Clear skies weren't part of this thriller in Luhansk or in London. She swallowed hard; it was eerie, out of an Arthur Conan Doyle novel. She desperately wanted to turn the page and end this nightmare.

Confronting the world's most powerful publishing magnate is your destiny, she thought, *pushing you forward at Papa's breakneck speed.* She frowned at her choice of thoughts.

Thinking of the possible consequences, she had hesitated at confronting Toll. It was her father who taught her to always meet the unknown head-on, though he had told her to '*be a man.*' She wanted answers about Alistair Rensenhaus for Adelaide … and for herself. The deeper she was drawn into this case, it seemed ever more relevant.

Her heart was heavy … Adelaide. She hadn't reported to work; no one had heard from her. Call after call brought only the bawl of an unanswered cell phone and a voicemail message. Fear crept into Kenna. She, not Adelaide, was the constant in this equation, the video, and BNC ... with everything leading to Sir Clifton Toll.

'You have no choice, leanbh,' Gran Lockwood had told her years ago. *'Once you cross the line, you accept what will happen as inevitable. If you have chosen to fight, you must follow through until you find all the answers ... the truth.'*

Of course, Kenna thought. But diving headlong into a fight had gotten Gran killed in Virginia. It was a lesson learned, no matter how cruel or hard to accept. *Don't make the same mistake; accept it and move on!* she scolded herself.

It was the last word of Gran's wisdom that hit the hardest ... *truth*. But doubt lingered at the edge of hell's abyss. A great deal of the spark that ignited her during her last conversation with Thurnbull was now gone. But there was no time to wallow in doubt.

She parked in front of the grand residence, immediately realizing Sir Clifton was a man who hungered for opulence, a contradiction to his outer shell at BNC. The home was a display of power and influence, a man who wanted all and demanded control of the most powerful weapon in the free world ... the press.

Trying unsuccessfully to conceal her wound dressings, she approached the front gate. A chill went through her as rain and fog thickened the air. A bright security light penetrated the sullen grey and illuminated her. She looked up to a security camera and rang the bell.

"Mr. Holmes would be pleased," she mumbled as the door unlocked and opened.

"Ms. Hannigan," Graves said in his best Boris Karloff. "He is expecting you."

He is? she wanted to say but didn't.

Graves unlatched the gate and held it open. His scowl followed her into the foyer, where he removed her overcoat and directed her up a sweeping grand staircase. Portraits of men and women lined the walls, yet none were family. *There's a story in that,* she thought.

The Victorian furniture's formality was appropriate here, though not to her liking. Several round-faced glass China hutches held ancient crystal and silver service settings, Oriental jade statuettes, and a collection of carved ivory, which she was fairly certain was illegal. Original oils lined the hallway: Botticelli's *Birth of Venus*, a *Self-Portrait* by Rembrandt, Valazques's *Maids of Honor*, and several she believed had been reported as lost or stolen during Hitler's Linz Project during the Second World War. *Are they originals?*

Graves opened the door to Toll's study. "Sir Clifton will be along momentarily, ma'am."

She entered, immediately humbled. Power filled this room with its grand décor and heavy wood and stone treatments. Eyes watched her from the fireplace mantel, porcelain statuettes of Odin, Thor, Frey, and several other Deities of Norse Mythology. Lust for history turned her to a glass-covered lectern and a large leather-bound book that lay open to the first handwritten, badly yellowed and frayed page, charred along the edges as if burned. The writing, however, was legible ... old German, the signature a slanted scribble with slashing abruptness in its capitals.

"The diary of a madman, Ms. Hannigan," Sir Clifton Toll said as he stepped through the doors in a three-piece Savile Row suit. Graves closed the door softly for effect.

"Adolf Hitler," she said as much as asked with a wince. "Is it authentic?"

"Some have argued not," he said, raising his aged but powerful hands to the room. "But, as you see, I entertain no falsehoods."

"Nor do I," she said.

"I see you are injured."

"Still on two feet, though," she said. "Why was the attack

that put me in this state edited from the riot piece?"

"A woman who comes to the point. Quite unusual but refreshing," Toll said. "I stopped nosing around the cutting room floor long before the advent of computers, Ms. Hannigan."

Toll moved to the sideboard and poured a whiskey neat. He smiled beyond the rim of the glass that touched his lips. *A challenge, this one,* he thought. After a sip, he settled the glass to the slab of granite desk and stared into her eyes … the same, he noted, that he saw in his own mirror daily.

"Shall we forego the formalities of getting to know one another," he suggested. *We already do intimately.* She agreed with a nod. "Tell me about this Luhansk video."

"A quid pro quo, perhaps," she said. "You sent me the police report on Yuri's killing … why?"

"There is an obvious link with Kovalev, Ms. Hannigan," he replied. "I want you to find it."

That he had not offered a drink did not escape her. It wasn't unusual but convinced her of something she hadn't considered. She was possibly facing the greatest gamesman of all, save Gran Lockwood. *Let the games begin.*

"Alistair reported to you about my video, no doubt," she said. "But he didn't get it out of Luhansk; there was no time before the Russians attacked the office."

"He mentioned a secret meeting in Luhansk," he said. "Right out of a John Le Carré novel, eh?"

"Textbook Russian FSB clandestine work, Sir Clifton," she said, avoiding the anger that filled her. "I believe my video provides the link between Kovalev's and Zelenko's murders."

"This *'textbook Russian FSB clandestine work'* interests me, Ms. Hannigan," he countered. "Please elaborate."

"A lot happened during that time. I need the video to refresh my memory."

"Yes, your injuries during the Russian assault." Toll smiled inside. *I like you, Ms. Hannigan.* "This video … what do you propose to do with it … if you locate it?"

She ignored his question. "You ordered Alistair's post-mortem in Ukraine; why not bring him here?"

"With the condition of his body," he said and paused. "You saw him … I believed it more prudent for the dirty work done there."

That's curious … 'dirty work', she thought. She had never told anyone she had seen Alistair's body pulled from the fire, not even Wiggy. *Why would he say that? To provoke another reaction?*

"I'm curious … why?"

"To protect his daughter, of course." He sipped the whiskey. "The video, Ms. Hannigan?"

"I won't know until I compare it with the Halibeck International folder."

Toll tensed, surprised but equally impressed. "A folder, you say?"

"I believe you were expecting Kovalev to deliver it," she said, pausing. "A quid pro quo on Halibeck International's activities in Ukraine and Russia."

Toll chuckled and swirled the whiskey around the glass with the agility of a brain surgeon. Given to temptation, he tilted the glass to his lips and drank the contents swiftly.

"You haven't seen this folder, yet you speak as if you have."

"No, I speak as if someone told me about it."

"Hearsay, then. You are a simple, finite creature, Ms. Hannigan," Toll said, not believing it for a moment and hoping to spark a rebuttal that did not come. *Brilliant self-control, Ms. Hannigan,* he thought, poured a whiskey neat and handed it to her. "The folder … to some, its value could be highest in its silence, if you follow."

He doesn't have it! She thought. "Perhaps we could

compare notes."

She has the video! He thought. "All in good time."

No threats, no innuendos about spending the balance of my days in the Tower of London, she thought. *That part of the game is to come.*

"And should I come across this folder first?" she asked.

"It's not a competition, Ms. Hannigan," he challenged.

"My grandmother said that every case is a competition … of right vs. wrong."

"I knew your grandmother, which was the main reason you were hired in Luhansk."

"Very large footsteps to fill, Sir Clifton," Kenna said, knowing she never could.

Toll rang a bell. Kenna remembered similar words from Alistair Rensenhaus in Luhansk. She finished the whiskey as Graves opened the door.

"I believe we understand each other completely, Ms. Hannigan," Toll said in finality, then to Graves, "Please show our guest out."

Without valediction, she walked out. Words escaped her. Confusion raced through her mind. *What the hell just happened? A vote of confidence or a warning?* She hurried down the steps ahead of Graves, grabbed her coat and helmet, and stepped out into the night rain.

She fumbled with the key to switch on the Honda and started it. For only an instant, she looked to the first-floor study window. Caesar stood over her and lifted his glass. Without acknowledging, she lowered the visor and flipped on her cell phone. She punched voicemail.

"Athena forgot to say, they put a couple bullets in me," Oleksandr's labored voice recording said. *"Could use your help."*

With anger bordering on hysteria, she roared into the darkness.

XXXVII

Deep within the bowels of the Embassy of the Russian Federation was a dedicated medical clinic, complete with operating bed and equipment. The facility was like any other sterile environment, brightly lit and all white, with stainless steel equipment trays and trollies. Many injured and wounded Russians had been treated here since the new embassy's opening.

Just because Perestroika succeeded didn't mean that spying on the West had stopped. In many regards, it intensified. Before the turn of the millennium, Russia had an economy to rebuild. And the fastest way to accomplish that was to steal technology. Such activities had been Medved's specialty when he entered the FSB. Combined with his predilection to killing, such expertise made him perfect for this job.

Awake and uncomfortable, Medved lay on the bed, partially covered by a sheet. A middle-aged Russian doctor and accompanying female nurse were annoyed with their uncooperative patient. The doctor had dealt with men such as Medved before and liked it no more now than the other times.

"The wound's not bad, Medved, but if you want me to stop the bleeding, lie still," the doctor insisted.

Medved's angry glare said how he felt. Stitched shoulder in a clean medical shirt, Svetlana walked in, ready for a confrontation. The volcano of mutual hatred erupted.

"Why did you go after Shwetz when I ordered you to find the reporter?" Svetlana demanded.

Medved's frustration mounted; he lifted to an elbow. "I don't report to you."

The doctor pushed Medved back to the bed. "Fight when I'm finished."

Medved ignored him and threw off his grip. "He caught you with your pants down, Svetlana. You need to pay more attention to business."

"And you, tricked by a phone swap," Svetlana said.

"You both survived. You should be happy about that," the doctor insisted.

"Shut up!" "Stay out of this!" Medved and Svetlana insisted at the same time.

"It's impossible to work under these conditions," the doctor said and moved away with the nurse. "Tell me when you want to continue."

"Do it now, doctor!" Medved demanded, then to

Svetlana said, "I'll kill them both. We now know they'll be together."

"You will do what I say!" Svetlana demanded.

Medved calmed. "My orders are from the president and don't concern you."

"Lyuba recovered the folder from Kovalev's safe," Svetlana insisted.

"She's here? You've seen it?" he snapped.

"I'm waiting for her call," Svetlana snapped back but understood Medved's point. "Once I secure the folder, my mission moves ahead!"

Dull silence filled the room. The doctor stepped forward and continued his work. Medved's objective finally hit Svetlana. Though angry with his deceit, she was relieved at his insistence on what he saw as his part of this mission. Just as she had planned it.

"You've never been after the documents," she thought aloud, as if surprised, which she wasn't. "Yuri Zelenko stole something else in Luhansk."

"That links everything," Medved said. "It wasn't on him when he arrived in London."

"So, we are right where we have always been … waiting," she said, as if at a loss, which she was not.

"Complete your mission, Svetlana. I will complete mine."

A little more time to keep him in the dark, Svetlana thought. "Then, do your job, Alexi. Don't return to the embassy until both have been eliminated."

Svetlana walked from the room with a mild Cheshire grin. In the hallway, Filipp came to her with a small, electronic black box in hand.

"How they knew where you were, ma'am," he said. "I have no idea when or how they got it on the car."

Svetlana examined the tracker. "A GPS real-time tracker … very sophisticated, Filipp. Put it on one of the other cars and have a man drive around the city."

In the surgery room, the doctor sighed with relief and tied off the last stitch. With discomfort, he ignored as best he could. Medved sat up on the edge of the bed while the nurse covered the stitches with a wound patch.

"I don't suppose it would do any good to tell you to take it easy for a few days," the doctor offered.

Medved didn't answer and accepted a clean shirt from Pyotr. Anger at a boiling point, Medved walked gingerly from the clinic with Pyotr.

"We could have captured the journalist, sir," Pyotr

offered.

"In time, Pyotr," Medved said. "She worked with both Rensenhaus and Zelenko in Luhansk. It's just possible he sent it to her."

Medved had heard stories of the young female American reporter behind the lines in Luhansk but had brushed them off as hearsay. He no longer would. It was time to learn more about this reporter … and why she was in Luhansk.

"What about Shwetz, sir?" Pyotr asked.

"Two cars, two men in each, Pyotr," he ordered.

"Where to, sir?"

"I'll know after I speak with Feodor," Medved said and slapped Pyotr on the shoulder.

Pyotr spun and hurried away. From the opposite direction, Feodor hurried for Medved with proud exuberance filling his face. Feodor spoke loud before reaching Medved:

"I recovered the numbers from the phone left at the warehouse. Rather sloppy of him."

"Get to the point, Feodor."

"He's gotten calls, which means he didn't inform others he was abandoning the phone." Feodor cleared his throat and relished this moment. "There are three numbers called recently. But there are several voicemails that will interest you."

Feodor handed Medved a piece of paper. For the first time that Feodor could recall, Medved looked up and smiled.

"Kenna Hannigan," Medved said evenly. "I was right, she's been working with Shwetz since Luhansk."

With a crumpled brow, Feodor asked, "So, he really is alive?"

"Through a coward's ruse, Feodor," Medved said. *One I will correct,* he thought.

"I tracked her phone and just got a hit … in Whitechapel … and she's on the move."

"I'll be in the car."

Medved and Feodor ran opposite directions.

XXXVIII

Blending with the darkness, the Brava rattled to a stop on the side street of Oleksandr's apartment building. In great pain, he eased from the vehicle and slung the Uzi over a shoulder. He looked up at the building with emotion … *not a mansion … but home.* Where he wanted to live in peace … until his nemesis interrupted his life … again. Now, everything had changed, and serenity had once again become chaos.

With great effort, he took the steps up to the building. It had been a long time since … the wounds reminded him why he left Luhansk.

He stepped into the empty foyer lit only by a dull flickering streetlight outside a filthy window. He glanced up the stairs, *give me strength.* With a slight grunt of pain, he grabbed the rail and took the step up. Climbing Everest without a sherpa, without oxygen, one step at a time … the fear of falling … no, of failing.

To hell with this, he growled at himself and forced his legs to take him up the stairs. At the top, he wanted to celebrate. Logic said, *get to the bed, call for help.* He reached for the room door and entered. The tick of the bell alarm clock echoed in the darkness. Outside the window, the black cat scratched the pane and screeched.

"Mrs. Kohut!" he said softly, believing he had yelled. Muscles weakened; he faltered to the side, not remembering the earlier phone call. "Mrs. Kohut?"

Oleksandr staggered and collapsed. He fell onto the unmade bed, gripped the bedspread but couldn't keep hold. He tumbled against the table. It crashed to the floor; beer bottles rolled away; the round bell alarm clock landed next to him … tick, tick, tick.

He stirred, angry and in pain … *shut the fuck up* … he slapped the clock across the floor and stared at his bloody hands. The streetlight outside the window flicked on and off, maddening him … he screamed, glaring at the clock … tick, tick, tick.

***

LUHANSK, UKRAINE—TWO YEARS BEFORE

In the destroyed neighborhood, on hands and knees, Oleksandr screamed, throwing aside the rubble of war with bloody hands. Tears streaked his face; beside him, a destroyed and half-buried bicycle; its rear wheel spinning, ticking. In the ground, a small hand appeared, then an arm; he clawed at the debris with great urgency.

'*Nadia! Nadia!*' he screamed.

A face appeared … Nadia, covered in blood, not breathing. He pulled her up, hugging her, and howled like a wounded wolf.

***

In the apartment, streetlight glimmered against Oleksandr's blank eyes. The alarm clock ticked. He reached out, but not for the clock … for Nadia. On the windowsill, the black cat shivered off the light rain.

At the rear of the building in the alley, a streetlight flickered a final time and popped out. Soaked from the ride, Kenna swung off the Honda across the side street. She looked at the rusted Brava pickup and glared up the rusty metal fire escape, remembering.

"Haven't done this since Luhansk," she whispered to herself.

She climbed the creaking fire escape, recalling the automatic weapons and explosions that had chased her to the rooftop two years before. On the first-floor landing, she slid a knife under the window to unlock it, pushed it up, and stepped inside.

On the floor of the apartment, Oleksandr jerked fitfully, struggling with the images that invaded his mind. A noise …

panic … he snapped upright and slammed the bed against the wall. He inhaled deeply, lifted blood from the side wound, and leaned against the bed. He lifted the bloody Glock pistol and checked the clip, empty. He tossed it and reached for another in his vest.

The hallway was empty and silent. Floorboards creaked with Kenna's steps. A door hinge squawked with a light breeze. She froze against the wall, then hurried past several doors. She pressed an ear against the last door before the staircase and knocked lightly.

Explosions filled Oleksandr's mind. He pulled himself to the edge of the bed. With great emotion, he mumbled, "Nadia … I'm sorry, my love."

Pain bit into him; he buckled and fell against the chair. He raised the pistol, frantically trying to insert a new clip. Vision faded in and out…

"Job's not done … should have …"

With shaking hands, Oleksandr tried to insert the clip. The explosion … no, a knock at the door; the handle clicked. Panic, weak, delirious …

"Nadia?" he asked, faltering.

Kenna stuck her head inside the room. "Oles?"

"Athena, they're coming," he forced out.

Oleksandr dropped the clip when the door opened. Kenna entered hesitantly, then in a rush. She knelt at his side, comforting him as much as checking his condition.

"Oles, come on, we hafta get you outta here."

"Athena," he said, delirious. "They want Nadia."

In a memory flash, Kenna relived *the explosion that sent Nadia into the great beyond.* With a deep heart, she helped Oleksandr stand; he yelled with pain.

"They already took her," she whispered in sadness.

Outside the window, three cars slid to a stop in front of the building. Medved and Pyotr stood from the Aston Martin; Vanya and a Russian guard stepped from a Corsa. Two armed Russians stood from a second Corsa. Medved waved the men to join him.

"They're here!" Kenna said, helping Oleksandr towards the door.

"Go … leave me," was his weak reply.

"We've been through too much, you old bastard."

"Old? Who you callin' old?" he objected, rejuvenating him.

Kenna helped Oleksandr out the door. They hurried towards the open window at the end of the hall. With Russian voices in the front, Kenna helped Oleksandr out to the fire escape landing. She turned back when the front door of the building burst open. Not hesitating, she stepped out.

At the bottom of the fire escape, Kenna ran across to the Honda. Oleksandr faltered and sat heavily.

Medved, Pytor and two Russians rushed into the apartment. The cat scampered out the window. He looked out the window at the side street. Two Russians walked along below and paused to examine the Brava pickup.

"He's here somewhere," Medved demanded and moved for the bathroom. "Check the other apartments."

Vanya and the other Russian hurried from the room…

In the alley, the two Russians saw Oleksandr, startled, and pulled weapons. Oleksandr saw them at the same moment. Something snapped inside, and with precise dexterity, he shoved a clip into the Glock and rolled to the side.

"Halt!" one of them yelled and fired into the air. "Stay where you are!"

Across the street, in the shadows, Kenna started the Honda.

Inside, Medved and Pyotr rushed from the room to the stairs down.

On the side street, both Russians turned on Oleksandr

and fired, hitting the building alongside him. Oleksandr's bullet hit a Russian; he faltered. The other Russian tripped over his falling comrade and fired wildly before hitting the pavement. Oleksandr fired, hitting him in the chest. Helmet dangling from the handlebars, Kenna accelerated across the street.

"Let's go!" she yelled. Oleksandr swung onto the Honda behind her.

"Should'a brought a car," he said softly.

At the front door of the apartment building, Medved ran onto the sidewalk. Kenna accelerated the Honda past. He drew down, but his vehicles blocked his line of fire. He ran to the street and aimed the pistol …

The black cat screamed and jumped onto the Aston Martin's hood, startling Medved for a moment. As Kenna swerved … he fired and missed.

Kenna leaned into the corner, then opened the throttle through heavy night shadows. Oleksandr held on but weakened. When the other Russians ran onto the street, there was no sign of the motorcycle.

Medved lifted his phone. "Feodor, any signal?"

"Yes, sir, going east from your location," Feodor responded on speaker.

On the Honda, Kenna slowed as they approached a busy roundabout and pulled on the helmet. Oleksandr tapped her shoulder.

"I need your phone."

"Not now," she objected.

She strapped the helmet while avoiding traffic. Oleksandr rifled her pockets and lifted her phone. He punched in a number and waited for an answer.

"On the way and need the doctor," he said and disconnected the call.

Kenna leaned the Honda into a busy roundabout and was about to ask about the call when Oleksandr tossed the phone into the fountain in the center.

"What are you doing?" she objected.

"That's how they tracked us, Athena," he said. "Now, unless you want Medved up your ass, get on with it!"

There's that name again, she thought and yelled, "Who the fuck is Medved?"

*

Pyotr started the Aston Martin; Medved's phone rang. He answered and listened. Dejected, he slapped the window.

"Signal just went dead, Pyotr."

Pyotr stopped and waved for the others to pull alongside. Vanya stopped the Corsa at his door.

Medved screamed into the phone, "Do a background. I want to know where she's been over the past two years." He turned to Vanya. "Go through that apartment. Shwetz might have left something that would tell us where he went."

*

On a motorway heading east, Kenna reached back with deep concern, trying to hold Oleksandr upright as he weakened.

"Once again, Oles, we prisyádka with the Russians."

"Better than theirs," he forced out. "Gives us … advantage."

"Not with you shot to hell."

"We can … fix that," he exhaled hard. "Limehouse Basin, Athena."

A smile inched across Kenna's face. "The captain … it's been a very long time."

A glare of confidence replaced doubt, and Kenna accelerated the Honda along the busy motorway.

XXXIX

In the overcast darkness of night, Kenna slowed the Honda and turned at a streetlight into Limehouse Basin. She eased the bike past a row of brick homes with attached storage units. The area was easy on the eyes, clean, not what one might expect in an East End working boat basin. Captain Evhen sat on a bucket at an open storage door; he stood and opened it fully. She stopped alongside and shut the Honda down. Evhen grabbed Oleksandr and lifted him from the rear with a grunt of pain.

"Miracle, he didn't fall off," she said.

"Not a miracle, Athena … determination," Oleksandr said between gritted teeth. "Lotta … work to do."

"Not for a while, Oles," she ordered.

Oleksandr howeled with pain when Evhen helped him towards the storage door. Kenna swung off and pushed the Honda behind Evhen as they entered the storage unit.

"Always chargin' in like the bear he is, eh Red," Evhen said to Kenna.

"What the hell happened, anyway?" Kenna asked.

"Think ya best save that for later, red," Evhen said. "But

Medved's a slippery sod, he is."

"Medved, everyone keeps mentioning him," she stated. "Who is he?"

"FSB, Athena," Oleksandr forced out. "Talk … later."

The riot and the Russian attacker … Medved … flashed across her memory. *My violent Russian friend is FSB,* she thought. *Now, it made sense.* She thought of Toll and wondered why he hadn't mentioned that the Russian Security Service was involved. Had he not known? She didn't believe that for an instant. *Dear God, the FSB,* she thought, *not again.*

"Do you have petrol, Captain Evhen?" she asked, leaning the Honda onto a kickstand.

"Cars don't run on air, Red," he said. "I'll take care of it once we've gotten our wounded warrior help."

"Where's the nearest hospital?"

"Other side of the flat," Evhen said and pointed to a door.

Both helping Oleksandr, Evhen led them to a door out of the storage room. When he threw it open, the smell of mold and dust, not fish, filled Kenna's nostrils. A tingle of unfamiliarity raised the fine hairs on her arms. The modified apartment living room was a sidewalk from the water's edge. Leaving little room to maneuver, it was filled with nets, lines, hooks, tackle, fish heads, and the jaws of prize catches. She couldn't make it out, but something told her this wasn't a working shop; it was organized chaos … for show.

"Not much different from Crimea, eh, Captain Evhen?" Kenna asked, assisting Oleksandr around the battered remains of an old ship's wooden helm.

"Just a lifetime, Red," he responded.

"Only man in London … we can trust," Oleksandr said weakly.

"That makes two," Kenna said, thinking of Wiggy. "Why didn't you ever contact me?"

"Nearly got me killed …" Oleksandr forced out, then breathed heavily. "Yer obsession … with Beck."

"He murdered my grandmother," Kenna said, not backing down. "Like your obsession over the Russian you call Medved."

She saw Alister Rensenhaus's face once again. At the same time, she heard Toll's words of advice: *'To some, its value could be highest in its silence, if you follow.'* Indeed, she did … and didn't like it if his intention was to hide the truth.

Oleksandr was right. Luhansk and the search for Beck had fueled her fervor, which became fanatic obsession compounded by trauma, and drove her to the brink of self-destruction. Consumed by that black hole of rage, she missed the inside game ... that she realized only now was Sir Clifton Toll's game ... until it was nearly too late. He had capitalized on her youthful zeal but had discounted her professionalism and work ethic. Sir Clifton had obviously not been trained by Dame Fiadh Dougherty-Lockwood.

They walked from the apartment into the still and silent night. The light over the walkway was out ... *by design, no doubt,* Kenna thought and inhaled the water. Dark and void of people, working and pleasure boats filled the basin, moored port-to-starboard. Along the apartments, they were moored bow-to-stern. A dim light flicked on from the salon of the aged fishing boat at the front of Evhen's flat. The metal gangway was old and rattled as they helped Oleksandr across.

There was nothing fancy about this boat. It was designed to look like a working boat, but Kenna sensed it was something entirely different. Unlike the air, it did not smell of dead fish. The deck was strangely void of debris, one would expect. There were no amenities, only a single round plastic table and four plastic chairs. It was, as well, void of a working fishing boat's equipment: no tackle, no nets, even the winches were for show. Evhen and Kenna helped

Oleksandr off the gangway, onto the deck, and to the steps below.

At the bottom, wearing a doctor's whites and a stethoscope over her neck, Mrs. Kohut stood patiently. Taken aback initially, Kenna nodded, understanding.

"My scalpel's waitin', Bear."

Oleksandr stirred, though somewhat delirious. "Don't let her … cut on me. God knows … what she'll take out."

"When did ya start believin' in God again?" Evhen asked.

"Bear, me doctor fees come cheap, but also come with me speeches. Ye know that," Mrs. Kohut said with a mouth of crooked, yellow-stained teeth. "Been fixin' this animal since we was kids? Ain't never been as bad as some of the men I pulled Russian lead out-a in Luhansk."

"No different … tonight," Oleksandr said in pain.

Mrs. Kohut met them at the bottom of the steps and did a cursory observation of Oleksandr's wounds. She pointed into a dimly lit room. Stepping inside, Kenna noticed this was no surgical ward or operating room. It was a room that also acted as a mess hall, a gambling den, a bar, or for any other purpose. They eased Oleksandr onto a wood *'operating table'*. To the side, a high fish cleaning table held a doctor's tools in a plastic tray.

"Taken more than a few chunks-a lead outta these two, sweetie," Mrs. Kohut said with full sincerity. "All balls, but no brains ta move outta a bullet's way."

"Kina hard to see 'em comin', love," Evhen said.

Mrs. Kohut placed an oxygen mask over Oleksandr's mouth and inserted an IV in his arm. She checked his vitals and slid the equipment stand close. Her concentration was fully on the work ahead while she spoke:

"Gettin' close to yer nine lives, Bear."

Before Oleksandr could respond, she injected him. His eyes fluttered; within seconds, he drifted to sleep. She taped his eyes shut and turned to Kenna.

"How ya holdin' up, sweetie?"

"Saw worse in Luhansk," was Kenna's solemn reply.

"Aye, we all did," Mrs. Kohut agreed.

"Always given me the worst job," Evhen objected.

"I don't remember you," Kenna said.

Mrs. Kohut patted Oleksandr's chest and motioned to Evhen. "Too busy patchin' the likes-a these two … came to the UK with this hunk, me brother."

"Brother?" Kenna said, surprised. "I didn't—"

"Ya don't know much for bein' a nosey reporter," Mrs.

Kohut responded and turned to the work ahead. "Now, be gone with ya. Me and Evi got work to do."

Wearing a surgical gown, Evhen joined them. He lifted the ripped shirt from Oleksandr's wound. Blood sprayed across his gown; he reached for the equipment tray.

"He's tellin' us what we gotta fix first, Evi," Mrs. Kohut said without emotion. "Pinch that off so's he don't bleed out."

While Evhen and Mrs. Kohut tended to Oleksandr, Kenna walked up the steps. The madness that began with a simple interview … no, Wiggy was right. This madness began long before she went to Luhansk in search of Anson Beck.

XL

The fishing boat salon was dark, with the same frugal decorating scheme as the balance of the vessel. Fixed benches ran along the sides; in the center were four plastic chairs around a plastic table. Kenna reached into the backpack but turned to a small television on the serving bar that separated a small galley. Its screen flashed with a strobing effect, changing scenes from a newsroom to on-location reports. She turned up the volume.

"And now to Stephanie, on location in Belgravia," a smiling boyish news anchor said.

Kenna was fixated as the events unfolded. Police stood at the plastic crime scene tape around Kovalev's apartment. A large crowd of observers and news people confronted them. The familiar crime scene-suited forensic experts entered with their tools of the trade. Others walked the street, placing plastic evidence tents at spent cartridge casings and the pool of blood where the Russian fell. A coroner's wagon hauled the dead Russian away. Cameras and phones flashed from every direction.

The television camera focused on a very attractive Black Female reporter holding a microphone. She listened to something in her earpiece, then smiled into the camera. *Three, two, one ...*

"This apartment in Eaton Square was the scene of a major gun battle earlier tonight, possibly between rival Eastern European drug gangs. We have seen one body in the street and a second brought out. Details are sketchy at this time ..." Stephanie paused, turning to a disturbance.

The mob of reporters behind her pressed towards the apartment. Stepping from the front door, DCI Attwood wore a crime scene protective suit. Though without sleep, he didn't show it. DS Jenkins followed, the signs of overwork darkening her eyes and expression. Attwood blinked against the bright mobile crime scene lights and stopped at the bottom of the steps to a barrage of questions and camera flashes.

"It looks as though DCI Attwood of MIT is giving a statement," Stephanie stated the obvious.

In a sudden rush, she followed the other lemmings towards the crime scene tape. The camera zoomed on Attwood at the head of the semicircle of reporters, all extending microphones, cell phones, and recorders like fans wanting a star quarterback's autograph and words.

"We have confirmation that the building behind was owned by Kostyantyn Kovalev—" Yelled questions

interrupted him.

So, that's where you've been, Oles, Kenna thought.

Attwood ignored the questions and continued, *"We have three confirmed dead. One was a suspect from the Kovalev killing earlier, his bodyguard who had suffered wounds at the stadium."*

Illya there, but why? Kenna wondered.

"Do you have his name?" "Why was he in the flat?" "Did he kill the others?" "What was his connection to the Kovalev killing?" "Was anyone else involved?" the reporters yelled in unison.

The questions continued as the reporters ignored Attwood's raised hand. Kenna had heard enough, as she was positive Attwood had, but she had an advantage … and turned down the volume.

She unzipped her bloody riding leathers and reached inside her backpack. As she lifted out the laptop, the courier envelope fell onto the table. She had forgotten about it and lifted it. Curious, she pulled the label across to open it. A memory stick wrapped in paper by an elastic band fell out. On the paper was printed in Yuri's handwriting: "Woman Born of Fire."

Staring at it, frozen for the moment, her heart raced. She

snapped open her laptop and turned it on. *Come on, come on, start …* she punched in her password. *Go, go, go!*

With shaking hands, she inserted the memory stick. The screen morphed into a phone selfie of Yuri Zelenko in a small, messy office. Kenna smiled at Yuri's infectious grin, then saddened, knowing she would never again see it in the flesh. He panned the phone around the room.

"Kenna, I pray this finds you well. As you see, not much has changed," Yuri said, paused, and the smile faded to a serious scowl. *"What follows is your video the night beyond no-man's land with Oleksandr. What I didn't get out was a file on Halibeck International, a CIA front company that was funded to a great extent by Kovalev's oil empire."*

Kenna paused the video and leaned back … *the CIA! But Kovalev?* She pushed play.

Yuri continued, *"Over the past two years, I worked hard to infiltrate the FSB as a double agent. I discovered the video was in the possession of an FSB operative named Alexi Medved …"*

Medved again, Kenna thought.

"Now in my possession, I have to keep a low profile before sending it via courier. If that fails, I will bring it personally. So far, I have not been suspected, but Medved is

a very resourceful and nasty man ..."

Which I know first-hand, Kenna thought.

"The master Halibeck document is with Kovalev," the video continued. *"Seek him out. The video and the file tie everything together. Be warned that Sir Clifton Toll is also in search of them. Remain cautious in dealing with him; he has been known to do work outside BNC, specifically for whoever occupies 10 Downing. I don't know what's in the file, but if Toll wants it ... it's big, very big. As Alistair always said,* 'The story of a lifetime, my boy.' "

Yuri lifted a bottle of Horilka and poured a shot glass full. He took a drink as if to calm his nerves. There was no smile now, just the unknown.

"Only God knows if I will get out of Luhansk, but I pray the video helps reveal their plan. My heart is heavy that I must place the burden of truth solely onto you, but my belief, as it was Alistair's, is strong that you will stop this insanity."

The screen went dark. Kenna paused it. *Burden of truth, Gran's and Papa's words again,* she thought. *Insanity ... yes, she understood that.* Why hadn't he just said what was on his mind? Puzzles, more fucking puzzles ...

She punched play. Darkness for a few seconds, then the screen morphed into a muddy, snow-covered, war-torn street. Date Stamp: "10 March 2020". *Unintelligible whisper as the phone image bounced, Kenna crouch-walking. The image lifted, focused on Oleksandr when he stopped and crouched low, observing the area, then moving forward.*

Kenna fast-forwarded the video and stopped just as …

Three Russian UAZ-469 "Jeeps" stopped in the street. Two men and two women in civilian clothes jumped out. Svetlana and Lyuba stepped out while armed drivers stood watch. The young lieutenant followed Lyuba inside. An armored Russian Tigr stopped; Novikov stood out.

No Medved, she thought. *Why weren't you there?*

Kenna fast-forwarded until the *Russians were inside the shack, gathered around the table lit by electric lanterns.* She slowed the replay, concentrating on the dark faces, some indiscernible. A diverse array of people: The first woman, a bit snobbish, pretty and thin with a dark jaw-length hairstyle. The second woman wore American blue jeans with a faded, tattered jean jacket and a tousled lob haircut. The two men, one with a distinct Aquiline nose and cropped blond hair; the second with a hoody pulled up while he moved for the table.

Kenna slowed the video once again. *The silhouette at the rear of the room moved to the edge of the light, but his face remained hidden in shadows.* In frustration, she zoomed on him. *Beck,* she wondered, *is that you? Medved?*

Frustrated, she stopped the video, ejected the memory stick, and wrapped it with the paper. She stood and opened the sliding door to the rear deck. The dark basin was quiet. She stepped out to inhale the stench of reality, dead fish. It wasn't that far removed from what she remembered of Luhansk, what she coined *"eau de death of humanity"*. She looked southeast, in the direction of Ukraine, but saw only darkness. It seemed fitting.

In a medical gown smeared with blood, Evhen stepped onto the rear deck with her. He lit a cigarette and offered her one. She shook it off but accepted a shot of Horilka. They toasted and drank in silence. Her sad eyes asked the silent question.

"He's been hit worse, Red," Evhen said. "Mrs. Kohut'll take care of him. Perhaps this will slow him a bit."

"A man doesn't shut down his Ferrari simply because you want him to slow down," she countered.

"Even if the Ferrari's engine is burned out?"

'I don't know what's in the file, but if Toll wants it ... it's big, very big,' she heard Yuri's words again.

"There's something I have to do," she said. "Hopefully, I'll return early in the morning."

"And, if not?"

"Then we'll never celebrate having gotten out of Luhansk alive, Evhen."

Kenna stared into the black abyss of the basin's water. It curled her upper lip as though she were flying at her father's breakneck speed on a one-way passage to hell. Smoke from Evhen's cigarette drifted past her nostrils; she recalled Luhansk, knowing hell was where this passage led and into the devil's grasp where she was destined to crash.

Without emotion, she threw the backpack on and walked from the boat.

XLI

At South Dock of Canary Wharf, Filipp held open the rear door of a new Russian Aurus Senat limousine. Svetlana stepped out to the streetlights and stretched exhaustion from her body. The yacht was well-lit, an all too welcome sight. What transpired in Eaton Square burned at her insides but had nothing to do with the wound. She had arrogantly waltzed into London, believing she was immune from retribution by the one man who swore to kill her.

The question begged: *how did Oleksandr know she was in London?* Logic said he was working with someone other than the reporter; someone with knowledge of her plans. That pointed inside her organization… but who? Everyone knew the price of betrayal. The gun battle was a mistake, a big one on her part and his. Now, every policeman in London would be searching for them. Regardless, she could not allow that to alter her plan.

"Filipp, park the car and come aboard."

Filipp hesitated, then said, "Might I suggest I return to the neighborhood, ma'am? Lyuba could be wounded."

"Not just yet," Svetlana said, thinking. "She's resourceful. If we don't hear from her by dawn, we'll both go."

"Ma'am, my apologies for saying so, but you should leave that work to Medved and me."

At any other time, she might have snapped for his insubordination. Tonight, she didn't have the energy. Besides, he was right. Her present state proved she wasn't superwoman, as much as it pained her to admit. She turned for the yacht.

Exhaustion disfigured her perfectly painted face; lines of age appeared. Days and nights blended. It wasn't physical exhaustion that seized her; it was the mental grind. She had never been charged with a mission that demanded her total focus and attention every moment… for nearly eight years. Her mind had been on full alert day and night since the annexation of Crimea. Sleep came in fifteen-minute intervals; she even dreamt of what was to happen the next day. There was no downtime, no relaxation. But her hard work and drive had paid dividends; she had discovered the CIA plan. It hit her hard that it could all be ruined by her own stupidity and arrogance.

I will not allow that to happen, she thought. She wanted a glass of wine … in fact, she wanted several.

Lyuba, she thought, *where are you?* There was something troubling her lover, and she was going to discover what it was. Lyuba's indiscretion aside, there was no room for mistakes on this mission. Medved had been right about the romantic interlude. She never should have lived out that fantasy, even though she had thought long and hard about it. The reason had been sound, at least to her... with Kovalev dead, she would take what was his, if only for one night. She owed herself that.

As she stepped onto the yacht, Sergey approached to give a report, as he always did. She waved him off.

"Tonight, silence and wine, Sergey," she said, removed the Toll folder from her handbag, and handed it to him. "Put that in the safe."

Sergey nodded and led her to the aft deck. He turned on two gas heaters and snapped fingers at the young maid. She stepped forward with a bottle of white wine in an ice bucket. Without speaking, she poured a glass, nodded, and backed away. Just as Svetlana lifted the glass, her phone rang. The tension on her face eased.

"Lyuba, where are you?"

*

Jubilee Park was situated a bit inland on the opposite side of South Harbor. On a bench, nerves on edge, Lyuba smoked a cigarette and glared at every person who passed. In a pocket of her overcoat, her hand never left the grip on her pistol. The small water fountain did little to ease the tension; its monotonous sprays of water seemed to heighten it. Behind her, a group of teenagers sang with music from an MP3 player.

Silhouetted by walkway lighting, robe rustling in a breeze like a medieval temptress, Svetlana approached from behind them. In the shadows behind, Filipp followed the obedient guard dog. Svetlana's glare locked on Lyuba, who knew there was no safe haven from FSB's highest-ranked female. She was prone to violent rages; the slightest misstep could send her over the edge. With diplomatic immunity, Svetlana could do whatever she pleased without threat of prosecution. Lyuba stood.

Tonight, they were not lovers. Tonight, two warriors walked slowly along the winding paths.

"Where have you been?" Svetlana demanded.

"It surprises you I am still alive?" Lyuba asked.

"What are you talking about?"

"Your assassin, the one in the dark hoody, failed to kill me."

"I have no intentions to kill you," Svetlana said. *Unless you betray me.*

"After the fight, I searched for the video and folder—"

Svetlana interrupted, "What do you know of these two items?"

"Medved searches for a video while you search for a folder," Lyuba said. "Similar to the one you have on the company Brac—"

"Silence!" Svetlana interrupted. "Do not speak that name in public. It's imperative the folder be returned to me. That was the transaction to take place with Kovalev."

You're lying, Lyuba knew. "Why is it so important?"

"Its contents are for my eyes only, Lyuba," Svetlana demanded. "If you find it, do not look inside."

"Others search for it, as well," Lyuba said.

"The Englishman," Svetlana said with rancor. *How do you know this?*

"Your hooded assassin killed Kovalev's bodyguard." She paused as two lovers strolled past. "Yet, he did not see me."

"Did you recover the folder?" Svetlana asked with a hint of panic. "Don't betray me, Lyuba."

Not don't betray our country, Lyuba noted, also knowing they were synonymous. Angry emotions erupted into words:

"My country ruined my family and worked my father to

death, Svetlana!"

"Your father drank himself to death," Svetlana challenged, pleased at Lyuba's burst of emotion.

Lyuba countered, "Our failed system beat him down!"

"Silence!" Svetlana interrupted and slapped Lyuba hard, then again. "You speak treason … for him, the father that beat you?"

Lyuba stiffened. "The work I do is for me."

With a menacing glare, Svetlana moved to where she could smell the fear on Lyuba's breath. *Or is it confidence?* she suddenly wondered.

"What I can give you is infinitely more permanent than any other offer."

'Can', not will, Lyuba noted. Unafraid, she said, "I told you before, I want my life back. If the price is this folder you value over life, then so be it."

Svetlana grabbed Lyuba by the coat and pushed her against the tree. Fire ignited in Lyuba's brain; she had played the docile, obedient soldier for the last time. Lyuba calmly slid a stiletto from her sleeve, snapped it open, and lifted it to Svetlana's ribcage.

"In less than a breath, I can impale your liver on my blade, Svetlana," Lyuba said evenly, pressing the knife against Svetlana to pierce clothing. "Release me, or I will."

"You would be better served helping me," Svetlana snapped without fear. "Bring me the folder."

"I don't trust Medved … or your hooded assassin." She paused. "I don't trust anyone."

Svetlana allowed a smile to crease her cheeks. She flicked her eyes to the side. At the edge of the clearing behind a tree, Filipp trained his pistol on Lyuba.

"A bullet in me assures the folder will be delivered to the Englishman," Lyuba lied. "And everything you've worked so hard for will be made public."

Shock filled Svetlana's face. "Then, help me, and I will give you what you want."

"How do you know what I want when you never asked?"

In an instant, Lyuba lowered the knife and darted into the trees behind Svetlana, using her for cover against a bullet from Filipp. He ran forward; Svetlana stopped him.

"We will allow her to do what I require, Filipp," she ordered. "She's smart and will see the error of her ways."

She turned to the fleeing shadow. *If you betray me, Lyuba, you will never enjoy your precious freedom.*

XLII

The hotel bar was brightly lit and done in rich, dark woods. Furniture and tables were evenly spaced and well appointed. At a table with his back to the wall, Wiggy finished a pint and motioned to the bartender for another. Images projecting from two laptops before him split his face in different shades of grey. On one laptop were frozen images of the riot and the interview with Kovalev on Wembley's pitch. Wiggy's attention was on the second laptop that ran Wembley's CCTV security footage.

Kenna was a free spirit, prone to travel her own path, but he was concerned. It had been several hours since he last heard from her. Every time he called; her phone went dead. *It could be anything*, he convinced himself several times. Now, however, he wasn't buying it. Wiggy didn't think of himself as a negative person, but at this point negativity was all he could muster. What infuriated him the most... there was nothing he could do about it.

His only recourse ... dive into work and stay focused.

Speaking to Tommy hadn't helped his mood. The lad was crazy with worry and grief; all his attempts to locate Adelaide had failed. He had gone to every hospital in a ten-kilometer radius of the stadium, had called every police station, and had viewed two Jane Bloggs in two morgues. It was impressive he had covered so much ground in such a short period of time.

"Hey, mate! She just walked in," the bartender said, motioning to the foyer.

"She'll have what I'm havin'."

Wiggy closed the laptops and walked out. Dragging with exhaustion, Kenna entered the brightly lit foyer. When greeted by employees, all she could muster was a smile. Wiggy cut her off before she reached the lift. He took her by the arm and led her towards the bar.

"The bar … tonight, Wiggy?" Kenna asked. "I actually feel like I could sleep."

"Sleep later, kid."

"I'd really like to go to the room, Wiggy," she said. "I need a shower."

"See, ye got a few new beauty marks," Wiggy said, not amused. "How many times I gotta tell ya to let me handle that stuff."

"They refused to wait until you got there," she said as they entered the bar. "Found Oleksandr, he's getting patched up. We'll go when he's up to it."

"Been ringin' ya all night."

Kenna lifted a burner phone and called Wiggy's number. When it rang, she said, "That's me, had to trash the other phone."

Wiggy pointed to the table with the laptops. As Kenna sat, he went to the bar and retrieved the two pints. Kenna rested her head on the table. Wiggy slid a pint across to her, revealing the handle of a Glock 22 in a shoulder holster.

"Where'd you get that?" she asked and sat upright.

"Barnaby had an extra lyin' about, complete with license," Wiggy said, opening the laptops to illuminate him.

"I won't mention that to DCI Attwood," she said. "Thought you'd be asleep by now."

"Normal people are," he said. "But then—"

"Nobody ever accused us of that."

"A couple-a these, and you'll sleep like a baby," he said.

"You might have to carry me up."

"Wouldn't be the first time, lass."

"A second laptop," she said, taking a large drink.

"Took yer advice. Tryin' to run too many things on one," he said and turned one to face her. "Rashon Hill's video got me to thinkin'. CliffsNotes, he ran around the stadium, then down to the pitch. In running up the steps, he heard the shot."

"Which would have been just before I was knocked unconscious," she said, coming alive while watching the video.

"He didn't come to the suite because he saw the man in the hoody…"

Kenna fast-forwarded to Rashon, videoing the hooded man running away. Illya, bloody and wounded, stagger-ran after him. Rashon followed into the parking garage. The hooded driver looked at Rashon just as he sped the Jaguar from the garage. Illya turned and saw Rashon; he aimed his pistol and fired just as Rashon ran away. Kenna rewound it to when the Jaguar sped away and froze it.

"The killer looked right at Rashon," she said. "So, he knew who had seen him."

"Unfortunately, we don't see him well enough for facial recognition," Wiggy said. "But keep that image in mind, and we'll run through the sequence."

On the second laptop, he flipped to CCTV from the front of Victoria Station. "Courtesy of Barnaby, when Yuri Zelenko was killed."

"That answers one question," Kenna said. "I was having my doubts when I learned that MI5 put a lid on his killing."

"He mentioned we should keep this close to the vest,"

Wiggy said. "Something about grounds for deportation."

The beer went down rough as she watched the execution. Even blurry and from a distance, the result was chilling. When the killer finished and was knelt at Yuri, he looked up when the security guard approached. Wiggy froze the image there, shrank the image, and moved it to the corner of the screen.

"The hoody, trousers, and trainers are all consistent," he said.

"What the security man said, *'a hoody's a hoody'*," Kenna said.

"Now, back to Wembley. Seen this so many times, me eyes are blurrin'."

"But something's bothering you, or you wouldn't keep going back," she offered.

He froze the outside stadium footage just as the Jaguar backed into Adelaide. He reversed it swiftly to when Illya put Adelaide in the Mini Cooper, then ran back inside.

"Look at the date stamp," he said. "She was in the Mini quite some time until the Jag drove from the garage."

"Illya's not hurt when he puts her in the Mini. Then, he runs back up to the suite just in time for Kovalev's murder," she concludes. "He either kills Kovalev and is wounded in the process … or is wounded outside where I am injured and chases the assassin down to the garage."

Wiggy points to the Jag as it sped from the garage. "Which is when the Jag roars out, the driver sees Adelaide, then reverses into her."

At extreme slow-motion, the Jaguar drove from the parking structure. Adelaide ran forward, waving her hands. The driver of the Jag turned.

Wiggy grumbled, "Doesn'a make any sense, her runnin' to the Jag. Runnin' away is what makes sense."

"Remember, she's injured. She could be yelling for help and didn't realize who was in the car until it was too late," Kenna suggested.

Wiggy froze the video and enhanced the driver's image as far as possible. All that could be seen was a fuzzy hooded image with no face. He returned to normal view and continued the video. The Jag hit Adelaide, throwing her against the Mini. Kenna cringed, feeling the pain that must have shot through her. The Jaguar stopped; the driver's door opened.

"Freeze it!" Kenna said and leaned close. "Now, slowly."

In slow motion, the hooded man … yes, it was a man …

stepped from the Jaguar.

"Freeze it!" she insisted. "Close on the hoody."

"Tried it, but it's just not clear enough to see him," Wiggy said. "Watch."

Wiggy started the footage and pointed to the hooded man. Just after stepping from the Jaguar, he looked up at Adelaide, then paused in mid-step.

"Why did he hesitate? I asked meself a hundred times?" Wiggy wondered aloud. "Wasn't the lights and sirens, that's after he drives off."

"Run it through again," she said, now fully awake, and took a drink that went down smooth. "Then, freeze when he hesitates."

As the video flicked across the screen, Kenna's eyes never left the images. Just as the hooded man paused, she tapped the screen.

"We missed it in real-time," she said. "Right there …"

"Yeah, saw it," Wiggy said. "Something distracted him."

"When Illya saw Rashon and fired at him?"

The hooded man turned to the garage, then jumped into the Jaguar. As he sped away, the wind from an open window blew off the hoody. Wiggy froze the image, capturing only the fuzzy back of the man's head.

"Which gave the Jaguar driver time to escape," Wiggy said.

"Dammit," Kenna said and dragged a finger across the screen.

Wiggy said, "Here's when Adelaide leaves."

The Jaguar weaved wildly. Adelaide pulled herself into the Mini Cooper and sped in the opposite direction.

"Again, in slow motion," Kenna insisted.

Wiggy paused and reversed the video to when the hooded man jumped into the Jaguar and ran it again.

"See it?" Wiggy asked. Kenna's blank expression answered him. "Didn'a think so. Watch the Jag, not Adelaide or our friend in the hoody."

Wiggy ran the video in extreme slow motion. Just before the hooded man got into the Jaguar, he looked at the garage, then flinched. Lunging into the Jag, he pulled his pistol. Tiny sparks ricocheted from the Jag the same time Adelaide pulled herself into the Mini Cooper. A flash of gunfire from inside the Jaguar. More sparks from the Jag, a hole splintered the rear window. The Mini Cooper sped away the opposite direction. Wiggy paused the video.

Out of breath, Kenna leaned back. "We concentrated too much on the people."

"Aye," Wiggy agreed. "Someone was shootin' at him from the garage."

"Illya … which gave Adelaide and Rashon an opportunity to escape," Kenna agreed. "Then, where the hell is she?"

"I'm lookin', but found how Illya slipped out," Wiggy said and continued, "Had DCI Attwood confirm that there's a private executive garage and exit from the stadium. Illya used it … Attwood found his blood inside."

"So, he drove out undetected," she concluded.

"Aye," he said. "I'm off my bloody game since this COVID stuff shut down everything."

"How so?"

"I went back and checked the other outside cameras around the stadium," he said. "The copper and Wembley security missed Illya driving away on the opposite side in a dark utility van. Barnaby's tryin' to locate it."

"I have to talk to Tommy," she said.

"When I spoke with him last, he was in the Media Room, somethin' about workin' to keep from goin' crazy with worry."

Before Kenna stood, Wiggy took her arm. "Ya won't be doin' no one any good if'n yer crashed from exhaustion.

He's in BNC. I'll phone and tell him to stay. They have security."

"Sometimes, I really do hate your logic, Jeremy Heffernan," she stated.

XLIII

Morning sun peeked through the hotel suite windows. Kenna walked from the bedroom in jeans, and sweater with riding leathers, and helmet. She poured a cup of coffee behind the bar and joined Wiggy. While staring at the screen, he motioned to a pyramid built of pencils and Blu-tack in the center of the table.

"The Grand Ole Dame's crime pyramid, lass," he said. "Made with pencils, why?"

"The Hatton Garden caper, she did an elaborate pyramid of metal, symbolic for the safety deposit boxes. At Congressional, the clues were behind the scenes, in the air, with apparently no links, so I did it with my thumbs and index fingers," she said. "Here, it's about the written word."

"How so?"

"Last night, I remembered something I didn't tell DCI Attwood," she said and sipped coffee. "Just before Kovalev died, he told me there was a folder in the Mandarin Oriental Hotel … what Toll was expecting to receive from him."

"A dying man's wish for ye to have it," Wiggy deduced.

"According to Yuri, the video and the folder tie everything together."

"Yuri? The lad's dead," Wiggy said.

"Damn, too much on my brain," Kenna admonished herself and lifted the memory stick from her leathers. "The video from Luhansk. He sent it to me via courier before he was killed. Watch it; we'll discuss it after you do."

Kenna moved for the door and paused as she opened it. "Don't forget Halibeck; I'll call you after the hotel."

*

Kenna stopped the Honda on Knightsbridge, across from the Mandarin Oriental Hyde Park Hotel, one of the most exclusive in London … which made it one of the most expensive. A call to Evhen gave her some comfort. Oleksandr was resting, which meant complaining about not being able to do anything, or so the background noise indicated.

Carrying the helmet, Kenna took the steps up under the canopy between tall, ribbed columns with Corinthian capitals. A uniformed doorman opened the deep red door trimmed in gold. His greeting was bright, cheerful, and well-rehearsed, finished off with the tip of his cap:

"Welcome to the Mandarin Oriental Hyde Park, mum.

Enjoy your time with us."

She strolled slowly into the grand foyer, ignoring the opulence, and concentrating on the people. During the night, she had thought Kovalev's words were broken gibberish from a dying man. The more she thought of them, the more they started to make sense. She found it curious that he had left the package here and not in his apartment safe. For whatever reason, the shoot-out proved his rationale was correct. Perhaps it was, as Wiggy suggested, his dying wish that she have it.

By coming alone, she was breaking the confidence with DCI Attwood. But she hadn't liked his pushy female Detective Sergeant. She seemed too eager to impress her superior, and people like that tended to hinder more than help. Kenna disliked pushy women like DS Jenkins, who insisted on force-feeding their opinions on everyone. Of course, she realized that many people saw her in that light. Often, that's what it took to get the job done. She thought of Jenkins for a moment … but her opinion didn't change.

Gran had referred to every crime as a grand 3-D puzzle trapped in a pyramid. Solving it required putting all the pieces together inside the pyramid. Some people, DS Jenkins, no doubt, would see it as childish. But very few people had solved as many crimes as Gran Lockwood.

Regardless of what others thought, this was a very elaborate puzzle. At present, all the pieces were spread out, with only the corners connected. The middle remained a mass of confusion … and she had no idea who sat at the top.

She moved through the extravagant hotel lobby and its beautiful furnishings and fixtures. Finely dressed staff walked through the guests without interruption. Like Toll's residence, Kenna felt the decor was over the top. She stopped at the finely appointed check-in counter to the disapproving glares of several guests. Ms. Chester, by her gold nametag, was 20-something with a broad smile, perfectly styled hair, fastidious makeup, and pressed suit.

"Welcome to the Mandarin Oriental Hyde Park. How may I be of service?" Ms. Chester asked in her rehearsed and welcoming tone.

Kenna extended her passport. "I believe Kostyantyn Kovalev left a package for me."

Ms. Chester smiled in the manner she was trained. "Do you have the claim check, Ms. Hannigan?"

"No, he didn't mention that," Kenna offered.

"Then, I'm afraid—"

"Is the manager available, Ms. Chester?" Kenna interrupted with authority.

Obviously trained not to contradict guests, Ms. Chester disappeared into a room behind the counter. In a few seconds, she followed Mr. Toft out. He was a tall, lean man in his 50s with the looks and attitude that *he just might own this place*, if only in his mind. He scanned Kenna's attire, none too impressed.

"So, you are here to retrieve a package but don't have the claim check," Toft stated more than asked.

"Yes, left for me by Kostyantyn Kovalev," she said.

With a nod from the omnipotent ruler, Ms. Chester moved to the computer and punched a few keys. Ever mindful of his guests, Toft put on a pleased façade while being abhorred by the presence of a woman in riding leathers … *certainly not their normal clientele*. It was obvious he would do whatever it took to get her out of *his hotel*.

"Let me take a look … Ms. Hannigan," Ms. Chester said, moving the mouse.

Several clicks later, a curious look crossed Ms. Chester's face. Toft joined her at the computer and lifted glasses to read. He wasn't pleased by what he saw, hesitated a moment to think, and cleared his throat.

"It was listed under your name—"

"Was?" Kenna interrupted.

"Earlier this morning, a woman presented a claim check and was given the package," Toft offered.

Time for improv. Kenna asked, "Is that how you do things here? Give packages intended for someone to someone else?"

"No, Ms. Hannigan," Toft stammered. "There must be a good reason."

"Do you have the person's name, Mr. Toft?" Kenna demanded in a loud voice.

"It appears it was his wife, Ms. Hannigan," Ms. Chester said.

"Wife?" Kenna objected. "He wasn't married. Just who was this woman?"

Toft didn't like her boisterous outcry. He nervously smiled at nearby guests.

"Could you describe her?" Kenna insisted.

Toft lifted his eyes; recognition flashed across his face. He was very nervous now … *the press in his hotel?*

"You're the reporter that was at Wembley when he was killed," Toft said, panic rising.

"One in the same. And right now, I'm following his path yesterday, and at some point, he was here … with that package meant for me!"

"Oh, dear God," Toft stammered. "I beg of you not to mention the hotel in your report."

"Then, tell me what the woman looked like," she insisted.

"We can do one better," Toft assured her. He talked while moving to the end of the counter. "Come into the back room, and we'll review the security video."

When they entered the security room, Toft's blood pressure lowered with Kenna out of the guests' sight. Toft stood behind a twenty-year-old computer operator while he ran the footage back to the time indicated on the claim check. He slowed it when a woman appeared on the screen at the check-in counter. He froze it when the package was delivered.

"Lyuba," Kenna said.

"You know her?" Toft asked.

"Of her," Kenna offered. "Are you sure about her being Kovalev's wife?"

From a printer, Toft lifted a printed sheet and handed it to Kenna. What she stared at in disbelief was a copy of Lyuba's Ukrainian passport.

"Lyuba Kovalev," Kenna said.

"Sorry we couldn't have been more help," Toft said.

Toft escorted Kenna from the room. He handed her a coupon for the hotel bar. She smiled and patted his hand.

"Is there any way to know what was inside the package?" she asked.

"Mr. Kovalev didn't detail the contents when he left it, I'm afraid," Toft said.

With thanks, Kenna walked through the lobby. Curious stares of *the other half* followed.

Lyuba, what is your game? Kenna asked herself. The doorman opened the door as she walked out. At the curb, Kenna sat on the Honda. It was then she realized she knew nothing about the woman who may now be the chief suspect … *in partnership with Alexi Medved*, she feared.

'*Beautiful and dangerous,*' Oleksandr had said in Luhansk.

If known killers, how had they gotten into the U.K.? What was their motive? Duty to Svetlana, her lover, according to Oleksandr? She punched Wiggy's number on her cell phone. It rang and went to voice mail.

"Wiggy, find all you can on Lyuba … she's presenting herself as Kovalev's wife." She hesitated, wondering what to believe. "Don't know if it's true but find out."

She disconnected the call and impatiently tapped

Bluetooth. "Call Tommy." *Answer, dammit, answer.*

"Hi, Kenna," was Tommy's impassive response.

"Anything on Adelaide?" she said over the traffic. He paused; she didn't like it.

"Nothing, absolutely nothing," he said in defeat. "I don't get it, here one minute, gone the next."

"Tommy, get your head outta yer ass and find her!" she yelled, slamming her clutch hand on the handlebar. "Stay there until I come in!"

Kenna disconnected the call and looked down the side street towards Hyde Park. Standing in the broken shadows of a leafless tree and smoking a cigarette was Lyuba. The Russian beauty made long, knowing eye contact, then casually turned and walked towards the park. Kenna started the Honda and eased it down the street to follow.

XLIV

Kenna stood from chaining the Honda at the edge of Hyde Park and followed Lyuba at a run across the park towards the Serpentine. The smell of the water consumed her, and she thought of Evhen's boat and Oleksandr. At the walkway, she turned to look both directions. Seemingly without a care, Lyuba sat on a bench in a tree's shade at the edge of the water. Kenna stepped to the bench; Lyuba revealed a concealed and suppressed pistol.

"You are either very brave or very stupid," Lyuba said, clicking back the hammer.

"I like to believe the former," Kenna said, unsure at that moment.

"Why are you following me?" Lyuba asked.

A thousand things flashed through Kenna's mind in an instant, Gran's wisdom at the fore. She responded:

"I believe we are after the same thing, and you got here before me."

Lyuba patted the satchel slung over her shoulder. "The folder on the American company."

"Have you read it?"

"Doing so is an automatic death sentence," Lyuba offered.

"I was told you don't fear death."

Lyuba silently agreed. "No more than you, I have a feeling."

"Those who willfully venture into the valley of death can't fear doing so," Kenna said.

A man and woman walked arm-in-arm along the water's edge. Lyuba motioned Kenna closer to her side. Lyuba smelled the soap on Kenna's skin and shoved the pistol firmly against Kenna's side. Staring into Kenna's eyes, Lyuba was impressed at no reaction … and no fear.

Kenna sensed Lyuba's immediate physical attraction. Their stares remained fixed, fire staring at gasoline. A man walked past with an English Bulldog; both ignored them.

"You have what you wanted, why wait?" Kenna asked to break the ice.

"Adversaries should meet face-to-face," Lyuba responded.

"Adversaries? We don't know anything about each other," Kenna offered with a half-truth. "How can we be adversaries?"

"Then, perhaps it was curiosity," Lyuba whispered.

"Two strong women driven by sheer will. Are we anomalies, Ms. Hannigan?"

"My father always said I was an enigma wrapped in an anomaly," Kenna said and motioned to the satchel. "What will the folder give you?"

"Freedom," was Lyuba's terse reply.

"From Svetlana," Kenna ventured. "And perhaps an Englishman? I see … you are lighting the candle at both ends, Lyuba."

Lyuba investigated her quickly, liking her, could fall in love with her under different circumstances. But that was never to be. In her world, perhaps both of their worlds, there was no room for attachment.

"Living between two dragons, Ms. Hannigan," Lyuba said with an undertone of sadness. "One must discover how to escape both." Her pause was brief. "Doing so could solve two mysteries, yours and mine."

Of course, Kenna thought, then said, "To use the information against both … or perhaps to pit them against each other. Yes, the latter, I think."

"Pretty and with an insightful mind. You are a rare breed, Ms. Hannigan," Lyuba said. "It's surprising it hasn't gotten you killed."

Nearly has ... and more than once in Luhansk, Kenna didn't say.

Lyuba chuckled at length. "Like when you ran away that night in Luhansk."

"So, you do remember," Kenna said with appreciation.

"I remember everything," Lyuba said, not boasting. "I could have easily killed you."

"Why didn't you?"

"It wasn't part of my mission," Lyuba said. "And, in part, why we are sitting here now."

"I can assure you police protection," Kenna offered.

Lyuba's chuckle was not of joy this time but of absurdity. "What can the police do against the most powerful governments in the world?"

"Nothing with only words, Lyuba, which is all you offer … words," Kenna stated. *But the press, on the other hand.* She pointed to the satchel. "I need proof, evidence."

Lyuba backed to arms-length, pistol still aimed at Kenna's side. She wouldn't fall into the clutches of another dragon, though this one was different, or at least played a lesser game of evil.

"You have evidence we can both use," Kenna continued.

"Is everything so finite to you, Ms. Hannigan?" Lyuba

asked, leaning away.

Toll had said much in the same, Kenna thought.

"Yet, I must play my masters' games, both of them. If I discover how to survive …" Lyuba continued, lifted a finger gun, and simulated shooting Kenna in the face. "Don't follow me again. You are far too beautiful to have it spoiled by a bullet in your forehead … Next time, I will not hesitate, or …" Lyuba checked both ways with a shrug. "Perhaps we will meet again."

Without urgency, Lyuba walked along the path beside the Serpentine. Kenna watched until Lyuba was in the sunshine beyond the trees. She exhaled hard with relief and walked out the way she entered.

'A great rugby match,' Alistair Rensenhaus had said of the opposing Russian and Ukrainian armies. *'With the number of dead being the score.'*

What's the score, Alistair? Kenna wondered.

XLV

Kenna walked through the sunlit lobby of BNC to the lifts. For what she believed to be the first time, she rode up alone. It was a relief not having the inquisitive stares of employees wondering what an outsider was doing in their midst, especially a Yank. She shrugged it off when the doors opened.

In the On-Line Reporters room, she noticed Tommy was not at his desk. She made eye contact with Corina as she lowered her phone, then stood to greet her.

"Ms. Hannigan, Tommy's in the Media Room," Corina said with a directional point.

"Actually, I'd like to see Mr. Thurnbull," Kenna responded.

The door to Thurnbull's office opened. Unlit pipe between his teeth, he said, "You Yanks might say that my house is your house or some nonsense, but this isn't America if you haven't noticed. We make appointments in the civilized world."

As Kenna walked in, Thurnbull turned to Corina. "Tea, if you will, Corina."

It was the first time Kenna had been in Thurnbull's

sanctuary. Without hesitation, she walked behind his desk and admired his wartime decoration. Even her father's office couldn't compare to the stuffy discomfort of her surroundings at that moment. Perhaps that was what had been bothering her, the case aside. She lifted the photo.

"Young men sent to do a job, Ms. Hannigan," Thurnbull said with a bulged chest. "A testy lot, Saddam's Republican Guard."

"So, I've heard," she said, but felt the need for more. "After your release from the military because of your wounds, you continued to serve … why?"

"If you reference my stint with S.I.S., simple, I was asked, Ms. Hannigan."

They took seats as Corina ushered in the tea service. A young woman just out of her teens prepared the tea to perfection and placed two cups on Thurnbull's desk coasters. He did not acknowledge her as she pushed the cart out.

"Is this about my service to the Crown?" Thurnbull asked.

"Actually, I want to know why my video of the riot was edited."

"Orders come down from on-high, Ms. Hannigan," Thurnbull offered. "Every piece, if not live, passes through the cutting room."

She was being lied to, but by whom? There was something on the video that wasn't to be shown … just like the video from Luhansk. Was that the real reason it had never been shown?

"What about Henson?" he asked. "The lad's mind's been anywhere but work."

"Are you married?" was her succinct question.

"Never found the time," he said. "And now, well, it's probably too late. And you?"

"The same, other than the late part," she offered. "What started as a search for my grandmother's killer has transformed into an international manhunt."

"That you initiated by going to Ukraine two years ago, if I am not mistaken," Thurnbull said with a snippet of insinuation.

"You were in Ukraine twice, as I recall," Kenna countered.

Well played, Ms. Hannigan, he thought. "Yes, in fourteen and two years ago, helping Rensenhaus on the coverage of Russia's aggression."

"Did you encounter Kovalev while there?" she asked, then added, "Perhaps on a personal level, more than business?"

"Both times, unfortunately, coincided with Russian advances," he said. "That put a clamp on travel into and out of Crimea."

"I sent Tommy the photos of six people for him to identify. I'd like you to look at them," she said more than asked. "To me, they are all suspects, but thought more sets of eyes might help identify them."

"You really don't want to be a sports reporter, do you?" Thurnbull stood, amused by his own dry humor. "No time like the present."

He opened the door and followed Kenna out. Walking through the reporters was like being on display in Macy's window. What seized her most was that not one reporter smiled. She did so, remembering Gran Lockwood's witticism:

'Smile, it'll make everyone wonder what you've been up to.'

As the curious eyes followed her, she believed she could hear the silent questions: *'Does she really like working with him?' 'Did they have sex in his office?' 'Lunch date and a quicky?'*

Kenna followed Thurnbull into Media Room #1. Tommy

sat at the table, his laptop and desktop in front of him, listening to his phone over an earbud. Running on the white wall was Kenna's video from Wembley as she fell and the assailant leaned over her. She felt the impact on her head again, subconsciously reaching for it.

"How's the head, by the way?" Thurnbull asked.

"Try not to think about it," she said.

"Thank you for your help," Tommy said into the phone and disconnected the call. With heavy eyes, he looked up to Kenna. "Adelaide's nowhere to be found. It's like she's disappeared."

"Her mother's still alive, isn't she?" Thurnbull asked. "In north Kent, as I recall."

"You know Adelaide?" Tommy asked with hesitation.

"I make it a point to know all my people's families, Henson. Like Hannigan's mother and father in Dallas." He shrugged to Tommy … *well?*

"I don't want to alarm her at this point," Tommy offered.

"Perhaps it's time to pay her a visit," Kenna said. "I'd be happy to go along."

"Good, that's settled," Thurnbull said. "Now, to these photos you sent."

Kenna's comfort level dropped when Tommy put the

photos of the men and women from the secret Russian meeting on the white wall. It was like being catapulted back through time. As he zoomed close, light flooded into the room from the door opening. Toll entered with his cane, paused at the door, and made brief eye contact with Kenna. She felt a game challenge coming from the master.

Thurnbull moved closer to the wall, clipping Pince-Nez glasses on his nose. Toll moved between Thurnbull and Kenna.

"Well, you're the two in the room that've been there," Toll insisted. They were expected to fill in the rest.

"I recognize the shot," Thurnbull said but appeared to grapple with the *where*.

"Really?" Kenna asked dubiously. "It's from my video."

Thurnbull paused, his mind clicking. "I'm certain of it … yes, something Rensenhaus must have sent from Luhansk."

"So, he looked at the video long enough to cut from it," Kenna concluded with curiosity. "Odd, he never told me."

"The men and women, Thurnbull!" Toll demanded. "What about the men and women?"

Staring hard, shaking his head, Thurnbull offered, "Nothing. Don't recognize any of these chaps."

Kenna pointed to Novikov. "What about him? He was odd man out, didn't seem like he fit in the meeting. And I don't mean just his clothing. His entire demeanor was off compared to the others."

"In what way?" Toll asked.

"He didn't want to be there," Kenna responded.

"Not a clear enough image," Thurnbull said, shaking his head. "No, none of them."

"Where's the entire video?" Toll queried calmly.

"Being analyzed by my partner," Kenna said.

"This chap you call Wiggy," Thurnbull said; Kenna nodded. "Then, I suggest we go review it with him."

Thurnbull spun to Kenna; Toll grabbed his arm. They made long eye contact until Toll spoke:

"You and I have something else to do, Thurnbull. Send Henson with Ms. Hannigan. Seeing how a professional does things might get his mind back in his work."

Tommy looked up, not liking what he heard. He shoved his laptop into a backpack, shut down the other computer, and turned for the door. As they walked out, Toll held Thurnbull back. The door closed.

"We have work ahead of us, Douglas," Toll said. "I want you to know how things really work around here … and who

I work with at Number 10.”

Thurnbull’s eyes brightened. “Your humble servant, Sir Clifton.”

“Save that for the Crown, Douglas,” Toll said.

*

Kenna and Tommy walked down the front steps of the BNC building towards the Honda. Tommy stopped her halfway down. Though his body language portrayed sadness, Kenna sensed anxiousness in his eyes. A contradictory mix, she felt for him. Confusion was never a comfortable state of mind.

“Did you sense anything odd about that meeting?” he asked. “I mean, why does Toll want me reviewing the video?”

“Another set of eyes, Tommy,” Kenna said, pulling away. “Come on, let’s go.”

As Kenna unchained the Honda, she looked up. Thurnbull stood at the window and lifted the pipe. Tommy joined her. She sensed before he spoke what he was going to say. *Adelaide!*

“Thurnbull was right. Adelaide might have gone to her mother’s,” Tommy said. “But first, there are a couple hospitals I haven’t been to. Cover for me.”

"Call me when you find her," Kenna said, looking back up to Thurnbull.

Tommy hurried to the curb and hailed a taxi. As he stepped inside, Kenna started the Honda. A movement in the rearview mirror captured her attention and then another across the street. Pytor, Vanya, Luka, and another Russian sat in a Corsa sedan. Behind her, exhaust puffing, sat the Aston Martin. Behind the wheel …

"Medved," she mumbled, "and all your apostles."

Life … more definitively … survival took on new meaning … it was now or never. As fear crept into her, Medved's presence also impressed her … a challenge in daylight.

She pulled on the helmet and riding gloves in preparation for the ride of her life, literally. A final glance at Thurnbull, whose expression changed to surprise. With a screaming tire on wet pavement, a springbok joining its herd, the Honda lunged into traffic. Behind, the Cheetahs roared after.

XLVI

In the wrong lane, Kenna passed a bus, then slid around a corner in front of it … *go, go, go!* Blaring its horn, the bus skidded to a stop to block the intersection. Medved slammed on the brakes, stopping the Aston Martin a few centimeters from the bus's front bumper. Pytor drove the Corsa over the sidewalk, crashed into a stand of bicycles, and accelerated onto the side street.

"Call Oles," Kenna yelled into her Bluetooth.

Oleksandr's phone went to voicemail, "You know what to do." A ding followed.

With controlled urgency, she said, "Oles, your old friends want to party again." She weaved around rubbish tips. "If I'm invited, I'm sure you are as well. Keep your eyes open."

Kenna roared the Honda through a narrow street that turned lazily. When it split, she took the right fork and glanced at the rearview mirror …

*

Driving all out a half block behind the Honda, Pyotr glanced into his rearview mirror. As the bus cleared the intersection, the Aston Martin lunged after them with bawling tires. Like a rally co-driver, Vanya pointed when Kenna swerved along the right fork.

"Right fork, right fork!" Vanya yelled at Pyotr.

Into his Bluetooth, Pyotr yelled, "Medved, take the left fork. We'll have her between us when she comes out."

*

Kenna's eyes flashed from the street to the rearview mirror as the Aston Martin took the left branch at the fork. Frantic, wanting to scream, she was alone … and vulnerable. *No, dammit, take control!*

She focused, slammed on the brakes, and power slid the Honda into a narrow alley. The bike smashed into a metal rubbish bin and sent it reeling down the alley. Passing, the rear tire knocked it against the building.

*

Pyotr's Corsa slid to a stop; the alley was too narrow to follow. Pistol in hand, Pyotr jumped out, yelling into his Bluetooth:

"She took the alley a block and a half from the split."

He aimed for the Honda's rear tire and fired.

356

The bullet ricocheted from the pavement; Kenna swerved. The Aston Martin slid to a stop at the exit of the alley. Pistol in hand, the Russian passenger jumped out. From the other end of the alley, Pyotr's second shot blew out the Honda's rear tire!

The Honda wobbled wildly out of control.

"Fuck!" Kenna yelled as impact was imminent.

Instinct … Kenna laid down the Honda, staying aboard like riding a surfboard. With screeching metal and sparks flying, the bike slid through the alley. She jumped free just before it slammed into the Aston Martin and the Russian. He screamed and collapsed. Kenna flew over the trunk. The bike spun out of control, smashed into a streetlight, and came to rest.

Beyond the car, Kenna landed hard, rolling like a rag doll. Bleeding from the leg, she jumped up and limp-ran along the extension of the narrow alley. Medved rolled down his window and aimed his pistol. Porch lights illuminated, doors opened, and people stepped onto their stoops.

Kenna screamed, "Call the police! Call the police!"

Leaving the injured Russian, Medved sped away just as

Pyotr slid the Corsa to a stop.

"Get in!" Pyotr yelled.

Vanya and Luka jumped out and helped the injured man inside. Pyotr turned to Vanya.

"Get after her on foot," Pyotr demanded. "Phone me when you've trapped her."

Vanya and Luka ran into the alley in foot pursuit while Pyotr roared away.

*

Breathing heavily, Kenna ran past an alley and jerked off the helmet. She turned back to Vanya and Luka a block behind. With a blank gaze, her eyes went to the alley. The roar of approaching car engines soured her expression.

Clear of traffic, Pyotr slid to a stop at the alley. Kenna panicked, *she's pinned in no way out*. She fought a sudden burst of anguish and ran into an intersecting narrow brick alley. She hurdled debris and rubbish bins, struck one, but gathered her balance and ran.

On the street, Medved's Aston Martin screeched around the corner backwards to a sideways stop. A foot patrolman halfway down the street turned and blew a whistle. As he ran for the Aston Martin, Kenna ran from the alley and turned that direction. Medved's suppressed gunshot hit the patrolman in the leg. He tumbled head-over-heels into the gutter.

Kenna hesitated in disbelief. Medved spun the pistol on her and fired; intentionally missing, the bullet ricocheted from the building. She stumbled to the side … and ran.

"Stop!" Medved yelled. "We just want to talk."

"Not listening," Kenna said to herself.

She sprinted into the next alley. Her arm brushed the corner bricks, tearing cloth and skin; she ignored it. Ahead, the Corsa engine roared.

Pyotr spun the Corsa across the next street to cut her off. The brakes locked; the car slid sideways and slammed into a parked car just as Kenna appeared. Tires bawled as Pyotr reversed hard. The Corsa slammed into the brick building and rebounded forward.

Screaming, Kenna ran past the rear bumper. Pyotr accelerated backwards. Torn metal brushed her calf; she stumbled, then hobbled into the street, barely maintaining balance, and ran.

Sprinting, Vanya slid over the Corsa's trunk while Pyotr pulled forward. Pyotr jumped out. The man in the rear took the driver's seat. Luka followed Vanya through the alley after Kenna. Jogging behind them, Pyotr punched his

Bluetooth:

"Alexi, another block to the east. She's a rabbit, this one."

Kenna ran around a lazy corner to the left that branched immediately into three different fingers. She stopped again, sucked air, and rubbed her leg and side. Staccato running footsteps and Russian voices from behind turned her. A distant siren brought an inkling of hope.

At an aged tenement, Kenna leapt up stone steps two at a time. She jerked on the entrance door handle … locked. She jumped over the railing and ran down a series of steps to a cellar door. A short prayer touched her lips when she grabbed the handle. The bolt clicked but stuck. She shouldered it hard; hinges shrieked, and dust exploded as the door crashed inward.

Entering the aged cellar, Kenna stumbled across the floor into a barrel. Kicking the door closed, she flipped on her cell phone light. Swiping away cobwebs with disgust, she hurried into the musty darkness of an adjacent room. Behind, the door creaked. She froze, turned off the light, and stopped breathing. *Why did I come in here?* She wanted to scream.

In the other room, footsteps preceded a cell phone light on the wall. She turned, moving silently, but bumped into a black iron kettle hanging from a nail. It clanged into several others, then stopped at her touch. She hesitated but a moment.

Waving the light across the darkness, Luka moved rapidly. Kenna slid through the shadows, then behind another wall in the direction of a heavy basement door. In darkness, she fumbled rapidly along the stone wall until her hand fell on the heavy door bolt. She startled and shrieked lightly when a rat darted along a head-high wall ledge and dropped onto her shoulder. Frantic and frozen, her breathing deepened. The rat sniffed at her ear like a distant steam locomotive.

Shock! Enraged, Luka was atop her. He wrenched her off balance and threw her against the wall. With a shriek, the rat flew onto him. Not losing his grip on Kenna, he beat the rodent away.

"Don't resist," he demanded.

"I'm not going anywhere with you!" Kenna yelled.

She kicked Luka's knee; he yelped, dropped the phone, and the light went out. He pulled a knife that flashed across her eyes, slicing the back of her wrist. Screaming but fighting the pain, she fell back and kicked at the knife as it streaked across her eyes. Anger overcame Luka; he lost control. He drew back high for a downward plunge. She lifted her helmet just as he slammed the knife into it. Falling aside, she released the helmet.

She kicked straight out into Luka's groin. He yelled but did not stop and beat the helmet off the knife, knocking pans out of the way. Kenna kicked out, screaming, moving to the side, throwing everything she touched. Kenna's hand landed on a long object. With a sadistic laugh, Luka lunged forward.

Kenna raised a potato fork an instant before his knife sank into her shoulder. The fork drove into Luka's stomach; he screamed. She twisted it for measure. In disbelief, Luka dropped the knife and gripped the wooden fork handle. He convulsed and fell at the fireplace hearth, bleeding, mortally wounded.

At the door, Vanya entered the cellar, angry, limping, holding his hamstring. He flipped on his cell phone light.

"Luka?" he said.

Kenna spun. She retched, covering her mouth, not realizing she had spread the Russian's blood on her face. She slid as quietly and swiftly as possible towards the basement door to the adjoining room.

Vanya's phone light scanned the outer room. "Luka?"

Kenna eased the door open and shoved her backpack through the opening. She forced the door open as much as possible, then squeezed through … almost. Head through the opening, she squirmed arms and shoulders forward. Exhaling hard, she pushed on the wall with every bit of strength … then, as if greased, popped through.

In the adjacent room, Kenna rolled to the side, pulled on her backpack, and leaned against the wall. Fear, adrenaline, anger, hatred, and sorrow rushed through her in an instant.

From the adjacent room, Vanya yelled. The phone light illuminated the crack in the open door. Kenna tensed as Vanya shouldered into the door hard; it slammed against a pile of debris, preventing it from opening. His head and a gun appeared at the opening. She grabbed a board; he spun the weapon. With all her strength, she hit him on the head. He fell with a grunt but struggled up again with a mumble. Kenna hit him again, then again; he collapsed, unconscious and bleeding. With great hesitance, she lifted the pistol and hurried to the exterior door.

Kenna eased the door open to light rain and closed it behind. Dirt and blood covered her. In the stairwell, she wrapped a kerchief around her wrist. With her teeth and a light whimper, she pulled a long splinter out of her hand. She retched, braced herself on the wall, and threw up.

Weakness overcame her and dragged her down to the steps. *'Never quit! Never rest!'* Gran Lockwood demanded from the past.

Kenna gathered resolve and splashed water from the steps to wash the blood and vomit from her face. Looking at the dark streets, she spun to a cell phone ring inside. Medved's Aston Martin roared down the street in front of the building and out of sight. She ran. Entering the opposite alley, she firmly gripped the pistol and spoke into her Bluetooth:

"Wiggy, call when you get this."

She had wanted to say more, but there was no need. Panicking, Wiggy accomplished nothing. She needed his mind on his work, not worried about her. Running, the pain in her leg worsened, and she reconsidered her logic, if only briefly.

XLVII

In the last traces of daylight, Kenna limped along a tree-lined street of middle-income brick terrace houses. She refused the pain and the control it wrestled from her body and mind. Light rain streaked the blood down her riding leathers like a macabre horror movie poster. Remaining in the shadows as much as possible, she avoided CCTV cameras.

A tear touched the corner of her eye for the dead, beginning with Gran Lockwood. With the body count increasing, who was next? She swept away the thoughts with the rain.

While in Luhansk, Thurnbull had insisted that her responsibility was to him and BNC. *The burden of truth and proof,* as her father and grandmother had drilled into her, fueled every ounce of her being. *If not for the truth, why do this at all?* Papa had demanded both, never one over the other. She had found it shockingly missing from Thurnbull's and Toll's diatribes.

Every set of eyes was a potential enemy. She screamed in her mind at every person she saw, knowing it should have been Toll receiving her wrath. She had been thrown amongst the wolves for slaughter. She needed time to think, to calm the anger, and avoid irrational decisions.

'Nothing can be accomplished without a plan,' Gran Lockwood had lectured.

Or, as father preached, *'Get yer shit together!'*

Having avoided the London tube and busses for hours, she made the long walk. When people approached, she ducked into an alley to wait. Those who saw her must have wondered at her looks, the blood, the injuries. She ignored the questions, even the offers of help.

As a youth in Gran Lockwood's Boston, she had ridden with Paul Revere, helped James Lafayette spy on the dreaded Redcoats, and flew Ben Franklin's kites. Dallas was home, but Boston was where life was given meaning, where, as she aged, she went to think. The short time she had been in London, that escape had become Adelaide's flat.

At the next intersection, she turned and hurried to the mews between terrace houses. She limp/ran through the darkness, avoiding the rubbish-bins. She stopped at the rear of an apartment with a smiley face on the door.

What's to smile about? Kenna asked herself and took the steps up. She lifted a key from under the rear mat. *Gotta change your security protocol, Addie.* She unlocked the door and entered the dark kitchen.

"Addie," she said, hoping, praying there would be an answer. There was none.

The kitchen was small, with matching tile countertops and floor. Kenna had often referred to it as matching Adelaide's pleasant state of being, not flashy, not boring. She hoped to have the opportunity to laugh with her about that again.

"Call Tommy," she said into her Bluetooth. The phone rang.

*

Tommy stood at the admittance window of "Northwick Park Hospital". He showed the attendee behind the glass a photo of Adelaide. His phone did not ring. The nurse took the photo and motioned Tommy to a chair. Expression stern, he turned to the waiting area, ignoring everyone else in the same situation, and looked at his phone.

*

Kenna emptied her pockets onto the kitchen table and said into her phone:

"Tommy, if you find Addie, don't come to her flat. Go to yours, her mum's, wherever. I'll ring later to discuss."

Kenna disconnected the call and removed her bloody,

soiled blouse. She punched a speed dial number on her phone. It rang …

*

In a dark, secure room with computer screens decorating the walls, Wiggy stood with Barnaby, reviewing footage from archival files. Pinned on the walls in several locations were signs: "CELL PHONES OFF". Wiggy moved to the screen as facial recognition ran against the silhouette of the killers in the hoodies. Both were perplexed and unable to compare them to the photo of Anson Beck next to it. Beside it ran another facial recognition program, comparing the hooded man in the secret Russian Luhansk meeting.

"Nothing," Wiggy said, frustrated.

"We're getting nowhere," Barnaby agreed.

"Let's change our approach," Wiggy said, "and compare what we have with the CCTV outside Victoria Station when Yuri Zelenko was killed."

"Guy in the hoody's too smart to look at the CCTV cameras," Barnaby said with finality.

"So, we compare body types, actions … how he walks, does he limp? Does he talk with his hands?"

"I see your point and like it," Barnaby agreed. "You should'a been a cop, Jeremy."

In Adelaide's apartment, Kenna spoke into her phone, "Wiggy, we have to get together with Oleksandr. Come to boat slip 23 in Limehouse Basin. I'm sending a text on something I want you to investigate. Keep it between you and me."

The darkness matched her mood while she walked through the living room. *Why do people have cell phones if they don't keep them on?* she wondered. She paused and inhaled. A frown creased her brow, thinking of Gran Lockwood's living room.

She stripped, stepped into the bathroom, and spun on the shower. As steam rose, she glanced at her face in the mirror. Steam slowly clouded her reflection … she blended into the smoke of war from Luhansk. Trying to ignore it, she stepped into the shower and sat on the floor.

*

The shower had been the longest she had taken in … well, she didn't remember. It gave her time to reflect on the madness that surrounded her. New wound dressings on her head and arm, Kenna came into the kitchen in a borrowed pair of jeans and a loose wool sweater. She pulled on the riding boots and tossed her filthy clothes and riding leathers into the washroom. She opened the refrigerator, lifted a bottle of wine, and took a big drink.

The attack flashed before her like the nightmare of Luhansk. Trembling, she startled when the dead man's face reflected in the dark windows, when a car's headlamps slashed through the glass like the knife's blade.

A frightened voice within said they would find her again. Weak, vacant eyes saw only the potato fork as it plunged into the Russian's midsection. *Luka* she remembered the other Russian calling for him. The name … of a would-be killer.

Why couldn't you have been Anson Beck?

She tasted only Luka's blood and her vomit. She took another drink of wine, but it did nothing to relieve the visions, tastes and smells. They remained as vivid as the snowy square and streets of Luhansk in the electric display of battle.

I didn't lose my nerve in Luhansk, she thought, setting the wine bottle on the table. She raised a trembling hand. *Why now?*

'When in doubt,' Gran Lockwood had told her, *'call on that stubborn desire of yours and use it as an alternate energy source. Never give up!'*

She reached for the wine bottle again, but her eyes went to a small white board on the wall. Printed in bright red marker ink was: *'It is always darkest just before the day dawneth'* by Thomas Fuller. She took a drink of wine and stared at the darkness out the windows.

Where the hell are you, Addie? She wondered.

With newfound resolve, she lifted a key from the wall beside the rear door and stepped outside. She ignored the light drizzle, locked the rear door, and slid the key under the mat. Attached to the rear wall stood a storage room. She unlocked the padlock and entered.

It was dark, the walls stacked with boxes. Kenna pulled an overhead string light that illuminated a sheet of canvas covering a motorcycle. She pulled it away to reveal a vintage 1970 Triumph TR6 Trophy. She affectionately brushed dust from it and filled the gas tank.

"Was hoping to get you back to the States before bringing you out … and never under these circumstances, old girl … but I need your help."

She snapped dust from aged riding leathers and pulled them on. Wearing an equally old skull cap helmet and goggles, she pushed the Triumph to the door. She primed it and kicked it twice; it started. Pleased, she stared at the bright alley light, and a smile inched across her face.

***

LUHANSK, UKRAINE - 2020

On a sunny day, Alistair Rensenhaus stood in front of the BNC company logo on the side of the aged office building. In one hand was a bottle of Horilka, the other a cigarette. Kenna sat apprehensively astride a Ukrainian Musstang 250 motorcycle. He waved her forward with the bottle. She eased the clutch out with too much power. The bike lunged forward; she lost grip on the clutch. Her hand twisted the throttle to full. The bike accelerated hard, popped a wheely, and threw her off the rear. The Musstang spun wildly in a circle, power subsided, and it twirled into the building close to Rensenhaus.

With a grand laugh, he turned the bike off and lifted it. Kenna joined him and took the bottle for a big drink. Without hesitation, she grabbed the handlebars again.

***

In the garage, Kenna let the blood flow through the engine while she checked a map on her phone. Satisfied, she placed it in her pocket and looked up to the bright alley light.

'Never enter a situation without preparing for the worst,' Gran Lockwood whispered from the past.

Kenna lifted the pistol from her backpack and shoved it

into her rear belt. With an intense grimace, she eased the Triumph along the narrow alley and paused at the street. There was no traffic, only darkness. With calm control, she accelerated between parked cars. She turned back, looked at Adelaide's apartment, and yelled in her mind:

I won't fucking give up until I find you!

XLVIII

Lyuba ignored the cold, damp air and pitch darkness of the abandoned parking garage. Echoing growls of lorries crossed the bridge overhead. She was playing a dangerous game; one she had contemplated for several years. Jammed between two colossal egos, she had formulated in her mind how to secure her future financially. That meant surviving, which, in turn, meant using every martial skill in her repertoire. Svetlana's threats revealed her true nature. Sir Clifton was more pragmatic, though equally dangerous. Neither could be trusted.

Busy eyes circled the decayed structure. Strewn at her feet and crumbling atop her, slabs of concrete leaned precariously against upright walls. Thick as blood, water drooled from spear-like reinforcement bars protruding from fallen sections as if impaling flesh. In the shadow of a streetlight, a crane's wrecking ball swung like a metronome. Cats scampered past inquisitively if only briefly seen. She wondered, with a grimace, if they were real.

Here, life seemed constant, perhaps a return to her childhood; outside was the unknown. She snapped the lunacy from her mind when headlights illuminated the darkness. The hum of the Rolls Royce's engine filled her ears. She lifted the P-96 semiautomatic pistol, chambered a shell, and switched on the safety. Like Kovalev, but unknown to most, Toll had a body count that preceded him to this meeting.

Edgar stopped the Rolls at the edge of the darkness and stood out. Leaving the calm chauffer persona inside, the bodyguard scanned the area while walking around the car. Satisfied, he opened the door. Toll stepped out and moved forward without fear, a man 30 years younger in his mind.

Hesitantly, Lyuba lifted a tightly bound leather pouch from her satchel. She untied the drawstring and placed it on a concrete slab. The rumble of a truck overhead sent a shock wave through the fragile structure. For a reason she could not explain, it calmed her.

"What I told you I would bring," she said.

Toll lifted the document. "How can I be certain you possess the balance?"

"By making the final payment," she said with confidence. "Then, I will produce it."

"Have you read it?" he asked.

"I have no interest in the games between you and Svetlana, Sir Clifton," she said. "What I demand is freedom, an option she will not guarantee.”

“And you think I will?”

“Let’s say your words have more allure.”

Toll nodded to Edgar. With a fighter’s stride, he walked for them with a package. He handed it to Toll, then rested his hand on the Walther pistol. The bodyguard’s eyes never left Lyuba. The attraction was not physical; he was calibrating the exact moment to kill.

“Stay your hand, Edgar,” she insisted.

“How do you—” he paused at Toll’s raised palm.

“All life’s problems are not solved with a bullet, my child,” Toll said to Lyuba. “Just the nastiest.”

“Svetlana, for example.”

“Perhaps,” Toll offered. “I have other plans for her … which involve you, of course.”

“Our agreement was for the folder,” she insisted.

“Our agreement is open-ended, Lyuba, and ends when I say it ends.”

Their conversation drowned out the slight movement of people approaching in the shadows. The crack of a pebble turned Edgar’s eyes an instant before Lyuba’s. Edgar pulled the Walther semiautomatic from his belt and took a protective stance in front of Toll.

"It appears our negotiation has just begun, Sir Clifton," Lyuba said, stuffed the envelope into her satchel, and ran.

Toll stepped towards the light and the sounds. There was no fear in his eyes; indeed, the only fear he had ever felt was of failure. Edgar led his master to a pile of debris where Toll stopped.

"I can smell your Ciel de Gum, Svetlana," Toll offered.

Pistol in-hand, Filipp stepped from the darkness just ahead of Svetlana. She hesitated and shoved her pistol into her handbag.

"I always gave you more credit, Svetlana," Toll said. "An ambush?"

"Lyuba?" she asked.

"She heard you before I did. A very illusive creature," he said. "You trained her well."

"Where is it?"

"If you speak of the Halibeck folder, it will be in safe hands shortly."

"Kovalev was bringing it for me," she demanded.

"Kovalev was bringing it to the highest bidder, my dear."

"I will have it," she demanded.

"In London, the rules of the game are mine, countess," Toll said without hesitation. "If you want it, then you must take it."

"Have it your way, Sir Clifton," she said and led Filipp away.

*

Edgar steered through traffic. In the rear seat, Toll opened his cell phone and typed in a text. *'It seems you are even more indebted to me now, my dear.'* He sent it; his phone swooshed. In a moment, his phone dinged with a message … Lyuba. *'I was thinking the same thing, Sir Clifton.'* Edgar stopped at a traffic light.

"Find her and that folder, Edgar," Toll ordered. "I have no intentions of paying for what is rightfully the Crown's."

"And her, sir?" Edgar asked.

Toll opened the folder and rifled through the sheets. On the final page, he paused. Stuck to the cover was a micro listening device. He angrily lifted it.

"Whatever the situation dictates," he said into the device and tossed it out the window.

*

In the darkness of a building alcove, Lyuba removed an earbud with a frown. Survival strained her face but a moment. She inhaled hard, thinking of her mother and father, and hurried away.

XLIX

The black water of Limehouse Basin was silent and still in the moonless night. Stars were hidden by heavy overcast that seemed a permanent fixture in the London sky. Kenna and Oleksandr sat on the aft deck of the fishing boat, a bottle of Horilka between them. Their silence and lack of eye contact emphasized heavy emotions.

It was time to bury the hatchet.

Kenna had brought up the past … what happened in Luhansk. It was an explosive subject but needed to be discussed. Nadia! Kenna left Luhansk shortly after her death, never knowing the truth of what happened. Oleksandr refused to discuss it. With his silence, his refusal to return her emails and calls, the animosity from afar mounted … but neither backed down; neither was willing to put the past to rest.

Neither had any idea that they had been so close together all this time. Had they known, perhaps the hatchet could have been buried long ago. But they didn't, and it hadn't been. Given present events, however, both knew that to succeed and survive, their animosity needed to be put to bed. Or at least shoved aside.

"My past is my failure," he said, pouring both a shot of Horilka.

"One of my grandmother's axioms was *'don't crucify yourself because of other people's actions.'*"

"Philosophical bullshit doesn't make it easier to swallow, Athena. I should have seen their betrayal."

"We both should have," she snapped. "But none of us can see the invisible, Oles."

He frowned, knowing it had been something entirely different. "It wasn't invisible. I was blind."

Her tone was curt; she was annoyed. "These people deal in realities, not analogies."

He turned, angry. "I know their fucking intentions, Athena! I've felt the edge of their blade more than once!"

"That doesn't excuse what you did!" she demanded. "Correction didn't do … Nadia!"

Crumpled fists held silent his response. Before they realized it, they stood nose-to-nose, breathing hard like two gladiators ready for battle. Her honesty dug to the quick. He was out of shape, drunk most of the time, and mentally unprepared to deal with the present … only dream of the past … where he had failed!

In frustration, he grabbed her, not to harm her but to

silence her. *Shut up!* was his silent demand. She knocked his hands away and kicked his leg out from under him. He went down hard on the deck with a shout of pain and pulled Kenna down with him. With little effort, he threw her to the side and rolled atop her with a fist recoiled to strike.

"What are you doing?"

Mrs. Kohut ran onto the deck, grabbed his arm, and put herself between his fist and Kenna's face. Anger boiled in Oleksandr, such as she had seen only on that horrible day.

"It's okay, Mrs. Kohut," Kenna said. "A discussion we should have had a long time ago."

"Nadia," Mrs. Kohut said.

"If you both don't learn to accept it, as horrible as it was," Evhen said from the salon door. "You will never survive."

Weak, the anger escaping him as swiftly as it mounted, Oleksandr rolled to the deck. Blood spotted the side wound dressing; Mrs. Kohut reached for it. He stayed her hand.

"Leave it," Oleksandr said. "And leave us. Athena and I aren't done talking."

"As long as it's talking and not fighting," Mrs. Kohut demanded, stood, and walked inside with Evhen.

Breathing hard, regaining control, both looked at the

black sky.

"Just like that night … remember," he said as much as asked. "With the Russians searching for us."

"Just like now," Kenna responded. "But there's more to it, Oles. It's no time for self-pity."

"Weakness is a trait of man," he said in a curt tone. "It is our gravest flaw."

"From those weaknesses, we must gain strength," she countered. "That is our greatest asset."

He lifted a palm, a sign of capitulation. "More philosophical bullshit, Athena. Let's just finish what's in front of us."

"Agreed, but this discussion isn't over until we both agree," she said. "You once told me that *'Hell hath a master, and that master be fear.'* " She took his shoulders and stared into his deep eyes. "Turn the pain of that night into power, Oles."

"On that, we agree," he said.

Kenna looked at the black sky, knowing she had stepped through the gates of fear once again. Facing the master chilled her as if standing at the final ring of Dante's hell.

In her mind, she saw him bleeding, remembering as well other bleeding men, wounded men, dying men … and the ten-year-old girl. Bodies littered Luhansk. Pain filled her, but not from the recent injuries … from the killing, the pain, and the sorrow.

She winced, hearing the mortars, the cackle of rapid gunfire, the bright flares seeking their position. Burnt cordite filled her nostrils as it had that night and many more, and a sense of defeat overwhelmed her.

Kovalev had said it best, *'You were in no condition to combat the Russian Army.'* None of them were.

Now, after two years of trying to forget, her eyes narrowed, and her breath engulfed the putrefied air of the present. She stared at the wounded man, a friend, seeing not a warrior but a father who had lost everything that night.

Her hand brushed her hair, feeling her own wounds; sweat dampened her brow. She tasted salt, like the ocean, and wiped it away. An imaginary wind blew hard against her hair.

"Not Luhansk, but hell nonetheless, where we're goin', Athena," he said with calm intent.

***

LUHANSK, UKRAINE—2 YEARS BEFORE

Bitter cold wind bit into Kenna's face as she ducked into the ruins of a destroyed apartment building. She knew the man at the back of the meeting had been Anson Beck; she had to prove it more to herself than the others. Oleksandr and Rensenhaus both warned her not to come across no-man's land alone.

She hadn't listened. The intel had been good from the source that informed them of the secret meeting. But Rensenhaus wanted further verification. Kenna decided not to wait and left after midnight.

A patrol of armed Russian soldiers marched along the destruction of war, speaking low, smoking cigarettes. She huddled in the shadows and examined a map. She eased from the hiding place to look for a landmark. Shock hit her. Not twenty feet away, where their source had said, stood Anson Beck, brash and arrogant.

She didn't know why, but she stood in the open and removed the hood from her head. His stare was of calm intent. Like at the farmhouse in Virginia, the calm broke in an instant.

Like a Wild West showdown, they both pulled pistols and fired at the same time. Her shot ripped through his free arm, spinning him. He fired again. The bullet ricocheted from the wall, blowing chards of stone across Kenna's side, ripping flesh. She screamed and fell into shadow. Soldiers swarmed into the area. A hand startled her and covered her mouth.

'Quiet, Athena,' Oleksandr whispered. *'I'll get you out of here.'*

He carried her from the destroyed building and through the snow.

***

Warm desire flushed Kenna's cheeks. It was refreshing to finally meet a man willing to accept his faults and failures as part of himself. But one also willing to fight them. She shook her head … *idiot* then spoke before thinking:

"Perhaps I am a greater fool than I thought, but I trust you, Oles," she offered. "The difference between then and now is we have home-field advantage … well, kinda."

He stood and helped her up. He handed her a glass of Horilka, and they toasted. "To an unlikely partnership, Athena, woman born of fire. May we be successful or die instantly, without pain."

They toasted again and drank.

L

An orange slice of sun appeared on the horizon, transforming Limehouse Basin from black to grey. Lights and people appeared on boat decks. Voices, a cough, and a laugh bounced across the water. An engine cranked to life; a bell rang; a dog barked. Music played over the rumble of a working narrowboat's engine. At the helm, a woman smoked a cigarette, steered the boat away from its mooring, and eased it away. She drank coffee; a man came from below and readied the craft for cargo.

Still in the shadows, Evhen's fishing boat was dark and silent. The captain sat on the aft deck with a cigarette, watching the sunrise. He longed for the mornings of Odessa most of all. His boats were now in Russian hands, the fate of his crews unknown. He hoped to return one day but doubted he ever would. Footsteps turned him.

Wiggy walked along the sidewalk between the water and the terrace houses. "Lookin' for number 23."

"What business you have?" Evhen asked.

"Between me and the woman born of fire," Wiggy said.

Evhen flipped a thumb over his shoulder. "Last I saw,

asleep."

"That's a rarity," Wiggy chuckled and paused at the gangway. "Permission to come aboard."

"Granted," Evhen said, extending a hand. "If you be Wiggy."

"Jeremy Heffernan if ya wanna be formal."

"Prefer not," Evhen said. "Take it she gave ya the nickname."

"Not for discussion," Wiggy said and stepped aboard.

"Tea or something harder if ya prefer," Evhen offered.

"Little early for the harder, but I'll take a rain check. Tea's fine."

Inside the salon, Kenna lay on a bench covered by an overcoat. Voices and a narrowboat's horn opened her eyes; her hand pulled the Russian pistol from beneath her. She sat up, wiping sleep from her eyes. A light flicked on; hobbling footsteps turned her to the stairway.

"Thought I heard you making noise last night," Oleksandr said as he entered.

"You should be in bed," Mrs. Kohut shouted from below.

"Been on my backside too long," he responded. "Besides, I'm hungry."

Kenna joined him in the galley and searched through the

cabinets. "How did the British empire conquer the world without coffee?"

"Tea and spices, Athena," Oleksandr said.

"Then, why is British food so bland?"

"So, yer a food critic now." Oleksandr paused, looking to the aft deck. "Visitor."

Kenna stretched and turned when Wiggy and Evhen entered the salon. "Our resident computer genius, Wiggy."

Mrs. Kohut joined them in the galley and pulled a can of instant coffee from the refrigerator. Kenna smiled. The men shook hands.

"Better than nothin', sweetie," Mrs. Kohut said.

"You heard from Tom Terrific?" Wiggy asked Kenna. "I've been calling and nothing."

"Said he was going to a couple hospitals, then to Adelaide's mother's, if he hadn't found her." Kenna accepted a cup from Mrs. Kohut. "I tried to talk some sense into him about developing a plan—"

"He'll go about it his own way, kid," Wiggy interrupted.

"Keep after him, Wiggy," Kenna thought aloud. "Don't want him vanishing into thin air, as well."

Oleksandr studied the wall behind Kenna. "You were busy last night."

"Had to do something while Mrs. Kohut stitched my arm."

A dozen sheets of E4 paper detailed a convoluted diagram. At the top was *'Victims'*, and listed, *'Alistair, Yuri, Kovalev, Wembley Guard, Illya, Nadia,'* with a line drawn to the side for *'Rashon Hill and Policeman,'* with a note: *'Saw too much.'* On another sheet: *'Ukrainian Survivors'* and their names, *'Oleksandr, Mrs. Kohut, Evhen.'* On yet another sheet: *'British'* and the names: *'Toll, Thurnbull, Tommy, Barnaby, Attwood, Jenkins, Carter.'* Below that, a sheet titled *'Russians'* and the names *'Svetlana, Medved, Lyuba, 5 Unknown at Luhansk Shack.'*

"You think we're suspects, Athena?" Oleksandr asked.

"Athena?" Wiggy asked.

"Goddess of War," Oleksandr said, then to Kenna, "Answer my question."

"You don't shoot well enough, from what I recall."

Kenna pointed to the diagram. She spoke as she pointed out the names and details on each sheet. On the sheet below the names:

"Alistair was shot and burned in Luhansk," she began, pointing on the same sheet beside it. "Yuri was shot twice, in the shoulder and leg, then strangled and a coup de grâce above the left eye. In the Wembley owner's suite, Kovalev and the Guard—"

"Wilkerson," Wiggy interrupted. "The lad's name."

Not skipping a beat, Kenna continued, "Both shot once in the heart. And then Illya, also a bullet to the heart."

"He'd been in a scrap, as well, kid," Wiggy said. "Broken ribs and a bullet wound in the leg."

Fighting pain, Oleksandr joined Kenna and pointed. "Nadia?"

"That's where all this started, Oles," she said. "She was there when the Russians raided the BNC office and killed Alistair."

"You don't have to remind me what happened, Athena," Oleksandr snapped, recalled the night before, and calmed.

"Think about what you saw, Oles," she said, placing a caring hand on his shoulder. "You were too frantic and grieving to see it; we all were."

Oleksandr's eyes narrowed, recalling that horrible moment he lifted Nadia's lifeless remains from the ground. He weakened and sat heavily on the bench.

"She was ripped apart by shrapnel," he said and paused. "Shot in the back. But why is she—"

"Let me walk through it, Oles, and you'll see," she said,

then to Wiggy, "Did you look up what I asked?"

Wiggy stepped forward, opening his laptop. He flashed to a document and showed it to Kenna. While she reviewed the screen, Wiggy continued for her:

"Sent for the Ukrainian pathologist's report on Rensenhaus's death. Wasn't the fire that killed him."

"A single gunshot wound to the heart," Kenna said. With a look of angry satisfaction that only Wiggy noted, she asked, "Are you sure of this?"

"I didn't write it," Wiggy insisted.

Kenna turned her attention back to the diagrams on the wall. The next pages detailed the identities of the Russians, the murder locations, the dates and times, and Halibeck International (CIA). Kenna went back to the report on Rensenhaus's death. In a flash of memory, she remembered his body taken from the destroyed building. There had been so much gunfire she hadn't seen what happened. It was staged to look like he was killed during the battle, but it was an assassin's bullet that ended his life, just like the others. But Yuri … his wasn't as clean or precise … as did Illya's leg and ribs. The others, all precise, a bullet to the heart!

"What did you learn from yer mind cobwebs, kid?" Wiggy asked of the papers.

"My thought process changed when you said you needed two laptops to track the complexity of this case."

"Now all I need's more hands," he countered.

Lines funneled down the pages to the last sheet. Printed in bold letters at the top was *'British News Corporation'*. Below that, *'Toll'*.

"All roads lead to Rome," she said, slapping the last paper. "The connections all lead to BNC."

"And to you, kid," Wiggy concluded.

"Yes, specifically, my work in Luhansk … for BNC," she said and turned to Oleksandr. "Our work there, Oles."

She drew circles around the victims with heart-shots and those not. Wiggy knew where she was going and completed the work for her. When done, lines connected all players with BNC, but through *'ASSASSIN'* and *'KILLER'*.

"Yuri was killed, and an attempt was made on Illya by an imprecise killer or killers," she said. "Like the men that attacked you at Kovalev's apartment, then later at your apartment, Oles."

"Medved and his Bolshevik hooligans," Oleksandr said.

"Kovalev, Wilkerson, Illya, and Rashon were all shot in the exact same spot," she said, drawing a heart and slamming the pencil through it.

"And Nadia?" Oleksandr asked.

"Is exactly what you know it is, Oles," Kenna said. "And has nothing to do with these."

"Then, what's it tell ya, Athena?" Oleksandr demanded.

"They have two objectives: the video we took of the secret Russian meeting and the folder Kovalev stole from Svetlana in Luhansk."

"Yuri said there was a link between the two, kid," Wiggy said. "That's what Barnaby and I need to work on."

"I agree with the objectives, but the killings seem random," Oleksandr said. "Doesn't seem to be a logical order."

"That's because they aren't being performed by one person. If Illya had survived, he could have told us we have two shooters, not one," she said with emphasis. "Similar objectives but different motivation. The heart shots seem personal and were certainly professional. Both achieving results but by entirely different methods."

"What's the next step?" Oleksandr asked.

"Don't say what I think yer gonna say," Wiggy demanded.

"We're gonna give the rats a reason to come out of the woodwork."

LI

Revving the Triumph's engine, Kenna was stopped at Knightsbridge, looking both directions. The conversation with Lyuba unfolded in her mind and gave meaning to her words.

'What can the police do against the most powerful governments in the world?'

Plural, yes, she had said *'governments'*, not government. Lyuba confirmed what Kenna suspected all along … these weren't just simple random killings. These killings were greater in magnitude and had security implications for not just the people involved but for their countries: Ukraine, Russia, the U.K., and the U.S., Just as she and Wiggy had detailed in their Kovalev crime scene sketches.

She punched Bluetooth; it went to voicemail. "Widen your scope, Wiggy. We've gotten into a mess between governments, not just men. And you were right, time to watch the darkness."

Kenna disconnected the call, crossed herself, and accelerated onto Knightsbridge. She turned through the open gates of West Carriage Drive. Her mind whirled as she sped through the barren winter trees that lined the street. She crossed the bridge over Serpentine Lido, passed the Serpentine Sackler Gallery, accelerated hard around a slow-moving lorry, then skidded to a stop at a red light.

A car stopped beside her; she turned. In the rear seat, a girl about Nadia's age gave her a thumbs up. Fighting back anger and sadness simultaneously, Kenna nodded. When the light turned, she leaned on the tank and, with a screaming tire, roared ahead of the other cars. In the Triumph's rearview mirror, the girl leaned out the window to watch.

She turned left at Bayswater Road and blended with traffic. At a line of police cars along the front security wall of the Embassy of the Russian Federation, she slowed and stopped. Confined to the opposite side of the street and off the roadway, a group of Ukrainian protestors carried signs. There was no yelling. Two men with barrels swept the last of the riot debris.

Kenna swung off and chained the Triumph to a streetlight. She stood in direct line with a CCTV camera, removed her goggles and helmet, and stared directly into the lens.

*

Inside a well-appointed Embassy office, Svetlana sat behind a large wood desk, staring at Kenna's image on a computer screen. A grimace of accepting the challenge creased her flawless complexion. *This could be fun,* she thought.

"Yes, that's her, Feodor. Well done," said the falconer into her speaker phone.

She disconnected the call, shoved a P-96 semiautomatic pistol into a shoulder holster, and winced while pulling on the tailored overcoat. She walked from the room, immediately followed by two armed guards. Meeting them, Filipp opened the front door. Svetlana walked out and was greeted by protesting voices across the street. She smiled inside, thriving on the animosity.

"Don't those vermin have homes?" she asked Filipp.

"We should give them one, director," he responded. "In a cemetery."

Svetlana walked to the security gate. Kenna stepped forward but was blocked by a Russian guard. With the wave of Svetlana's hand, he backed off. Kenna moved to where the barred gate was all that separated them. Silent stares welcomed a fight.

"Why are you here?" Svetlana demanded.

"To find Kovalev's killer," Kenna said without emotion.

"You're looking in the wrong place."

"All indications point to someone in this building,

Svetlana," Kenna said.

"I would never kill him," the chiseled features said. "At one time I loved him."

"So, I've heard. What happened?" Kenna asked.

"Two clashing egos," Svetlana said, wondering why she answered at all.

"What I meant was what happened that resulted in someone killing Kovalev?"

"I'll not do your homework for you, Ms. Hannigan," Svetlana said.

"Perhaps you should. It might help clear your name or the name of others in the embassy if what you say is true."

"Why shouldn't I kill you now?"

"Because you want what I have," Kenna said.

"You are brave," Svetlana said, admiring that quality without showing it. "I could kill you and fly home a hero."

"Doesn't seem like your style," Kenna countered. "Unlike Lyuba."

Taken aback, Svetlana gathered herself. "And what do you know of her?"

"We had a nice long chat outside the Mandarin Oriental."

"A great place for lunch or a drink."

"Both, I'm told," Kenna said. "Bit outta my price range."

"I would have thought your friend Kostyantyn would have treated you."

Kenna smiled. "To my knowledge, you are the only one standing at this gate that slept with him … unless one of the guards did."

Kenna relished the anger that instantly narrowed Svetlana's eyes. But she didn't come for a childish tit-for-tat.

"I know why you're in London, Svetlana," she lied.

"How naïve to think you can read my mind," Svetlana said with a smile.

"Then, enlighten me."

"Secrets never pass these lips, my foolish American journalist," Svetlana said with conviction. "In my country, the Gulags are very cold this time of year."

As is Leavenworth, Kenna thought. "Perhaps we could discuss a means to settle this without more bloodshed."

Svetlana's silent sneer told of her true intentions. "Yet, blood is what defines us."

"Without it, the world would be without people like us," Kenna said.

"Avoiding bloodshed is simple," Svetlana said with

intent. "Return what is mine."

"Funny, I thought it was Alistair Rensenhaus's," Kenna countered. "There are people here that will stop you from leaving."

"Such as you?" Svetlana said, finding humor in that. "Had we met in Luhansk—"

"Oh, but we did," Kenna interrupted. "The night you met with the others in the shack. Remember? I have you on video."

"So, that was you," Svetlana said with surprise, thinking of Medved. *Why didn't you tell me, Alexi?* "I will have that video."

"You have killed many people—"

"I have killed no one," Svetlana corrected.

"An order to kill is no different than pulling the trigger," Kenna said. "One, you will eventually pay for."

"I approach all assignments with open eyes," Svetlana hissed. "Had my men done their job in Ukraine, you would not be standing here."

Kenna's Cheshire grin allowed her thoughts to sink into Svetlana. She motioned to the policemen and guards.

"Nothing like a good cat fight to keep the boys interested, eh, Svetlana?"

"I prefer to eat what the lions kill," Svetlana said.

"Yes, your lion, Alexi Medved."

"Bring what is mine, or it will be you," Svetlana warned.

"Yes, the Halibeck International folder and the video … correction, my video." Kenna turned and walked away from the gate. She stopped halfway across the street. "But you'll have to come outside the zoo for that. And bring lots of gold."

Curiosity filled Svetlana as she watched Kenna speed away on the Triumph. She turned to the Embassy's front door.

"Filipp, have Medved meet me in the rear garden," she commanded. "Lyuba has made a decision."

He silently agreed and lifted his cell phone.

*

Gas burners warmed the embassy's rear garden. It was perfectly manicured with grass and flowers during the warm months. This day, it was barren of both, a brown that matched the stone security wall that enclosed them.

Smoking a cigarette in a holder, Svetlana sat across from Medved, some distance from other embassy staff. Only they knew how their mutual hatred had begun. And for both, it would remain between them. Afterall, how could they defend mutual betrayal? How could they resolve mutual betrayal?

"Alexi, we need to stop this childish squabble and concentrate on our mission."

She was old enough to be his mother, but that hadn't mattered to either. In fact, it was an erotic fantasy for both, as if a mother was making love to her son, an Oedipus Complex between adults. In the beginning, their love affair had been passionate, like a tsunami ripping across the ocean. Their nuclear orgasms had been mind-boggling.

'Why do you suppose we ended up here?' she had asked him two years ago in Luhansk.

'We seek the same,' he had replied. *'Death.'*

Everything fell apart when transferred to Luhansk, the end of the fucking world, the end of romance, the end of any feeling of life. The solution to their differences was, of course, simple … blood, which neither wanted.

"Do you suppose the garden is still there?" she asked.

Medved's hatred of life itself boiled within him, and he motioned around them. "All gardens die, Svetlana."

"The one given of life," she said, for the moment sad. She whisked the emotion away like blowing out a candle. "I believe the reporter has what you're after."

"The video," he said, mind concentrating on Kenna's image and thought, *I should have killed her in the street.*

"And Lyuba has the folder," Svetlana said. "Have you spoken to her?"

"Not since Kovalev's apartment."

"She's trying to make a deal with the British newsman." She hesitated at the next thought. "You were right, Alexi. The journalist is working with Oleksandr."

"It's time to take off the gloves, Svetlana," he said. "All three must be taken out, or our mission is in jeopardy."

She had always been the thinker when it came to their work. But when muscle was required, she wanted Alexi Medved by her side. She needed a little more time to complete the tasks required and needed him on a leash until then.

"Find Lyuba first," she insisted. "I want to verify who she's working with."

"I'll put Feodor on it and find her," Medved said and stood.

Svetlana took his arm, stopping him, and demanded, "Don't kill her; bring her to me! She has the folder, and I want it."

"The journalist?" Medved asked.

Svetlana thought a few seconds, then nodded. "Both, Alexi. Bring both … alive."

Walking away, Medved lifted his phone …

*

Medved and Pyotr stood at a computer station with Feodor and a young computer geek. As the geek worked the keys, images filled two screens directly in front of them. One held a map of London, which Feodor enlarged.

"In the cell phone left by the Ukrainian, the call memory was deleted," Feodor said. "But I recovered the history. The phone was used to call two other numbers several times."

"Did you locate them?" Medved snapped impatiently.

"Both phones have calls that bounced off a cell tower in Limehouse," Feodor said, circling it on the map.

"The fisherman," Medved mumbled.

"Evhen Chayka," Feodor said and pulled Evhen's image onto the screen. "Was Shwetz's partner in Odessa. Both came to London two years ago. He has a fishing boat moored at Limehouse Basin."

LII

With a cup of tea untouched on his desk, Thurnbull drummed his fingers against his laptop. With his mind elsewhere, he scanned the videos taken by Kenna and the still photos of the people in Luhansk. Kenna told him there was CCTV of Yuri Zelenko's killing, but MI5 had put a lock on it. MIT had also sequestered the video from Rashon Hill's phone. How could he finish his work if the information was not available?

It was unlike Henson to disappear from work. This girlfriend … not wife, he noted mentally … was getting in the way of him doing his job. Henson was the key; Thurnbull wanted to know what he was doing to get his head around work. Without the proper mental attitude, Henson was worthless to him.

Dammit, he cursed himself, *get control!* He threw on his overcoat and opened the door.

"Corina, I'm going to the gym," he said. "I need a workout to get my brain functioning."

As Thurnbull walked out the door, Corina lifted the phone. "Mrs. Pemberton …"

*

The red brick two-story quadraplexes backed against the Enchanted Woodland of Dartford in Northern Kent. It was a clean and quiet neighborhood that fronted a small park and playground for children. Today, there was no laughter; there were no games. It was empty, as was the main street entering, with cars parked along the sides and in designated places.

A white Vauxhall Vivaro panel van eased along the street in no particular hurry. In the passenger seat, Barnaby Scriven held his phone, staring at the GPS map, and pointed directions an instant before the irritating female voice instructed them:

"In one hundred meters, turn right."

The driver, a younger man in a suit not all that dissimilar to Barnaby's, flipped on the indicator and turned. Wiggy and another agent sat in the rear seat, anxious. Calm and collected, Barnaby watched the neighborhood, mentally noting everything.

"We have no idea what we're going to find, so be alert," he ordered.

Wiggy loosened his leather bomber jacket; the agent unbuttoned his overcoat. Beneath them were Glock 22 semiautomatic pistols in shoulder holsters.

"Hopefully, we won't need those," Barnaby said.

"Aye," Wiggy agreed, turning to the street. "Just bein' a good Boy Scout."

"You were never a Boy Scout, wouldn't have let you in," Barnaby said deadpan.

Wiggy lifted his cell phone and scrolled for a number.

*

Thurnbull sat in his Jaguar F-Pace in the darkness of the parking garage. He stared at the gym bag on the passenger seat, hesitated, then lit his pipe. He needed a clear head to work through this problem. Multiple murders, Russian interference, and his top man AWOL. And where was Hannigan? It was her mess, to begin with … all about the bloody video from Luhansk. If he could only get his hands on that …

The cell phone rang over the car's speaker and startled him. "Thurnbull."

*

Wiggy watched out the window at the empty street. "Mr. Thurnbull, this is Jeremy Heffernan, but Kenna calls me Wiggy."

"Oh, right that," Thurnbull acknowledged, tension

easing. "What can I do for you?"

"Kenna asked me to inform you that she heard from Tommy. I'm going to collect him now."

"Why didn't she ring me?" Thurnbull asked. "I'm out of the office and would be happy to help."

"No problem, I'm almost there," Wiggy said. "He's a bit skittish. Paranoid about someone being after him, with his girlfriend missing and all. Apparently, he's afraid to come out of hiding."

"Never known him to be afraid, a damn good soldier in his day."

"All the same," Wiggy offered, "Kenna said it has to do with the video and how it links with the murders. Was pretty hush-hush over the phone."

Then Tommy's seen it, Thurnbull said to himself, perking up. "When you're with him, let me know. I need to speak with him."

Wiggy disconnected the call and sent a pre-written text; his phone swooshed.

*

In the parking garage, Thurnbull walked from his Jaguar with the gym bag and punched a speed dial number. It rang and went to voicemail.

"This is Tommy Henson. Leave a message." Beep.

"Henson, call me when you get this," Thurnbull ordered. "We need to discuss Hannigan's video. You're key to this piece being done right, my boy. Ring me."

*

The driver eased the Vauxhall Vivaro panel van to the side of the street and stopped a half block from the residence. Barnaby checked his weapon, as did the others.

"Jeremy, you're with me in the front," Barnaby ordered. "You two lads to the rear garden. No one in or out, but we want this to be quiet."

"Let's pray everything's normal," Wiggy said.

"Oxford is considering removing that word from the dictionary," Barnaby quipped.

The four men stood from the van and walked for the building, like coming to pay a visit. Passing in front of an adjacent duplex apartment, they paused when a young woman opened the front door with two young children. Barnaby flashed his badge and a pleasant smile.

"Please wait inside, mum."

Without hesitation, she turned the children inside. Barnaby waved the two agents to the rear. They cautiously hurried around the side of the building towards the rear. On

408

the front stoop, Barnaby rang the bell, no answer. He knocked several times.

"Mrs. Rensenhaus, this is Supervising Agent Barnaby Scrivens of Security Service. We need to have a chat." Barnaby knocked again, then turned to Wiggy. "Appears no one's home."

"Or can't answer," Wiggy said, looking through the windows; there was no movement. "Turn yer eyes if ya don't wanna watch."

Wiggy lifted a kit from his bomber jacket and, with little effort, picked the lock. He eased the door open. With pistols at the ready, he followed Barnaby inside.

"Mrs. Rensenhaus, this is Barnaby Scrivens of Security Service; hello," he said to no answer. "Henson?"

Wiggy opened the rear kitchen door. The other agents entered. One remained at the door while they went through the entire two-story flat. It was perfectly kept, with no sign of a struggle. Indeed, there was no evidence anyone had been there other than the fact they knew someone had. They met near the front door.

"This makes no bloody sense," Barnaby said.

Wiggy disagreed silently. He lifted his phone and punched Kenna's number.

Weaving through traffic on the Triumph, Kenna punched Bluetooth. "This is Kenna."

Wiggy followed the other agents out to the street. He turned back to the apartment as if to be sure it was empty. Barnaby stood at the neighbor's apartment, speaking with the young woman, the children clinging to her.

"Just went through Adelaide's mother's house," Wiggy said. "No one here and no sign that anyone has been here for some time."

"Keep looking, Wiggy," Kenna said. "Adelaide must be somewhere. And, hopefully, where you find her, you'll find Tommy."

"Or vice versa, kid," he offered and stepped into the van. "I'm on it. Have more work to do."

Wiggy disconnected the call just as Barnaby stepped inside. The driver started the van and drove away. The young woman stepped from the apartment, shaded her eyes from the sun, and watched them.

"Neighbor hasn't seen or heard anything for several days," Barnaby said. "She thinks Mrs. Rensenhaus went on vacation."

"Then, why would Tommy think Adelaide had come here?" Wiggy asked.

"A question we'll need to ask him once we locate him," Barnaby said.

Wiggy lifted his laptop from the leather satchel and opened it.

"I missed something when we reviewed the stadium CCTV video, Barnaby," he said, angry with himself.

"Have the perfect place to brainstorm," Barnaby said.

"Long as it has whiskey," Wiggy said. "Kenna's dependin' on us."

LIII

Kenna stopped the Triumph in front of Sir Clifton Toll's mansion in the heart of the city. When she shut down the engine, she looked up and listened. Unlike Gran's Boston estate, there was no wind through the trees, just the multiplicity of street sounds that defined the megapolis of London. Both were equally hypnotic.

She looked at Toll's residence differently than she had before. She understood its necessity and the reason he wanted … no, demanded … this showpiece of opulence. It was the same reason her father lived in a mansion on 40 acres in the Southlake section of Dallas. When the players of life's power game died, whoever had the most toys won.

She thought of Wiggy's call. They couldn't accept finding nothing. She demanded positive thoughts, but it was more and more difficult. Adelaide was out there … enough said … if anyone could find her, it was Wiggy.

With satisfaction, Kenna turned when Graves opened the entrance door into Toll's toybox. With her tools of the trade, the helmet, and backpack, she entered.

*

In his private office, Toll, the private citizen, knew he

could, for the most part, avoid public scrutiny and bureaucratic meddling. As controller of the largest private press organization in the kingdom, he could fight off those wanting to invade his fiefdom. His army was the watchful eye of his reporters ... his *information gatherers.*

Alistair Rensenhaus had been the best, his finest asset. But even Rensenhaus had his flaws and had left this assignment, of them all, unfinished. Rensenhaus had been the one exception to Toll's clean workspace rule. Given his proclivity to slovenliness, the old warhorse managed somehow to report as Sir Clifton and, thus, the Crown demanded. In a selfish way, Toll wondered if Kenna Hannigan could replace Rensenhaus. But, then again, could anyone?

For four decades, BNC had been the funnel through which clandestine information of national consequence had squeezed undetected past other press agencies. He alone decided a story's worth, and the publication of same fell solely on his shoulders and the Prime Minister. Just because a story wasn't published didn't mean it wasn't newsworthy. His episode in Argentina was a prime example, which ended in the private celebration of his knighthood.

Kenna Hannigan's video in Luhansk had fallen into this realm. Kovalev's killing and the riot at the Russian Embassy added spice to her newsworthy stories. He knew she was a tad naïve, as they all were at that age, but he could mold her.

A knock at the door. Graves entered ahead of Kenna, she resplendent in the aged riding leathers, frazzled hair, and a warrior's grimace. Toll smiled inside; he had been right about this woman ... *more guts and drive than most men I know*. It had been those qualities that produced the video in Luhansk, not the camera. And he knew without a doubt it would be her determination that would locate and bring him the Halibeck folder.

Behind the desk, Toll smoked a cigar, a tumbler of whiskey on a coaster at the tips of manicured fingers. Without asking, Kenna went to the sideboard, poured vodka into a shot glass, and downed it. Without watching, a smile lifted the corners of the old man's eyes.

Obstinance can, at times, be one's greatest asset, he thought.

"I asked you here because I wanted to discuss your conversation with the Russian woman named Lyuba," Toll said.

"Yes, outside the Mandarin Oriental," she said. "An interesting ... and in many ways, frightening woman. But that isn't why I came."

You are good, Ms. Hannigan, Toll thought. *When pushed, you push back.* "My house, my rules."

"If you haven't learned by now, Sir Clifton, I don't play by the rules." Kenna poured another drink, sat in the parlor chair across from him, and sipped it. "What my grandmother taught me, *first one to warm the insides; the second to savor.*"

"A wise woman," he said. "Alright, Ms. Hannigan, today we'll play without rules."

Which is a rule in and of itself, she thought. The small victory warmed her as much as the vodka. It was time to *shake the trees and see what falls out.* She began:

"Halibeck International and its head, David Camden … ignoring the CIA involvement for the moment. What was Kovalev's involvement with the company and Camden?"

"If you know that connection, you undoubtedly have everything at your fingertips, Ms. Hannigan," he said. "There is much I can't say because of national security."

"A newsman speaking of national security," she said, confronting him head-on. "Which means it's true … you work hand-in-glove with 10 Downing."

"When necessity demands," he responded, unsure why he had.

"Such as what happened in Luhansk two years ago."

"Should you decide to share the mysterious video with me, we can talk." He paused and finished his drink. "Until then—"

"My grandmother," she interrupted, "told me the greatest asset at our disposal was history. Nothing has been done that hasn't been done before."

"Scientific accomplishments aside, I take it," he said.

That drew Kenna's investigative stare and smirk. *What I would have given to hear you and Gran in a conversation.*

"I speak of criminal enterprises, Sir Clifton."

"Is that inference that Halibeck committed illegal acts?"

The smile and stare again, *of course.* She changed direction like changing lanes on the motorway.

"You arranged the autopsy on Alistair in Ukraine. Why didn't you report the truth on how he died?"

Toll's mind whirled, impressed by her resourcefulness. "That's a matter for the family, not the public."

"Then, why wasn't his daughter told he was killed by a gunshot, not the fire?"

"If this is simply an inquest, my dear, we can stop here," he said. *Yes, I need to keep that mind of yours working,* he thought. "If you want to discuss the present situation, then proceed."

"Alistair's killing, my time in Luhansk, and yes, the video are all related to the present situation. If you can't see that, then you're lying or blind."

"I see perfectly well, Ms. Hannigan," Toll responded without emotion. "And I never lie."

"How can I contact David Camden?"

"To what end?"

"He met with Kovalev just before the killing. I'd like to know what was said."

"It's right in front of you, Ms. Hannigan," Toll guided her like the master manipulator he was. "You're approaching this like firing a shotgun when you should be using a rapier."

Sir Clifton's word games were mind-numbing, but Kenna refused to bend to them. She would get to Camden one way or another. She lifted the photograph of Lyuba receiving the folder in the Mandarin Oriental from her backpack and slid it across the desk.

"Lyuba received a package at the Mandarin Oriental."

His silent, *what of it?*

"The Halibeck International folder you seek," Kenna said. "Kovalev left it in the hotel for me, but she beat me to the punch. Did you know they were married?"

Absurd, he did not say. "Yes, the fake passport she used to enter the country."

"If you knew that, then why allow her in?"

Toll stood for another drink. "Because, my inquisitive American friend, she is an intricate piece of this game. Without her, victory is not assured."

Game? Victory? To Sir Clifton Toll, this was another box to tick, another square on the gameboard. He scanned the photo with feigned interest. He knew Lyuba perhaps better than them all; she sensed it. The way his eyes altered when seeing her image. He inhaled and closed his eyes, reflecting. When his eyes opened, it was like he had discovered life on another planet.

Kenna understood. Gran Lockwood taught her *it's more important to sense and feel the truth than see it.*

Toll looked into Kenna's eyes, understanding what was behind them. He was looking into his own soul. She had been a step ahead of them all. He wanted to embrace her but knew there remained much work to do. Perhaps when this was all over …

"Then, Ms. Hannigan, I suggest you find her," he said. "And bring me the folder."

As Kenna walked out, she appreciated Lyuba's brazen

courage. She was bartering with her two masters, vying for everything, her life, knowing either would kill her without a thought. *Such courage in such a beautiful young woman,* she thought. It was an admirable trait while also being terrifying.

LIV

Secluded in forty hectares of dense woodlands and surrounded by a ten-foot-high stone wall topped with concertina wire, the three-story 60-room mansion at the end of the winding cobblestone drive was completely isolated from the city that surrounded it. To ensure that isolation, it was further enclosed by a web of electronic surveillance equipment and guards, both human and canine. The wrought iron gate was opened only to specific visitors, both offered or forced to accept the hospitality of the British government.

Vehicles shuffled in night and day as would any to the home of a prestigious land baron. The guise of normality … and affluence … was staged for the benefit of a curious public. Had one peered over the wall or through the gate, they would see gardeners working the grounds and drivers polishing cars. They would not, however, see that each such "servant" received instructions through a receiver tucked into their ear and carried beneath their jackets a semiautomatic pistol. With window shades drawn tight enough to block out all view from outside, someone with binoculars could not see beyond the glass to notice there were neither maids nor butlers within. The curious onlooker would not know that his face was being recorded on a permanent digital video record and that within seconds, his appearance was being cross-checked against all known criminals, terrorists, and agents of foreign governments.

As if on a delivery, a white Vauxhall van stopped alongside the security cameras at the stone-pillared entrance. The driver swiped a card against a reader; the gate with the crest and name "LANE'S END MANOR" in ornate metal opened. With the only sounds being that of the engine and stones crackling under its tires, the van proceeded to a second checkpoint secluded in the trees.

The driver and Barnaby rolled down their windows. Both were asked several questions by a stocky armed man with a short-cropped black mustache. Two other armed men circled the van with a dog, sniffing the body panels. Search complete, the mustached man signaled the driver forward.

"Somethin's got their hackles up," Wiggy said from the rear seat.

The van broke into the sunlit clearing that held the ten-fireplace, three-story stone manor house at its center. The driver did not stop at the front door; he circled to the rear and parked in an outbuilding that a century before had housed the Earl's prize riding horses and now housed modern man's equivalent. Guards electronically rolled shut massive wooden steel-reinforced doors, and they stepped out.

Barnaby led Wiggy down a series of steps and across the drive underground through a tunnel. At the tunnel's end, Barnaby swiped a security badge; a sliding steel security door opened with only a whisper. Two armed guards led Barnaby and Wiggy to a stainless-steel lift.

"A step up from the no-smoking lounge, Barnaby," Wiggy said.

"Same rules apply here, Jeremy."

A lift opened without noise. The four passengers rode up to the ground floor; the door opened. Barnaby led Wiggy down the polished hallway. People with security badges passed without speaking.

"With things getting heated, thought it was time to step up activities," Barnaby said.

The three-hundred-year-old structure's interior had been gutted to support sophisticated listening devises and transmitters that reached the world over or entered the confines of an individual's residence in London … more often than the Crown's subjects dared to think. The once lavish hand-carved wooden architecture had been replaced by a maze of plastic computer terminals, glass enclosures, clean white rooms, and static-free hallways. Fixtures were items chosen not for comfort but for function.

"Thought it was time to see just how good your work is, Jeremy," Barnaby said and opened one half of a three-meter-tall double door. "You've been monitoring this Kovalev situation from the beginning. That insight will come in handy."

Wiggy was awestricken. It wasn't a time to ask questions. Barnaby had ushered him into the inner workings of MI5. Even with their friendship and working relationship, he never thought he would be here. *If only the Grand Ole Dame could see,* he thought.

What had once been the estate's formal ballroom was now symmetrical rows of computers with a myriad of large screens on the walls. Though conversations were on-going, the interior was designed to mute noise. It was like hearing through an apartment wall. Beyond that, each cubical was, in and of itself, a quiet room.

No one looked up from their work as Barnaby escorted Wiggy through the room. He paused at a cubical. Barnaby motioned to the chair before a cadre of computer and electronic communication equipment and two keyboards.

"I want one of these," Wiggy said.

"You now have one," Barnaby responded with a slap on

the back.

A young, bulky male pushed a serving cart toward them. Without speaking, he handed Barnaby two shot glasses and a bottle of Jameson Irish Whiskey. Barnaby uncapped the bottle and poured the glasses full. They toasted and drank.

A young and pretty, thin female who had *computer geek* written on her expression joined them at the cubical. Wiggy was taken by the depth of her dark eyes and the effortless glide of her moves. He shivered inside, as he hadn't since meeting Agent Edelman in D.C. She handed Barnaby a sheet of paper.

"I did as you asked, sir," she said, "and tracked the Mini Cooper from the stadium."

"What did you find?" Barnaby asked.

"May I?" she asked, motioning to the terminal. Wiggy gave way as she brushed past. "When the Mini left the stadium … well, I'll let the video do the talking, sir."

The CCTV at the stadium ran with Adelaide weaving the Mini away. It flashed to a street CCTV that captured the Mini swerving wildly through a red light, hitting a parked motorcycle, then swerving onto a side street.

"She's losing consciousness," Wiggy said. "I've been there."

"Exactly what I thought," the woman said, placing a hand on Wiggy's arm. "Watch …"

Wiggy looked into those deep eyes. She was young enough to be his daughter, olive-skinned with a Mediterranean smile and long dark hair tied in a bun. Surprise filled him, as did attraction.

"What's yer name, lass?"

"Isidore," she said softly.

"My apologies," Barnaby said. "Jeremy Heffernan, meet Isadore Andreas, the best we have."

I have no doubt, Wiggy thought. "The Ancient Egyptian goddess of life, moon, and magic, with a Greek surname … manly or warrior. Interesting combination."

She smiled, surprised and impressed. "My great-grandfather was a merchant mariner."

"Perhaps we could have a drink sometime, and you could tell me how you arrived in London," he said, not knowing why.

The smile, the twinkle in the eyes. "I'd like that."

He turned to the video as the Mini swerved to the side of the street and came to rest against a building. Wiggy punched Kenna's speed dial and motioned to the screen.

"What happens after this, my Egyptian Goddess?"

LV

Kenna walked from Evhen's flat cum storage room to the pitch darkness of an overcast night. She imagined *"The Hound of the Baskervilles"* in the background, but the night held only silence. Many of the boats that had filled the basin over the weekend were gone, either at work in a canal, a river, or in the Channel. She stopped on the gangway and spoke into her Bluetooth.

"We're in place, DCI Attwood. Seems like a perfect night for it." She paused, listening.

"This is a costly exercise if you're wrong, Ms. Hannigan," DCI Attwood said.

"If they come, it won't be for tea," Kenna responded and disconnected the call.

Smoking a cigarette, Oleksandr limped onto the rear deck of the fishing boat. His free hand was wrapped around a bottle of Horilka, his fingers clinching two glasses. Ready for the unexpected, slung at his side was the Glock 17 in a shoulder holster. He uncorked the bottle and poured doubles into the glasses.

Kenna walked the gangway to the deck. Though her instructions had been clear, she knew that Oleksandr would be here when she returned … and she knew the basis of his obstinance. *Not obstinance,* she corrected herself. *Revenge* was his motivation, pure and simple. She sat heavily in the chair and raised her glass in a toast.

"Cheers," "Budmo," they said at the same time and clinked glasses.

As she lowered the glass for a refill, her phone rang. She lifted it and looked at the face.

"Wiggy," she said to Oleksandr, then into the phone, "Give me some good news."

In Lane's End Manor, Wiggy sat at the computer console like a kid in a very large candy shoppe. He had never been near such sophisticated equipment.

"Barnaby's been keeping secrets from us," he said. "Brought me to their information gathering center. You wouldn't believe this place."

"So, he sees the significance of our efforts," she said more than asked.

"Isidore isolated Adelaide's Mini on city CCTV cameras and tracked it after it left Wembley," Wiggy said.

"Who's Isadore?"

"Works for Barnaby, young and intelligent; you'd like her."

"What's it with you that attracts the virile women, Wiggy?" she asked. "No time for romance."

Virile? He thought, looking at Isadore, and lied, "Never gave it a thought. As soon as I review this, I'll edit it and send the pertinent stuff."

"I'm with Oleksandr on the boat, waiting to see if my ploy worked," she said.

"Keep that backside protected, kid," he said. "Don't want your father gettin' bad news this week."

Kenna chuckled, disconnected the call, and took a sip of the Horilka. Wiggy's advice was sound as ever. He was seldom wrong about what to expect. She had never thought of him as an extension of herself, but in a way, they were of each other. Gran had fused them together and made them inseparable.

Oleksandr set a plate of bread, meat, and cheese on the table. Kenna eyed it with hesitation, not remembering the last time she ate. She grabbed a piece of bread, thinking of Adelaide.

"No butter?" she said without thinking.

"Sorry," Oleksandr said, standing. "I'll get some."

Kenna stopped him. "Sorry, a giggle I had with Adelaide the last time I saw her. God, I hope she's alright."

"Your man Jeremy's on it," he said. "We have our own problems."

"Not problems, Oles, opportunities," she corrected.

Oleksandr patted her hand and poured two fingers into her glass. Emotion touched the corner of Kenna's eyes as it seldom did. A tear clung to her eye lid but a moment, then tumbled down her cheek. Leaving it untouched, she bit into the sandwich.

We'll find you, Addie. Dammit, I don't care what you've done, we'll find you.

She swallowed the sandwich with her emotions. "Evhen does understand what may happen to his boat?"

"Was him that suggested it," Oleksandr said. "Doesn't run anyway; hasn't had an engine since he towed it here."

"I wondered why it didn't have a name. Then, why's he kept it?"

"For nights just like this. We both knew our past would catch up with us."

"We never discussed it, your past, that is," Kenna said.

"Me and Evhen go way back to when we were kids," he said. "Been partners ever since. Hell, he married my sister."

"Mrs. Kohut?" Kenna asked. "But her married name."

"Was her first husband's," Oleksandr said. "They both

lost their spouse in the Russian incursion of '14."

"Ergo, the hatred of all things Russian," Kenna concluded. "You were supposed to leave the boat with them."

"You think I'm gonna miss out on puttin' that dog Medved down for good?" On sudden alert, Oleksandr set his glass down. "Besides, too late; they took the fuckin' bait."

Their eyes went to the end of the row of apartments and storage units. Shadows approached stealthily. He lifted his pistol. He and Kenna moved swiftly into the salon. She pulled the pistol from her rear waist and sent a pre-arranged text, *'They're here.'* Her phone swooshed.

The group of armed silhouettes in black hoodies crouch-walked stealthily towards the fishing boat. Approaching from behind, DCI Attwood led a team of Specialist Firearms Command officers from the shadows. At the other end of the apartments and storage sheds, DS Jenkins crouched in the shadows with five other officers of the Specialist Firearms Command.

Kenna's phone dinged with a text message, *'Now.'*

Oleksandr flipped a switch. Spotlights from the boat illuminated the approaching Russians at the apartments. Yelling orders, the Specialist Firearms Command converged on the armed intruders:

"Drop your weapons!" "Stop where you are!" "On your knees!" "Do it now!"

Within minutes, the Russians were on their knees and handcuffed. Two officers gathered the weapons, extra ammunition, clips, and other evidence and placed them into evidence bags.

Kenna and Oleksandr walked from the boat and joined Attwood and Jenkins. Two paddy wagons backed to the end of the row of apartments. Flashing lights illuminated the arrested Russians as they were loaded inside. The doors were shut, and the wagons driven away.

"Thank you, DCI Attwood, DS Jenkins," Kenna said.

"How did you know they would come tonight?" Attwood asked.

"Woman's intuition," she said. "DS Jenkins can tell you all about it."

"Why didn't you just leave the basin?" Jenkins asked.

"No petrol," Kenna said with a smile she shared with Oleksandr, then to Attwood, "What'll happen to them?"

"Held until their embassy undoubtedly declares diplomatic immunity."

"And sets them free," Oleksandr said.

"Yes, but also deported," Attwood said.

"Plenty more where they came from," Oleksandr said.

Attwood and Jenkins shook their hands and walked away. Kenna waited until they had driven from the basin and turned to Oleksandr.

"You noticed who wasn't in the group," she said.

"Medved," he responded. "This was his play as much as ours, Athena. He's gone after the woman with the Halibeck folder."

"How do we find her before he does?"

As they turned for the fishing boat, Kenna's phone dinged, followed immediately by a ring. She looked at the face, surprised, and answered.

*

Cell phone to his ear, Wiggy stood behind Isadore at the computer terminal. Barnaby slept in a chair behind him. Isadore's fingers flashed across the keyboard, using the thumbpad to track a highlighted circle on the screen across a map of London.

"Look at the message, kid," he said with excitement. "Isadore's tracked the van—"

"What van?" Kenna interrupted.

"We were wrong about the van. It wasn't Illya," Wiggy

432

offered. "Just look at the video. You'll understand."

"Tell me."

"Stop talking and get going!" he shouted. "Isidore may have found Adelaide!"

He disconnected the phone and, for a reason he couldn't explain, kissed Isidore on the forehead. Still working the screen, she smiled.

*

Walking onto the rear deck of the fishing boat, Kenna pulled up the image in the message. The Mini weaved through traffic … camera switch … the Mini ran a red light, barely missing another car … camera switch … the Mini slows abruptly, weaves to the side of the road, and eases to a stop against a building. The driver, Adelaide, is face down on the steering wheel.

Wiggy's voice came over the speaker, "By the time stamp, the following occurred fifteen minutes later."

A dark Vauxhall van stopped at the rear of the Mini. A man in a dark hoody walked from the van to the Mini, pulled Adelaide out, and dragged her towards the van. Kenna gasped; it was the first clear image of Adelaide's bloody face.

"What is it, Athena?" Oleksandr asked.

"We have to go," she said, panic filling her. "Wiggy's right, it's Adelaide!"

She grabbed her riding leathers, but Oleksandr stayed her hand. "Not on that. We'll need more room if we find her."

Hurrying across the gangway, Kenna called Wiggy. "Have you found the final destination?"

"Working on it … went south—"

"Halstead," Isadore said calmly in the background.

"Got it," Kenna said. "We're on the way; call with the final destination."

LVI

23 FEBRUARY 2022

Intermittent through light fog and the trees, sunlight peaked over the horizon. Kenna snapped awake in the passenger seat of Oleksandr's aged Vauxhall Brava pickup. Her nose crinkled when she glared at the overflowing ashtray and whiskey flask on the seat. Oleksandr stood outside, soaking up the sun and smoking a cigarette. She opened the door for fresh air and stepped out.

"Morning treats you well, Athena," he said.

"Your blindness is noted, Oles," she said and stretched.

They stood on an isolated stretch of single-lane, paved country road. She imagined horse-drawn wagons delivering goods from the working fields a hundred years before. In her mind, the land baron yelled at his workers. She snapped the nonsense from her thoughts … *focus*.

She coughed up cigarette smoke and spit. Oleksandr tossed her a bottle of water. Catching it, she remembered catching the football in Wembley. It seemed so long ago. With gratitude, she took a big gulp.

Hookwood Road was farm country. Estates of various sizes lined the narrow road, from a few Hectares to several hundred, Kenna imagined. The houses were far enough apart that what happened inside would never be heard by the neighbors.

Was that the 'why here'? she wondered.

"A long way from Wembley," Kenna said.

"Been up and down this road a dozen times and haven't seen a dark van," Oleksandr said.

Kenna looked at Wiggy's text from the night before. "Wiggy said the last CCTV sighting was when the van turned off Rushmore Hill. It has to be one of these houses."

"We might have to go door-to-door."

"If that's what it takes," Kenna agreed. "Let's make it a baker's dozen."

They got into the pickup, and Oleksandr started it. It rattled and vibrated until *the blood got pumping through it,* as Oleksandr had said. He pulled onto the narrow road and drove slowly.

At each property, Kenna lifted binoculars and focused on farmhouse windows and grounds. Farm country in Texas, the hands would be at their duties with the sun. She had to believe that farming in England was no different. As Oleksandr drove by a wood gate, she placed a hand on his arm.

"Pull up where we can't be seen from that house," she said.

Oleksandr pulled to the side of the road by a high hedge row. Kenna stood out and went to the flimsy wire fence; she leaned on a post. Slowly, she passed the binoculars across the property several times. She handed them to Oleksandr.

"Take a look at that farm," she said. "No activity, though it's daylight. From the looks of it, the equipment hasn't been used. It could be for show."

Oleksandr looked through the binoculars just as the dark Vauxhall Vivaro panel van pulled from the barn. Without stopping, it accelerated down the long gravel drive.

"He's coming out now, tag number LM21 WLD."

It disappeared behind the thick trees and shrubbery that lined the drive. Just before the paved road, it appeared in a clearing. Behind the wheel, the driver wore …

"That's our man," Oleksandr said. "Dark hoody … can't see his face." He spun to Kenna. "We go now, we can stop him."

Kenna lifted her phone. "Call Wiggy's cell." The phone rang.

"Yer up bright and early," Wiggy said from a chair in Lane's End Manor.

"The van's on the move again," she said with urgency. "Track it from where you lost it last night. Tag number LM21 WLD."

"What you gonna do?"

"See if Addie's in this farmhouse."

A hundred meters down the road, the van turned the opposite direction and accelerated along the paved road towards London. Oleksandr hurried for the pickup and lifted out the Uzi.

Reminiscent of their time in Luhansk, Kenna followed Oleksandr down the driveway towards the isolated farmhouse. There were no lights inside; there was no movement. Close, they paused at the edge of the clearing. Kenna lifted the binoculars and scanned the windows.

"No movement," she said.

"Stay with me, Athena. Strength in numbers," he insisted.

Blood pumped wildly in Kenna's veins, igniting her scalp like the fire of her namesake. She lifted the Glock from her back belt. *What the hell was she doing in a spy's game?* she wondered. Thurnbull had been right. She had put this all into motion when she went to Ukraine in search of Anson Beck, or whatever his Polish name was. But, as Gran said, she had accepted what happened as a given. Now was the time to move forward.

Kenna's hands sweat. Though moistened by morning dew, rusty hinges of a backyard gate squawked when Oleksandr pushed it open. They hurried across the clearing towards the farmhouse's rear door. At the stoop, he paused and listened; silence was the answer.

Deep planter boxes extended the full width of the white-shuttered windows and overflowed from rainwater. Yet, all the plants were dead. Kenna listened, hearing nothing beyond the drumming of her heart. She ignored it.

Oleksandr reached for the door, but Kenna stayed his hand. She lifted out a lock-picking set, chose two tools of the trade, and picked the lock. She eased the door open.

"See you went to the same school I did," he whispered with a smile.

"My grandmother," she whispered in return and swallowed the lump in her throat.

They stepped inside the dark, empty utility room. Jasmine filled her nostrils as she slid to the inner door and glanced through the glass. Squinting into the dark shadows of the kitchen, she froze. Silence filled the house. *Something is definitely off,* she thought.

She eased open the kitchen door and stepped inside; Jasmine overpowered her. The electric water kettle clicked off. Both snapped their weapons that direction. *Someone's here!*

She moved slowly across the small kitchen, a slight squeak of wet shoe soles against the floor. She paused to listen briefly, then passed through another door into a formal dining room. Several blotches of dull light guided her onto a handwoven throw rug past an oval dining table, China hutch, and chairs.

This could have been any family's residence in England. And she imagined the rustling sounds of children and adults gathering for dinner, silver clinking against China, a football game on the telly in the background. She cursed this fraud of normalcy.

Something scraped the floor overhead. Both snapped weapons to the stairs; Kenna sucked a short breath. Oleksandr moved to the stairs before her. Frozen at the edge of the large throw rug, she turned slowly. Drops of water rolled from the tail of her jacket, striking the floor like a smithy's hammer strikes an anvil. Moist palms and fingers tightened on the pistol. The scrape, however light, came again.

On her toes, she moved to the staircase, a step behind

Oleksandr. With a deep breath, she peered around a wall only to find more darkness. *If someone's here, why's the house dark?* she asked herself. The question repeated itself as they took the first step up. Aged wood creaked lightly, though resounding in the confined space as if Elizabeth Tower had chimed in the front room.

Oleksandr paused and strained to see the top of the stairs but could not. With each cautious step, the gun remained raised to fire. A different sound, a shuffling this time; they froze. It continued as though someone was rifling a drawer or a file cabinet.

They timed their steps now to match the noise until they reached the top of the stairs. At the landing, dark spots passed before her eyes, playing tricks on her. She blinked hard.

'Never fear the darkness,' Gran had told her. *'Nothing exists that is not there in the light.'*

Kenna leaned against the wall, fighting a churning stomach, fighting to gather control. A thick throat blocked a swallow and demanded a cough. Her nose itched. Sweat beaded her face, and she turned sharply as a clamor from the adjacent room interrupted her thought.

There was no time for hesitation, no time for indecision. Those things had brought about failure; now was the time to regain control of life. Away from Sir Clifton, away from everyone else. She was in front of Oleksandr now and touched the doorknob. She moved to the side, leveled the pistol, and threw open the door.

Jasmine overpowered her; her stomach retched. She fought back the bile that lurched forward from the base of her throat. She leaned back against a wall. With a penlight, Oleksandr illuminated the room. The shuffling again, this time from a side door. He eased the door open, aiming the pistol inside.

In a walk-in closet, a small fan rotated back-and-forth. Zip-tied to a chair, Adelaide was covered with blood, badly beaten, and unconscious. Kenna moved past Oleksandr and checked her vitals.

"She's alive," she said with hesitant glee.

A light breeze whistled through a partially open window. A window shade rattled. Oleksandr snapped the gun that direction, then moved quickly to it, looking outside. He returned the gun toward the far end of the room.

"Something's not right," he said softly.

Kenna flipped open a switchblade and cut the zip ties from around Adelaide's bloody wrists and ankles. Tears of anger filled her face. She eased Adelaide from the chair and carried her from the closet.

Wind howled, seemingly on cue, stronger than before, and pushed open a curtain to lay a long, narrow streak of light across Adelaide's face.

"Let's get her out of here," Kenna said.

"Someone's still in the house," Oleksandr said cautiously.

The throaty engine of a sportscar filled their ears. At the window, Oleksandr lifted the Uzi to fire, but it was too late. The Jaguar F-Type roared from the barn, fishtailing, spraying the drive with pebbles, and sped away from the house.

"The fucking Jaguar from the stadium," he said.

"We have other pressing matters, Oles," Kenna said, lifting Adelaide. "Help me get her downstairs, then go get the pickup."

Oleksandr lifted Adelaide's arm over his shoulders and wrapped his hand around her waist. They carried her to the staircase and eased her down the steps.

"Why the hell would they do this to her?" he asked but knew the answer.

"I can't wait to ask 'em," Kenna said, anger consuming her. "One thing's for certain. I was right. There are two of 'em."

LVII

In a small, cheap hotel room on the ground floor, Lyuba sat at the window that overlooked the front street. Lack of sleep had caught up with her. She nodded, barely able to stay awake. She walked to the aged sink in the toilet room and splashed water on her face. Moving back into the bedroom, her eyes went to the "Halibeck International" folder on the bed. She lifted it and grabbed the cover; she hesitated, *no!* She threw it onto the mattress.

Her call to Toll had gone to voicemail. She knew the old man's game as well as he did. He was trying to weaken her resolve. For her, though, the sooner she got the folder out of her hands, the better. She needed sleep, a shower, and a change of clothes, but she couldn't risk being out of touch with what was outside. It would only be a matter of time before either Toll or Svetlana came for her. To survive, Svetlana had to be killed or captured.

Lyuba knew Svetlana, the lover, would allow her to live in peace, but Svetlana, the FSB director, would not. The key question was, which took precedence? Lyuba knew the answer. She refused to live the balance of her life, looking over her shoulder. To accomplish that meant a confrontation with Medved at some point. And then there was Sir Clifton Toll.

One dragon at a time, she thought.

She had begun this dangerous game without a true exit strategy. The emotions eating at her stomach reinforced the folly of her ways. She subconsciously lifted her P-96 semiautomatic pistol, ejected the clip, then reinserted it, chambering a shell. She flipped on the safety and slid it back into the shoulder holster.

Rule #1, she remembered her training: *Never be stationary for more than a few hours when evading the enemy.*

She shoved the folder into the leather shoulder satchel, pulled on her overcoat, and walked from the room. At the front desk of the 18th-century renovated house's living room, she stuck a £50 note under the bell and tapped it. The ring still vibrated through her ears as she walked out. At the counter, a large, round woman with a toothless smile and scarecrow hair lifted the note with a smile.

"Come again, love," she yelled as the door closed.

Lyuba's eyes were on the move as she stepped onto the street. *Rule #2: Never stay in the same location twice.*

Medved weaved the Aston Martin through heavy traffic and passed when possible. His patience with this city, with this mission, was wearing thin. Svetlana was stringing it out to infuriate him. Had it not been for their past relationship, she would have been dead a long time ago, either by his hand or Oleksandr's.

Medved tapped the car phone screen. "Call Feodor." It rang over the speaker.

"Yes, Medved," Feodor said from his desk in the embassy security room.

"What have you heard from Shwetz or the American reporter?" Medved asked.

"Nothing since the last tracking," the computer genius said. "They've obviously switched to burners. But I've been monitoring Lyuba. She's made several calls to the British newsman."

"Which one?" Medved asked and turned, coming out of a roundabout.

"Sir Clifton Toll."

Medved's anger peaked, and he slammed a fist on the steering wheel. "The bitch is betraying us. Where is she?"

"On Warrington Cresent, north of the embassy," Feodor

said. "Take the A5, the best traffic right now."

"Call with any changes in her location," Medved said.

He spun the Aston Martin across traffic and turned onto the A5.

*

Lyuba walked the sidewalk through Little Venice. Boats sat idle along the shoreline of the basin, awaiting tourist season. No business today.

A sportscar's engine roared; she looked up. The Aston Martin spun her direction at the end of the street. She reached for her pistol but paused when people left a flat across the street. She turned at a run as the Aston Martin sped directly at her like a supernatural demon.

She ran across the street and, without slowing, lunged over the fence that surrounded the residences. An alarm sounded; she didn't stop and ran between the residences into the rear garden. A man with a cricket bat hurried from his home.

"You there, what are you doing?" he yelled.

She ignored him and climbed the stone security wall into the neighbor's garden. The second batsman of the cricket team hurried out; she passed him at a run, dodging his hapless swing, and climbed to the top of the wall. She paused and looked over.

The batsman approached. "Are you in trouble, lass?"

If only you knew, Lyuba thought. She glared at him and dropped over the wall to the sidewalk. She ran across the street and into a bakery. She paused, the hypnotic smell of freshly baked breads and pastries overpowering her senses. The screeching tires of the Aston Martin turned her to the front.

She didn't pause and ran through the rear of the bakery. Kitchen help yelled and cursed. She knocked a chef's assistant from her path and hurried for the rear door.

She broke into a narrow pedestrian alley lined with metal rubbish bins. *Rule #3: Use all your senses, not just your eyes.* The sportscar's engine was to her left; she ran to the right. As she did, she realized just in time it was an echo through the alley. She lunged to the side …

Behind Lyuba, passenger window down in the Aston Martin, Medved fired the suppressed PB 9mm pistol. The bullet ricocheted from the building. Staying in the shadows, Lyuba crouch-ran towards the other end of the alley. The Aston Martin roared away with screaming tires.

Lyuba sprinted to the end of the alley, hailed a taxi, and jumped in. "Hyde Park, double quick."

*

In the outer executive office of BNC, Mrs. Pemberton removed a clip-on earring and answered the desk phone, "Sir Clifton's office."

"Sir Clifton, please. Tell him it's about Kovalev," Lyuba said.

One of those foreign names, Mrs. Pemberton thought. "One moment, please," she said. She placed the call on hold and punched the intercom. "A foreign woman calling about the dead Ukrainian, Sir Clifton."

"Send it to Thurnbull, Mrs. P.," Toll yelled with a cough from the office. "I have no time for their gibberish."

She punched the line. "Sir Clifton is unavailable and asked that I will redirect you to Mr. Thurnbull."

*

Thurnbull walked through the parking garage with his gym bag when his phone rang. He looked at the face, frustrated, but answered:

"Yes, Corina, what is it?"

"Mrs. Pemberton phoned Mr. Thurnbull, says there is a foreign woman wanting to speak with Ms. Hannigan," Corina said.

"Text me the number, and I'll call immediately," he said.

Thurnbull double-quicked through the parking garage. At his car, he threw the gym bag in the rear and jumped in. Starting it, he looked at the phone screen and punched in the number.

"This is Thurnbull."

LVIII

Oleksandr drove the Brava pickup through the gate of Lane's End Manor and stopped at the second security checkpoint. With a curious look at the vehicle and Oleksandr, the guard waved them through, then spoke into a shoulder walkie-talkie.

"How's she doing?" Oleksandr asked.

Kenna sat in the rear seat, covered with blood, Adelaide's head on her lap. "She hasn't moved, but she's breathing."

At the rear of the manor house, Wiggy, Barnaby, and a medical team waited. Oleksandr stopped beside them and jumped out. Wiggy jerked the door open and helped Kenna out.

"Are you hurt?" he asked.

"No, it's Addie's," she said and moved aside.

A large male EMT reached into the cab as a female EMT got in the opposite side and managed Adelaide's legs. A third technician rolled the gurney to the Brava and set the brakes. They gently lifted Adelaide from the pickup and placed her on the gurney. While the male strapped her to the gurney, the female wrapped a blood pressure cuff around her arm. Kenna kissed Adelaide's forehead as the EMTs wheeled her inside.

"She'll be fine," the female EMT said. "We'll take care of her."

Wiggy took Kenna by the arm. "Come in, we'll get you cleaned up."

"There's no time," she said and pulled away. "Did you follow the van and Jag?"

"Just the van, the Jaguar passed through the net somehow or never came into the city."

"Could be in Portsmouth by now," Oleksandr said.

"What about Tommy?" she asked.

"Nothing," Barnaby said. "We've checked every known address."

"I'll come with you," Wiggy said.

"No, keep on it. Oles and I will do the field work," Kenna instructed.

"Where you going?"

"To find the key to this puzzle."

As Kenna and Oleksandr stepped into the Brava, her phone rang. She had him wait and rolled down the window. She answered on speaker.

"Mr. Thurnbull, what can I do for you?"

*

Alone in his vehicle, Thurnbull looked at the street outside the parking garage. A bead of sweat rolled down his forehead onto his cheek; he ignored it.

"I just received a call from a young woman who said she wants to meet you," he said.

"Did this woman have a name?" Kenna asked, having a good idea.

"Sounded authentic, thick Eastern European accent, said she knew you from Luhansk." Thurnbull lifted a notepad. "I'll text the phone number she gave. Is this about Kovalev?"

"Won't know until I speak with her, sir."

*

Kenna disconnected the call. Her phone dinged; she pulled up the number, inserted Wiggy's number, and pressed send. Her phone swooshed; his dinged.

"Find that phone, Wiggy," she said. "It might be Lyuba reaching out for help."

"Or to lure ya into Svetlana's trap," Oleksandr said.

"Anythin' else?" Wiggy asked.

"Pray Addie wakes and can tell us who did this to her," Kenna said, then hit her forehead. "Almost forgot, what about Adelaide's mother?"

"Seems the neighbor was right; she was in Spain. On the way home now."

"At least she'll have a bit of good news when she arrives."

Oleksandr drove the pickup towards the gate.

*

In the Jaguar, Thurnbull lifted his phone and hit a speed dial number. He anxiously waited while it rang.

"Mr. Thurnbull's desk," Corina answered from her desk in BNC.

"Have you heard anything from Henson?"

"No, sir," she said, obviously shaken. "It's rather scary, first his girlfriend—"

"Bloody unusual," he interrupted. "Do we have anyone else who can track a phone?"

"I can, sir. Tommy showed me how," she said.

"I'll text a number," he said. "Find its location and let me know where it is. Ms. Hannigan is stepping into water she may not be able to swim."

Thurnbull started his vehicle.

*

At her desk in the BNC On-Line Reporters room, Corina was anxious at her computer and pulled up a program. At the same time, she lifted the desk phone and punched an exchange.

"Mrs. Pemberton, Mr. Thurnbull asked that I locate a phone. I'll text the number. Just thought you should know."

LIX

Much to Kenna's annoyance, Oleksandr smoked a cigarette and drove the Brava pickup along the busy street into the heart of the city. There had been a lot to absorb in a short period of time. Why kidnap Adelaide and torture her? They, whoever they were, just killed people before, but they kept Adelaide alive.

Why? jabbed at Kenna's insides like a dagger. Her phone dinged; she looked at the message.

"Wiggy … the last known location of the van," she said to Oleksandr.

She pressed the address to pull up the city map.

"In 100 meters, turn south on the A5," the mechanical GPS voice said.

"What's on yer mind, Athena?" Oleksandr asked. "Thought we were going to see the mysterious caller."

"She can wait," Kenna replied. "I want to find that van."

Approaching the intersection, the tick of the turn indicator kept a beat while the Brava rattled to a stop at the light. Oleksandr threw the cigarette out the window. He winked at Kenna and didn't light another.

"Last pack," he said.

"And just when I was thinking of starting," she said in jest to lighten the mood. It didn't.

*

Grey overcast outside darkened the parking structure. The Vauxhall Vivaro's wet tires squealed on concrete. Wearing a hoody, the driver eased it into a stall and stopped. He turned off the engine and headlights and opened the door slightly to get out. His phone dinged.

He lifted the phone; the light illuminated him … a tap on the front windscreen … he looked up … a tall, thin man in a dark hoody with a suppressed pistol aimed at him … the driver panicked … the assassin smiled.

The assassin's bullet entered the driver's heart before he could flinch. The driver doubled over on the seat; the phone dropped.

*

Window open, relishing the fresh air, if there was such a thing in London, Kenna pointed down Bayswater. This was becoming a very familiar stretch of road. Oleksandr made the turn on a green light and accelerated with other traffic. To their left was Hyde Park, where people strolled in the cool air of day.

Kenna tried to remember the last time she had gone for a walk just to relax. It would have been with Gran Lockwood, but then, it wouldn't have been relaxation. It would have been work training. She forgot about it.

"In one hundred meters, turn right onto Queensway," the GPS directed them.

"You know where we are, eh, Athena?" Oleksandr asked, turning.

It wasn't lost on her that they were a morning stroll from the Embassy of the Russian Federation. A few hundred meters from Bayswater was the Queensway Parking garage.

"On the right, you have reached your destination."

Oleksandr slowed and turned into the garage. He eased the pickup through the darkness and passed parked cars. At the rear of the garage, parked in the final stall, was the dark Vauxhall panel van. Oleksandr stopped behind; they hesitated. Kenna stood from the pickup, checked the surrounding area, and lifted the Glock from her rear belt. Uzi slung at his side under the overcoat, Oleksandr stood out and limped to her side.

"Rather brazen of 'em leavin' it in the open," she said.

They eased around the sides towards the cab. She noticed the driver's door was open slightly; the cab was lit by the interior light. Seeing the spider web break and hole in the windshield, Kenna lifted the pistol. She opened the door; her heart sank. Saddened more than startled, she backed away. Oleksandr reached inside to check on the man.

"Hasn't been dead long. Still warm and limber," he said, rifled the victim's pockets, and straightened with a photo. "Had this, though, Anatoli Novikov."

"Perhaps the next victim," Kenna said.

"Or just maybe who's been doin' all this, Athena."

Kenna's phone rang; she answered. "Yes, we—"

"Finally got a match from the video on your phone in Wembley," Wiggy interrupted. "You aren't going to believe who it is."

Angry sorrow filled Kenna; she nodded and shook her head as she disconnected the call. It made sense now; the two killers had been working together, not separately. They were both at Wembley that day, one to assassinate Kovalev, the second to provide backup in case trouble happened. It had been the backup man who had wounded Illya and knocked her unconscious … this poor dumb bastard on the front seat before them.

Kenna tapped a contact on her phone. Thinking of Adelaide, she wanted to mutilate the man on the seat but held back. As the phone rang in her ear, she said to Oleksandr:

"You need to get out of here. I'll deal with the police and take a taxi to Evhen's boat." An answer on her phone. "DCI Attwood, this is Kenna Hannigan. I just found Tommy Henson."

*

Kenna discussed what she knew with DCI Attwood, how they came across Tommy's body, and why. He hadn't been happy but had been understanding. That she was always at the wrong place at the wrong time was becoming her norm … at least to him.

The assassin hadn't bothered taking Tommy's weapon. It was, undoubtedly, the 9mm pistol used at Wembley. This possibly solved the blood question: the other two samples outside the owner's suite were Illya's and Adelaide's. If a fourth type was found, it would undoubtedly be Tommy's.

She hadn't waited for the coroner to take Tommy away. From what she had seen of Adelaide, he had gotten off easy. The question whirling around her brain was the same, with the exception that one name was now complete in Gran's puzzle. But one question still bit at her: who had Tommy Henson killed? DCI Attwood would be able to tell her that.

She sat in the taxi, almost wishing she was in the stale

cigarette smoke-laden air of Oleksandr's rattling Brava pickup. Or even having a Horilka with Alistair Rensenhaus in the smoke-laden air of the BNC Luhansk office. Nerves on edge, she found herself watching to see if they were followed, checking every person on every corner when they stopped at a light.

Wiggy was digging into Tommy's past, but Kenna believed she knew it. It would be dark, filled with uncertainty, much like Anson Beck. What was it that had driven him to capture and torture a woman he said he loved? A constant for men such as him … and Beck … first and foremost, they were liars. Damn good liars. She had been wrong about Tommy and fought with it inside her brain. How had she been so blind? How had they all been so blind?

She remembered Oleksandr's similar question about Nadia. Her phone rang to snap her from the thoughts.

"Sir Clifton. I take it you've heard of Tommy Henson?"

At his desk in BNC, Toll glared at his game board. "Old news, I'm afraid, Hannigan. Our favorite female Russian assassin is looking for you."

"Svetlana, I expected it," Kenna said.

"No, Lyuba. She wants to meet and will ring … take the meeting," he instructed. "Oh, and Ms. Hannigan."

"Yes?"

"Take a gun."

LX

Kenna stood with Oleksandr and Evhen in the fishing boat salon. She stared at the wall of papers that outlined the crimes. She had plugged Tommy Henson's name onto the sheets … "Kidnapper" … "Murderer". If Tommy's background was sordid, Wiggy would find it. Still, there was something missing; it was gnawing at the base of her brain.

Mrs. Kohut set a plate of meat, bread, and cheese on the plastic table. She brought a medical kit to the table and changed Kenna's old arm wound dressing. Kenna stared at it, remembering the cellar, the rat, and the man she killed. *Yes, that she killed,* she thought.

'Blood will stain your hands, leanbh,' Gran Lockwood had said in the snow on her 18th birthday. *'Accept it or don't go into the work.'*

She had accepted it then, but she had yet to kill someone … an act that would be on her conscience forever. *It was his choice,* she reasoned. *It was the life he chose.* Just as Tommy Henson had chosen his. *A single bullet to the heart,* she remembered.

She tapped the Bluetooth, "Call Wiggy's cell."

In the computer room of Lane's End Manor, Wiggy sat

at the keyboard, playing with his new toy. He hesitated when his phone rang, then punched his Bluetooth.

"They've sedated Adelaide to get her body fluids to normal levels," he said. "I'll—"

"Anything on Tommy's background?" she asked.

"Still working on it," Wiggy said. "Very little, no violations, no school records; hell, the guy was a ghost."

"Keep looking and let me know," she said and disconnected the call.

Kenna stormed out to the rear deck. *Killers, not a single killer,* she screamed in her brain. *Two, one organized and precise, the second a madman on the loose.* Of the two, the former fit Tommy. Kovalev … yes, Tommy had been in the stadium. The madman? Medved, the Russian assassin. Illya had been at night. Yes, Tommy could have been at Kovalev's apartment after the gun battle. She strained her mind, trying to remember where Tommy had been when Rashon Hill was killed.

All with a single bullet in the heart … just like Tommy was killed. He wasn't the organized, precise killer. Could the Russian be playing two positions in this game? Was that possible?

She slapped her head. *Why kidnap Adelaide? What had*

she known? Or was it what they thought she knew?

Halibeck International flashed through her mind. Alistair Rensenhaus had stolen the file from Svetlana and was going to send it to Sir Clifton. It was never sent. She was told it was destroyed in the fire when Alistair was killed. Yuri Zelenko confirmed it had not been. Kovalev brought it to London to barter. *Madness!* She stomped into the salon and walked up to Oleksandr.

"Tell me everything about the night Alistair was killed," she demanded.

"You were there. You know what happened," Oleksandr said.

Alistair Rensenhaus, a single bullet to the heart, she thought of the autopsy.

"I was thrown aside by an explosion in the office," Kenna offered. "When I looked up, you were there, standing … and did nothing to help Nadia. I see it like it's happening now. I will never forgive you for that."

"You aren't alone," he offered.

"What's that mean?"

"How can I ask others to forgive me when I can't forgive myself?"

Oleksandr sat heavily in the chair and poured a shot of

Horilka. In anger, Kenna moved for him. She slapped the drink from his hand. Dammit, she wanted answers! Mrs. Kohut stepped between them and stopped her.

"Complete your mission, sweetie, and you will understand," Mrs. Kohut said. "Whether you accept it is up to you."

Kenna spun from the salon. "I'll call with the meeting place. See if you can be there this time."

LXI

Kenna sat on the Triumph, staring at the Tower of London. Traffic and pedestrians passed unnoticed. When the distant Elizabeth Tower bell announced a new hour, she didn't flinch, didn't really register.

Why was it that no one would talk about Alistair Rensenhaus's killing? Why was everything so secretive about that day? A body burned unrecognizably, an autopsy in a foreign land authorized by the Executive Director of BNC? Secrets held from the wife and daughter who go missing and one tortured?

Her phone buzzed; she punched Bluetooth.

With the clarification of two murderers, it became more than she could manage alone. But there was something else gnawing at her. It wasn't just two murderers; it was the way they were killed … more importantly, she now believed why they were killed, taking her back to the most important element of murder … the why.

She'd been through the cadre of emotions and trust issues. Contrary to how she preferred to do things, she had to rely on Oleksandr for part of the field work. He had to be her shadow and do it without being seen or heard … at least until the right moment.

Every case had two essential elements: who you could trust but, more importantly, who you couldn't. Now, the only man she trusted without question was busy with his own assignment. She didn't like being on an island alone, but there was no other way. Doubt trickled into her mind: *Could she trust Oleksandr to be there when the proverbial defecation hit the oscillator?*

Her phone rang, interrupting her thought; she punched Bluetooth, "Who's this?"

With Evhen driving the Brava pickup, Oleksandr winced in pain when it turned the corner in front of a double-decker bus.

"Where are you?" Oleksandr asked.

A hint of relief eased Kenna's whirling mind. "Staring at my future residence, the Tower. Are you coming?"

Oleksandr countered, "Somebody has to keep you from killin' yerself."

"Lyuba wants to meet alone."

"She's Svetlana's lapdog; you can't trust her."

"She wants freedom over slavery," Kenna said.

"Remember, Medved's out there, so keep that damn pistol handy," Oleksandr said.

Medved … she had almost forgotten about him. Was it a coincidence, or did he really fall by the wayside? No, his intentions were clear, and Kenna believed she knew why. They were after the same objective.

"Medved wants the folder more than me," she said. "And there's a reason. There's something inside that folder he doesn't want the world to know."

"We'll do what it takes to get it," he said. "Evhen and I will stay in the shadows. Phone when you know where and when."

*

In the security room of the Embassy of the Russian Federation, Medved and Pyotr stood behind Feodor. On the computer screen, Feodor highlighted a location on the map of London and pointed to it.

"Lyuba, I'm positive of it," Feodor said.

"Don't lose her this time," Medved demanded.

"It was a computer hack that's been corrected," Feodor offered. "She's in The City and has been for quite some time."

"What's she doing there?" Medved wondered out loud.

"Several possibilities," Feodor ventured. "It's close to British News Corporation, also close to where Sir Clifton

Toll lives, and not far from the yacht in Canary Wharf."

"She's fucking with our heads," Medved said. "Call me with any change in her location."

In the hallway, Medved and Pyotr were met by Vanya with a bandaged head and arm and two other Medved clones. Together, they hurried for the rear of the embassy.

*

Kenna sat on the Triumph in thought. She hated the idle time more than anything, wondering what and when was to come. It did no good to think about it, but it was impossible not to. Her phone dinged; she looked at the text message. She tapped the Bluetooth and kicked the Triumph to start it.

"Call Oleksandr's cell," she said and accelerated into traffic. It rang, and he answered. "The Black Friar in The City in half an hour."

"We're on the way," Oleksandr said from the front of the Brava pickup." Evhen started it with a rattle and accelerated away from the curb.

*

With a soldier in the passenger seat of the Aston Martin, Medved steered through heavy traffic. The phone rang over the car system; he tapped the phone screen.

"Talk to me, Feodor."

“The Black Friar in The City.”

LXII

Kenna eased the Triumph across Fleet Street and rode along busy Farringdon Street. A sense of history greeted her as she rode through the heart of The City. Just before River Thames and Black Friars Bridge sat a rectangular corner building, 174 Queen Victoria Street. Black Friar pub was built on the grounds of the Dominican Order of the Black Friar, established in the 13th Century. The proprietors had kept the old-world theme inside and out.

Kenna eased the Triumph onto the walkway and stopped at the entrance to the underground. Before turning it off, she checked all directions. Eyes still watching the area, she chained the Triumph to the railing.

Loud voices, some business, others there for pleasure, buzzed from the people at the tables on Black Friars Court. A motorcycle aficionado gave her a thumbs up. Attention moving from vehicle traffic to the people at the tables, she received no contact stares. The building had three doors along Black Friars Court, all with historical significance. The corner door had been where the landed gentry, the upper class, entered. The middle door had been for women to take away their drinks since they were not allowed to enter. The rear door had been for the proletariat, the workers, to keep them segregated from the upper-crust clientele.

At the middle door, Kenna paused for a woman carrying two pints. She stepped into an ornately decorated pub of marble and deep wood. *Times have changed,* she thought. Filling the pub was a mixed bag of clientele, several rungs above the working-class confines of the Blue Boar. Artifacts from the ancient Dominican Order hung on the walls, including brass murals depicting the monks' lives. It struck her as curious that in all murals, the monks' faces were hidden by their habits. Inscriptions above the arched doorways separating rooms read like a book of knowledge: "SILENCE IS GOLDEN" and "WISDOM IS RARE", all chiseled in old English style lettering.

Sitting at the long half-circle bar, Lyuba made eye contact. Neither was comfortable with the other; Kenna studied her but did not sit. She noted Lyuba's hands were on the bar, not on a pistol. It did nothing to ease the tension that filled her.

'I could have easily killed you that night,' Lyuba had said in Hyde Park. In a memory flash, Kenna recalled Lyuba coming from the rear of the shack in Luhansk, followed by the lieutenant. The lieutenant's face flashed before her. She froze in thought …

"Your mind is elsewhere," Lyuba interrupted the thought.

Kenna snapped away from remembering the video and hesitated. *Why?* Kenna leaned against the bar with a chair separating them. Handsome and young, the bartender wiped down the spot in front of her.

"What'll it be, lass?" was his polite question.

Kenna pointed at Lyuba's glass of clear liquid … vodka. He lifted a glass and checked it in the light for cleanliness. Kenna watched with a smile, remembering her first drink with Alistair Rensenhaus.

"That's okay," she said and indicated the bottle. "That stuff kills all sorts of bugs."

"Just don't want it to be you," he said and filled the glass, then Lyuba's, and turned away.

"I should thank you for not shooting me in the back in Luhansk," Kenna said and lifted her glass for a toast.

"No sport in that," Lyuba said with a grin. *Yes, I could easily fall in love with this red-headed Yank.*

"In the meeting, Svetlana was given—"

"This," Lyuba interrupted. From her satchel, she lifted a thick folder titled in gold "HALIBECK INTERNATIONAL" and slid it across the bar. "Kovalev paid handsomely to have Rensenhaus steal it."

Kenna ignored the connection as her mind flashed to the meeting in the Luhansk shack. Anatoli Novikov, different from the others in dress and demeanor, handed Svetlana the "HALIBECK INTERNATIONAL" folder.

Kenna did not touch it; did not look at it. "Did you finally read it?"

"Don't need to," Lyuba offered. "It's what Sir Clifton Toll has strived to recover since you videoed the exchange."

So, he hasn't seen it, Kenna thought. "What's in here worth killing for?"

"You aren't naïve, Ms. Hannigan. Men kill for many reasons, from nothing to everything," Lyuba said. "But this particular folder? Secrets, Ms. Hannigan, from both sides of the globe."

"Yes, Sir Clifton Toll, Kovalev, and Svetlana," she said.

"And your friend, Alistair Rensenhaus."

"He was the first killed for it." Kenna studied it, *CIA cover.* "Toll and David Camden."

Lyuba placed a hand on Kenna's, relishing the touch of her skin. "Their reach is long, Ms. Hannigan. They control the destiny of everyone around them … and some that aren't."

"What does that mean?"

"Alistair Rensenhaus discovered it too late. I hope you don't."

Both spun to a raucous commotion outside. Medved slid the Aston Martin to a stop on Black Friars Court at the side door. Pyotr slid the Corsa onto the sidewalk at the front door. Medved and the Russian disciple jumped from the Aston Martin with guns raised. Pyotr, Vanya, and another Russian jumped from the Corsa. Patrons screamed and scrambled from the tables on Black Friars Court. Some jumped over the fence; all ran away from the pub, lifting cell phones. Waiters stood at the doors outside, unsure what to do.

Inside, panic. Lyuba jumped up and pulled a pistol. She shoved the folder to Kenna, downed her drink, and kissed Kenna on the lips.

"You now control my life, Ms. Hannigan," Lyuba said and hurried around the bar. "Don't forget, Toll owes me!"

Kenna swiped the folder from the bar and shoved it into her leathers. She and Lyuba moved away in opposite directions.

Medved stepped through the middle door; patrons shoved past at the door and slowed him. The handsome bartender jumped over the bar and stood his ground at the door. Without hesitation, Medved slammed the pistol against his head; the bartender fell unconscious. Pyotr rushed through the front, hit, and threw a man and woman outside. Tables crashed; glasses shattered.

Lyuba ran the length of the bar and turned into the kitchen. Kenna ran into a small adjacent dining room towards the third door.

Medved yelled to Pyotr, "Get Lyuba! I'll get the reporter!"

Pyotr and Vanya rushed behind the bar with the other Russian. Another bartender lifted a cricket bat from beneath the bar. Pyotr didn't hesitate and shot him; the bartender collapsed. They stepped over his lifeless body in pursuit.

In the kitchen, Lyuba pushed staff to the side. They screamed and fled when Pyotr crashed through the door, brandishing the pistol. A young female cook cowered on the floor; he tripped over her.

Medved and his disciple rushed through the pub and into the separate room. When they reached the last room, the disciple looked outside through the stained-glass window. Kenna hurried to the Triumph. He knocked a table away and ran for the last door.

At the Triumph, Kenna fumbled with the chain lock. The

disciple ran from the rear door and tackled her just as the lock snapped free. She fought and kicked, but he pinned her to the pavement. Medved walked up with smug confidence.

"I have many questions for you," he said.

The roar and rattle of an old vehicle turned him. Medved screamed upon seeing Oleksandr as the Brava pickup slid onto Black Friars Court and slammed into the Aston Martin, blocking its path of escape.

Inside the pub at the rear of the kitchen, Pyotr threw open the office door. Shock! Sitting patiently on an office chair, Lyuba pointed a pistol at him.

"That was a mistake," she said and fired twice, hitting Pyotr in the chest, spraying Vanya with blood, and knocking both down.

On Black Friar Court, sirens approached from all directions. Oleksandr fired from the Brava pickup and winged the Russian disciple. His grip on Kenna faltered; she beat him off and rolled to the side. Medved fired but hit the pavement. She kicked his knee as he fired again; the bullet ricocheted from the pavement next to her ear.

From the Brava, Oleksandr fired, hitting Medved in the leg knocking him against the Triumph. Medved fired and hit Evhen in the chest above the Kevlar vest; he yelled and dropped. Oleksandr climbed from the Brava to Evhen's aid, pulling him behind the vehicle and leaning him against the building.

Medved slammed the pistol against Kenna's head, knocking her down. He slid the folder from her leathers and rifled her pockets. With urgent satisfaction, he lifted the memory stick.

At the Brava, Oleksandr told Evhen, "Stay here, Athena, and I will take care of this."

In the kitchen, Lyuba stepped from the office, fired, and hit Vanya. The Russian disciple fired several times. Hit in the leg, but not badly, Lyuba collapsed. As the Russian approached, she rolled over and shot him in the head. Bloody but able to stand, Lyuba hurried to the rear door and hobbled out to daylight.

Kenna gained her senses as the Russian disciple snapped open a switchblade. She shot him in the face and spun to Medved as he kick-started the Triumph. She fired and hit him in the shoulder; blood sprayed the bike. He faltered but accelerated away.

Evhen yelled at Oleksandr, "Go! I'm alright!"

"He has the folder and video!" Kenna yelled, jumped up, and weaved for the Brava.

Oleksandr pulled Kenna into the Brava. With an assortment of squeaks and rattles, Oleksandr reversed from the Aston Martin and accelerated after the Triumph.

LXIII

The Triumph roared around and through heavy traffic on Queen Victoria Street. Medved wasn't an accomplished rider but kept the Triumph upright. He weaved around, stopped traffic at the first red light, swerved across to the wrong lane, and missed a lorry by less than a meter. Blaring horns didn't slow him.

Several cars behind, the Brava rattled and puffed blue smoke. Steam hissed from the radiator. Oleksandr slowed. Kenna slapped his arm, urging him forward. She pointed to the wrong lane.

"Go! They'll get outta the way!"

Oleksandr weaved around the stopped cars and didn't slow at the red light. He crossed back into the proper lane at the same time Medved did several cars ahead. A taxi came from an office building in front of them; Oleksandr didn't slow. He hit the taxi, knocking it to the other lane. The driver slowed, yelling and waving for Oleksandr to move to the side of the street. When Oleksandr didn't slow down, the taxi driver stopped, jumped out, and flipped him off.

The street narrowed. Parking lanes on both sides were lined with busses. From the Triumph, Medved looked into the rearview mirror. Fighting the pain, he swerved through the heavy traffic. At the next traffic light, he bounded over the median, crossed the street, and roared onto the sidewalk. People jumped from his path, yelling.

In the Brava, Oleksandr slowed at the light and pounded on the steering wheel. Not waiting, he crossed into the other lane. Vehicles swerved to avoid them as he accelerated through the red light.

"He's going for the footbridge!" Kenna yelled.

At a construction barrier, Medved swerved back into traffic, hit a bicyclist, and both spun. The Triumph came to a halt, facing the Brava that roared for him. At full throttle, he spun the Triumph one-eighty with a roar of pain. Oleksandr swerved to miss the bicyclist and sideswiped a parked car. The Brava was close, very close.

Kenna yelled, "Run him off the road!"

"But your bike?" Oleksandr said.

"It's a piece of fucking metal!" she yelled. "Crash into him!"

She jerked the wheel too late. Medved weaved the Triumph between car barriers onto Peter's Hill. Screaming pedestrians jumped from his path. Oleksandr slid the Brava to a stop at the footbridge entrance. Brandishing weapons, they jumped out. People screamed and fled.

With a smile of smug satisfaction, Medved powered the Triumph through the buildings and onto the footbridge over the Thames. He didn't look back.

Oleksandr grabbed Kenna and moved swiftly for the Brava. "I'm betting Medved is a creature of habit, especially wounded. I have a good idea where he's going."

Approaching sirens filled the streets. As they sped away, several people filmed them with their phones.

"We're about to go viral, Oles," Kenna yelled.

*

In the Russian Embassy Security Room, Svetlana stood behind Feodor, both eying the screens. It was all coming to a head just as she planned. Though the final few hours were the most critical, confidence was high; she had accomplished her objective. Feodor brought up an image of police vehicles arriving outside the embassy.

"Alexi phoned earlier to say he had the folder and video, director," Feodor said and removed a headset. "Police radio traffic indicates they are looking for him. You should go now."

In a way, Svetlana was saddened by Medved's actions. His angry streak and desire to settle the score with Oleksandr might have cost him his life. Or, worse yet, landed him in a British dungeon for the rest of his days. On the way out the door, Svetlana grabbed Filipp.

"We are very close to accomplishing our mission, Filipp. Do you have everything?"

"In the car, ma'am," Filipp said. "What about the folder and video?"

"Medved has them," she said.

"And Medved?"

"Is doing exactly what he wanted to do." *And what I anticipated,* she did not say.

Without hesitation, both hurried down the hallway. There was no nostalgia in her eyes, no fond farewells to the embassy staff. Now, it was a mad dash for survival, a game she had never lost.

*

Weaving violently, weakening, Medved slowed the Triumph at the end of the footbridge over the Thames. He stopped and looked back, confident Oleksandr and the journalist were not coming on foot. He tapped his Bluetooth.

"Call Feodor," he said with a cringe, ripped off his undershirt, and tucked it against his shoulder wound. The phone rang in his ear.

In the security room, Feodor frantically answered, "Medved, everyone's—"

Avoiding glares by nosey on-lookers, Medved interrupted, "I'm wounded … send someone out to bring me in."

Feodor didn't like what he was about to say. "We can't. The British are forming a two-block radius around the embassy. They are hunting for you."

"How do they have my name?" Medved wondered aloud, then spit in anger. "The journalist."

With determined hatred, Medved accelerated the Triumph away slowly. "Is there anyone outside the embassy? What about Pyotr?"

"Shot dead inside the pub. The others, as well," Feodor offered. "I'll find someone to help."

"Have them meet me at the safe house," Medved said and turned the Triumph into traffic.

*

Inside Lane's End Manor, the security room was abuzz with activity. Every screen had a view of The City. The screen in front of Wiggy followed the Brava as it weaved through traffic. Wiggy tapped computer keys and turned to Barnaby. On the screen, a tracking light indicated a connection.

"Isadore, you still on the Triumph?" Wiggy yelled.

Isadore looked over her cubby with a smile. "How could I be on it if I'm here?"

"You know what I mean," Wiggy said.

"He's at the south end of the footpath bridge over the Thames," Isadore said, and with a giggle, added, "I'll stay on it and feed you his location."

"Have a hit on the Russian director's cell," Wiggy said. "She's calling Moscow."

Barnaby slapped his shoulder. "Get that number," then to a computer geek behind him, "Shut down all international cell calls to Russia."

Wiggy looked up with surprise. "You can do that? Oh, I definitely want one of these."

Barnaby moved to the large screen on the wall in front of Wiggy. The five unknown people from the Luhansk meeting were centered.

"Now, let's take a look at these five."

"I've identified 'em," Wiggy stated and brought their dossiers up on the screen. "All but the last man."

Barnaby allowed a rare grin. "You just made my day, Jeremy. The next round's on me."

Wiggy's phone rang. "Yes, Kenna, you okay?"

*

Oleksandr took a sharp corner to avoid traffic …

"It doesn't matter!" Kenna yelled into her phone. "Tommy was the young lieutenant at the meeting in Luhansk; look at the photo! He was a fucking Russian spy! Which means—"

"That his accomplice was, as well," Wiggy said. "I'm on it."

*

Svetlana sat in the rear of the Aurus Senat limousine while Filipp steered through heavy traffic. Frustration mounted as everything moved in slow motion. Ahead, the flashing lights of construction vehicles. She cursed the phone and tried the number again.

"Why didn't we know about this construction?" Svetlana screamed.

"The GPS didn't indicate it, ma'am," Filipp offered.

Svetlana's line with Moscow went dead. Panic filled her; she tapped her phone as if that would help. Paranoia struck her; she glared at the construction work.

"Hello? Sir, are you there?" she said into the phone. "Filipp, get us out of here!"

In the security room of Lane's End Manor, Wiggy and Barnaby smiled when the line went dead.

"Shut down in mid-call. That won't make her happy," Wiggy said.

"Good man," Barnaby agreed. "Now, let's locate our favorite female Russian spy so we can have a chat with her. I know someone who will want to be in on this."

Barnaby scrolled through his contacts and punched a number. "Yes, this is Barnaby Scriven of MI5. Put him on, if you will."

"He's not in the office, but I will connect you, Agent Scriven," the female responded.

With a hint of pleasure brightening his face, Barnaby took a sip of whiskey. He perked up when David Camden answered.

"Agent Scrivens, it's been a long time," Camden said.

"We're tracking your favorite female Russian spy and look to have a chat with her," Barnaby said. "Thought you might want to join in."

"I'm occupied at the moment," Camden said. "Pass on details, and I'll make it if I can."

LXIV

Oleksandr guided the Brava pickup around a traffic circle and shifted into a higher gear. The small engine wound tight, gaining speed with the pressure of his foot. He swerved around slower cars, aiming the vehicle through each available opening as if a dart thrown at a bull's-eye. His hands gripped the wheel with intent, his glare defiant. Kenna dared look at him as the buildings flew by.

"Is it gonna make it?" she yelled, pointing at the steam from under the hood.

"We'll run it 'til it dies."

Neither liked the parallel, with one fine line of exception. There remained a shred of hope now where a deep void had existed a few days ago. That hope lived in something outside her control, however. It was held by the obsessed man driving them towards their destinies, perhaps in a last-ditch effort to reach salvation and rectify the mistakes of the past … for them both.

Kenna didn't like this situation, not being in control, complete control, but knew she had to fight until the end. But what, dear God, was to be the price? Death?

You're a fool! She screamed at herself. *You're a damn*

fool!

Oleksandr stopped the Brava a half block from the front of the red brick warehouse door where Evhen had placed the phone. Scanning the rooftops and windows, they hesitated inside the pickup for a few moments. Seeing no danger, he chambered a shell in the Uzi and flipped off the safety.

"What is this place?" she asked.

"The Russians use it for various reasons," Oleksandr said. "Safety off … this is the shit that puts hair on your balls."

Armed and ready for action, they stepped out. Oleksandr reached behind the front seat and lifted out a canvas satchel. With caution, they eased towards the partially open warehouse door. Adrenaline rushed through Kenna when they reached the Triumph on its side. Blood smeared the tank and handlebars, but it was in good shape.

"Unless they get shot off," Kenna said, flipping off the pistol's safety.

What the hell are you doing here? She screamed in her mind. *You should be in Boston, making snow angels in the field … or a snowman … anything but this!*

At the door, Oleksandr held Kenna back, then kicked the door open. Automatic gunfire from inside riddled the door and walls.

"Medved!" Oleksandr yelled. "Just want to talk."

"Come inside, and we'll do just that, Shwetz!" Medved yelled in pain from inside.

"It's been a long time, Alexi, my old friend."

"Yes, you were supposed to be dead," Medved said and fired at the door. "Come on, let's do this!"

Oleksandr lifted a smoke grenade from the canvas satchel, pulled the pin, and snapped the handle. He waited a few moments, then tossed it into the opening. The canister rolled across the floor and exploded, spraying the room with dark grey smoke.

The ten-meter square room was a storage area of car parts, file boxes, and old office equipment. Medved coughed, turned away from the door, and stumbled towards the darkness of a rear room. As he moved from the dissipating smoke …

Oleksandr and Kenna rushed through the door. Squatting alongside tall metal shelves, they hesitated and scanned the area. Kenna moved forward; he held her back. She turned; he motioned for silence, then pointed to an ear … *listen.*

A rat, the size of a cat, scampered past inquisitively. Kenna ignored it and shook Oleksandr's sleeve. She motioned that she would circle around. Before he could object, she moved that direction.

Medved walked into a torture chamber, complete with chains, harnesses, tables, and blood stains. He ignored his wounds and passed a table with the tools of the torturer's trade.

"I should have killed you in Luhansk," he yelled.

"Who? Me or Oleksandr?" Kenna yelled from another room.

Medved snapped the direction of her voice. They were maneuvering to get him in a crossfire. He hobbled swiftly across the room to a row of storage shelves.

"You've always been a coward, afraid to face me," Oleksandr yelled from the front room.

Kenna moved rapidly but stealthily into an adjacent room, found a door, and pushed it open. "Why did you kill all those people, Alexi?"

Medved laughed. "Fishing in the wrong river, like most journalists. And blind."

Kenna hesitated. *Was it possible?* "Then, why are you here?"

"This is between me and him, Athena," Oleksandr yelled.

Enough of this machismo shit, Kenna thought. She eased past stacks of tables and chairs. In the other room, Medved leaned against a brick wall with a clear view of the opening into the next room. Oleksandr eased for the door, sensing Medved's location by his voice.

"I always thought you would come for Svetlana, not me," Medved said.

Oleksandr eased to the opening with Medved's position and remained behind the wall. Gathering anger, he kissed the Uzi … *it's time.* He stepped out and fired into the room on fully automatic. When the clip emptied, he shouted:

"When I'm done with you!"

Medved blindly returned fire. At the front of the warehouse, a Corsa slid to a stop. An armed Russian disciple jumped out and ran inside.

"Alexi, more men are on the way!" he yelled from the front room.

Oleksandr turned back to the approaching running footsteps. Though weak, using the wall for support, Medved moved rapidly towards the opening.

On the opposite side of the room, Kenna stepped out and followed Medved's silhouette in the hazy light. Oleksandr stepped out from around the opening. Medved stepped from behind the wall. The other Russian's footsteps were now cautious, approaching slowly.

In the open, Medved and Oleksandr hesitated in a silent duel, pistol-to-pistol, gladiator-to-gladiator.

Those who are about to die salute you!

"I've waited for this since you killed Nadia," Oleksandr said from the side, surprising Medved.

Kenna appeared, ready to speak, when both men moved and fired.

A solid impact threw Medved backwards. For a lengthy instant, his mind held the pistol, but he didn't fire; he couldn't. Hand still wrapped firmly about the pistol, Medved dropped backwards against the wall, tripped, and fell inside the adjacent room.

The Russian disciple ran in from the front room, firing at Oleksandr. Without hesitation, Kenna fired and hit him in the chest, throwing him back. Dead.

Oleksandr was on the floor, blood on his forehead. Kenna squatted at his side and felt for a pulse. He jolted awake and lifted the gun but paused, realizing it was her. She helped him up as an electric garage door lifted in the adjacent room.

"Stay here," he ordered.

Oleksandr walked into the adjacent room. On the floor, Medved bled from a new chest wound, this one fatal. He reached for the door of a mint condition 1967 Jaguar E-Type roadster. He weakened, lost his grip on the handle, and collapsed against the door. Oleksandr walked up and kicked away Medved's gun.

"You should have left Nadia out of it," Oleksandr said, tears streaming down his cheeks. "You lied and said you wired her to explosives, you bastard! My child!"

"Had to … stop you," Medved forced out, weak.

"But I agreed," Oleksandr yelled. "And you killed her anyway."

Medved looked up. "Such are … the fortunes … of war."

Kenna entered the room behind Oleksandr as he screamed and fired into Medved's forehead. Kenna took his arm.

"Why … why did he do it?" she pleaded.

"Nadia followed him after he met with someone. Medved recognized her." Oleksandr hesitated and wiped away the tears. "She was about to tell me who he met when Medved shot her in the back. When you saw me, she was already dead."

Kenna's heart collapsed … as an electric shock hit her.

"I was wrong … dear God."

Sirens closed on them. Oleksandr jerked the keys from Medved. Kenna removed the Halibeck International folder from Medved's bloody shirt, then the memory chip from his pocket.

All this death for a folder and a memory stick, she thought.

"No hunk of metal here; it's a classic," Oleksandr said of the XKE. "Always wanted to drive one."

"You're assuming it'll start," Kenna said, stepping to the passenger side.

Oleksandr jumped in, ground the starter … nothing. He ground the starter again … nothing. He stood out and kicked the door closed.

"Guess it's me and the old Brava to the end," he said.

As sirens neared, they ran to the front of the warehouse. Kenna lifted the Triumph. She and Oleksandr made pleasant eye contact.

"One more thing to do," he said.

"Svetlana … don't kill her, Oles," Kenna said.

"You, as well, Athena," he said, stepped into the Brava, and started it. "I'll buy the Horilka when we're finished."

With a final glance at each other, both realized the

friction between them was gone. As Oleksandr roared and rattled away in the Brava, Kenna started the Triumph. Helmet strapped and backpack on, she sped from the warehouse and the sirens. She tapped her Bluetooth.

"Wiggy, Medved's dead, but we aren't done," she said. "Barnaby has a lot to do, and I need you to do something."

LXV

Kenna hurried into the hotel suite and threw her helmet and goggles onto the sofa. Wiggy sat at the table, staring at the two computer screens. On one screen, Isadore sat at her console in Lane's End Manor.

"Can you get it all done, Issi?" Wiggy asked.

She smiled on-screen. "No problem, working it now. I'll ring when it's done. TTFN."

Isidore disengaged the connection. The screen went black for a moment, then to documents Wiggy had researched. Kenna grabbed a beer and joined Wiggy at the table. She lifted out the "HALIBECK INTERNATIONAL" folder.

"Issi," she said seductively. "Doesn't take you long, Wiggy."

"Aye, kid, a female magnet, that's me," he chuckled. "Now, to what matters."

She dropped the folder before him. "Scan it all, then put it in a secure folder only you can access. Then, email a copy to my father and tell him to do the same."

"He'll want to know what's in it," Wiggy advised.

"Put in the message that if we survive, we'll come to Dallas, drink some Texas potato vodka, and discuss it."

"And you think that'll appease him?"

"If you tell him it's getting us one step closer to Anson Beck, it just might."

It was a devious grin that creased his cheeks. "A little white lie never hurt anyone."

She pointed to one of the computers. "Get me on FaceTime with Toll."

"If he answers," Wiggy said, pulling up the FaceTime logo and connecting.

"He's waiting," she said. "Baited the hook on the ride here."

*

Sir Clifton Toll sat at his desk; Sir Keegan Benton-Smythe stood beside him, both anxiously awaiting the connection. The computer dinged a connection, and Toll accepted the contact. Wiggy's image came into view, which surprised Toll.

"You must be the one she calls Wiggy," he said.

"I am at that, Sir Clifton," Wiggy responded. "I'll put her on before she throws something."

Kenna took the seat beside Wiggy. Anxious at his desk,

Toll stared into her eyes.

"Why didn't you come here?" he demanded.

"I am a cautious woman, Sir Clifton," she said. "We all want to survive this."

"You have nothing to fear from me," he said.

Kenna ignored him and held up the "HALIBECK INTERNATIONAL" folder for Toll to see. His attention and attitude shifted in an instant.

"Svetlana's plan, or so Lyuba said," Toll offered. "I have that folder."

"You have part of it, Sir Clifton," Kenna said. "That's why I'm calling and not there. You need to react now!"

"To what?"

"There are five nuclear suitcase bombs in five cities. Wiggy's sending the locations now."

On the other computer, Wiggy punched send. His computer swooshed as the secure email was sent.

In Toll's study, Benton-Smythe was already on his phone. "We have a critical alert, repeat, a critical alert. Hold on the line."

Toll printed the email and handed it to Benton-Smythe, who continued, "Emergency contact to Paris, Berlin, Washington, and Warsaw. Imminent terrorist threat of nuclear detonation." He paused. "Send it with the locations and names I will provide." He covered the mouthpiece. "What's the fifth city?"

"London," she said matter-of-factly. "But MI5 is taking care of that."

"Security Service? Why the bloody hell have you involved them?" Benton-Smythe objected.

"Because it's their help that got us here, Sir Keegan. Nothing MI6 did," Kenna said with enough emphasis to drive her point home.

"Rensenhaus was a genius, Sir Clifton, "Kenna said. "This was the last move of a Russian chess master, Svetlana, but his work helped us prevail …" she paused. "Not unlike your game board."

While Benton-Smythe provided phone guidance to his people, Toll remained fixed on Kenna's words. *What a fascinating young woman,* he thought. *You are definitely cut from your grandmother's mold.*

"And what do you know of my game board?"

"Your mistake was not realizing that all this began with Chernobyl's meltdown in 1986."

"The missing plutonium," he said. "We knew about that early on."

"But not what was done with it. The CIA and the NRC never reported the shortfall."

"The only record of what happened to the bloody stuff was in Camden's clean-up brief," Toll said, attempting to hide his surprise. "Apparently, until this."

"If we are to believe Svetlana, Camden's oversight was intentional, part of his plan to dismantle the USSR. The report verifies that the CIA planted suitcase bombs in five major Russian cities to be used if he failed."

"Are you implying the CIA was going to blow up Russian cities if Perestroika failed?" Benton-Smythe asked, multi-tasking.

"I wasn't there; I don't know the rationale behind it if there was any, or even if it's true," Kenna said, then continued, "What I do know is the suitcase bombs were why Kovalev wanted to buy Halibeck. He wanted to protect Ukraine from a Russia invasion."

"So, Svetlana discovered what happened to the missing plutonium, and she's turned it around to use on us," Benton-Smythe concluded.

"How in the bloody hell do you know that, Hannigan?" Toll snapped.

"My video shows Svetlana giving the suitcases to her co-

conspirators in Luhansk. Her plan, as Rensenhaus details in the folder, lays it out."

"Then, where the bloody hell is she?"

She ignored him. "This is what Yuri and Alistair died for, sirs."

"God help us, dirty bombs in five major cities," Benton-Smythe said in disbelief and disconnected his call. "Why would the Russians risk taking the stuff through Ukraine?"

"Two reasons, I believe, Sir Keegan," Kenna said. "The CIA would call it plausible deniability, and easy for the Russians to blame Ukraine for what happens."

"What happens?" Toll asked.

Kenna lifted the folder. "You see, all the murders, though pertinent to us, were an elaborate ruse by Svetlana to have us chasing after the killers, the folder, and the video. She wanted our attention away from her mission."

"The bombs," Toll concluded.

"Her mission was to establish a counter measure to keep NATO from responding to their ultimate plan," Kenna said and finished the beer. "Which is to finish what they started in 2014 … invade and occupy Ukraine."

"So, where is the bloody mastermind behind all this?" Toll insisted.

Kenna smiled. "About to meet an old friend."

Kenna shut down FaceTime.

"You know what I need?" she asked of Wiggy.

"As soon as I get the documents from Issi, I'm on it," he said.

Kenna grabbed her satchel, helmet, and goggles and moved for the door.

LXVI

In a huge traffic jam, the Aurus Senat limousine was stopped. In the rear seat, Svetlana grew anxious. She hadn't heard from Medved and accepted the inevitability that he, or Shwetz, or both had met their demise. Her phone dinged; she looked at the text message.

'Enjoy your journey. Contact me via normal channels when safe.'

Sadness, not fear, overcame her when she finished reading. He had unwittingly played an important part, another smokescreen to aid in her plan. She needed a body count to keep the British and the American journalist off balance. She prayed he survived, but in reality, it didn't matter.

If he survived, their mole would remain in place; if he didn't, she'd find another. This one hurt, though. In her heart, she believed she could have loved that man. She brushed aside the emotion like a piece of lint … and did not respond.

*

A dozen Army and police vehicles arrived at South Dock from different directions. Armed soldiers and police went shop-to-shop, escorting patrons and workers away from the area. A perimeter was established around the Russian yacht, *"Worldly Light"*. In civvies but wearing a Kevlar jacket, Barnaby Scrivens led a team across the gangway and onto the aft deck. He was joined by the supervisor of the Explosives Disposal Unit.

Barnaby showed him Kenna's photo of the street in Luhansk while she was running from the shack. Soldiers from the Tigr carry suitcases, all exactly the same, inside the shack.

"The suitcase is what we're looking for," Barnaby said with confidence. He motioned to two strong-armed soldiers who held Sergey, restrained and cuffed, and pulled him forward. Barnaby showed him the photo. "Where is it?"

Sergey was stone-faced, his eyes glaring at Barnaby with a silent, *fuck you!*

"Have it your way, my stupid Russian friend," Barnaby said. "Co-operate, and you just might get a ticket home. Don't, and I guarantee you will never see daylight again."

Special agents of London's Explosives Disposal Unit walked the gangway onto the yacht with two dogs. The guards and crew were handcuffed, led down the gangway, and loaded into armored and heavily guarded paddy wagons. Clad in heavily armored suits, bomb disposal experts boarded. Sergey led Barnaby and the supervisor down the steps below deck.

*

Filipp stopped the limousine alongside a private jet outside the hangar. Parked at the jet's front landing gear was the old beat-up Brava Pickup. Svetlana looked out curiously, then realized too late what was happening. Four blacked-out Chevrolet Suburbans surrounded the Limousine. Eight suited and armed British MI6 agents stepped out. Svetlana panicked momentarily, then accepted reality … her escape plan had failed.

"Just do as they say, Filipp," she said, reaching forward and placing a hand on his shoulder. "You are in no danger."

Another Suburban slid to a stop behind the others. David Camden disconnected a cell phone call and approached her window; she rolled it down. His haughty grin told her *the gig's up.*

"Svetlana, how rude of you to leave without saying hello," he offered.

He lifted the door handle. Svetlana stepped out with her own haughty grin. She lifted a black cell phone from her handbag. Camden looked at it curiously, not concerned.

"Yes, the second phone to trigger the device," he said.

"Afraid that won't do you any good. At Sir Clifton's instructions, Lyuba was kind enough to disarm the device enroute to London."

"Lyuba," Svetlana said and cursed under her breath. "There are others."

He pulled up the message from Benton-Smythe. "Yes, concerning that …"

*

PARIS

Police cars with flashing lights surrounded an aged warehouse. Police dragged a bloody dead Woman with a dark jaw-length hair style from an aged warehouse. Suitably clad, the bomb squad walked from their armored truck and entered.

*

BERLIN

Plain-clothes officers pulled a bloody unconscious man with a distinct Aquiline nose and cropped blond hair from an apartment building. A bomb disposal officer followed with the matching suitcase.

*

WASHINGTON D.C.

In the darkness of early morning, FBI agents swarmed a

delivery van that sat alongside a park bench in front of the White House. Two agents dragged out a bloody, unconscious woman in American blue jeans with a faded, tattered jean jacket and a tousled lob haircut. An agent exited the van with the matching suitcase.

*

WARSAW, POLAND

Police swarm into an apartment building at Mila 18. Antoni Brzezicki, aka Anson Beck, ran from the rear of the building with a large suitcase, jumped into a Mercedes roadster, and sped away. A bomb expert walked from the building with a bag the size of a suitcase; he lifted out the matching suitcase. When they opened it, what they found was magazines.

*

On the tarmac in London, Camden lit a cigarette and offered one to Svetlana; she declined. "All but one arrested or dead. Thought we could discuss the man in Warsaw."

Dejected but fighting it, Svetlana moved to board the private jet. Two MI6 suits blocked the steps up. Camden stopped her and motioned to the blacked-out Chevrolet Suburban.

"The only place you're going is with me," he insisted, took her arm, and held firm when she tried to jerk away.

With smug self-assurance, she said, "I have diplomatic immunity, Camden."

He pulled her to the Suburban, where another armed British agent opened the rear door.

"I suppose that would be relevant if anyone knew we were detaining you," he said. "I assure you, no one will." He motioned to the open door. "Please, I insist."

Two other agents removed Filipp from the limousine, handcuffed him, and shoved him into a trailing Suburban.

Svetlana was taken by surprise when she entered the vehicle. Flipping on the overhead light, Oleksandr faced her in the rear seat, smoking a cigarette.

"The CIA, Oleksandr?" she yelped. "I never thought you'd stoop that low."

"We have a mutual interest."

"Killing me," she said, almost pathetically.

He clasped her hand, not releasing it. "You have no idea how long I have wanted that, even though you were the mother of my child."

"There was no room for you and Nadia in my work," she said without emotion. "Why do you think I involved Medved?"

"What a bizarre and sad world you live in, my dear,"

Oleksandr said. "You somehow believe that justifies killing your daughter?"

"Then, why am I here … with the man I put two bullets in?"

Oleksandr gripped her hand tight until Svetlana winced with pain that creased her painted face. *It should be your throat*, he thought, wanting it to be. Camden slid into the vehicle beside her.

"Provide MI6 and the CIA what they want on the man in Poland," Oleksandr demanded. "If not, they have agreed to turn you over to me. You have until we reach the British safe house to decide."

"That's all you want?" she asked.

"About now, the British Foreign Secretary is informing your ambassador we have captured a rogue FSB agent that conspired in a wild plot to start World War Three," Camden said.

"And that, my dear, is just the beginning," Oleksandr concluded.

Camden chuckled and tapped the driver's shoulder; the Suburban doors locked.

"And you, Mr. Camden, have some questions to answer about Luhansk, as well," Oleksandr said.

As British agents entered the Russian jet, the line of
Suburbans sped away from the hangar.

LXVII

In the stained, aged riding leathers, Kenna smiled at Graves as she walked into Toll's study. Benton-Smythe sat across from Toll. Standing at the sideboard, Thurnbull poured vodka into a cocktail glass and added a splash of soda.

Surprised, Kenna said, "Mr. Thurnbull, I wasn't expecting you today."

"He's Alistair's heir apparent in Luhansk," Toll said. "I thought he should sit in on this. We were waiting on you to discuss the Halibeck folder. Did you bring it?"

"I'm sorry, Sir Clifton, but Medved destroyed it and the video before we arrived."

"Damn shame that," Thurnbull said with a smug, relaxed exhale.

Toll and Benton-Smythe locked stares, both curious, but remained silent. *She was up to something.*

Kenna ignored their curious stares and turned to Thurnbull. "Are you alright, Mr. Thurnbull? You seem to be slumping more than usual."

"Slumping?" Thurnbull asked.

"Must be from the wound in Iraq … the back, if your service record is accurate."

Thurnbull took a sip and glared at Kenna over the top of the glass. "A minor nuisance."

"But you can't stand up straight, right?" she asked.

"Hannigan!" Toll insisted. "We don't have time for small talk. The bloody Russians!"

"Yes, of course," Kenna said. "The folder was Rensenhaus's detailed research on Svetlana's entire operation, including the moles she planted in London."

"Moles?" Benton-Smythe questioned. "Elaborate, if you will."

Kenna opened her laptop to a frozen frame photo of the meeting in Luhansk. She turned the computer to Thurnbull.

"The image Rensenhaus sent to me," he said.

"The odd man out is Anatoli Novikov, the head of Russia's nuclear program," Kenna said. "Before the Berlin Wall came down, he worked with Camden and the CIA to create the plan. When Perestroika succeeded, and the USSR crumbled, Camden no longer needed Novikov. It ruined Novikov, so he sought another partner to take out his revenge and found a willing accomplice in Svetlana."

"We would have eventually identified him," Toll said.

"The folder and the video weren't necessary," Kenna continued. "It was an elaborate ruse by Svetlana to keep us going a thousand directions while she implemented the plan."

"The suitcase affair," Benton-Smythe said.

"Accomplices were needed, so she recruited outside," she said and pulled up a series of photos from Luhansk.

"Here, in Luhansk 2014," Kenna continued. "Svetlana, Novikov, and there, off to the side … Tommy Henson, or should I say, Foma Heraskov. He's also at the shack, the Russian lieutenant who followed Svetlana and Lyuba inside.

"Though he was involved in the dirty work and deserved what he got in a way," Kenna continued, "it bothered me until I put it together. You see, part of Svetlana's plan was that she convinced her accomplices that Alistair was alive."

"The autopsy provided evidence to the contrary," Toll said.

"There's no mistaking it; he's dead," she agreed. "That's why Tommy got close to Adelaide immediately upon entering London. He was ordered by Svetlana, his handler, to discover if Alistair had sent her the folder for safekeeping. It began innocently enough. When Adelaide went to Wembley to confront Kovalev about her father's death, Illya intervened and beat her, then dragged her out to her car."

"This is all very fascinating, Ms. Hannigan, but where are you going?" Thurnbull asked.

"Yes, to the point, Ms. Hannigan," Toll ordered.

She eyed Thurnbull like aiming a pistol and continued, "Svetlana ran it all. Even Medved was a ruse designed to throw us off the track."

"So, Tommy … Foma, whatever his name, and Medved are both dead. The suitcases have been recovered. Does that end it?" Benton-Smythe asked.

"That brings us to the relevance of the Halibeck folder," she said and turned to Thurnbull. "Why don't you tell us about it, Mr. Thurnbull."

"Me?" Thurnbull stammered. "I've never seen it."

"Of course, you have. You were in Luhansk when Svetlana received the original from Novikov."

Like a razor pressed against everyone's throat, silence filled the room. Kenna pulled up the photo of the secret Russian meeting.

"It took a long time for facial recognition to pull it up, but that's you in the rear, with the hoody."

Toll and Benton-Smythe were breathless; the latter reached for a pistol. Thurnbull remained statuesque at the sideboard, unemotional, eyes fixed on Kenna.

"That's absurd, libelous rubbish," Thurnbull countered. "My war record speaks of my loyalty—"

"As Sir Clifton says, let's get back on point," she interrupted. "The pipe, Mr. Thurnbull, you are never without it, and it's there in the photo. The house where you and Tommy interrogated Adelaide reeked of the Jasmine tobacco you smoke."

"There's no truth to it; all circumstantial," Thurnbull stammered, sweat beading his forehead. "It'll never hold up in court."

The door opened, and Wiggy entered with a leather gym bag. He dropped it on Toll's desk and lifted out a satellite phone.

"Then, perhaps this will," Wiggy said. "The sat phone you used to contact Svetlana and Medved. I also have the call Yuri Zelenko recorded that he made to you, informing you he was coming to London. A minute later, you called Henson, who it's been confirmed killed Yuri. The hoody with the sailor's hitch on the drawstrings and blood stains. I imagine forensics will match the blood."

Wiggy paused, glaring at Thurnbull, wanting to rip his head off. "Suffice it to say, Thurnbull, that they'll stick you in a very deep and dark hole for the rest of your days. May they be many and miserable."

Thurnbull's eyes spun about the room, fixing on a target … Kenna. He reached for a pistol in his overcoat but hesitated when Wiggy pressed the Glock against the back of his head. Benton-Smythe pulled a Walther from a shoulder holster and aimed.

"Ease that out and drop it on the floor," Wiggy demanded.

Confusion filled Toll. "Douglas, why? I gave you everything."

"You gave me nothing," Thurnbull growled.

With a swift movement, Thurnbull dodged to the side, pulling Kenna with him as a shield, and jerked free the pistol. Without hesitation, she slammed her heel against the arch of his foot. He bawled, pressed the pistol against his chest, and fired. Blood sprayed Kenna and the glass case holding Adolf Hitler's diary; he collapsed atop the case then fell.

Kenna knelt beside him, seeing that the shot missed his heart. In half shock, Thurnbull's breathing was labored, hollow, wheezing; blood ran from his mouth.

"Why didn't you kill me in the stadium?" she asked.

"Never part of the mission … didn't think you'd

investigate.”

“Your underestimation was your downfall,” Kenna said with a hint of pride.

“You don’t want … to be a sports journalist, do you, Hanni …”

Thurnbull’s muscles relaxed, his breathing stopped, as did his heart. Kenna closed his eyes. There was no satisfaction in Douglas Thurnbull’s death, just as there had not been in the death of Bernard Altmann. It was, as Gran often said, *the pepper on the ice cream.’*

“True to the end, through the heart,” Toll said.

“No,” Kenna disagreed, “he didn’t have one.”

“What put you onto him, Ms. Hannigan?” Benton-Smythe asked.

“Several tells,” she offered. “The physical defect appeared on the CCTV footage. Then, the hoody with the sailor’s knot on the drawstrings.”

“His background didn’t check out,” Wiggy said. “Most damning was that he met Novikov back in ‘14. It’s documented in another photo with Svetlana, Medved, and Tommy.”

“But he told us they had never met,” Kenna said. “What clinched it was the pipe and the tobacco at the farmhouse.”

Graves entered the room and covered Thurnbull's body with a sheet. He walked to the sideboard, poured a whiskey neat, downed it, and moved to the door.

"I phoned the police, sir," Graves said and walked out.

At the windows overlooking the courtyard, Benton-Smythe talked on his cell phone. Toll poured three drinks at the sideboard and handed one to Kenna and Wiggy.

"All along, you knew about my Luhansk video," she said to his surprise.

"National security often requires unconventional measures, Ms. Hannigan," Toll countered.

"Spoken like the great dictators over time, Sir Clifton," she responded.

Benton-Smythe disconnected his call, poured a whiskey, and downed it. "All but the Yank … ah, the American in Warsaw."

"Let's hope Oleksandr gets it out of Svetlana," Kenna said.

"I take it the folder and video weren't destroyed, Ms. Hannigan," Toll concluded. "I will have them."

"A lot of blood for words on a page and a few images, Sir Clifton." Kenna poured drinks for her and Wiggy. She continued:

"I have the originals in a private location and will provide them when I hear Lyuba has been paid in full."

"I'm not one to barter," Toll demanded.

"Without her, we never would have succeeded," Kenna said.

"I can have you both arrested and thrown in a dungeon," Toll threatened. "I suggest—"

"You know my father," she interrupted. "He's safeguarding a copy of those documents for me. Should what you threaten happen … well, I doubt you want the Crown to learn that a twenty-first Century Kim Philby operated under your noses."

"And you, Ms. Hannigan, what is it you want for the video?" Benton-Smythe asked to diffuse the tension.

"What my grandmother always accepted, Sir Keegan," she said. "The gratitude of a satisfied client."

"I should have seen this," Toll said at Thurnbull, angry with himself.

Kenna handed Toll a whiskey. "The blind aren't always the first left in the dark, Sir Clifton."

"Yes," he agreed. "Your grandmother's wisdom, no doubt."

"No, that one was all mine," she said.

The grandfather clock chimed Midnight. Surprising Kenna, Toll took her hand.

"You are quite good at this game, Ms. Hannigan. You should consider changing avocations."

"That's the difference between us, Sir Clifton. You see manipulating, even destroying peoples' lives as a game. I think of football as a game." She toasted him. "Think I'll stick to reporting on that."

Kenna drank the whiskey and walked out with Wiggy.

On the street in front of the Toll mansion, Kenna looked up to a clear sky.

"First stars I've seen for some time, Wiggy."

"Since I've been here, as I recall," he agreed.

"How'd you get here?" She held up a hand to stop him. "Don't tell me … Issi?"

"The lass offered; I accepted."

"Where is she, then?"

"Said somethin' about a room," he said with a smile.

Kenna slapped him on the shoulder. "Good go. Hop on, I'll drop you."

"Drop ain't the kinda word that'll convince me to get on this contraption," he said.

Kenna kicked the Triumph to start it. She revved the

engine and lowered her goggles.

"As Gran said, *'We've chosen the fast lane, get on and enjoy the ride.'*"

With hesitation, Wiggy swung on behind. As Kenna sped away, Wiggy let out a great victory howl … or was it a scream of fear?

EPILOGUE

With bright sunshine through the windows of Toll's study, the honorable knights of the British empire, Sir Clifton Toll and Sir Keegan Benton-Smythe stood at the sideboard with glasses of his best whiskey, neat … of course. What other way was there? Toll looked down at the courtyard.

"Do you think we'll remember any of life's challenges in death, Keegan?" he wondered aloud.

"Never gave it a thought, ole boy," Benton-Smythe said.

That was the only exchange of small talk between them that either remembered. They toasted their reflection in the glass and took a sip, savoring it. Toll moved to the desk and flattened the gameboard on the surface. With a diamond-studded Conway Stewart fountain pen, he checked the final box.

"Checkmate, Mr. Putin," he said and lifted the glass.

He handed the gameboard and the Halibeck International folder to Benton-Smythe, who tossed them into the fire. They drank … not sipped … the whiskey and watched them burn.

*

BASEL, SWITZERLAND

A Rolls Royce Phantom stopped in front of UBS bank, a five-story white stone corner building that beamed in the bright sun. The female driver got out, circled the car, and opened the rear door. Wearing a long dress and fur coat to cover her wounds and with the aid of a cane, Lyuba stood from the rear with the driver's help. The driver lifted out a briefcase, extended the handle, and handed it to Lyuba.

"Wait for me here," Lyuba said.

"Yes, ma'am," the driver said. "You have me all night."

"I'll see if I can come up with a surprise for later," Lyuba said, thinking briefly of Svetlana.

Lyuba brushed a hand across the pretty driver's face and turned for the bank entrance. A middle-aged doorman opened the door, tipped his cap, and she stepped inside.

*

The yacht *"Worldly Light"* cruised the Thames past Parliament. On the aft deck, enjoying a day of sunshine, Kenna toasted Horilka with Oleksandr. Bandaged from her injuries but in good spirits, Adelaide sat on a deck recliner beside Ian from the Blue Boar. Wiggy and Isidore, Corina and Barnaby toasted with Champagne. Leaning on a crutch,

525

arm in a sling, and wearing a new captain's cap and sparkling white uniform, Captain Evhen stood with Mrs. Kohut just outside the yacht bridge. Kenna and Wiggy moved to the railing.

"The Polish police just missed Beck in Warsaw," Wiggy said.

"After this pleasure cruise, I guess I know where we're going," Kenna responded.

"Do you suppose he has that fifth suitcase?"

"Let's hope not," Kenna said. "He's crazy enough to start WWIII."

***

BOSTON—10 YEARS BEFORE

A cold winter night with a bright, full moon. On the veranda of Gran Lockwood's estate home, she and Kenna were bundled near a roaring fire pit. Gran Lockwood read from a red leather-bound book with no title, no cover. On the spine was imprinted: "Museum of Modern Art – Paris 2010".

'Silence became the dreadful breath of an end to battle, the reality of defeat for the vanquished, and celebration by the victor,' the Grand Old Dame said and closed the book.

'What does it mean, Gran?' Kenna had asked.

***

On the yacht, Kenna lifted the glass of Horilka to Wiggy, "To bringing a case to a victorious conclusion, be it the capture of an art thief … or a murderer."

"Or two," he concluded.

*****

Russia invaded Ukraine the morning after the arrests. The West responded with sanctions and rhetoric. The fifth suitcase and courier were not recovered … was this the reason?

THE END